PRAISE FOR LESLIE HORVITZ AND *CAUSES UNKNOWN*!

"Calling *Causes Unknown* a pulp thriller is like calling *The Brothers Karamazov* a mystery. Although there are enough clues and action to satisfy the most jaded airline travelers, Horvitz writes with skills that far transcend his chosen genre."

—*Inside Books*

"Horvitz weaves an intricate plot replete with murder, corruption in high places and romance."

—*Publishers Weekly*

"Leslie Horvitz has written several novels over the past ten years. Each has a ring of truth and plenty of top-notch suspense."

—Baker & Taylor's Hot Picks

EXAMINING THE BODY

The bed was king-sized and unmade. The body of the deceased was propped up in a sitting position against the wall a short distance away. He was clad in a bright red sweatsuit jacket, with the zipper front undone to expose a blue Izod short-sleeved pullover with a button-down collar. Blood, now dried into a rusty color, trailed along the wall for maybe five or six feet. There was a partially congealed pool of blood below the head. The gun was in his hand.

Gail had only to grab hold of the deceased's arm to see how flaccid it was. Rigor mortis had passed off some time ago, leaving the same way that it had come: the eyelids first, the feet last. He'd been dead at least thirty-six hours, possibly longer.

Kneeling down next to the victim, Gail inspected the bullet hole in his chest. The bullet had gone through the jacket and the pullover. From the look of the wound she guessed that the gun was about one inch away when it had discharged.

The entrance wound of the second bullet was located in the right temple. The exit wound she found behind the left ear. She made her notes: no marks around entrance wound, no singeing of hair, no powder tattoo marks, no blackening of the flesh, no rebound bruises. Rebound bruises would have indicated that the gun had been fired from some distance.

"It's pretty unusual for a suicide to shoot himself twice, isn't it?"

CAUSES UNKNOWN

LESLIE HORVITZ

LEISURE BOOKS NEW YORK CITY

A LEISURE BOOK®

November 2006

Published by

Dorchester Publishing Co., Inc.
200 Madison Avenue
New York, NY 10016

ISBN 0-8439-5795-6

Visit us on the web at www.dorchesterpub.com.

No es sueno la vida. Alerta! Alerta! Alerta!
Nos cameos de las escaleras para comer la tierra humeda
o sublimos al filo de la nieve con el coro de las dalias muertas.
Pero no hay olvido, jni sueno:
carne viva. Los besos atan las bocas
en una marana de vans recientes
y al que la duele su dolor le dolera sin descano
y al que teme la meurte la ilevara sobre sus hombros.

(Life is no dream! Beware and beware and beware!
We tumble downstairs to eat of the damp of the earth
or we climb to the snowy divide with the choir of
        dead dahlias.
But neither dream nor forgetfulness, is:
brute flesh is. Kisses that tether our mouths
in a mesh of raw veins.
Whomsoever his woe brings to grief, it will grieve
        without quarter.
Whom death brings to dread will carry that death on
        his shoulders.)

—Garcia Lorca, *Unsleeping City*
  ("Brooklyn Bridge Nocturne")

CAUSES UNKNOWN

PROLOGUE

Asleep, Evan Keeler dreamed of subways. A retired motor-man, he'd long resigned himself to these dreams. Subways had gotten into his subconscious, and there was no way to escape them. Awake, he shot up in bed, suddenly alert. He was sure he'd heard a car door slamming. Dogs were bark-ing furiously, but then, late at night dogs always barked like that, crazy in heat or hunger, he didn't know which. There was a sound of rain, a rat-tat-tat, like a machine gun against the rafters of his two-room house. But he was listening for another sound.

First he detected voices, then footsteps. The rain, how-ever, muffled their steps against the worn, rotting planks of the pier that ran from the road past his house down to the channel. It sounded as if two men were talking in hushed, urgent tones. But Keeler couldn't for the life of him under-stand what they were saying.

Evan Keeler was in his early eighties. His body suffered from mysterious aches—arthritis had put crimps in his hands, and his circulation was bad. Many a winter day he had no feeling in his fingertips or his toes. His plumbing was shot. Just about nothing worked the way it was supposed to. Worse, with his wife dead for fifteen years, he was terribly lonely. He didn't need trouble. And what was going on outside, he was certain, was trouble.

The voices and the footsteps grew louder; then, after a time, they began to recede. Forcing his stiff limbs to function, Keeler got out of bed. Even though it was late in June, the early-morning air held a bone-chilling dampness. He went to the window, putting on no lights, and looked out.

And saw nothing. Not at first. In the drizzle, the nearby houses, the pier, the water, and sky had gotten blurred; it was all grays and blacks out there, featureless, with barely a hint that there might be some kind of color in the world. But he could still catch the sound of the footsteps, and so he knew that they were out there, that it wasn't just his imagination.

He stepped over to the other window, parting the curtain enough to peer out, no more. This window held a better view of the channel, and from it he could make out the end of the pier. Keeler's weathered yawl was tied up there, creaking rhythmically in the sullen waters. Keeler was now able to see that there were three people, not two as he'd surmised from the voices.

Two men and a woman. The woman was between them. She had long hair and was wearing only a shirt and shorts and no shoes, which was something he found very strange. She should know better than to go out on a night like this dressed in so little. It looked as if the two men were holding her up. She was not doing very well at maintaining her own balance anyhow.

They were standing—precariously—at the end of the pier. Something was happening, but Keeler couldn't tell what. He strained his eyes, willing them to take in more than they were capable of doing.

But he still couldn't be certain of what was happening. It was damned frustrating. The best he could tell, the woman had fallen. The two men hoisted her back up, but no sooner had they done that than they flung her into the water. He registered the sound of a splash. Was this a trick played on him by his ruined eyes? Had this really happened? Had they pushed her in?

The two men, both in trenchcoats, one with a hat on, the other bareheaded, with an umbrella, stood at the end of the pier for a few moments longer, as if they were waiting for the woman to surface. Then they turned around and started back the way they'd come.

Terrified that they would catch sight of him, Keeler quickly pulled back from the window, taking refuge in the shadows. His heart struck up a fearful, dangerous rhythm. He could not draw a proper breath. They were coming closer, their pace measured, unhurried. But they were not talking; they had said all that they had to.

From what Keeler could judge, they were right outside his house now. He was convinced that he was finished, that they would burst in and kill him. He waited, huddled in the corner, shaking like mad. But after a few moments passed the footsteps resumed. He felt like a damned fool.

Two car doors opened and slammed shut. A motor came to life. Keeler risked another look out the window. Headlight beams struck the window, nearly blinding him. Then the car was gone. He wouldn't have been able to say what the car looked like, except that it was dark and indistinguishable, just like everything else in the world on this night.

He couldn't get back to sleep. He kept thinking of the woman, whoever she was, and what had happened to her. He deliberated over calling the police. But he didn't like the idea; he wanted nothing to do with the police. He reasoned that it was better to say nothing. It wasn't as if he could save anybody or bring that woman back to life. No good could come of it. Even after making his decision, though, he still couldn't get back to sleep.

Finally, at around five in the morning, he got out of bed for the last time and made some instant coffee. The rain was almost gone. He stepped outside to have a look. In the gathering light, he spotted something beneath his feet.

It was blood the rain hadn't managed to wash away. It was definitely blood, fresh and bright red. Some color had come back into the world, after all.

PART ONE

CHAPTER ONE

The first thing that Joe Stopka did when he discovered that his wife had four kids back in the Dominican Republic that she hadn't bothered telling him about was go and get a drink. It was one of those unbearably hot Sundays in the city, almost completely emptied of its population. The evacuation had begun Thursday afternoon as jitneys circulated through the neighborhood, collecting people for the Hamptons and Fire Island. By Sunday there was hardly anyone around at all.

McNally's had just opened for the day, and Stopka was the only customer. Though he was a man with a hulking build, there was something soft and vulnerable about his face. His dejection was immediately apparent to the bartender, who without a word set a double shot of vodka in front of him.

Stopka threw the drink back. The bartender refilled it. Stopka was ready to talk. "Stopka needs money."

"We all do," the bartender agreed. "What's the matter, The Brandenberg isn't paying you enough?"

The Brandenberg was the condominium tower down the block, at Sixty-ninth Street and Second, where Stopka was employed as super. He'd been there for ten years, long enough so that he could count on reasonably good tips at Christmas, but not much more.

"It's not that. It's my wife . . . Maria."

"What's wrong? She getting on your case already? How long have you been married? Two months?"

"Three and a half," Stopka said despairingly. "This morning, out of the blue, she announces she has four kids living in Santo Domingo and that I'd better get ready because they'll be coming up here to live with us in a couple of weeks."

The bartender looked astounded. "Four kids? And you didn't know nothing about them? All this time and she was holding out on you?"

Stopka nodded sadly. "Guess she figured she'd queer the marriage if she said something to Stopka before. Now what I got to do is get a hold of a lot of cash quick. You know what it's like supporting one kid—think of four!" The very thought caused him to drain his glass and signal for another.

"You ever think of divorcing her?"

Stopka glanced up at him with an aggrieved look on his wide, flushed face and said, "Divorce Maria? Why the hell would I want to do that? I love her."

When he returned to The Brandenberg, Stopka was screaming mad, his rage fueled by alcohol. There were a million things he wanted to say to his wife. But she gave him no opportunity. "That crazy woman up in fifteen-K has been calling up every five minutes complaining about the smell in the hallway!" she shouted from the kitchen, where she'd taken refuge. "Now she's saying she's seeing bugs up there, too. You'd better go check on it. I'm getting tired of giving excuses for you."

"Mrs. Moskone, you mean?"

"Moskone, that's the one."

Stopka's head ached. He felt as though he'd been bludgeoned. He regretted the vodka he'd drunk and wanted most of all to lie down and take a nap. Mrs. Moskone was a pain, and her nagging drove him crazy.

The Brandenberg was a luxury building, immaculately kept, and there was no reason for there to be any strange smells, and certainly no possibility of bugs, except for those that infested Mrs. Moskone's imagination.

In a way that Stopka didn't like to admit, he felt sorry for the woman. Growing old in the lap of luxury wasn't such a great deal when one got right down to it, not if one were alone like Hannah Moskone. It wasn't her complaints that got to him so much, it was her neediness. Once she'd lured him to her apartment, she kept him there as long as she could, hoping to tempt him with nauseating concoctions she insisted were Bloody Marys. No matter how pressed he was for time, Mrs. Moskone refused to let him go. It was as though, after he left, she feared she'd never lay eyes on another human being again in her life.

Strangely enough, there *was* a peculiar odor in the fifteenth-floor corridor that assaulted him as soon as he got off the elevator. It smelled like garbage that hadn't been disposed of properly. Aside from Mrs. Moskone, all the other residents on the floor were away for the weekend, or else they surely would have complained about it, too.

No sooner had he rung the bell of 15K than Mrs. Moskone, a shrunken figure in her worn housecoat, opened the door. "Thank God, at last," she said. He might have been the redeemer the way she welcomed him. "You smell it? It's been like this since seven this morning when I got up. I thought maybe it was the plumbing. That was what happened last March, you remember, when the pipes started leaking in fifteen-G."

"I smell something," Stopka acknowledged. "I have to go see where it's coming from. I'll let you know as soon as I find out what it is." He was hoping to escape from her as quickly as possible.

"But that's not all. Did you see the bugs?"

"Oh, yes, the bugs," Stopka said resignedly. "No, I didn't see them, Mrs. Moskone."

Mrs. Moskone screwed up her face in disbelief. "Well, then," she said indignantly, "that must have been because you didn't look for them. I told your wife there were bugs loose. I told her to call an exterminator. I don't know what's wrong with you people. And with the kind of money I pay for maintenance, it's a crime."

Accustomed to this sort of abuse, Stopka gave an apologetic smile and stepped back. "Let me go check it out, Mrs. Moskone, okay? Let Stopka see what the trouble is."

He didn't really succeed in escaping. Mrs. Moskone remained at the door, following him with her eyes. "There, don't you see them?"

Though she was well into her seventies, maybe older, age had done nothing to impair her eyesight. Stopka dropped his gaze toward the apricot-colored carpet and instantly saw what she was talking about. He took in two, then three, of them.

"Damned roaches," Mrs. Moskone muttered.

Stopka hesitated to tell her that they weren't roaches. They were maggots.

Stopka traced the maggots—and the foul odor—to the door of 15C, Alan Friedlander's apartment. He felt Mrs. Moskone's sharp eyes on him but refused to look back. When he failed to elicit any response by ringing the bell, he tried knocking. It was difficult concentrating; all that kept coming to mind was the thought of those four kids in Santo Domingo.

He decided that he couldn't wait until Alan returned to investigate. He only hoped he wouldn't need to call a locksmith. Residents usually preferred to put in their own locks, which defeated the purpose of his carrying a set of master keys.

But only one lock had been secured. Opening the door, Stopka was nearly bowled over by the smell. Jesus! This was worse than anything he could remember. It made him want to retch. Reflexively he began breathing through his mouth. Advancing through the apartment, his heart pounding, he gradually became aware of how soaking wet his shirt was getting. No question he shouldn't have had that vodka to drink.

There were many more maggots inside, dozens of them, scrambling out of his way as soon as he opened the blinds to let in the sun. He crushed one underfoot, grinding it into the carpet. When he lifted his foot he saw that it was still twitching. The fucking things didn't die so easily. Stopka finished the job.

Friedlander, like a lot of people who'd come into money suddenly, was hot on big-ticket items: a personal computer, a Rolex watch, a JVC super VHS camera, an elaborate home entertainment center with a screen that wouldn't have looked out of place in a movie theater, a BMW convertible, even a gold-and-onyx lacquer pen by Cartier worth nearly a thousand dollars—all accessories that would confer status on their owner, at least in his own eyes. Even the plants looked expensive. They weren't ordinary house plants by any means; they were plants that might have come out of the Amazon jungle: thick, sprawling growths that seemed to Stopka to have something sinister about them—the more so now that they were all dead. Everything used to be white in the place: the walls were white, the ceiling was white, the tiled floors were white. But the white wasn't quite as clean as he remembered from his last visit; it had begun to fade, to gray a little, and it was stained—with blood.

He hesitated for a moment, then proceeded through the kitchen and around past the bathroom in the direction of the bedroom. He thought he was prepared for what he was going to see. He was not.

Even without knowing the exact address, Dr. Gail Ives would have had no difficulty in locating The Brandenberg. Three squad cars and an ambulance were parked in front of its glass-and-pink-stone facade. She seldom saw many cops around on her previous investigations, but then, she was new to this. Maybe this was someone important, a politician or a celebrity whose untimely demise would turn out to be the major event on this airless summer day. She was keen with anticipation.

The doorman appraised her with a doubtful look, seeing at once that she wasn't a resident of The Brandenberg.

"I'm with the chief medical examiner's office," she said, displaying her credentials.

If she'd thought that this would be sufficient to dispel his skepticism, she was mistaken. He had the look of a man who believed he was being taken in by an elaborate scam. He reached for a phone and called up. He seemed surprised to discover that she was expected.

The Brandenberg's lobby struck Gail as overdone. Designed to be stately and ornate, with its pink marble walls, its chandeliers and mirrors, it had ended up looking like a museum gallery, sterile and cold.

There were more mirrors in the elevator, so that one wouldn't lose sight of oneself for more than a second. The same music that was being piped into the lobby followed Gail up to the fifteenth floor. It was a song from the sixties called "Comedown (So Long, Good-bye)," which she liked enough so that under other circumstances she might have ridden up and down in the elevator until it was over.

As the elevator door slid open, she found herself looking into the face of an elderly lady who stood at the door to her apartment, her hands knitted together, an expression of consternation on her wrinkled face. Gail's appearance caused her to raise her eyes. She smiled conspiratorially, as if to let Gail know that she was in on a wonderful secret. Gail suspected that she was seeing more excitement today than she had in years.

An officer with a round red face—what Santa Claus would look like if he drank too much and didn't like kids—opened the door to 15C for Gail. She nearly reeled from the stench. There was an odor death had when it had progressed for too long. The officer smiled thinly at her reaction.

She identified herself, but the cop didn't seem interested. He walked back into the room and let her follow. He approached a balding, weary man with hooded eyes of about fifty who was standing in the kitchen, which was just off to the right. There was a quick, whispered exchange at which point the balding man looked toward Gail. He motioned to her.

"My name's Ralph Mackie," he said. She could tell instinctively that he wasn't going to be impressed with anything she had to say. He was looking for experience in her eyes and not finding it, wanted nothing more to do with her.

She told him her name, thinking that in five minutes he wouldn't be able to recall it.

"You don't look like the type who's cut out for this line of work," he noted. She decided that this didn't deserve the courtesy of a reply.

Gesturing in back of him, he continued the introductions. "We have a male Caucasian, thirty-one years old. Name's Alan Friedlander. Gunshot wounds in the head and chest. Thirty-eight-caliber weapon, one-hundred-fifty-eight-grain ammunition. No signs of breaking and entering, no signs of a struggle. We're treating it as a probable suicide."

Gunshot wounds? What was this? This wasn't the kind of case they'd want her to handle. There must have been a mistake, a mix-up of names and assignments. "Who else is here from the medical examiner's office?" she asked, hoping he wouldn't pick up on her nervousness.

"You're the only one."

"Well, when is an examiner expected?" In cases where foul play was even a remote possibility, an examiner was routinely dispatched to the scene. It was believed that by viewing the circumstances in which the body was found, the examiner would have more to go on when it came time to perform the autopsy.

Mackie shook his head. "So far as I know, you're it. We weren't told that anybody else from the M.E.'s office would be coming."

Gail was stunned. This was crazy. She wasn't prepared to take on this responsibility herself, not without the supervision of an examiner.

Of the ninety thousand deaths that occurred every year in New York City, approximately thirty thousand of them were turned over to the chief medical examiner's office for investigation. The death didn't necessarily have to be suspicious, just medically unattended. Violent deaths naturally merited attention. Because there was no way for the medical examiner's office to handle such an overwhelming caseload with its salaried employees alone, it turned to residents and interns who worked in local hospitals, recruiting them as medical investigators on a per diem basis.

The truth was that as a resident, Gail already had enough drama and death to cope with without taking on a second job; it was insane to run herself ragged like this. Certainly she wasn't particularly interested in pathology or becoming a medical investigator on a full-time basis. But she was in desperate need of every last cent she could lay her hands on; otherwise, there was no way she could possibly keep up the payments on the one-bedroom apartment she'd purchased eight months before.

Theoretically, Gail's shift began at midnight and ran until eight in the morning three days a week. But because this was a summer weekend, with the city abandoned by all but the homeless, the crack dealers, and the dead, it came as no surprise that the M.E.'s office would call on her. What *was* a surprise was that the case should turn out to be something like this.

As a rule, medical investigators were assigned only to nonsuspicious cases: the heart attack victim on the street or the widower who expired alone in his shabby apartment, for example. So Gail had had no reason to believe that what awaited her at The Brandenberg Towers was anything other than routine—or as routine as death ever got in this city.

But what was she going to do? Walk out? She could call the M.E.'s office, but already Mackie was urging her forward. The place smelled wretched, and the detectives wanted to finish quickly. "Take a look at the stiff, make your notes, and we'll do the rest," he said.

There was no question that the detective sensed her unease, and that infuriated her. Somehow it became important to her to gain back the initiative. She asked the first thing that came into her mind. "You said you're treating this as a suicide. Did the deceased leave any note?"

He shook his head. "We didn't find any. You ever seen one of these before?" He obviously knew the answer already.

Not about to give him the satisfaction, she replied flatly, "I've seen my share."

"Well, then, you should know that in most cases they don't leave any notes. In the movies they do; in real life, maybe one out of every five or six will leave a note. The majority of them probably figure they've said all they had to while they were alive."

"I suppose suicide's a pretty dramatic message in itself."

Mackie nodded. "Got that right."

The stench was working on Gail. Although the air conditioning was turned on full blast, the oppressive heat couldn't be entirely defeated any more than the smell. She was beginning to feel nauseated, but if she was going to be sick, it would not be there, not in front of Mackie and his men.

The apartment opened up, turning into a living room more tastefully decorated than Gail had expected. On the walls she recognized prints by Liechtenstein and Klee and a gouache by somebody she couldn't identify. She noticed a photograph of a young man in tennis whites, with an enviable tan and windswept hair, his arm loosely draped over a brunette with a huge smile. They looked like a couple out of an ad in *Town and Country*.

Following the direction of her gaze, Mackie said, "That's Friedlander—in better days."

"What does—did he do?"

"Investment banking, stocks. See the Quotron?"

"Quote what?"

"Quotron. It gives you a readout of stock prices."

The Quotron, its screen empty of profits and losses, rested on top of a Baldwin piano.

As he escorted Gail toward the bedroom and the body, Mackie seemed to have adopted the role of host. For now this was his apartment, this was his dominion.

She asked if he'd spoken to any witnesses.

"There aren't any," Mackie said. "The last time anyone saw him was Wednesday afternoon coming home from work. Nobody saw him go out again."

In the living room a lab technician was dusting the french doors for fingerprints. The doors led out to a terrace large enough on which to grill a steak. The bedroom was straight ahead. Spots, smudged and gray, were visible against the thick cherry rug. She knelt down to see what they were, put a finger to one spot, and lifted it up to her eyes. Dirt. That was all it was, just dirt. Out of the corner of her eye she saw a procession of white maggots crawling along the carpet in her direction. She quickly averted her gaze.

Portable lamps, temporarily installed by the police, had thrown the room into a blinding glare. It reminded Gail of a film set, all that was needed now was a director. Three officers were clustered around the body, looking as if they were waiting for something to happen. Certainly not the resurrection. A police photographer, his body twisted into some impossible contortion, was holding his camera over his head so as to get the right angle.

Gail's entrance drew some quizzical stares from the cops. She nodded to them. They wished her a good afternoon. She wondered what kind of a good afternoon they had in mind.

The bed was king-sized and unmade. The body of the deceased was propped up in a sitting position against the wall a short distance away. He was clad in a bright red sweatsuit jacket, with the zipper front undone to expose a blue Izod short-sleeved pullover with a button-down collar. Blood, now dried into a rusty color, trailed along the wall for maybe five or six feet. There was a partially congealed pool of blood below the head. The gun was in his hand.

One officer finally went into motion and looped a shoestring through the trigger guard of the gun and gingerly lifted it up, keeping the muzzle in a safe position.

Gail had only to grab hold of the deceased's arm to see how flaccid it was. Rigor mortis had passed off some time ago, leaving the same way that it had come: the eyelids first, the feet last. He'd been dead at least thirty-six hours, possibly longer.

Now Gail took a closer look at Friedlander's face. It was in the midst of putrefying and the flesh had a puttylike aspect to it; his face might have been a mask that was about to drop off. In his glazed eyes Gail read not pain so much as vast astonishment that this thing should have happened to him, of all people. Just about all resemblance between him and the man in the photo in the living room had disappeared. He smelled, literally, like shit.

Kneeling down next to the victim, Gail inspected the bullet hole in his chest. The bullet had gone through the jacket and the pullover. From the look of the wound she guessed that the gun was about one inch away when it had discharged. Her conclusions were based partly on what she remembered from the textbooks, and also from her experience with gunshot cases she'd seen in the emergency room. Some of her conclusions, though, were pure guess-work.

The entrance wound of the second bullet was located in the right temple. The exit wound she found behind the left ear. She made her notes: no marks around entrance wound, no singeing of hair, no powder tattoo marks, no blackening of the flesh, no rebound bruises. Rebound bruises would have indicated that the gun had been fired from some distance.

Now that she was preoccupied by the examination itself, she was no longer so anxious, becoming confident that at the very least she wasn't in danger of bungling this completely.

"It's pretty unusual for a suicide to shoot himself twice, isn't it?" Gail glanced back at Mackie.

"Believe me," Mackie said, "I've seen stranger things."

She understood from the detective's expression that he didn't regard it as unusual as all that. People were capable of accomplishing improbable, even impossible, actions, and it was high time she got used to it. Again she was being made to feel the burden of her inexperience. Mackie wasn't someone easily fooled. He wouldn't occupy the position he did if he could be: He knew.

She noted high-velocity blood spatter on the victim's right hand, right arm, and right thigh. She took swabs of both hands for the paraffin tests and neutron-activation analyses that were likely to be run. The tests should go a long way toward proving whether the victim had in fact shot himself.

When she asked Mackie if he had any idea whether Friedlander was right- or left-handed—something that would be important to establish, owing to the direction of the wounds—he said that it was obvious. He must be right-handed if they'd removed the gun from his right hand. Maybe this wasn't the sort of question she, as a medical investigator, should be asking; she wasn't sure. In any case, it was clear that he was growing irritable, and who could blame him with this stench and the maggots beginning to crawl out of the various holes in Friedlander's body? Still, she was anxious to do a thorough job.

There were other injuries to look for: bruises, abrasions, and cuts, even other bullet wounds that might have escaped detection. But aside from several fresh scratches on his wrists, she found nothing.

Now she turned her attention to the fingernails. Any scrapings—of blood, dirt, hair follicles, or other material—could prove vital to the investigation. Say a follicle of hair found under the nails failed to match the victim's, why, then there was a chance it might belong to an assailant—if there was an assailant.

But all that Gail could extract from under these fingernails was caked dirt, which she removed with a file and placed in a plastic bag. Labs in the M.E.'s office would later subject the dirt to a chemical analysis. Maybe in the dirt, invisible to the naked eye, something of significance would turn up.

She examined his feet last. They were bare and clean—no smudges on their soles. But what caught her eye was the reddish coloring of the feet, clear evidence of post-mortem lividity. When all circulation ceased, the blood responded to gravity, settling into the lowest regions of the body. The clotting of the blood essentially "fixed" the characteristic reddish stain within five to six hours after death. The lividity in the feet was an important sign. It indicated that Friedlander had been moved after he died.

If she needed further proof, she had only to take a look at the way the blood had stained the wall behind Friedlander's head. Blood spots could be read like a language by a trained eye. There were six common shapes that blood spots could form: drops, smears, splashes, spurts, trails, and pools. A blow on the head, for instance, would produce either circular drops or a stain resembling an explanation point. A freshly wounded body, it if was moved, would almost invariably leave behind a dribble of blood and a pool where it was finally deposited.

Gail should have been able to find blood spatters from the head wound radiating out for a couple of feet, had Friedlander shot himself in the position he now occupied. But all she could see, hard as she searched, was the telltale dribble of blood extending beyond the body along the edge of the wall until it came to an abrupt stop. She looked more closely at this stretch of the wall, trying her best to understand why there should be no more blood.

"It's been washed away," she said.

"What did you say?" Mackie asked.

"I think somebody washed the blood away here." She put a finger to the spot.

"Is that right?" He looked to where she was pointing, but she realized that nothing was going to convince him. She felt suddenly light-headed and very tired.

"It's possible that he was shot elsewhere and then moved here," she said a little more tentatively than she'd intended.

The way Mackie was looking at her, she expected him to explode. She imagined that his wife must have walked out on him years ago. But when he replied, it was with a surprising calm. Still, the calmness was deceptive and came as no relief. "Well, then, what you're going to have to do is put that in your report."

"Do you still plan to treat this case as a suicide?"

Mackie's eyes met hers. "When the autopsy is completed and we see what we've got, we'll decide." He hesitated, then added, almost as if it were an afterthought, which it obviously was not, "What we do from now on isn't your concern. You've done your job here."

CHAPTER TWO

Reaching back in his memory, Michael Friedlander came up with the date September 10, 1971. That was the last day he had been in New York City, having left, he'd thought, for good. He'd made up his mind to cut all ties, burn all bridges, start life anew. After nearly twenty years he was on his way back, staring numbly out of his bus window at stretches of Route 95 that he'd assumed he'd never have to look at again.

For the last five years New Hampshire had been his home. Before that it was San Francisco, before that, L.A., before that a small impoverished village on the shore of Lake Panahachel in Guatemala. Before that . . . well, what difference did it make? It was painful to go rummaging about in his memory trying to reconstruct his past.

But he couldn't help it; memories kept surfacing, unbidden and certainly unwanted. March 14, 1983, was the date that came to mind next. That was when he'd last seen his brother. Alan showed up a couple of days before he was set to leave San Francisco, another place he was intending to leave for good. His apartment, like his life, had never given the appearance of being settled to begin with. When his brother arrived, the place was in complete tumult, crowded with boxes and milk crates, with scarcely any room to move. Alan said he was on a business trip and could stay only for a few hours. But it had been so long since they'd seen each other that he didn't want to pass up the chance. Even then Alan basked in an aura of success; money was as anxious to move in his direction as it was to steer clear of Michael.

As soon as Alan walked through the front door, it was obvious that Michael could no longer depend on their age difference to balance things out. Michael had squandered his seniority in the pursuit of misguided dreams, succumbing to all temptations except the one Alan had given in to: money. Somehow Michael had always assumed that there'd be enough of it around, that he'd always get by, as indeed he had, and that sooner or later his ship would come in.

Alan was clearly uncomfortable. It was only with great restraint on his part that he refrained from parroting the words their father would have said: *Get your life together for Chrissakes, settle down, find a job with a future. For that matter, find a girl with a future.* Alan never thought much of the girls his brother found, and no wonder. They were very nearly as crazy as he was.

But Alan had been diplomatic, so much so that Michael suspected he was acting on behalf of their parents, maybe thinking he could play mediator. Michael's relations with his parents, once tempestuous, had turned cold and uncommunicative. Alan must long ago have replaced Michael in their affections. It was on their younger son that they'd pinned their hopes; it was Alan they looked to for their grandchildren and, Michael was sure, it was Alan whose name figured prominently in their will.

For all his reservations, Alan insisted on lending money to Michael, even though he must have known the prospects for getting it back were slim if not nonexistent. Michael never asked for the money, but periodically he would open his mail to find two or three hundred dollars—always cash, never a check—from his brother. There were times when he had no idea how he would have made it if it weren't for those unpredictable "loans" of Alan's. As of last month, he owed Alan close to seven thousand dollars. It had always been his intention to pay Alan back. Now it seemed he would never have the chance.

What had begun as an overcast day had turned into a moonless night. The man next to him was too big for his seat and, even dead asleep, squirmed in an effort to escape its confines. Everyone else around him seemed to be sleeping, too. Michael had the feeling that he might be the only one still awake in the world—aside from the bus driver. He didn't know what time it was since he never wore a watch. It was dark; that was all that mattered. For great distances there were no towns, no hamlets, nothing at all that gave off any light. All Michael could see in the window was his own distorted reflection, which made him look much like the ghost that his brother had become.

He would doze off, then wake suddenly, jolted into consciousness by an abrupt motion of the bus, a defiant squeal of brakes. Shaken so abruptly back into consciousness, he'd think, *Something's wrong, but what is it?* And then he'd remember. His brother was dead.

Michael's fitful sleep was finally extinguished when he opened his eyes to drink in thousands of bright lights. Fluorescent colors seeped over the pavement and dyed the skin of the people moving at an impossible pace along the streets. People were everywhere. He'd forgotten how many people there were. Some were leaning out of windows, calling down to furtive gatherings on street corners. At every intersection there were men with squeegies in hand, ready to clean windshields for a quarter. They moved fast, ambushing any driver too slow on the uptake to avoid them. What got to Michael, though, were the men slumped in doorways, nodded out, without the will or the interest to extract the needles from their arms. As if in accompaniment to all this frenzy of making a buck and getting high, salsa and rap music erupted from the open windows and boom boxes, horns wailed, sirens rose and fell, signaling a temporary truce in what was a continual state of emergency. Michael was home.

The Port Authority Bus Terminal was altogether different from what he remembered although his memory, he knew, was an unreliable, treacherous thing. The immense building had obviously undergone extensive renovation so that now it resembled an airline terminal, which Michael guessed was some improvement. He listened for piped-in Muzak but heard none. Many of the benches, he noted, were occupied by people who weren't on their way anywhere; apparently this was all the home they had.

* * *

Finding the coffee shop across the street from Bellevue wasn't a problem, but for ten minutes Michael couldn't bring himself to go in. His mother, and for all he knew, his father, too, would be inside waiting for him. He wasn't sure how he was going to face them. Finally he couldn't stand it any longer. He had to get it over with.

It took him several seconds before he spotted his mother. Her features were distorted in grief, her face taut and white. Her neatly coiffed hair, which Michael had remembered as brown, was now full of gray. In front of her was something that looked vaguely like custard, which she'd barely touched. Suddenly she became aware that he was there. A half smile flickered across her face, for the moment returning some of her lost years to her. Michael went over to her table and without a word took hold of her. *How fragile, how insubstantial, she feels*, he thought, *like she could be gone tomorrow.* His mother kissed him, then quickly separated from his embrace, saying, "Oh, dear, I've got lipstick on you. Let me wipe it off."

And before he'd had a chance to utter a word, she did just that, using the same piece of Kleenex to wipe the tears that had begun to gather at her eyes.

"Sit down, Michael. Have something to eat. You must be tired after your trip."

Yes, he thought, considering that it was a trip that had lasted more than sixteen years, he was very tired.

"Your father's still across the street. When you're finished, we can join him."

"They haven't done the autopsy yet?" Michael was surprised. His mother had gotten hold of him early in the afternoon, and he'd naturally assumed that in the intervening hours all the formalities would have been completed.

"Dr. Magnus—the medical examiner—they had to get in touch with him, and so it was a while, you know, before he could get to examine Alan. I don't think it'll be too long now." She gave Michael a scrutinizing look. "You've been well?"

"I've been okay."

"It's good to see you. I'm glad you could come. It's been too long."

"Yes," he agreed, "it's been too long."

"But I'm not so sure about the beard. You looked fine without it, you have a nice face."

He shrugged. This was no time to start arguing about a beard. "Maybe I'll shave it, then." He was anxious to find out about Alan. All his mother had told him over the phone was that he'd been discovered dead by his own hand and that he should come at once to New York, nothing else. But he sensed that he'd better wait. When the time came, his mother would tell him. Obviously the time wasn't now.

The first thing that Michael remarked on when he entered the building housing the medical examiner's office were the words engraved in marble. He was certain he could have figured out what they meant if only he'd paid attention in his high-school Latin classes. The words were: TACEAT COLLOQUIA. EFFUGIAT RISUS. HIC LOCUS EST UBI MORS GAUDET SUCCURRERE VITAE. Something about laughter should cease, he believed, something about the dead helping the living. He couldn't make much more sense of it than that.

His mother appeared to know where she was going. He followed, suitcase in hand; he must have looked as if he was moving in.

But no one moved into this place unless he was dead; that was just about the only qualification necessary. From the lobby they proceeded into another room. Michael had a glimpse of police and people like his mother who wore their suffering so openly that there could be no mistaking the reason for their presence there. But most of what Michael saw was a blur; a thick haze seemed to hang between him and the rest of the world, impenetrable and endless.

Then they found themselves in a private room, a waiting room, much too brightly lit. His father was approaching him from across the room, his hand held out for Michael to take. Michael was prepared for a taller man and he didn't know whether his father had actually shrunken or whether it was his memory that was at fault. His hair was nearly gone but the eyes were the same, and the way they questioned, and even accused, his son was the same, too.

Michael took his hand. The grip was hard, signaling, if nothing else, some sort of acceptance. The prodigal son returned. "Thank you for coming," Paul Friedlander said. "I didn't know whether you could make it."

Michael looked to his mother but she had locked her eyes on her husband. Maybe, Michael thought, he deserved his father's reproach, but not now, not now.

"What do they say?" his mother asked, taking a seat in the corner, digging through her pocketbook for a mint, taking one for herself, offering the other to Michael. "How long do they say it will be?"

"Not long," replied his father. "It shouldn't be long now."

To Michael it seemed almost unimaginable that his father should be put in the humiliating position of having to wait for word from some higher authority. All of his life he'd regarded his father as the ultimate authority, sometimes a benign dictator, more often a despot, but always the person he had to answer to. Nor was he alone in this. Hundreds of other people looked upon his father the same way. Kroll, Friedlander, Geddes, and Lichter was one of the city's top corporate-law firms, cannily accruing power and influence by brokering deals no other firm dared to touch. But apparently when it came to his son's autopsy, he was incapable of exerting much influence at all.

Michael took a seat next to his mother. His father refused to sit, preferring to pace, his eyes directed toward a panel located on the wall across from them. "What are you doing with yourself these days, Mike?" he asked wearily.

"Not much," he said. "Just fixing up my house. It's an old house; it goes back to the eighteen hundreds. It needs a hell of a lot of work." It needed so much work, in fact, that at the rate he was progressing, it wouldn't be finished until the next century.

His father nodded. "Doing any work? I mean, do you have a job of any kind?"

For all Michael knew, his father might still hold out hope that he'd resume his medical studies where he'd left off, finally apply himself to something substantial. But that wasn't in the cards. "I was doing some importing," he answered, "selling rugs and jewelry I picked up in India."

"Oh, you were in India?" his mother said. "When were you there?"

"About a year and a half ago, just for a few weeks."

"Alan was in Hong Kong last year. He was always on the road. Whenever we'd plan on a vacation, we'd ask Alan where we should stay. Isn't that right, Paul?"

"What was that?" Paul looked at her distractedly.

"I said that when we planned our vacations—"

She didn't get any further. For just then the wall panel slid open to expose a glass chamber. There was a faint electric hum: machinery kicking into motion. His mother hid her face in her hands. Paul looked blankly ahead. At the same time the door behind them opened and a man wearing a white coat stained with blood and smelling of formaldehyde walked in. He was a man of about forty-five, slender and dark, with sharp features. He moved quickly, energetically, his eyes taking them all in. His hands, Michael noticed, were strong, the fingers narrowly tapered, the hands of an artist.

"Dr. Magnus, this is our other son, Michael," his mother said. To Michael she added, "Dr. Magnus is the chief medical examiner."

Magnus nodded and shook Michael's hand, trying out a smile that was quickly gone. He turned his attention to Paul. "If you'll step up to the window here, please, Mr. Friedlander, this shouldn't take long. But we need to verify the identification."

Mrs. Friedlander clung to her son, but while her body was trembling, there were no longer any tears in her eyes. She held herself with dignity, bracing herself for the shock.

"We installed these viewing rooms some years ago so that the bereaved wouldn't have to go into the morgue," Magnus said. "This way you at least can have some privacy."

It was possible that Paul didn't hear, with his entire attention focused at that moment on the empty chamber. The gurney with Alan's body was just now coming into view. Michael looked hard, almost as if he needed to memorize what he saw. He wanted to feel something, but the only thing he felt was empty. That wasn't his brother—that was a bloody, decomposed cadaver. His brother was long gone.

Then he stole a glance at his parents. In their eyes he read horror and incomprehension—that much he had expected. But there was a question in their eyes, too. And Michael knew very well what the question must be: Why is it Alan who's lying there, when all the time we were thinking that if it had to be anybody it should have been Michael?

CHAPTER THREE

It was nearly midnight, more than an hour after the Friedlanders had gone, when Kurt Magnus began Alan's autopsy. The autopsy was performed in one of the three basement autopsy rooms reached by a central circulating corridor that led from the mortuary bay.

Tonight Magnus was using only one assistant, a deputy examiner named Francis Holmes who'd been working for the M.E.'s office for as long as anybody could remember. Holmes had participated in thousands of autopsies—perhaps more than Magnus had—and his manner was brusquely efficient, even a little bored. Death had no surprises left in store for him except, possibly, the manner in which it would come for him. He was a wiry man in his early sixties, with an owlish hairless face and glistening pink skin. Magnus understood that he'd once trained to be an artist and actually displayed a fair skill at painting models from real life. But somewhere along the line real life failed to hold any more interest for him.

They started out by radiographing the head. Since it was evident that the bullet had exited out of the back of the head, Magnus wanted to see whether any fragments remained lodged inside the skull. Wet plates were ready in a few minutes and showed no dense metallic shadows, sparing him the necessity of going in search of fragments, an observation he transcribed into the microphone installed at the base of the table. Sometimes a stenographer would be present to take dictation, but not tonight.

He then proceeded to reflect the scalp—drawing away the skin so that he could get at the skull, or what remained of it. This was done according to a procedure dictated by cosmetic considerations. Magnus used a knife to describe a single ear-to-ear incision across the scalp. This way he could part the scalp into two large flaps, pulling one flap back toward the rear of the head, just as if it were the hood of a windbreaker, and dropping the other half over the face. But the subgaleal tissue that connected the scalp to the skull resisted Magnus's efforts to separate it.

Magnus was left with no alternative but to place his thumbs under the flap and pull it back by force. The tissue gave and the scalp tore away to expose the white of the skull itself.

To remove the skullcap he chose to use a handsaw. While the skull had to be sawed through completely, Magnus had to take care that he didn't cut too far and risk damaging the brain tissue itself. Final separation was achieved by hammering the cut out with a chisel.

They were down to the dura matter, the outermost protective membrane of the brain. To obtain the traction he needed, Magnus inserted a blunt hook called a dura elevator, which resembled a small spatula, into the saw cut. Because the brain had been so shattered by the impact of the shot, it was now possible for Magnus to look down straight into the skull cavity itself. He began to dictate his findings: "It appears as if at least a third of the brain tissue, posterior cerebral tissue, and some of the cerebellar tissue has been blasted out."

He paused to make a further inspection before resuming: "There is a large deficit in the right occipitoparietal area. . . . I am able to see the back of the head quite well. There are multiple fractures of bones of the calvarium bilaterally. These fractures extend into the base of the skull and involve the floor or the anterior fossa on the right side. . . . There are enormous cracks radiating downward and outward from margins of the large deficit in the top portion of the skull extending to the base, plus numerous others on the floor of anterior and middle fossas on the right. . . ."

He was about to go on when Holmes interrupted him, pointing to the entrance of the autopsy room, where a man was standing staring at them with an implacable gaze fixed on his coarse features. A large man, he was wearing an ill-fitting corduroy jacket, with a wide blue-striped tie that had become all askew. In his right hand he held a worn leather briefcase. Holmes shot a questioning look at Magnus, puzzled, even dismayed, at this intrusion. Clearly this man didn't work there, nor did he appear to be an authorized visitor.

"Can I help you?" Holmes asked, stepping away from the table, ready to send the man packing.

But Magnus moved to stop him. "It's all right, Francis, let me go speak to him. It'll just take a moment." He realized that his voice was quavering, but he couldn't help it.

Francis frowned with incomprehension. He must now be wondering whether the two men knew each other, and if so, what possible connection they could have. Francis was extremely judgmental when it came to sizing up an individual; he believed that someone's manners and clothes marked him for what he was. And it was certain from the unhappy expression on his face that he'd found this man wanting in both respects. Why Magnus would lower himself to bother exchanging words with this stranger was beyond him.

No greeting was expected or given. "Follow me," Magnus said, doing nothing to disguise his irritation. He didn't even so much as glance at the man. Out of the corner of his eye he registered Holmes's scrutiny. *The hell with him,* he thought.

Magnus went straight to the men's room. A few moments later the man joined him.

"Lock it, please," Magnus instructed.

The man complied, but he seemed to be deriving some amusement out of the medical examiner's discomfort.

"It smells better than it did the last time," the man observed. "Somebody clean it, or what?"

"I told you I didn't want you coming here while I'm at work. What are you doing here, anyway? We didn't have any arrangements to meet."

"For somebody who's making out like a bandit on this, I don't know why you're raising such a fuss. We just felt that you deserved a little more for your trouble, Dr. Magnus. If you have any objections, take it up with the boss. I got nothing to do with it."

He turned from Magnus and, placing his briefcase on the tiled floor, went ahead and took a long leak. Magnus just stood there, uncertain whether he should say anything more.

"That's better," the man said, zipping himself up. "Enjoy your night."

Only after he'd gone did Magnus reach down and open the briefcase the man had left behind. It was all there, as promised. The bills felt new and crisp in his hands, as if they were hot off the press.

CHAPTER FOUR

There was nothing about the design of the house Paul Friedlander had purchased in 1961 to make it stand out in any way. Many times on his way home from a party, admittedly drunk but not so far gone as all that, Michael had been unable to recognize it. There must have been well over a hundred houses set on two-acre tracts of land that were identical to theirs. But if it was altogether lacking in style or originality, the house had increased phenomenally in value over the years, something in which his father took immense pride, as if unconscionable inflation were his doing.

There was some comfort to be taken, Michael supposed, from the dull familiarity of the neighborhood. Perhaps in the daylight he would notice some changes, but at two-fifteen in the morning this section of Bellmore, Long Island, looked exactly the same as he remembered from his childhood. Few lights were on in any of the houses, which was to be expected; like his father, these people had to be up early to make the commute into the city.

Scarcely a word had passed between Michael and his parents since leaving the medical examiner's office. The silence was terrible. Music would have been welcome, even the news, but the radio was left off. Who needed other people's bad news? From time to time his mother would say something, but she was careful not to touch on what they had just seen. It would be a long time, Michael knew, before each in his own way could deal with the sight of Alan dead, his head blown open. It was one thing to accept Alan's death in the abstract, but seeing the body like that—even for just those few moments—made it into something final, something inescapable. Whenever Michael shut his eyes, he could still see Alan's face, the skin waxen and half fallen away, the rusty ring of blood around the wound, the blood caked in his hair. But his eyes were closed and Michael was sorry about that; he would have liked to have looked into them one last time.

Lights were blazing in the Friedlanders' house. Michael's first thought was that this day of terror hadn't ended and that the house was being burglarized. But that wasn't the case at all. As soon as they pulled into the driveway, a woman opened the door. Michael couldn't make out who it was because of the way the light behind her threw her into silhouette. But as soon as his mother rushed into the woman's outstretched arms, he realized that it must be her sister Janet.

Janet was six years older than his mother and resembled her not at all. She was taller and bonier, a woman with few expectations, and it showed in her face. Seeing Michael, she swept him up in her arms, moistening his face with her tears.

Janet's husband, Buddy, rose from the couch when they walked in, tamping out his cigar in the ashtray at the same time. Buddy was an accountant but he had the look of a cosmetics salesman who expected to have the door slammed in his face. He greeted Michael indifferently, as if he were used to seeing him every day.

Almost from the moment they entered the house his mother was ready to go to work. Anything to provide distraction. "Let me go and get you some more coffee," she said to Janet and Buddy.

"No, Rachel, you just sit and make yourself comfortable," Janet declared in a voice that brooked no protest. "Buddy and I will take care of everything. We're here as long as you need us."

Paul took a seat across from Buddy, who was now relighting the cigar he'd abandoned a minute before. "It was terrible, Buddy," his father began. "It was worse than I'd imagined it would be."

Rachel slumped down on the couch next to Buddy but then grew too restless to stay there. "I think I'll go help Janet," she said, her voice quavering.

Michael didn't know what he should do. As if by instinct, he found his way to the liquor cabinet. A drink would be hard on him, he knew, but he could think of nothing else.

Conversation, such as it was, came fitfully, uneasily. Nobody was talking about Alan. Everyone was hanging on the phone call from the medical examiner's office, almost as if they expected to hear that miraculously Alan wasn't dead at all. When the phone did ring, it might have been the loudest sound in the world. On the fourth ring Paul sprang from his chair, released suddenly from a spell. The phone was on the other side of the wall from the liquor cabinet, so Michael could hear every word his father said.

"Yes, this is he. . . . Yes, I understand . . . I see . . . I see. . . . Then there's no way that it could be . . . ?" He fell silent for several moments. "Yes, yes, of course. No, I'm grateful, thank you, Doctor. . . . Certainly I'll let you know. . . . Good night."

"Honey?" Michael heard Rachel's questioning voice.

"That was Dr. Magnus."

"What did he have to say?"

"He's sending me a copy of the report in the morning, but he wanted to let us know tonight."

"That was thoughtful of him," his mother said.

"He said that his autopsy confirmed what the police told us."

"That Alan—?" His mother didn't want to, or perhaps couldn't, finish the question.

"Yes, I'm afraid so. There doesn't seem to be any question in his mind."

"What does that mean?" Janet broke in. "What happens now? Is that it?"

"If the medical examiner found no reason for the police to investigate further, then . . . then nothing happens. There's nothing we can do. . . ." He cast a puzzled glance at Michael, who'd come into the room. "I guess it's over."

The funeral took place the following day at one-thirty in the afternoon. Michael was late; he didn't mean to be, but there was something in his nature that rarely permitted him to turn up anywhere on time—even for an event as important as this one. His breathless arrival drew a withering glance from his father. His mother just looked relieved that he'd appeared at all. Unable to sleep, he'd gotten up early and gone for a long walk, trying to sort things out. While he hadn't managed to sort out much of anything—it was even possible he'd only gotten more confused—his walk had taken him much farther than he'd planned. By the time he'd returned his parents had already left for the funeral home. He was a little surprised himself that he'd made it.

His parents were standing at one end of the room together with Janet and Buddy, receiving condolences from people Michael presumed were relatives and friends, almost none of whom he recognized. He decided that the younger mourners were Alan's associates from Colony Saxon Securities. More than their youth, their glowing tans and stylish clothes gave them away.

He had no difficulty picking out Alan's intended without any problem, though. Nancy looked just like the sort of woman his brother would have chosen to marry: a classy brunette, but nowhere as beautiful as Alan probably thought she was. She possessed a pretty doll-like face that might go over big in Charleston or Cedar Rapids, not in Manhattan. Michael had an idea what would happen: She and his mother would try to keep up a relationship of sorts, there'd be phone calls, maybe a lunch or two, and then Nancy would meet another man and little by little fall away.

"Michael, it's good to see you after all these years," said a balding, bespectacled man, grasping both his hands. "It *is* Michael, isn't it? I'm Lou Waterman. Judge Waterman?"

Dimly Michael remembered him. Judge Waterman was one of those friends of his father's who could always be counted on for favors. What those favors were Michael never knew. It was all related to the firm's business, which his father never brought home with him.

"I was very close to Alan, you know," Waterman said.

"I'm sorry, I had no idea." Michael wondered how long he could continue to be this polite and formal. His tie was choking him. He couldn't recall the last time he'd worn one.

"It was horrible what happened to him, just horrible. It's worse when you don't know why a brilliant boy like Alan with everything going for him should do such a thing." He shook his head in consternation.

"I don't know," Michael said. "Maybe he didn't."

The judge regarded him questioningly. "I'm not sure I follow you. Maybe he didn't what?"

"Maybe he didn't kill himself."

The judge looked bewildered, unsure whether Michael was serious or not.

"I realize it must be painful for you. But then, you and Alan weren't really in close touch, were you?"

"No, but—"

"If you'd like to talk about your brother, I'd be happy to have you over for a drink sometime. Your father knows where I live. Come around whenever you like. I'm retired now, so it's not as if I'm pressed for time."

"Maybe I will, at that."

There was no further opportunity to talk with so many others wishing to offer their sympathies to Michael. It seemed to him that even after he'd gone to the trouble to shave for the occasion, they had no more idea who he was and what role he occupied in the Friedlander family than he had of them. For years Alan had been the "Friedlander boy"— the only Friedlander boy. And now came this complete stranger to usurp his rightful position.

Out of the corner of his eye he saw Nancy sneaking occasional glances at him. He had a feeling, without their ever exchanging a word, that he knew her. She would be like all the other women Alan took out, one of a set. Even in these sorrowful circumstances he could see that she was judging Alan's business associates in the hopes of finding a suitable replacement.

Nothing about the funeral—not the liturgy, not the consoling words from the pulpit sprinkled with appropriate quotations from Job and the Book of Leviticus—reached Michael. He was indifferent to the entire proceedings, which he somehow viewed as a sham. To him, it seemed amazing that people could so easily accept his brother's death. Why weren't these people angry? Why weren't they ready to kill?

Certainly they all seemed to be in agreement that it was baffling why a young man like Alan who had so much to live for would want to commit suicide. But that was as far as it went. Nobody seemed to consider the possibility that maybe the autopsy report was wrong, that maybe he hadn't shot himself. It was this blind acceptance of theirs that incensed him. At least someone should be demanding an explanation. Maybe, Michael thought, it was easier for all concerned this way.

The funeral service over, he began walking—alone—

toward the limousine that was to take the immediate family to the cemetery. Somebody was calling his name. Looking around, he saw Nancy.

"Do you think we could talk after?" she asked breathlessly.

"I guess so. Why?"

"Because there are some things about Alan that ... well ..."

She had a slight but rather engaging Southern accent.

"I'm not sure I could be of much help, though. I didn't know my brother well." He suspected that she, too, was looking for an explanation and figured that he might be able to provide one.

"I know that," she said impatiently. "I was just hoping that somewhere along the way he might have mentioned something about ..." She paused and shot a furtive glance in the direction of the mourners collecting in front of the funeral home. "Well, about that woman."

"What woman?"

Nancy threw him a reproachful look. "Oh, you must know what I'm talking about. That woman Alan was fucking at the same time he was fucking me."

CHAPTER FIVE

Now that the funeral service and the burial had taken place, everyone expected that Michael would be on his way back to New Hampshire. And he'd gone to sleep in his old bedroom that night prepared to do just that.

But he awoke suddenly after a short but surprisingly restful sleep. Somehow he didn't feel tired at all. On the contrary, he was fully alert, ready to get on with the day. From the softening grayness in the sky he guessed that it must be an hour or so before dawn. His room was half buried in shadows. He listened but heard nothing; the house was impenetrably quiet.

He'd decided that he owed it to his brother, and to himself, to discover why Alan had died. He remained steadfast in his conviction that Alan couldn't possibly have killed himself. But even supposing he had, at least he could find out why. If he couldn't give Alan back the seven thousand dollars, at least he could do this much. Once he had his answer, then, he told himself, he would go back home.

How he would go about this, what actual steps he needed to take, he had no idea. But he was certain that something would occur to him as he went along. For now what was important, what was crucial, was to begin.

His logic seemed to him so unassailable that he somehow expected that his parents would approve of his idea. Or at the very least not oppose it.

Seeing him at the breakfast table when he came downstairs, his father assumed that he wanted to get an early start.

"Are you all packed?" he asked without much interest in the answer.

"I'm not going back just yet. Probably I'll be moving to the city." Actually, he hadn't given it any thought until that moment.

"Oh?" His father was putting a couple of slices of bread into the toaster. "Do you want some?" he asked.

"I've eaten, thanks. Mom still upstairs?"

"Let her sleep, she could use it."

So, obviously, could his father. He looked monumentally tired.

Up until this point Michael had counted on his mother being present when he presented his plan to them. He expected that she might prove more understanding, more sympathetic. But alone with his father, he was more hesitant.

"What do you plan on doing in the city, Mike?"

"I'd like to stay at Alan's for a while. I thought I could be of some help getting things in order." It was a pretext, but one that he believed his father might accept.

His offer, though, seemed only to heighten Paul Friedlander's skepticism about his motives. "I don't believe we'll have any trouble settling Alan's affairs on our own."

Michael didn't know whether he was hearing the lawyer speak or his father. "I'd like to do something for you and Mom." He was anxious to impress upon his father that he meant well, that he was willing to work at a reconciliation, and what more propitious occasion to do that could there be than this one?

It was possible his father recognized that Michael was making a gesture and that maybe it would be better not to dismiss it out of hand. "Well," Paul Friedlander said after a short silence, "let me think about it."

Later that day Michael moved into his brother's apartment in The Brandenberg. He didn't have much to move, and it wasn't as if he was planning to stay long. As far as his parents were concerned, his job was to sort through his brother's effects, determine what was worth keeping and what was not, make sure to record for tax purposes the articles he chose to give to charity, and finally to show the apartment to people interested in buying it. An ad listing the apartment was going into next Sunday's *Times* at an asking price of $425,000.

Michael had never lived in an apartment valued at half that much and doubted he would have the chance again. By the time he arrived, all evidence of his brother's violent end had been eradicated. Restored to a more or less pristine state, it looked as if it had never been lived in. Michael had been expecting to find the apartment permeated by his brother's presence, but it turned out that there was no one's presence there at all.

No sooner had Michael made himself a drink than he began hunting through the apartment for any letters, photos, financial records, receipts, or souvenirs that many people routinely collected. He came up with pathetically little. The afternoon following the funeral his father had come by and removed what personal effects of Alan's he could find. Michael had gone through them later on, after his parents had gone to bed, and found next to nothing. No diary, no journal—that would have been expecting too much. Alan had no time to write things down. He was a memo man, a computer man. The dozen or so letters that Alan had troubled to save didn't amount to much, either: they included a couple of thank-you notes, some business correspondence, an insistent letter from Macy's disputing Alan's claim that he'd paid up an overdue bill on a sofa for $2249.99, and a letter from Nancy, postmarked in the Bahamas, saying that while she was having a lovely time, she couldn't wait to get home and see him.

He was convinced that more revealing documents must exist somewhere. Certain that Alan must have hidden them away, Michael looked and looked. A hot hazy western light had settled over the city by the time he finished. If the swizzle sticks from Bandito's Mexican restaurant, the three Amex receipts from Bloomingdale's, Paul Stuart, and American Airlines, or the pair of ticket stubs from the Baronet collectively had a message to convey, he for one couldn't comprehend it.

But what made no sense to him was why there should be a whole stack of videotapes—*Ghandi, The Empire Strikes Back, Flashdance, Suspicion, Rocky IV, Body Heat, Dirty Dancing,* and *Children of a Lesser God* among them—but no VCR. He also located two boxes of 3M floppy discs—both unopened—but no computer.

He got on the phone to his mother. "Do you know whether Alan owned a VCR? He has plenty of videotapes here."

"I don't know. I guess he did." She sounded impatient and probably a little irritated, too. What Alan did or did not own must have seemed beside the point to her.

"What about a computer? Did he have a computer?"

"Maybe. I can't remember. He was always talking about getting one, but I don't know whether he did or not."

"When you were visiting him, did you happen to notice a computer here?"

"I honestly don't remember, Michael. Maybe your father

does. You can try him later. He's with your uncle right now, and I'd prefer not to interrupt them. Why does it matter?"

"Because they're not here is why."

"So they're gone," she said. "So what?"

Perhaps it didn't matter at that. The only conclusion he could draw was that in the days before Alan shot himself, he'd done more than just put his affairs in order; he'd wiped the slate clean, destroying his records and discarding his possessions. But that wasn't like Alan. His brother was not someone to discard his possessions, not without replacing them with something better.

Although Michael was discouraged, he was by no means done. He had drawn up a list of people to talk to, people who knew his brother. He began by calling the 19th Precinct and asked for Lieutenant Ralph Mackie. According to the police report, he'd been the one in charge of the investigation.

"Mackie?" The officer taking the call didn't sound as if the name meant anything to him. "Wait a minute." Several seconds went by while he attempted to find out what had happened to the detective. When he came back on the line, he reported that Mackie wasn't in.

"Well, when can I reach him? What time does he come on tomorrow?"

"Mackie isn't coming in tomorrow. He doesn't work here any longer."

"Was he assigned to another precinct?"

"No, he retired."

"How can I get in touch with him?"

"I couldn't tell you that. I don't know."

"Who would know?"

"Beats the hell out of me," the officer said. "Maybe if you try tonight, somebody at the desk might know." Then he hung up.

It wasn't a long list that Michael had put together; in fact, there were only four names on it—Mackie, Judge Waterman, Colin Gray, one of Alan's colleagues from Colony

Saxon who'd introduced himself at the funeral, and Nancy Melanby. He decided he'd try Nancy next.

"I was just thinking about you," she said when he identified himself. "I was wondering if you were ever going to give me a call."

He said that he could come by and see her any time she liked. "When would it be convenient for you?" He was new at this sort of thing, unaccustomed to making plans and setting up appointments. In the world he'd been living in these past several years, people just sort of showed up when they felt like it.

"Are you doing anything now?"

"Not especially."

"Then why not come by? I could use the company."

Nancy's high rise was called The Bogata; it was a taller, sleeker version of The Brandenberg wrapped in tinted glass. Nancy's apartment led onto a terrace from which it was possible to see half the Upper East Side. She had her hair pinned up against the heat and was wearing a white linen shift that draped her like a Bedouin.

They sat out on the terrace drinking white wine. An easy-listening station was tuned in on her radio, which was something Michael could have done without. He still couldn't make up his mind whether she was as vapid as he'd thought, or whether she was anxious to conceal her intelligence for fear that men might otherwise fail to appreciate her.

Of course, she wanted to talk about Alan. "Nobody else knows this," she started by saying, "but I don't think I would have married Alan. Don't get me wrong, I loved him, but that only gets you so far, don't you think?"

"I guess."

"See, we were going in different directions. When we had our charts done, Christy said we were incompatible."

"Christy? Who's Christy?"

Nancy looked a little surprised that he wouldn't know. "She's the woman who did our charts. They're expensive, a hundred and fifty dollars each, but you'd be surprised how accurate they are. Alan's chart showed that there would be trouble for him around this time—his planets were in the wrong place. His stars were out of alignment."

"I can believe that," Michael said. "You know, Nancy, you never did tell me what you do."

"For a living, you mean?"

"Yes, for a living."

"Well, I'm a fitting model."

"A fitting model?" Michael had never heard of anyone being a fitting model before.

"We're the models they use to see how clothes fit before they manufacture them. I'm a perfect ten." She smiled happily at the notion.

Michael had begun to see her in a whole different light. "A perfect ten?"

"Yes, a perfect size ten. You can't imagine how difficult it is keeping yourself in shape, watching your diet every minute. Gain a couple of pounds and you can lose a job. Even so, it's a bitch. The way it's going now, they're going to replace me with a computer."

From what Michael could see of her body, more emphasized than concealed by her Bedouin shift, he couldn't quite imagine how a computer could replace her.

"They can program in the measurements for the sizes. Then all they have to do is push a few buttons and they can see what a sweater or a pair of slacks will look like on someone. It's cheaper than we are. It's the wave of the future. Say, would you like some goat cheese? It looks awful, but it has a real interesting flavor to it."

Michael declined. The wine was enough. "You told me at the funeral that you thought there might be some other woman in Alan's life. Was that why you wanted to call the marriage off?"

"That's putting it rather delicately, Michael. I didn't think you were so discreet. What I said was that he was fucking somebody else while he was fucking me. Ginny, I think her name was. Jean or Ginny, something like that. He kept denying he was seeing her, but a woman knows these things. It's like a sixth sense. You can tell when a man's hiding something like that. It was such a shame because when Alan and I met he was so open, so much fun to be with."

"How did you meet exactly?"

"At a benefit dance at the St. Regis. It was for muscular dystrophy. Or maybe it was for multiple sclerosis; I'm always getting those two confused." She looked at Michael as though she expected him to enlighten her as to the difference. Then she went on. "But then he began to change. He was always under a lot of pressure. You know, with the market and his clients he constantly had to be on his toes. It was like he was living and breathing the market night and day. How long can you keep up that kind of pace? But even so, why did he have to go out and buy a gun? Even if he lost a million dollars on IBM, is that any reason to buy a gun?"

"He didn't tell you why?"

"He said it was for protection, that in a city like this you never knew. He began taking lessons. On television he saw an ad for this place in the Village where they'd train you. Ex-cops run it."

"How many lessons did he take?"

"I don't know. How many lessons do you need to know how to put a gun to your head and pull the trigger?" Obviously she believed that he'd killed himself, just as everyone else seemed to. "I think it was burnout that did it. It got so that I hardly knew who he was anymore. It could have been the drugs, of course."

"Drugs? What drugs?"

"As far as I know, all he was doing was ampicillin hydrochloride. Or maybe it was ampicillin trihydrate. Whatever it was, he was taking a lot of it. They can't sell it in this country—it's illegal."

"What does the stuff do?"

"It makes things go away. Reduces fevers, things like that. Did you know that your brother was a hypochondriac?"

Now that he thought about it, he supposed he did.

"The ampicillin made him feel better."

"How did he get hold of it if it was illegal?"

"Well, he was always going off on business trips—Europe, the Caribbean. So he must have had sources abroad for it. Toward the end he was going away all the time. I'm sure he was taking his girlfriend with him."

"Alan didn't leave you his computer by any chance, did he?"

She shook her head. "No. Why should he? I wouldn't know what to do with it. I don't like computers much, as you can imagine." She stared off into space, a dreamy look in her eyes. "You know what I'll never forgive Alan for?"

"No. What?"

"For what happened to Samantha."

"Samantha?"

"My German shepherd. Alan never liked her. He said that it wasn't right to have a dog in the city. But it was more than that—he didn't like dogs in general. Remember that Porsche he owned for a while? Before the BMW?"

Michael said that he'd seen none of his brother's cars since the secondhand Impala he'd bought off the lot for a hundred bucks when he'd gotten his driver's license.

"Oh, well, he had this beautiful silver Porsche for a year or so. One night he let Samantha loose while I was at work and ran her over."

More than anything else he'd heard about his brother, this shocked him. "Alan deliberately ran over your dog?"

"He said she was getting on his nerves and he couldn't stand it any longer. Only, you see, he didn't kill her—not right away. All he'd done was break her spine. He wouldn't let me take her to the A.S.P.C.A. to have her put down, so we had to wait up all night and watch her die. It was ghastly. It was like I said—something had happened to change him. I don't think he even knew himself. If you ask me, I think he's better off dead. At least now I can get another dog and won't have to worry."

CHAPTER SIX

In summers as hot as this one, the city took on the appearance of a war zone abandoned by all but those unfortunates nobody bothered to warn of the danger. In more temperate seasons, these desperate people could lose themselves in the crowd, taking refuge in their anonymity with all their lusts and weaknesses. But with the streets lying so empty they stood out. Their need for solace and pleasure was too palpable to ignore; there could be no pretense, no coyness. Their bodies, half-naked and soaked with sweat, longed to tremble under a stranger's touch. Their eyes boldly stared into the eyes of each passerby, their gaze demanding a response. Are you the one? Are you the one?

He had no name, or rather he had many names, just as he had many professions, many backgrounds, many pasts. He moved among the unloved and undesired like a fish in water. He wasn't only a predator, although he was certainly that; he was a searcher. In his lifetime, only one person had mattered to him, only one person had ignited a spark in him, had made him feel alive. And until he found somebody who could make him feel alive again in the same way, his search would go on, ceaselessly, relentlessly. He believed that he would only have to look in someone's eyes and he would know. He would know.

This Thursday evening, while it was still light, he was sitting by the fountain at Lincoln Center. Lights were coming on on all sides of the plaza, tracing patterns of beige and gold on the pavement. Cafés teemed with life; theatergoers in high spirits moved purposefully toward "Mostly Mozart" and *Pagliacci*. The women looked splendid in white and black, the men handsome and in command of their lives. But as showtime approached, it became easier to pick out the ones who were left behind, who came there to be touched by the glitter, to feel briefly a part of the excitement. These were people without money or without a lover or companion; these were people who surrounded themselves with their loneliness. These were the people the man by the fountain was looking for.

The woman he approached was probably in her early forties; she was short and plump but by no means fat. Yet he could tell that she was self-conscious about her looks. She was wearing a black top and a flounced skirt and gave every appearance of wanting to have an important event to attend. It was obvious she had nowhere to go, not tonight, maybe not any night.

"Pardon me. Would you be interested in a ticket to hear Alicia de Larrocca?"

She raised her eyes toward him wide with astonishment that he should be speaking to her. Then suspicion flashed into her eyes.

But when he told her that his sister hadn't been able to make it and he was stuck with the extra ticket and what a shame it would be to let it go to waste, the suspicion began to fade. Besides, she would be thinking: *What a nice, refined young man he seems, so beautifully dressed, and so good-looking.* He could see what type of impression he was making on her; it was the impression he made on practically all the women he struck up an acquaintance with this way. She couldn't take her eyes off him, not until he met her gaze directly, and then her face colored and she turned away.

"Well, I don't know. . . ."

She wasn't bad-looking, actually, though it was obvious to him that she believed otherwise. She wore her hair too short, like a boy's, and there was such an eagerness to please in her eyes that it undoubtedly scared men away.

"Are you doing anything else right now?" He could hear the ringing of the bells inside Alice Tully Hall summoning ticketholders to their seats.

"No, but . . . I'm afraid I couldn't afford—"

"Forget it. My sister paid for it, so it's not like I'm out the money. It would be my pleasure, really. If you want to repay me, why don't you buy me a cup of coffee afterward?"

The ticket proffered in his hand almost seemed to cast a spell over her. She hesitated, but in another moment he knew he would have her.

By the time the last exquisite strains of Mozart's *Piano Concerto Number 21* had died away, she was breathless with excitement, absolutely enthralled. Her name was Molly Gitelman; she was divorced and worked in a public-relations firm. "There's no future in it," she told him. "I really have to find something else to do."

There were thousands of people out there like her; they didn't care for what they were doing, they weren't getting ahead, they weren't making enough money, and they were tormented by the thought that they should be pursuing another goal in life if only they could figure out what it was.

For Molly he had decided that he would be Dan Morris, a playwright who'd achieved success in regional theaters in the South and was now trying out his luck in the big time. He told her the names of his plays—*Easy to Remember, Last Man Out*, and *Incandescence*—knowing that she wouldn't possibly recognize them. How could she? He'd made up the names on the spot.

He suggested that they go to The Ginger Man a few blocks away to continue their conversation. Molly was so exhilarated by the turn her night had taken that she was of course in no mood to end it.

The Ginger Man was crowded, as he'd hoped it would be. That way, if anyone should come around asking questions later, the waiters would be unable to recall the gentleman in the white jacket and matching slacks, much less describe him.

Molly was voluble, bubbling over, unable to stop talking, maybe because it had been so long since anyone had troubled to listen to her. "My husband, Philip, just hated going to concerts. He hardly listened to music at all. It didn't bother me when I was going out with him, but later it really got on my nerves, especially when he refused to let me go off to a concert even with a girlfriend. You can't imagine how incredibly jealous he was."

He genuinely felt sorry for her. She was stuck in a rut, and it would not change. Even if she should ever gather the courage to leave her present job for one that paid slightly better, nothing for her would ever improve. The man she imagined for herself, the man she imagined *him* to be, would never come along on a white charger to rescue her. Growing older, she would try to fight off the bitterness. Friends would drop away, particularly the ones who'd achieved better marriages than she, stung by her unarticulated resentment. Her air of determined optimism would begin to seem more and more false even to herself.

When they were done with their drinks, he asked her if he could take her home.

"I live uptown, near Columbia," she said uncertainly.

"Well, I don't mind driving you back. My car's parked just around the corner."

"Are you sure it won't be taking you too much out of your way?" She would never want to inconvenience anyone.

"Really, it's no trouble at all. I'd be delighted."

"Well, okay, sure, that's very nice of you, Dan. Just so long as you don't mind."

Fifteen minutes later he was pulling up in front of a drably respectable brownstone. It was a building without a doorman on a street that seemed to have gone to bed early. She began searching through her bag for her keys. "I'm sure they're here, I know I put them in here," she said.

"Hey, Molly."

"What?"

"Are you up for something different? I mean something exciting, something that you've never imagined before?"

She gave him a wary, disappointed look. "What did you have in mind?" Of course, she assumed that this was nothing more than a come-on.

"A sacrament."

This threw her. She had no idea to what he was referring. "It's kind of like a ritual."

"What kind of a ritual?" She was still under the impression that he was talking about sex.

"A private ritual, a religious ritual, Molly. It's something that means a great deal to me. Nothing would give me greater pleasure than for you to share it with me."

She was uneasy but intrigued. "Does it take long, this ritual? I have to get up for work tomorrow."

"Not long—a few minutes, really. And it's very simple to do. If you don't want to do it, just say no."

"Well . . ." Again she was hesitating, but he knew what her answer would be. It was this moment that he treasured, when everything hung in the balance, when it could go in either direction. It was the moment when a person chose life—or its opposite.

"I guess so, if it's not going to take long," she said. "Why not?"

"Why not, indeed?" he agreed, reaching to take her hand.

CHAPTER SEVEN

"I was really sorry to hear about your brother," Colin Gray said as he led Michael back into the maze of offices of Colony Saxon. "It was one of those things you hear about happening to somebody else, something you read about in the papers. You never think it will happen to someone you know. It was a shock to all of us here."

Colin was in his early thirties, another member of his brother's generation. He looked younger, though, and baby fat still clung to his face; and while it was likely he paid a great deal of money to keep his blond hair tamed, it had a way of falling into disarray whenever he made any sudden motion of his head. He was no one Michael would trust with his money—if he had any.

"The timing of your brother's death is really unfortunate," Colin said.

"Why? Is there any good time?"

Colin paused and gave a little nervous laugh. "I'm sorry, I didn't mean it that way. What I meant was that the market's going through such an incredible period right now. There's so much money pouring in. Your brother would have loved being in on it. He just craved excitement, and it's a thrill a minute down here. You know, whenever anybody would tell him that the Dow couldn't go any higher, he'd scoff at them. Wait until all the institutions get into this, he used to say. They keep holding back, thinking that they're playing it safe with bonds, but after a while you've got to figure their clients aren't going to be satisfied with their measly ten percent. They'll be wanting to see some real profits."

Michael's head was already spinning when he'd come in there. Maybe it was the heat, maybe it was life, but whatever the case, the hermetic atmosphere of these offices wasn't helping. On all sides of him, in cramped little cubicles, men and women sat bathed in the greenish glow of computer terminals, watching endless sequences of numbers and abbreviations come flying across their screens, typing in orders, answering calls, but evidently not quickly enough—phones were ringing everywhere unanswered.

"You know, if you have any extra money lying around you should really consider investing it—get more bang for your buck."

Extra money? Michael thought, astounded. Lying around? He wasn't sure he'd heard right. "Excuse me?"

"Well, you know, I could help you out. I don't care if you only have four or five thousand salted away."

No doubt, to Colin's mind, four or five thousand dollars was peanuts, scratch. That anybody wouldn't have had even that much to put into a six-month CD or a promising penny stock was a thought unlikely to have crossed his mind.

Michael had to strain to be polite, not make some wisecrack. He had to keep in mind that he needed Colin to help him. "At this point I really don't have anything—"

"Well, if you ever decide to do a little investing, do give me a ring. Why don't you take my card?" It was possible

Colin thought that Michael had the money but was reluctant to let him know he did.

"What is it my brother did exactly, Colin?"

"Same thing I do. He was a securities broker. He traded for the company and for his own accounts."

"Do many of the brokers here travel a lot on company business?"

This drew a laugh from Gray. He might have assumed Michael was joking. "Jesus! I wish. No, the brokers don't travel as a rule. Maybe to a company conference in Norwalk or White Plains, but that's as exotic as it gets. What made you think we do any traveling?"

"Alan's fiancée was under the impression that he was always out of town on company business."

"Ah, well, he took a lot of personal days, but so far as I know, it had nothing to do with business."

"Was there somebody else my brother was seeing?"

"Look, I was a good friend of Alan's. We used to go drinking together; we belonged to the same health club." Was Michael to understand from this that the two were joined in some secret business fraternity, that confidences once given could not be disclosed even after death had intervened?

"Listen, Colin, I don't want to pry, I just want to find out what happened to him, why he died the way he did."

Colin gave him a long, appraising look, taking his measure. Then he said, "Tell you what, let's talk later, okay? Let me have your number and I'll give you a buzz." His smile was intended to reassure Michael, but Michael took no reassurance from it. Michael didn't trust him, but he supposed it worked both ways: Colin probably wasn't sure whether he should trust Michael.

They now entered an area where traders, their faces rapt in concentration, sat in swivel chairs at a long table studying the movement of the markets on their individual terminals. A row of offices lined the corridor to their right.

"I'll show you your brother's office." Colin motioned him forward.

It was an office like all the others; it had a large gray desk with a hardwood top and a window view that would have allowed Alan to stare out at the Battery and the Statue of Liberty. But there was one major difference between this office and the others they'd just passed—it had been thoroughly cleaned out.

"What happened to all his papers, his records?" Michael asked.

Colin scanned the office, then opened and closed the desk drawers. "That's funny. Everything was here yesterday when I checked. Hold on for a sec. Let me call Personnel."

While Michael followed the tortuous progress of a tug into the harbor, Gray made his call. "This is Gray down in Trading. Can you give me an idea what happened to Friedlander's papers?"

Several seconds of silence passed during which Michael imagined bureaucratic wheels grinding into motion.

"That's Friedlander, Alan: office two-one-seven-four; extension eight-seven-eight-two. He doesn't work here any longer. As of five o'clock on the fifteenth. That's right." He waited for a while, alternately cracking his knuckles and stretching his fingers. A nervous habit of his. Then he said, "Well, thank you, I appreciate it." There was a strange look on his face when he turned back to Michael. "You're never going to believe this."

"What is it?"

He was shaking his head in bewilderment. "It seems that Alan's papers were seized this morning as evidence."

"What are you talking about?"

"The Feds took all his papers. No one seems to know whether it's the SEC or the FBI."

"The FBI?"

"You want to know something? I'm beginning to think that your brother might have been involved in some very deep shit. Who knows? Maybe he decided to get out while the going was good."

*   *   *

Heading home, Michael was so discouraged that he could think of nothing else to do but stop and have a drink at what was now his local watering hole, McNally's. What an ass he'd been to think that on his own he could have penetrated the mystery of his brother's death. He didn't know this city any longer, he didn't know how it worked. Any connections he'd once had were gone. Even the look and feel of the city were different. Old landmarks had vanished—some razed, others transformed and reopened under new names. What had happened to Dr. Generosity's or Max's or Stanley's? Where had Shakespeare's gone? When had Slugs shut down? Glitzy bars, full of big potted palms and magenta and lavender lights, had replaced them. The men who came into these places were smartly dressed and all reminded him of Colin Gray. The women with them were unapproachable and frighteningly beautiful. One look at them was enough to bring despair to his heart.

About the only place he felt comfortable in were places like McNally's. McNally's offered its customers the melancholy solace of nearly every neighborhood tavern he'd ever been in. Only regulars came in there; there was no attraction for anyone else. The women, even the ones in their thirties and early forties, had something broken about them. They drank as good as or better than the men and sat for hours wreathed in cigarette smoke. Whenever one looked with interest in his direction, Michael inwardly shuddered, dreading a tale of bitterness and lost opportunities, perhaps a drunken attempt at seduction.

But he sat there because he could think of nowhere else to go and because he was unwilling to face going back to Alan's apartment.

A man entered the bar. It wasn't until he'd gotten closer that Michael realized it was Stopka, The Brandenberg's super. Stopka was a dark, graceless man of uncertain extraction. There was a sly, knowing air about him that caused Michael to keep his distance. He sidled up to the bar, still not seeing Michael, and began speaking to the bartender in a harsh whisper. The bartender, however, made no effort to keep his voice down. They were talking about money—not an unusual subject for conversation in this city. From what Michael could gather, Stopka had something to sell—something hot—and, while the bartender was apparently interested in making a purchase, the price didn't appeal to him at all.

After a while Stopka, despairing of reaching any agreement, simply gave up. It was only then that he noticed Michael. His face lit up upon seeing him. If he sensed Michael's coolness toward him, he didn't respond to it. Clapping Michael on the back, establishing familiarity where none existed before, he sat down next to him.

"What do you think of this heat?" he asked, motioning to the bartender.

A glass of pale vodka materialized in front of him. "Get this man whatever he wants. On Stopka." Stopka was anxious to show Michael how magnanimous he really was.

"I'd like it if it wasn't like this day after day," Michael said, resigned to having a few words with the super now that he'd bought him a drink.

"Where you come from?"

"New Hampshire."

"Not so hot up there, I think."

"No, but you get a hell of a lot of mosquitoes."

"Oh, yeah," Stopka agreed, "those mosquitoes are killers. They can keep you up all night. You keep slapping and slapping but nothing you do gets rid of them, I know. You don't have no problems now with the mosquitoes, do you?"

No, everything was fine, Michael assured him. No mosquitoes, no roaches, no flies—and no maggots. "You're doing a fine job; everything's nice and spotless."

Stopka smiled proudly.

"Your brother, he is a very good tenant, no problems. What a shame such a thing has to happen to him." Stopka sounded sincere, which was a surprise to Michael. Maybe he'd misjudged the man.

"Mrs. Moskone, she isn't driving you crazy?"

"So far, no."

"Sometimes she can be a pain in the ass." He shook his head in wonder at it. "She is on the phone with me all the time. 'Mr. Stopka, do this, Mr. Stopka do that!' First it's her stove it doesn't work properly, then it is the toilet it is not flushing. It makes me crazy. She drinks, all day she drinks. But it is the loneliness that is bad. Drinking okay, but loneliness, it is the worst."

Michael agreed. Loneliness was the worst.

"That is what is so much a surprise about what your brother did. He is not so lonely, I think. He has girlfriends, very nice." His eyes glimmered, and his gold-toothed smile hinted at some lascivious memory.

"How many girlfriends did Alan have?"

"Two, I think. One is a brunette, the other is a redhead."

The brunette must be Nancy. It was the redhead who interested him. "Would her name have been Jean—or Ginny?"

"Stopka doesn't know their names," the super shot back, as if Michael had in some way offended him. "I see him with this woman in the lobby, sometimes he comes in with her late at night." He rolled his eyes up to emphasize to Michael how little he knew. Now his voice dropped. "She is pretty, but she is a dirty little girl, Stopka can always tell."

"What do you mean, dirty?"

"You look at her, you know that she fools around. It is written all over her. It is in her eyes, it is how she moves. Her hips, her ass. You see the way she moves, you know." Cupping his mouth with his hand, as if he was about to confide an important secret, he added, "She wears a tattoo on her shoulder. I have seen it many times. A tattoo of a flower. But not just any flower. Inside this flower there is a cross, a crucifix. Tell Stopka, what kind of girl is this?"

The impression Michael was getting of this mysterious girlfriend was that she was Nancy's exact opposite, a sort of anti-Nancy. Maybe Alan used one to balance out the other. Anytime life grew too stiff and dull and the need for excitement came over him, he could always give Ginny a call.

Then when Ginny's craziness wore him down, it was back to Nancy and her easy-listening music. Michael was beginning to think that he and Alan weren't so different after all. They both craved drama and tumult in their lives; they both even gravitated to flamboyant and adventurous women. It was just that Alan had been a great deal more successful in keeping his craziness hidden.

"Stopka, suppose I wanted to find out more about this girl. What would you suggest I do?"

Stopka thought for a moment. "Do you have money to spend?"

Michael had some of his own and more from his father, which was to go for expenses connected with settling Alan's affairs. "Yes, I do. Not a lot, though." He assumed that in return for some hard cash Stopka was prepared to divulge far more than he'd revealed so far.

He was wrong. "Do you have a pen?" When Michael produced one, Stopka began to write on the back of a cocktail napkin. "This man is very good. He finds out anything you wish to know. You tell him Stopka sends you."

The name he'd scrawled was Nick Ambrosetti. "What is he, exactly?"

"He is a detective. That is what you need, no? A good detective. I tell you he is a miracle worker. When my wife disappeared, he found her for me." Stopka snapped his fingers. "Like that, he finds her."

"Your wife disappeared?"

Stopka threw his head back, laughing. "Not my Maria. Sometimes I wish she would disappear, but she never does. No, I am talking about my first wife. She disappeared eleven years ago."

"What happened to her?"

"What happened? After Nick finds her she disappears again, but this time I am too wise to send anybody to look for her. Some people, it is better they don't come back, no?"

CHAPTER EIGHT

When Magnus arrived at the railroad flat, several minutes late, he was wearing a raincoat against possible thundershowers that had been predicted for days but still hadn't arrived. Weariness that went beyond a mere lack of sleep showed in his eyes. For a few moments it seemed as if he wasn't really aware of the attention he was drawing from the throngs of police, paramedics, and members of the press. He was the star there. Everyone was waiting on him. It took him a while before he spotted Gail off in a corner and acknowledged her with a faint smile.

A detective began to brief him as to what he would find in the adjoining room. Directly in back of him the terrified landlady was attempting—without any success—to comprehend what he was talking about. She was Hispanic, about fifty, a buxom woman bursting out of her summer dress. When it occurred to her that she was being ignored, she broke in on the detective, nearly shouting, half in Spanish, half in English. All that Gail could catch of what she was saying was that the tenant was a nice boy, a quiet boy, and there was no way in the world she could have believed him responsible for something as abominable as this.

Halogen lights threw the room into such stark relief that it no longer seemed real anymore. Kate Parnell from Channel 7 Eyewitness News was setting up for an interview with an upstairs neighbor, a carpenter in his early thirties obviously delighted to be in on all the excitement. A man from CityVision Cable TV was thrusting his boom mike into the face of a harried detective. "Is this the work of the Chopper?" he asked. The detective, shaking his head, replied that they would all have to wait and see what the medical examiner said.

Nobody seemed to know whether the Chopper was real or a convenient fiction concocted by the media to account for three or four especially brutal slayings. It was true that earlier in the month a severed arm wrapped in rice paper had turned up in the Rambles in Central Park and that a headless torso was found in an unclaimed trunk in Grand Central. Two unsolved killings in the Bronx, marked by savage mutilation, had also been attributed to the Chopper, though without any tangible evidence to connect them to him. Police spokesmen quoted in the papers had scoffed openly at the existence of such a pathological murderer. But the idea that there was such a Chopper had taken firm enough hold on the public imagination that it would need more than a few reassuring words from the police to dispel it.

Making his way through the tumult, Magnus approached Gail. Oblivious to the commotion around him, he took her aside and said, "I'm glad you could take the time to come, Dr. Ives. Ordinarily I wouldn't have pulled you away from your work, but I think that you might benefit from seeing a case like this."

So many lights and cameras were trained on both of them now that she felt a little like a celebrity herself. Just a few minutes before she'd been on the sidelines, another investigator in an army of investigators. But now she was basking in the same spotlight that Magnus was. It was unnerving; this wasn't a routine case for a medical investigator any more than Friedlander's had been. She could only speculate on why Magnus had chosen her in particular.

She'd heard that every so often Magnus chose one investigator and took him—or her—under his wing. For the first time it occurred to her that this was why he'd asked specifically for her; perhaps he intended on turning her into his disciple. It wasn't an honor she was looking for. On the contrary, it made her feel a bit guilty since she had no interest in this work other than a certain natural curiosity and a desperate need for money. Nor could she judge what his expectations might be. She couldn't deny, however, that the prospect of a continued association with Magnus intrigued her. There was no telling what might come of it.

At the sight of the medical examiner, the police moved aside for him—and Gail—to pass. The regard with which the police held the chief medical examiner was clearly visible in their faces. He was the ultimate detective, after all, the man who could, from the study of hair and blood and semen, solve many of the crimes that had them completely baffled. There was an attraction to power that Gail had never quite understood before. She began to see how it could become addictive.

Gray late-afternoon light spilled into the room where the body lay. The police photographer had finished with his work and stood at a good distance from the corpse smoking a cigarette. Forensic experts were bagging stray evidence and dusting for fingerprints that they probably had little hope of finding. Later they would have to vacuum everything, including the body, for hair fibers and specks of blood that might help them trace the identity of the murderer. But in the center of the room nothing had been disturbed; it was as if the body were an altar that could only be approached reverentially, demanding awe in the face of the violence that had been visited on this place.

Magnus paused about half a dozen feet from the body, his practiced eye taking in the scene, relating the context to the crime. Once the body was removed, there was no restoring the tableau to its original state; everything would become secondhand. The crime would be dissected and analyzed in parts: in the morgue, in police laboratories, in interrogation rooms, and perhaps eventually in a courtroom. Only now was everything they had to work with spread out before them—everything, of course, except the perpetrator.

The body was that of a woman, and she'd been dead for some time. Magnus stepped closer. The body was facedown, covered with a striped sleeveless dress that had been hiked up over her thighs. Blood was congealed in her thick coiled hair. Snapping on latex gloves, Magnus knelt down beside her, motioning Gail to do likewise. Detectives loomed over them, taking notes. "Look at her left hand," Magnus said.

The thumb and two fingers were gone—from all evidence, bitten away.

"Rats?" Gail asked.

"Look closer. You can make out the teeth marks."

"Human?"

Magnus nodded. She would have preferred rats. "The murder must have occurred at least a couple of weeks ago," he continued. "You see how the hands and the legs are in the process of becoming mummified?"

When Magnus attempted to lift the head for a glimpse of the face, the back of the head fell away. A portion of the skull bone, disintegrating already, shattered on the floor. The detective standing directly above Gail took two steps back. "Jesus!" he muttered.

Maggots seethed out of the vault of the skull. It looked as if a million of them had made their home in it. Gail forced herself to look without flinching. She realized she was anxious not to disappoint Magnus. He, alone in the room, seemed unperturbed; it was possible that he'd expected this to happen. "Obviously a blunt object was used to smash her head in—probably with a single blow."

"And that was what took the back of her head off?" Gail asked.

"No, it inflicted heavy damage, but the action of the vermin loosened it. I'd say that there were three successive layings of blowflies. You see how fat and indolent these maggots are?"

Gail shook her head dazedly. They didn't seem so indolent to her.

"It's only in the third instar that you see them this lazy."

Maggots were a key indicator of the length of time a body had been decomposing. In warm weather they could lay waste to a body in ten days. Known to hatch as early as the same day they were laid, the first-instar maggot shed its skin after eight to fourteen hours, the second-instar maggot after two or three days. The third-instar, or fisherman's maggot, continued to feed voraciously for the next five to six days before settling into the pupa stage.

It was going to take a full twenty-four hours with the body immersed in Lysol solution before the maggots could be killed off and the autopsy begun.

The face was a puffy, rotting mess, its features so formless as to make it impossible to make any definitive judgment about what it had once looked like. There were five stab wounds visible in the front of the head. "I would say that these were made by a right-handed person striking down and from the front," Magnus noted, still with no emotion in his voice. "Here. What do you see?" He lifted the right arm so that the hand and wrist were faceup. Two large gashes were present.

"More stab wounds. I'd say she was trying to ward off the blows."

"Exactly." Magnus looked pleased with her response. "Now take a look at the skull from this angle. Observe how far these stab wounds penetrated."

"It doesn't look far at all."

"What would you conclude from that?"

Gail considered this for a moment. "I'd say that the wounds might have been painful but probably not serious enough to disable her."

"Good. Perhaps in time she might have collapsed from wounds with this shallow penetration, but not immediately. She would have been in a position to try to resist her attacker."

He then went on to note the crush fracture of the right cheekbone.

"If you follow these six long fissures radiating away from the gap at the back of the skull, you'll see how the paths confirm the downward motion of the blows. What do you surmise from that, Dr. Ives?"

"I guess she would have had to be lying down when the blow came."

"Correct." He studied the mutilations more intently. "Now this should help us. See the way these knife wounds are shaped? They're beveled. It looks as if the knife had been driven into the head, then turned or twisted before it was removed. If we can ever find a knife that could produce a wound like this, it might take us one step closer to finding the killer."

Gail looked again at the wounds, but she lacked the discerning eye necessary to see what Magnus had just pointed out to her. She nodded dumbly, though, as if it were clear to her as well.

"Do we know who she is?" Gail asked.

"Not a clue," Magnus answered. "The police have failed to find any form of identification. That's something we're going to have to work on once we run our tests."

The dress came away easily. The woman's chest and abdomen had been slit open to reveal thousands of maggots swarming inside the wounds. Parts of her breasts and thighs had turned white and foul-smelling, and oily to the touch from adipocere formation. Ordinarily adipocere formation, characterized by stiffening and swelling of body fat, wouldn't have occurred so readily but for the heat. The summer heat was bad enough, but three generations of maggots, with all their frenetic activity, had also contributed their share.

Drawing the dress down farther, Magnus examined the pubic area. "There's some bruising of the thighs here," he said, "but the deterioration of the body is too pronounced to determine whether she was raped. At this late date vaginal swabs wouldn't do any good."

Magnus rose to his feet and whipped off his gloves.

"I'm done here, Lieutenant," he said, addressing the detective in charge. "You can remove the body now. But be very gentle; we don't want to drop bits and pieces of her along the way."

As the medical examiner started to leave the apartment, reporters surrounded him. "Dr. Magnus! Dr. Magnus! Please, a few questions, Dr. Magnus!"

"How long has she been dead?"

"Maybe three weeks, maybe a little less."

"Is this the same M.O. that the Chopper used in the other cases?"

Patiently Magnus explained that the other cases—the arm in Central Park, the torso at Grand Central, the Bronx mutilations—were still open, so there was no way for him to know whether they were the work of a single murderer.

"I for one wouldn't want to speculate whether there is such a person as the Chopper," he emphasized.

"But on the other hand, Doctor, you're not necessarily denying that he exists," another reporter pressed.

Magnus conceded the point. He knew just as well as the others assembled in the room that this particular death would never have brought out the press in such numbers had it not been for the conviction in people's minds that a demented killer like the Chopper was at large. Otherwise, it would have been one more senseless death among many and surely not worth getting excited about.

No doubt many people were afraid that somebody like the Chopper actually existed, Gail thought, but there were probably many others who needed to believe that he did.

Magnus broke off the questioning and proceeded out into the hallway. There he seemed to remember Gail and motioned to her. "I expect we'll be performing the post tomorrow or the next day. I hope you can attend."

He didn't wait for her reply but was instantly in motion, down the stairs, keeping one step ahead of a reporter who was hurling questions at him he didn't want to answer.

It was only a few minutes after he'd returned to his office when Magnus learned that a detective named Sorenson from the 6th Precinct—Greenwich Village—was waiting to see him. Sorenson had brought him a package. It was a small package that evidently had been opened and inspected. It was just the right size for chocolates.

"We recovered no latents from either the paper or the box," Sorenson said, "nothing to identify who sent it. It was in with the mail, but there weren't any stamps on it. It didn't come through the postal system."

Magnus raised his eyes at Sorenson's doleful face, suspecting that his expression would be the same even if he had good news to convey.

"Surprise, surprise," Magnus said, lifting the cover. Inside the box he found two fingers and a thumb. He would have to see whether they matched, but he had no doubt that they belonged to the body he'd just examined on West Twenty-fifth Street.

There was something else inside the box. With a pair of forceps Magnus brought it out into the light. It was a nipple, the tissue raw around the edges. A tooth mark was barely distinguishable.

This hadn't come from the body he'd just examined. He didn't need to go back and check; his memory was quite clear on that score. The hand had been mutilated, not the breasts. This could only mean that the nipple had come from someone else, someone they had yet to find.

CHAPTER NINE

Louis Waterman lived high up in a building on Park Avenue in the Nineties that had the look of a fortified castle. Under the vigilant eyes of security guards, Michael walked in through a courtyard, then turned to the left, where an elevator was waiting to speed him up to his destination. The elevator man waited until Michael was admitted, watching him scrupulously, before beginning his descent.

Michael was greeted by a kindly black woman with a faint Caribbean lilt to her voice. He assumed that she was the judge's housekeeper. "You will wait a minute, please. I will let Judge Waterman know you are here," she said.

Standing in the oak-paneled vestibule with its umbrella stand and framed nineteenth-century Hudson-school landscapes on the wall, Michael realized that he did not feel as much out of his element as he'd imagined he would. On the contrary, the seductive combination of old money and tradition worked to make him feel right at home.

The housekeeper returned to tell him that the judge would see him. "Please come with me."

She led him down a narrow passageway into a magnificent sunlit room. The judge was seated on a sofa, a book resting in his lap. Behind him in the window Michael had a view of town houses and modern high rises, old and new money competing for the same airspace, the same sunshine. "Isabel," the judge said, "please bring our guest whatever he'd like to drink."

"An iced tea if you have it."

"We have everything you could want," Waterman said. His face had a disturbing pallor to it, and he looked much frailer than Michael remembered from the funeral. But then the light had not been good, nor had Michael been at his most observant.

"How do you find New York?" the judge asked.

"It's altogether changed since I left it. I can't say whether I like it now or not."

"But I'm told you're planning to stay on at least until your brother's apartment is sold."

Michael admitted that this was so. He began to feel anxious. Up until this point he'd gone under the assumption that Waterman wanted to see him for family reasons, maybe because he felt an obligation to his father. But it occurred to him now that this meeting wasn't just a formality, that Waterman had something more in mind.

"You weren't very close to Alan, were you?" He knew the answer to this question and continued without waiting for Michael to reply. "It's understandable why you might not be satisfied with the way things have worked out."

Isabel entered so quietly that Michael failed to notice her until the iced tea was set down in front of him. A moment later she was gone.

"I don't follow you, sir."

"Well, it's come to my attention that you've been trying to find out additional information about how your brother died. . . ."

How the hell did he know? Michael wondered. Just what kind of sources did he have? "I don't know what you've heard, but it doesn't seem to me that it's out of line to question a few people about something like this. Nobody else bothered to; they just accepted what the police said on faith." Too late he realized he'd raised his voice. In such a setting, it seemed almost blasphemous.

The judge held up his hand to calm him but gave no indication that he was displeased. A small smile even came to his lips. "You always did have trouble with authority, I remember. But sometimes there's nothing wrong with that. In certain circumstances, it might even have its advantages. If I were in your position, I might very well do the same thing. I'd certainly want to get at the truth."

"Just to clarify things, sir, what exactly have you heard?"

"Oh, not much. Just that you've made some inquiries at Colony Saxon and attempted to get in contact with Detective . . . Mackie, I believe is his name."

Michael was about to ask how he knew about his "investigation." He didn't see how the information could have come from his father, but who, then? Colin Gray? Nancy? Somebody in the police department? Then he decided not to question him; the judge was never going to reveal his sources.

"And what have you learned so far?"

"Well, to be honest with you, I haven't really gotten anywhere."

"You must have heard about the seizure of Alan's papers from his office."

"I heard about it, yes, but I don't know why they were seized. I don't even know which agency it was that took the papers."

The judge nodded gravely. "I'm informed that it is the SEC. Perhaps other regulatory agencies have been brought in on it. I couldn't say. Apparently some suspicion exists that various brokers at Colony Saxon were playing fast and loose with their clients' accounts."

"How do you mean, fast and loose?"

Waterman's response was interrupted by a furious spasm of coughing that caused his body to tremble and drained the blood from his face.

"Are you all right, sir?"

Michael started to move to help him, but the judge shook his head, reaching for a glass of water, which he quickly drained. After a few moments more he recovered sufficiently to resume.

"It's one of those damned summer allergies, I'm afraid. Forgive me. Now, you must understand that I am not privy to the SEC's investigation, so I can only hazard a guess as to Alan's involvement. It's very possible that he may not have had anything to do with these irregularities. Perhaps the SEC is on a fishing expedition. Perhaps all they want to do is gather evidence so that they can bring charges against active brokers. But obviously we're dealing with something very sensitive here."

"I'm sure it's sensitive," Michael said, bristling.

"Am I right, then, in assuming that you intend to pursue your present course? You have no plans to return to New Hampshire?"

"Not until I'm satisfied I've found out why my brother died."

"Yes, I thought you'd say that. I admire your spunk. But I wonder whether you will get anywhere if you pursue this on your own. The way you're proceeding with this, you might only succeed in upsetting a great many people to no apparent purpose—including your parents." He let that sink in for a moment before going on. "Also, bear in mind how easy it is even for a trained investigator to destroy evidence inadvertently or scare a witness into recanting his testimony. You might only accomplish the exact opposite of what you mean to do. Do you understand what I'm saying?"

"Yes, I suppose I do."

"I'm told that many years ago, while you were here, you were in some sort of difficulty with the police. It was over drugs, am I correct?"

That seemed a terribly long time ago, but it still grated, it still hurt. "The charges involved drugs; the reality was politics. The police had a special intelligence unit that I'm sure you knew about. . . ." For all Michael knew, Judge Waterman might have sanctioned its actions.

Waterman cut him off. "Be that as it may, I'm not interested in dredging up the past. What concerns me now is your reputation. Even after the passage of all those years, it's possible that people may look at you as a troublemaker. I'm sure you've changed, but you're up against an enormous problem. Suppose you discovered that the police were mistaken, that Alan didn't take his own life. We can construct a thousand and one scenarios. But suppose you do come up with the truth—who will believe you?"

"I think people will believe me." He wondered about this, but he wouldn't let the judge know of his doubts. "I'll make them believe me," he said, hoping his voice carried conviction.

"I understand you're renovating your house in New Hampshire, is that right?"

"Yes, but what's that got to do with it?"

"See, if it were me, I'd make a mess out of anything I tried to build. I'd leave that up to you. By the same token, I couldn't attempt a criminal investigation, either. I would naturally seek out a professional service."

"I've already gotten in touch with a private investigator," Michael said.

"Oh, I see." He smiled. "Maybe people don't give you enough credit, Michael. I didn't realize you could be so persistent."

"It *is* my brother we're talking about."

"Do you mind telling me the name of this investigator? In my years on the bench I've encountered quite a few of them, you know."

"I'd rather not say, actually." It was embarrassment that stopped him; he feared that the judge would know who Ambrosetti was and find his choice absurd. Especially considering the source of the recommendation. An alcoholic superintendent.

"Michael, would you be willing to take advice from an old man?"

Michael thought it only polite to say he would.

"If you've made up your mind to pursue this business . . ."

"I have."

Again Waterman offered him a faint smile. ". . . even against better judgment, then at least think about acquiring the services of an agency that's reputable, an agency that can get the job done."

"I'm not that familiar with all the agencies—"

Waterman cut him off. "I know you're not. That's why I'm proposing to put you in touch with a private investigatory agency that I believe to be the best in the business. It does its job thoroughly and discreetly. If there's anything we don't know about Alan's death, they'll be the ones to find out about it."

"I appreciate it, sir, but there's the matter of the money—I have only so much to spare."

"Forget it, Michael. You're family, just like Alan was. I helped him. Did you know that? I got him his position at Colony Saxon. So why shouldn't I help you out? In a situation like this, we have to help one another out." He reached for the phone. "Let me call the agency right now and see whether someone can fit you in today."

Three hours later Michael was sitting in what passed for the reception area of the Fontana Security Agency. It had taken the judge only a few words to set up the appointment in spite of the short notice. But whatever Michael had expected from Waterman's description of the agency, it certainly wasn't this. Situated on the ground floor of a pre-World War II apartment building on East Thirty-third Street in surprisingly modest quarters, it consisted of five rooms, all of which, from what Michael could see of them, were simply appointed with bulky metal desks and filing cabinets. No computer terminals were in sight. Half a dozen men kept coming and going, occasionally talking in boisterous tones to one another, but it was impossible for Michael to tell just what sort of positions they held in the agency. The receptionist, an obese woman of indeterminate age who sat at the desk in front, was the only person who seemed to be working, mostly answering calls. Telephones were constantly ringing, but she had a studious way of ignoring them until she was good and ready.

In back of her, tacked on a cork bulletin board, were a dozen photographs of children and adolescents. A sign above these photos said simply: MISSING. Michael looked into their faces, full of innocence and acne, and read their names: Lynda Medeiros, Will Poppy, M. Whedon, Eddie Lupica. . . . He wondered what had happened to make them vanish and whether they would ever turn up again.

The detective who was taking his case was named Max Farrell. He was a big, square-shouldered man with knitted eyebrows that fixed on his features a look of fierce intensity. Michael guessed him to be in his early fifties. When he spoke, it was with a rasping voice. A file was open in his hands, but there seemed to be hardly anything in it. Picking up a ball-point pen, he said, "Now tell me all about yourself, whatever you think is relevant." Before Michael could so much as get the first word out, though, Farrell added, "But what I want to know most of all was why you got into such a shitload of trouble here back in 1970."

Evidently Farrell had already taken the time to familiarize himself—to a degree, at least—with Michael's history. So Michael told him the story, not in exhaustive detail, but making sure to include the relevant facts. He was in his second year at Columbia Medical School when he fell in with campus radicals. Soon he was so busy demonstrating against the war, lining up new supporters, raising money, and going on strikes that his work began to suffer.

"Med school's a bitch, people tell me," Max agreed. "Every day, they say, is like a final exam. You get behind, you're fucked."

That was true enough.

"But it says here," Farrell went on, lowering his eyes to one of the documents in front of him, "that the cops busted you for possession and trafficking of controlled substances."

Michael tried to explain; the drugs were nothing, the

drugs were bullshit. It just made the job easier for police than if they had to convict him on charges of fomenting insurrection. Eventually the charges were reduced, and he escaped with probation and a fine. "In any case, the police were spying on us, violating the law at every turn to build a case against us. If they hadn't reduced the charges, they would've lost on appeal."

Farrell didn't look convinced. "Well, it seems to me that that's a lot of trouble for the police to go to just to make a bust." He narrowed his eyes. "You wouldn't have been conspiring to blow up a Selective Service branch, would you? Nothing like that?"

"Look," Michael burst out, "I thought we're supposed to be talking about what happened to my brother two weeks ago, not about what happened to me way back in 1970. That's fucking ancient history!"

"You know who you're talking to? Know who I am? Know who all of us that work here are? We're goddamned ex-cops. Don't think you can jerk us around." He was waiting to see Michael's reaction.

"Hell, then, I don't think we have anything more to talk about." Michael was about to storm out when suddenly Farrell began to laugh.

"Jesus Christ! Take it easy. I just wanted to check you out is all. Relax, sit down. Don't you see? I'm with you. We're on the same goddamned side now."

Michael, still seething, sat back down. He had to admit that Farrell had done more digging than he'd expected. Maybe it was his way of showing Michael how thorough he could be. Michael didn't have to like the man, after all; what counted was that Farrell find out the truth.

"I'm sorry, but you've got to realize I need to know everything I can about you if I'm going to work on this case. Information that doesn't mean bullshit to you could explode in our face one day if we don't know what we're getting into. We need to be prepared for every eventuality. We want to know the lay of the land before we start out. That make sense to you, Mr. Friedlander?"

"I guess." He was still a long way from being calmed down.

"I understand, but it'll go better for us both if you put just a little trust in me, okay? Maybe as we work together you will. But for now let's talk about your brother."

It was a little after eight by the time the interview was over. Michael became aware of how quiet the office was. The phones continued to ring but less and less frequently. As Michael stood up to go, he heard a commotion out in front. A moment later a man in a light blue summer jacket materialized at the doorway. His hair, which he wore slicked back, glistened under the pale light of Farrell's office. His eyes were bright and alive. He was slender, and not very tall, and moved quickly, with athletic grace. While he wasn't handsome in a conventional sense, there was such alertness, such confidence, in his Levantine face that it was difficult for Michael to take his eyes off it. He smelled of expensive cologne and soon the rest of the office did, too.

"What have we here, Max?" was the first thing he said.

"This is Mr. Friedlander," Farrell said. Evidently no additional explanation was needed.

"Ah, Lou Waterman's friend," the man said, bridging the distance between them and clasping Michael's hand. "I'm Ray Fontana."

This, then, was the owner of the agency. Fontana radiated vitality. The air seemed to be charged by his presence. "Max is a good man. He'll do a top-notch job for you. But if he doesn't"—he leaned toward Michael as if he meant to impart some great confidence to him—"if he fucks up, you come to me and I'll find you somebody else."

Farrell, still seated behind his desk, didn't react, but maybe that was because he was undoubtedly used to banter like this from his employer.

"I'm telling you the truth now, Michael. If there's anything the police didn't find, anything they overlooked, we'll get hold of it. Max tell you we've got a lot of men from the force working here?"

"Yes, he told me."

"That's why we're the best in the business. We've got the know-how, we've got the connections, we've got all that experience behind us. The police fuck up, a layman would have no way of figuring it. But we can spot it right away. Isn't that right, Max?"

Max grunted. Yes, that was right.

"Then, if we do come up with new evidence we think should be acted upon, we'll hook you up with a lawyer you can count on—not one of these shysters you see hanging around Centre Street trying to cop some business. I want you to be happy. I want all our clients to be happy."

Michael said, a little more cautiously, that he hoped things worked out well for them both. He figured that this would probably bring the meeting to a conclusion. He was wrong.

Fontana suddenly brightened. Michael had the feeling that this was how he got when a new idea hit him. "Hey, Michael, are you doing anything now?"

"Not especially."

"Then maybe you'd like to join me and some friends of mine. We're planning on getting a bite to eat. Then who knows, maybe we'll hit a few clubs, check them out. You game?"

Michael wondered whether this was how all new clients of the Fontana Security Agency were treated. But he was perfectly willing to go along for the ride. A night with Fontana would seem to hold some promise to it.

CHAPTER TEN

It wasn't that Fontana's entourage had a tendency to grow larger—nearly a dozen people at one point—but rather that it changed with such regularity. Suddenly Michael would look around to find that there was a new face staring at him from across the table. He was being encouraged to do a great deal of drinking. There was no end to the drinking. Every time his glass was empty it would be replenished like magic. Even in transit the drinks continued, poured out of bottles of champagne that sat waiting for them packed in ice, the customary amenity he supposed was to be found in all stretch limousines.

They'd started at the China Grill in the CBS Building. The place was huge—it might have been a block long, with jade-green walls and huge eggshell-colored light shades suspended from the ceiling. In its marble floor Michael could read quotations from Marco Polo. It was there that a party of five blossomed into a party of eight. Although Fontana insisted on ordering for the table, he barely touched his food once it came. He had no time to eat. He needed to talk, and not just to the people at the table, but to others seated elsewhere in the room.

The man at Michael's right, a short man with a gnomish face and sandy hair, also turned out to be an employee of Fontana's—but not for the security agency. "No, I'm the manager of his trucking firm. We're based at JFK, but we also work out of LaGuardia and Newark."

"I didn't know he owned a trucking firm."

The man, who gave his name as Frank Brice, said that Fontana had his fingers in more ventures than he could possibly imagine. "He's got part interest in a cable company called City Vision, he's got real holdings all over the goddamned country; then there's his rental-car company, Quick Auto. . . . I could go on, but you get the picture. Every year he gets involved in something new. He's restless, you see, he always needs to be cooking up some new scheme or he isn't happy. Three years ago he ran for office—for State Senate—as a law-and-order candidate for the G.O.P. Came within three hundred votes or so of winning, too. That's not to say that he isn't in tight with the Democrats. He goes wherever the action is."

Fontana might have been in his mid-forties, five, six years older than Michael. It was unsettling to realize that while Fontana was busy building an empire and undoubtedly amassing a fortune, all that Michael had managed to accomplish was to build a house in New Hampshire that wasn't even finished yet. Thoughts like this caused him to drink with more determination.

"But really, when you stop and think about it," Brice went on, "he probably has more political clout being out of office than he would have if he'd won. See those fellows over there he's talking to?"

Michael glanced across the room at a table where two couples were listening intently to Fontana's words.

"The one on the left is Jason Parnase, the first deputy mayor. The other one maybe you've heard of—his name's Bernie Cook."

"The columnist?" Michael asked, looking at the husky, somewhat rumpled-looking man.

"The same. Ray gives him stories from time to time. Ray does favors for both Bernie and Jason, and naturally they do favors for him. It works both ways. Believe me, Ray holds a lot of sway in this city. I don't know what connection you have with him—"

"I'm a client of his security agency." That sounded safe to say, neutral, giving nothing away.

"Well, you couldn't be in any better hands. The kind of connections he has, you need to know something, you want something done, he's your man."

Fontana signed for the check, scarcely bothering to look at it, much less total it up to see if it was correct. The cost, Michael imagined, was close to what he used to make do with for a month when he lived in California.

Then they were off and running. Their first stop was Possible 20, a hangout—he was told—for dealers, studio musicians, and cops from Midtown North, and with two of whom Fontana was now deep in conversation.

A woman who'd attached herself to Fontana's party along the way, a diabolically pretty woman who in some inscrutable way belonged to a squat, unhappy-looking Italian named Mario something, sidled up to Michael. "You'd be surprised how the cops love Ray. He's made so many busts—on his own—over the years. No one can keep count anymore. Oh, he's helped out the cops lots of times. Did you know that he even stopped a hijacking of a Pan am jet one time? Nearly wasted the son-of-a-bitch who did it. They had to pull Ray off the guy."

"You're making him out to be some kind of superman," Michael said.

"It's just the way he is, a living legend. You don't get many of those these days. Besides, he's good to people, he helps them out. Hell, he'll give you the shirt off his back if you're in need."

Michael looked over to see that Fontana was again making a show of his generosity. Apparently it wasn't enough for him to pick up the tab at the China Grill. Now he was buying a round of drinks for everyone he'd brought with him—and a number of people he hadn't.

"So how did you meet Ray?" Michael was sure that this woman had her own little story to tell.

"Through Mario."

"Oh, and how did he meet Mario?" Michael shot another glance at the sullen man who stood off in the corner, glowering at them.

"The way Ray meets a lot of his friends—he busted him."

It was an odd crew, all right. By the time they arrived at the Zulu Lounge, walking directly in without having to endure the indignity of waiting in line, Michael had managed to learn the identities and occupations of half a dozen members of the Fontana entourage. It was curious that none of them appeared to have anything in common with anyone else. There was Brice, of the trucking firm; there was Mario, who worked nights, but not tonight, as a security guard for Fontana's cable TV operation, presumably as a way of redeeming himself from a life of crime; and there was Mario's pretty girlfriend, whose means of earning a livelihood was tough to pin down. A woman of somewhat more substance named Kathleen Fuerbringer said she was an interior decorator. She was especially fond of Fontana because he'd given her free rein in fixing up his new penthouse. "I show him what I've got in mind, he says yes or no, but mostly he says, 'Surprise me,' 'I don't like it,' 'I'll let you know.' But so far we've gotten along splendidly. Ask him about the antique chairs I bought for him in Indonesia."

Michael was also introduced to a young freelance writer who said he was under contract to *Manhattan Inc.* to do a piece about Fontana, as well as to a nervous middle-aged man who said he was trying to raise money for an Off-Off Broadway play he hoped Fontana might back. He complained that he'd had an appointment at five to see Fontana and still hadn't had a chance to speak to him. It didn't look like he'd have an opportunity any time soon the way things were going. It was twelve-thirty, and there was no sign that the party was letting up. Nor did Fontana give any impression of running out of steam.

Fontana's party was escorted to a table in the rear, which overlooked the dance floor. The Zulu was obviously very popular with nubile young women, most of whom appeared to be barely out of their teens. In the steamy darkness, broken periodically by strobes, they probably looked more heartbreaking than they would in broad daylight as their faces and limbs turned glossy with sweat from their frantic gyrations.

Fontana had taken a seat next to Michael. He ordered three bottles of Korbel champagne to be brought to their table as well as a dozen glasses—three more than were needed.

But it was only a matter of minutes before Michael understood what Fontana's purpose was in requesting these extra glasses. He filled each of them with champagne and then set them almost at the edge of the table, where someone dancing by could easily reach up and grab one. A warm smile from Fontana signaled his intentions to the women who caught on to his game instantly. "Nice buns, nice gams," he would say over and over, observing the girls who danced by him, waiting for the bait to be taken. "Nice buns, nice gams." And then the bait was taken, and before Michael knew it, two of the women he'd been staring at for the last half hour were sitting across from him, butting their bare knees against his. But their eyes were focused entirely on Fontana.

Fontana was playing raconteur now for the benefit of his newest guests—Tanya and Dawn. "You ever hear of Murph the Surf? No, he was before your time." Michael had a feeling that most things—Hula Hoops, the moon landing, the Tet Offensive—were before their time. "He did this job, stole one of the biggest pieces of ice in the world, the Star of India. Ice, you know? I'm talking about a diamond, a big fucking diamond. From the National History Museum. Guy I know, used to be Murph's chauffeur, told me a story; I don't know whether it's true, but I like to think it is. He says that after they pull off the theft they go into some saloon and sit down and Murph tells the bartender to buy a round for everyone in the house. And the bartender looks at him, suspicious-like, and says, 'How are you going to pay for it?' And Murph reaches into his jacket and pulls out the Star of India and rolls it down the bar and says, 'With that!' "

Everybody at the table was laughing along with Fontana, even people at the far end who, with the din of the music, couldn't possibly have heard what he'd just said.

Then Fontana turned to Michael, his face suddenly taking on a very somber cast, and said, "That kind of daring is largely absent from the world today, don't you think? I like action, you can see that, I like to party." Here his gaze returned to Tanya and Dawn, who clearly didn't know what to make of any of this but were willing to play along and see what came next. "But I've studied up on some things. You'd be surprised. I'll try one out on you: 'Of all the forms of illusion, woman is the most important.' Know where that's from?"

"I have no idea," Michael responded.

Fontana smiled slyly, delighted to have the opportunity to clue Michael in on the answer. "Or listen to this: 'Wine, flesh, fish, woman, and sexual congress—these are the fivefold boons that remove all sin.'"

Michael could tell Fontana derived enormous pleasure from reciting these lines, wherever the hell they were from.

"It's from an ancient Mahayana text," Fontana said. "Are you familiar with what Buddhism is all about?"

"A little, not a great deal." Michael wondered whether Fontana had now launched into a discussion of Buddhist philosophy because he thought it might impress him—or impress the two girls, who were really quite baffled by now—or simply because it was just something he felt like talking about at the moment.

Fontana knocked off what was left in his glass of champagne. He was really wound up. "Here's another one for you. 'Stars, darkness, a lamp, a phantom, dew, a bubble . . . A dream, a flash of lightning, and a cloud: Thus should we look upon the world.'"

"I suppose that's from a Mahayana text, too?"

"You got it, baby. You know how sometimes you're reading something and it hits you in the gut? It's what you had on your mind all the time, only put into words better than you could have ever done yourself. Each time I pick up any of the books about Eastern religions I feel it, it hits home. You're looking at me like I'm crazy."

"No, I don't think you're crazy."

"I can't talk about these things with too many people. But see, with me it's not enough to just keep plugging away, putting in time on this planet. You have to realize that it's all illusion, that there's only one reality out there."

Michael still couldn't make up his mind whether this man was joking or not. Maybe it was all the champagne that was inspiring him into such bursts of metaphysical frenzy. "And what exactly is the only reality, Ray?"

"What do you think, Michael? It's the void. The Big Zero."

Michael never got a chance to pursue the subject any further because Fontana then became distracted by Mario and his old lady, who were getting ready to leave.

"The night's still young. Why are you going?" Fontana protested.

Michael had the feeling, though, that the moment they were gone he'd have forgotten they were ever there in the first place.

"Stick around, Mario."

"No, Ray, we have to split. We'll catch up with you later."

Dawn, with her streaked hair spilling over her face, leaned over toward Michael with such an abrupt motion that it caused her dress to pull free from her naked breasts. "Does he go partying like this every night?" she asked, looking back at Fontana.

"I don't know. I've never met him before tonight."

Brice, who was looking very shaky from all the vast quantities of alcohol he'd been putting away in order to keep up, decided to answer. "Every night," he said, a certain awe in his voice, "he goes out like this every night."

"When does he sleep?" Tanya asked.

"He doesn't," Brice replied.

"Well, how does he do it, then?" Tanya pressed.

"Tell you what, when you figure it out, you let me know. I haven't any idea how he does it. We call it the Fontana Experience."

Fontana, catching the sound of his name, directed his attention back to the corner of the table where Michael, Brice, and the girls were sitting. He grinned. He knew how one went about killing off thoughts of the Void. "More champagne, anyone?" he asked.

CHAPTER ELEVEN

"I couldn't talk the other day, not in the office. People I work with like to stick their nose in everyone else's business. The old saying's only half right—it's not only time that's money, it's information. And as soon as anyone feels any heat at all, they panic. Ever since the Feds cracked down on insider trading it hasn't been the same. I'll tell you, it's a sobering sight to see your boss taken out by the FBI in handcuffs—makes you think twice. But here I figure I'm okay. Nobody I know would come to a place like this."

Gray might have been alone among his colleagues at Colony Saxon Securities to have any appreciation for painting apart from the value to which it could appreciate. He'd arranged to meet Michael at the Whitney Museum early in the afternoon.

Yet now that he was there, he seemed only mildly curious about the art on display. He passed Rauschenbergs, Rothkos, Schanbels, Hoppers, Katzes, and Calders without giving them so much as a glance. One of Warhol's iconographic portraits of Marilyn Monroe caused him to stop and look, but only because he seemed to recognize it from a picture in a magazine.

"I'm glad you got in touch with me," Michael said. He felt it better not to add that he wished they could have met on another day when he wasn't suffering the agony of a hangover.

"That woman you mentioned . . ."

"Jean?"

"Ginny. Her full name's Ginny Karamis. I met her a few times with Alan at Flutie's, where we used to go drinking after work. He seemed confused, your brother—I mean, about her. He didn't know whether to keep her his dirty little secret or to show her off. He told me they were just friends, but anybody could see it was more than that. He said that they had a kind of business arrangement worked out between them."

"A business arrangement?" Michael had not been thinking along those lines.

"Exactly my sentiments. She didn't exactly strike me as somebody you went into business with. You wouldn't find Bear Stearns rushing to grab her off the street, anyhow. Her version of a dress-for-success outfit was a leather jacket and a miniskirt. She had incredible legs, though, I'll say that for her. Nice tits, too."

"Did you ever find out just what kind of business dealings they had with each other?"

Gray shook his head. "Alan wouldn't tell me. He just said that it had nothing to do with the company, that it was something just between the two of them. He more or less implied that she was involved in some kind of private venture company, but that didn't strike me as very plausible, either. I had to figure it was a line he was feeding me so I wouldn't get the wrong idea. Now I wonder."

"Why is that?"

"The other day when you were at my office, I told you that some federal agency had taken Alan's financial records from his office in connection with an ongoing investigation."

"It was the SEC, wasn't it?"

Gray threw Michael a surprised look. "Where did you hear that it was the SEC?"

They were now just walking through the galleries, seldom troubling to glance at any of the prints or paintings. They now found themselves surrounded by a series of paintings entitled "Endangered Species." A panda was giving them the once-over as they strolled in front of it. "A friend of my family told me," Michael replied.

"Well, maybe the SEC is involved in it, but I heard it was the federal organized crime strike force."

"What?" This was much more serious than he ever could have imagined. "You're joking."

But one glance at Colin told him this was not meant as a joke.

"I only found out yesterday, which is why I called. I figured maybe I owed it to Alan to tell you."

"What exactly was going on down there?"

"I wish I could lay out everything in front of you, but all I know is what I hear secondhand. Colony Saxon's one big rumor mill. Hell, the entire Street is. People lose their shirts on rumors, some of them. Others act on a rumor and in a day they've socked in enough to retire to the Riviera. You never fucking know."

Now that Colin had qualified his remarks, he felt free to

advance his theory—based on whatever rumors and insinuations that had reached him—as to what the Feds might
have uncovered.

"What it looks like, I'm sorry to say, was that Alan was routinely siphoning money out of his company accounts. He was
check-kiting between three—maybe four or five—accounts.
No one is sure, probably not even the Feds themselves."

Listening to this, Michael was thinking, *What happened to
the fair-haired boy? What happened to the Alan Friedlander
everyone loved?* He was also wondering why anybody
pulling down two hundred fifty thousand dollars a year
needed to get involved in this kind of shit. Was it greed? Or
was it just that old familiar lust for excitement that Michael
knew so well?

"Whose name was on those other accounts?"

"I don't know. One was something like Valdesto Indus-
tries. There was another called Perry Shield Investment
Group. You can bet your ass they existed only on paper,
though—just letterheads and mailing addresses. In some
places, you know, that constitutes reality. The whole thing is
really very complicated. You don't put a scheme like this together overnight. It takes work and imagination. Plus, it has
to be a system that'll maintain itself, because unless it's carefully devised, it'll fuck up and you'll be left holding the bag.

"But what it looks like Alan did was to write a certified
check on one account for deposit in one of the other accounts. He could get away with it because he was counting
on his position at Colony Saxon to back him. He figured nobody was going to look at his balances to see if he actually
had the money. The certified checks in turn created the illusion that he had the funds to cover the earlier checks he'd
drawn."

"When he didn't in fact have those funds?"

"Oh, no, he had the funds, all right. Not at first, when he
started doing the kiting. But later on he did." Then he paused
before adding, "It was just that they didn't belong to him."

"How much money do you think was involved?"

"You mean all together?"

"All together."

"Well, I've been hearing some serious numbers floated about. I may be way off base, so don't hold me to it, all right? But what they tell me is that it's in the neighborhood of ten, fifteen million dollars."

"Fifteen million dollars! Jesus!"

Colin's eyes darted around. Even at the Whitney, that bastion of American art, he couldn't be too certain he was safe from prying ears. "I told you, that may be completely out of whack."

"But it was a lot."

"Yes, it was a lot."

"Tell me, Colin, do you know whether anybody else at your company was involved in this kiting scheme?" he asked, recalling Judge Waterman's suggestion that Alan might have been only one of several brokers targeted by federal investigators.

"So far as I know, it's just Alan. But you'd never know it from the atmosphere down there. It's hot and heavy; boy, you could cut a knife through it. I wish I didn't have to get back, to tell you the truth. For all I know, half the people I work with might be sitting in a paddy wagon right now. But I have a hunch that the Feds aren't going to find what they're looking for in Alan's papers. Alan wasn't dumb. He wouldn't have kept any records of illegal transactions lying around his office. Have you checked the apartment?"

"Believe me, I've looked everywhere for anything that might help me understand what went down."

"And you've found nothing at all?"

"Nothing."

"Well, those records have got to be somewhere. Even a mathematical genius couldn't run an operation like that without keeping any records."

If the records couldn't be located, Michael reasoned, maybe the girlfriend could.

"What about Ginny?"

"Yeah, well . . . I have a feeling she might have had something to do with this shit. That's why I said that maybe Alan was telling me the truth when he said they had some kind of business association."

"What could she have had to do with it?"

"How the hell would I know? Don't get me wrong, I think he was fucking her, too. They had that look that gave them away. But there was this other connection, too—this money thing."

"You have any idea how I can find this Ginny Karamis?"

Colin stopped in front of "White Car Crash, 19 Times," another Warhol work but one that appeared to interest him less than Marilyn had. He considered the question for a moment. "I haven't the slightest, but I'll tell you one thing—you find her and you'll probably find out why your brother ended up with a bullet in his head."

As soon as he left Colin, Michael went to a phone booth and called Max Farrell. It was obvious that he was never going to make any headway tracking Karamis down by himself. He reasoned that he ought to tell Farrell what he'd learned and let him handle it. It would be a good test to see how the detective performed.

He got through to Farrell right away, which he took as a positive sign.

"Heard you had quite a time the other night," Max said as soon as he came on the line. "How'd you like our boy Ray?"

"He's . . . unusual." That seemed to be the right word. "I liked him fine."

"Well, what can I do for you?"

Michael told him. First about the siphoned-off money and the investigation, and then about the possible involvement of Ginny Karamis. After he finished he was surprised by the long silence that followed. For a moment he thought that maybe something had gone wrong with the connection.

"Jesus Christ goddamn!" Max finally said. "Didn't you listen to anything I told you?"

"What's wrong?" Having called Farrell in the belief that he was contributing something to the investigation, Michael couldn't understand why he'd drawn the detective's wrath like this.

"What's wrong? Do I have to spell it out for you? Who's the dick here? You or me?" He was waiting, expecting an answer.

"I realize you are, Max, but—"

"Good, we've got that straight. Now what did I tell you when you were here in my office? You want to mess up this investigation? Is that what you're trying to do, Mr. Friedlander? Christ! You're like a bull in the fucking china closet. Now, in the future if you think there's somebody I should be talking to, don't be a smartass and try playing private dick. Come to me and tell me, okay? Then we'll take it from there. You decide otherwise, let me know and I'll get off the case, that clear?"

Chastened, Michael said that he would mend his ways in the future. He thought this was the end of it, but there was more.

"So who was your source? Who told you about Ginny and the check-kiting business?"

"I'd rather not say."

"Balls, you'd rather not say! How the hell do you expect me to follow up on this information if you don't tell me who gave it to you? If you're going to shut me out of this investigation, then forget it, man, I don't want anything to do with the damned thing. Got it?"

Michael could see his point, but he was loath to disclose a source. He knew Colin would be infuriated if he did. Still, he had to admit that Max would probably obtain far more information from the broker than he'd managed to do. He told Max the name.

CHAPTER TWELVE

It was natural for the residents of Broad Channel to be upset. Many of them liked to fish, and now the fish were dying, so no wonder they'd begun to believe that the water was poisoned. Urgent phone calls were made. Health authorities came to inspect the situation. State environmental people were called in.

Taking a look at all the hacklefish, whiting, porgies, and

fluke floating belly-up on the water's scummy surface, putrefying in the heat, these various officials admitted that they
had no idea what could be the cause of it. They did the inevitable thing—they took samples of the fish and samples of
the water and then went back to their labs to test them.

Broad Channel was a strange, anachronistic place, an en-
clave of ramshackle houses and rickety piers reached by al-
leys named, with self-deprecating humor, Broadway, Fifth
Avenue, and The Bowery. Although it was a part of New York
City, the area had more in common with a small coastal settlement that might be found in Maine or Massachusetts.

Practically to no one's surprise, the battery of lab tests performed on the fish and the water turned up nothing—no
virus, no bacteria, no evidence of raw sewage, no industrial
pollutant or reagent that could account for why so many fish
had died. The more superstitious held to the idea that this
was some kind of pestilence, a portent of worse to come.

After nearly three weeks of dead fish, Evan Keeler finally
decided that he'd better call the police. He knew what was
down there in the water and he had a feeling he knew why
those fish were dying the way they were.

Two officers responded to the call, arriving an hour later.
They found Keeler on the dock gazing into the water, a woe-
ful expression on his face as he contemplated what must be
down there. One identified himself as Officer Finn, the other
as Officer Catrillo. Both were young, which was reason
enough for Keeler to be leery of them. It was Catrillo who
asked most of the questions.

"Now, Mr. Keeler, I want to be sure I have this right,"
Catrillo began. He spoke slowly, exercising the patience he
no doubt believed was warranted in the presence of the
aged. "You said that on the night of the eleventh you were
awakened by the sound of a car."

"It wasn't the car itself," Keeler said. "It was the sound of
car doors slamming and the voices."

"Where was the location of the car in relationship to your
house?"

Keeler gestured to his house, located about twenty yards

away, then indicated a point at the beginning of the pier, hard by the road.

"That's where they parked the car?" Finn asked.

"That's where they pulled up."

"Do you think you could tell me what make of car it was?" He shook his head, sensing his questioner's disappointment. "Too dark to see."

"About what time was this?" Catrillo wanted to know.

"Maybe three, three-thirty in the morning."

"There were two men?"

"Two men, one gal. First I thought they were helping her along. Then I saw that wasn't what they were doing at all. They must have been dragging her."

"Did you get a good look at either of the men?" Catrillo asked. "Could you identify them if you had to?"

Keeler shook his head determinedly. "No way, it was too dark, I told you. Anyway, my eyes are shit. No, sir, I couldn't identify them."

"What happened then?"

"Well, they walked down to the end of the pier."

"Dragging this woman?"

He nodded. "That's what it looked like they were doing."

"Then what did you see?" Catrillo pressed.

"I can't swear on it, but to me it looked like she fell. But maybe not. Whatever happened, I'm certain about what they did next. They picked her up and threw her off the damned pier." That didn't seem to be quite enough. He decided to add, "And then I heard a splash."

"A splash?"

"A big one."

"They threw this woman off the end of the pier? You're sure about that now?"

"I'm sure," Keeler said curtly. Now that he'd come forward with his story, he resented anyone's questioning its veracity. "Then they walked back to their car and rode off."

"You didn't hear any shouts, any cry for help?"

Keeler again shook his head. "After that splash there was nothing."

"Why did you wait so long to get in touch with us about this, Mr. Keeler?" Finn asked.

"I couldn't believe what I'd seen, you understand. I thought in the morning maybe everything would come clear. Sometimes that happens in the mornings—some sun and some coffee, and you get rid of all the cobwebs in your mind. But it never did happen, after all. Things never did become clear."

They weren't inclined to accept this, he could see that.

And so he said, "I was afraid. I was afraid of those men. I thought they might come back."

"What changed your mind, Mr. Keeler?"

"Well, I've been giving it some thought and I decided that maybe what's killing these hacklefish and porgies had something to do with that gal they threw down in there. And I was beginning to miss my fishing, you see. That's what did it."

That afternoon was a circus in Broad Channel. Nobody could remember anything like it. While police collected onshore, frogmen dove off patrol boats in search of a body in the murky waters. Dredging operations were commenced. The air was electric with anticipation. This wasn't like Manhattan or Brooklyn, where murder was almost routine, something that could be, more or less, absorbed into the ebb and flow of city life. Here everybody's attention was fixed and unshakable. What had been until that morning the secret of Evan Keeler belonged to everyone now. His terse account of an unknown woman's death had in a few hours' time been transformed into a legend, a morality tale. Stories circulating among the crowd, usually in excited whispers, told of a shootout, a desperate chase, a victim's terror and final martyrdom. Those who'd spoken before of divine retribution now talked of seeing the dead woman's ghost wandering desolately along the piers. There was talk, too, of blood that no rain would ever succeed in washing away.

Throughout the afternoon they waited. The waters were flat and gray. The patrol boats for long stretches of time seemed to be standing still, their contours gradually blurring in the haze of summer heat. Nothing was in motion except for the sea gulls hovering above the searchers in hopes of new sustenance.

Close to nine o'clock, when it was apparent that efforts would have to be abandoned for the day, something became snagged in one of the nets. Men on the deck of the patrol boat began to haul it in. They'd been disappointed before: So far for all their work they'd been rewarded only with rubber tires and fragments of a long-sunken fishing sloop. A hush descended over the onlookers, who strained in the dwindling light to see what would come to the surface.

Something amorphous, pulpy, only vaguely organic in appearance rose into the last beige light of day. Draped in marsh grass, it gave every appearance of having been gnawed at by fish.

This formless pulpy mass, once the marsh grass and the crustaceans could be removed from it, revealed itself to be human, very like the remains of the woman Keeler had observed being flung into the water. There was, however, only one thing to identify her: Though it was very faint and partially nibbled away, a tattoo could still be made out on her right shoulder. It was a tattoo of a crucifix surrounded by the fading petals of a flower.

Although the body of the unknown woman—named Jane Doe for the time being—had been recovered in the borough of Queens, it came under the jurisdiction of the chief medical examiner's office in Manhattan. The M.E.'s office in fact was responsible for all coroners' cases in four of the five boroughs. Brooklyn, with its own office, was the sole exception.

In spite of the marked deterioration of the body after prolonged immersion in water, Magnus still had little difficulty determining the cause of death. The head, minus most of the skin, was relatively intact, and it was the head that had sustained the fatal injuries. While the body had been gutted by a knife, Magnus suspected that this was done after she was killed so that decomposing gases wouldn't build up in the stomach and cause her to float to the surface. The fatal injury, though, had come from a gunshot wound.

He judged that she'd been in a seated position, with the shoulders bent forward, when the shot had been fired. The bullet had glanced off the shoulder, causing only superficial injuries, before striking the left side of the head. The fissured fracture he observed was a direct result of impact.

Finding no singeing of the hair, no powder "tattoo" marks, nor blackening of the flesh, he concluded that the weapon had to have been fired from some distance.

X rays had already indicated that he would discover fragments of the bullet in the brain. Sawing open the skull, he exposed the devastated region of the head. After tedious excavation he located and extracted the fragments.

"I have just removed two fragments of metal from the brain," he dictated into the microphone, hoping that his voice remained steady. "One fragment measures seven by two millimeters, and an additional fragment measures one by three millimeters. Both were taken from the left side of the brain and have been placed in a glass jar containing a black metal top, which was thereafter marked for identification."

Following the signing of a proper receipt, he would see that this jar was placed in the care of the police department for ballistics tests.

In criminal cases, every item of evidence had to have a chain of possession—a demonstrable record of custody that began at the crime scene and ended only in the courtroom. That was why even the officer who would be entrusted with the fragments was obliged to scratch his initials into each of them. The reasoning behind these precautions was to prevent someone from either tampering with or mislaying the evidence.

There was, however, another piece of evidence that Magnus couldn't let the police see. It was the evidence provided by the tattoo on the woman's shoulder. As soon as he'd seen the tattoo, he knew at once who this woman was. Throughout the postmortem he kept casting surreptitious glances toward Holmes, wondering if the deputy examiner sensed how nervous he was. But Holmes didn't seem to notice. Magnus was determined to do nothing that would betray himself. Above all, he couldn't let on that he had any idea of her identity.

The police Missing Persons Bureau was conveniently located in the same building that housed the chief medical examiner's office, and it was this division that would assume the responsibility of identifying Jane Doe. In the absence of any usable fingerprints owing to the body's deplorable condition, the tattoo would obviously be the best way to make the identification.

"Francis," Magnus said when they were ready to cover the body up, "would you mind doing me a favor and making sure that these fragments get to ballistics? I don't want there to be any delay."

Holmes scowled. This wasn't part of his job, and he clearly resented being asked. But he took the jar containing the fragments and without a word left the autopsy room. That was all that Magnus wanted—to get him out of the room.

Now he was alone with Ginny Karamis. It had been a long time since they'd last been together. He never expected their next meeting to be this way. But he couldn't indulge himself in remorseful thinking or in wishing that things had not worked out the way they had. It was too late for that. Using a small blade, he cut away the tattoo. The cadaver was in such appalling shape that one more small mutilation would never be noticed or recognized for what it was. Of course, no mention of the tattoo would ever appear in his report. With the tattoo's removal, Magnus prayed that any connection he may have had with Jane Doe had ceased to be.

When a bullet spiraled through the barrel of a gun, it picked up an impression of a pattern of marks on the barrel's interior. Every one of these "rifling patterns" was unique, which was why it could serve to identify the gun from which it was fired. If the bullet hadn't been hopelessly mangled, the pattern engraved on it could be "read" and, under a comparison microscope, matched with other bullets discharged from the same weapon.

The next day, when he came into his office, Magnus was given the ballistics report on the fragments lodged in the brain of Jane Doe, though he certainly wasn't expecting any positive matches. He assumed that the murder weapon was untraceable, long since disposed of; that was his experience when it came to cases like this, anyhow. But in this instance he was wrong. To his surprise, ballistics experts had been able to establish an exact match. The .32 bullet discovered in her head had come from the same gun found in Alan Friedlander's hand at his death.

CHAPTER THIRTEEN

Nearly a week had gone by and Michael was becoming impatient. It was the 27th of June, almost two weeks after his brother's death. Nothing was happening. Farrell promised action; he said he was actively pursuing the case but so far had failed to produce any results. Michael took it as a bad sign when he couldn't get him on the phone and his calls were not returned. He understood that these things took time and that Farrell had other pressing cases, many that might have precedence over his. But the one thing that Michael lacked was time.

Having assumed that the sale of Alan's apartment was going to take months, he was dismayed to find that things were moving much more quickly. The real estate agent had led a score of prospective buyers through the apartment even in the short time since Michael had been there. Five of them had put in bids. Of these five, his father favored a young woman probably because she'd just graduated from Harvard Law and was starting out at Cromwell, Sullivan, in the fall. She'd struck Michael as mousy and neurotic and he'd taken an immediate dislike to her. She didn't have the money herself, but her parents were buying the place for her as a kind of graduation present, so that wasn't going to be any problem.

If the sale went through, the paperwork, he was told, could be completed in three weeks, by mid-July. And then he would have to leave town or start looking for another place to stay, something he couldn't see himself doing, not without a lot more money than he had.

Time was his enemy in another way. The more the weeks wore on, the more likely it was for the evidence in his brother's death to grow stale. Chances of finding witnesses and locating Ginny Karamis would diminish. Every day he opened up the papers anxious for some news item that would give him reason to think that his brother's death wasn't forgotten. Even if it was bad news, at least it would be something. Certainly he assumed that it wouldn't be long before there was some word about the federal investigation into the check-kiting scheme Colin had told him about. Yet he never found any mention of it at all; maybe the investigators were keeping the whole thing under wraps until they were ready to hand down indictments. Or maybe Colin had not been telling him the truth.

It was the threat posed by the Chopper, and not by unscrupulous financiers on Wall Street, that seemed to hold the news columnists in thrall. There was every expectation that another mutilated corpse—or a part of one, at any rate—would turn up in some improbable location. And there was almost no expectation that the police could track down the madman responsible. For those who were not his victims, he provided a certain kick, like the weather, a subject of conversation among strangers, a break from the summer doldrums.

It was bad enough that Michael kept running into people who seemed to want to talk about nothing but the Chopper. Worse, people were constantly advising him to stop being so obsessed about his brother's death. Give it a rest, they said. It was summer, they never ceased to remind him, and things inevitably slowed down in summer. People were on vacation, and even those who weren't took long weekends. One way or another, no one was around when needed. It was ridiculous to agonize over the situation. Why didn't he take it easy, go to the beach, work on a tan? Maybe after Labor Day, they said, he'd see some movement on his brother's case.

When it came time to meet Nick Ambrosetti, Michael began to have second thoughts. Maybe he shouldn't be doing this. Farrell would be outraged to learn that he'd gone behind his back, even if it was only to talk to another detective. But in the end he decided that he had nothing to lose.

It was Ambrosetti who had suggested they meet in Michael's neighborhood. From the conversation they had, Michael couldn't tell whether Ambrosetti actually had an office. All he said was, "You'll find I move around a lot." That didn't sound too reassuring.

Although Ambrosetti had described himself for purposes of identification, Michael had a feeling he could have picked him out regardless. He was sitting in a booth way in the back of McNally's, the only customer who wasn't at the bar watching the Mets–Cardinals game. He was a thick, ruggedly built man in his fifties with graying hair, unkempt and overgrown in back. His serge jacket looked uncomfortable and, indeed, he was sweating profusely. His eyes were dark and ringed with shadows. He looked as if he might turn out to be a monumental drinker, but the only drink in front of him was a club soda with a slice of lemon in it.

Almost from the moment Michael sat down across from him he said, a little apologetically, "I'm trying to stay off the sauce." His voice held a slight nasal quality to it, the voice of someone who'd grown up on the streets of New York.

They exchanged a few words about Stopka. Ambrosetti remembered him as a nut case, always in need of money, a chronic skirtchaser, but cunning in his own way, smarter than people gave him credit for.

"He said you located his wife—one of his wives—for him years ago."

"I can find just about anybody," Ambrosetti said with a conviction that heartened Michael. "You told me over the phone that this has to do with the killing of your brother."

"Officially it's been ruled a suicide."

"But you don't believe it?"

"I know my brother was involved in some very bad shit, but I can't believe that it led him to kill himself."

"Just what sort of very bad shit?"

Michael told him, sparing Ambrosetti no details. He related his interview with Judge Waterman and how he'd come to be hooked up to Ray Fontana's agency. He was waiting to see a reaction on Ambrosetti's face, but Ambrosetti's features had settled into an expression of grim detachment; it didn't appear as if anything Michael said was going to alter it.

"I know who Fontana is," was all that Ambrosetti bothered to say. But even from those few words Michael gathered that Ambrosetti didn't hold Fontana in very high regard.

"I wanted to be honest with you," Michael said. "And if you don't want to take on the case, I can understand that, too. I'm not sure about what's going to happen with the Fontana Agency. My inclination is to drop them unless this guy Farrell can turn up something soon. If you'd like, I can wait and see what happens and then get in touch with you."

"I don't see any sense in waiting," Ambrosetti said. "So far as I'm concerned, you can hire as many detectives as you want. See who delivers the goods." There was no question that he believed he'd be the one. "You saw the autopsy report?"

Michael nodded. "I've seen it, but I don't have a copy to show you."

"No problem. A copy should be on file. What about the results of the chemical tests?"

"What tests are you referring to?"

"Neutron, paraffin, antimony—the tests they do for gunshot residue. It's how they tell whether someone fired a weapon or not. They should have done tests on both Alan's hands as a matter of course."

"And if the tests turned out to be positive?"

"Then there's a good chance it was a suicide. Sometimes people off themselves whether you like it or not."

"The fact is, I don't know whether they were even done. I don't remember seeing any mention of neutron or paraffin tests in the autopsy report anyway."

"Well, that's something else we're going to have to check out." He was getting this down on paper. "What about this Karamis woman you told me about?"

"I have no idea what happened to her."

"From what you tell me, she sounds like a broad a lot of people aren't going to forget so quick. So maybe I can pick up her trail." He closed his notebook. "Now, about my fee . . ."

"I don't have a great deal to spend."

"Figure it this way. Give me, say, three hundred to start, and we'll work the rest out as we go along. Sound fair to you?"

Three hundred dollars Michael could deal with. It sounded fair enough.

Michael remained in the bar after Ambrosetti departed, reading a copy of the *News* somebody had left behind. Bernie Cook was inveighing against the police in his column, calling on the mayor to find another commissioner, somebody who could finally rid the streets of the dope peddlers, muggers, and hoodlums who were intent on turning the city into their private battleground. The paper was filled with full-page ads and pull-out supplements for special Fourth of July sales. With everything else that had happened, the approach of the holiday had nearly slipped his mind. He didn't like it; holidays caused delays, and were a convenient excuse for a lot of people not to get anything done. Besides, he was in no mood for celebration. Then on page fifteen Michael's eye was caught by a headline that read:

WALL ST. BROKER DROWNS IN ACCIDENT

No sooner had he read the first sentence—"A thirty-two-year-old strockbroker for Colony Saxon Securities died yesterday in a drowning accident off Quogue, Long Island."—than he knew who it would have to be. The deceased, the item related, had swum too far out. It was as if he was trying to make it to Ireland, a witness said.

CHAPTER FOURTEEN

For years Manhattan had turned its back on the water that surrounded it. When the great ocean liners and the passenger ships stopped coming, the docks and the piers fell into disrepair. Vast empty stretches extended along the West Side of the island, desolate places where the indigent and the hopelessly demented encamped. There were times when adventurous twelve-year-old boys riding their bicycles would be ambushed by predators and killed. It would later come out in the papers that the boys had been taunting their victimizer, hounding him in his shelter of cardboard and corrugated metal.

Below Fourteenth Street, still heading south, one would come across a succession of piers reaching into the Hudson. They were obviously unsafe; warning signs were posted and barriers erected to keep people off them. But sun worshipers ignored the signs and the barriers and settled down with their blankets and radios as if they were at the beach.

The Morton Street pier had a mixed crowd of men and women; the Bank Street pier was more conspicuously gay. At the very edge of the Bank Street pier, men felt free to go naked; all through the hot weekend afternoons they'd loll around and watch the sailboats and Circle Line boats pass by, delighting in the shocked expressions they would sometimes draw from the people standing on deck.

One Saturday afternoon early in summer, a young man appeared on the pier, responding to the same old urge, a blanket draped over his arm, a book that he did not intend to read grasped in his hand. It wasn't any news to him that he could excite such desire in these men who, while affecting indifference, were obviously following every move he made. Their reaction was predictable and even, sadly, somewhat disappointing. It wasn't so much that his body was superbly formed or that his features were exquisitely arranged or even that there was such desire in his eyes. It was more than that; for, by being in possession of such uncommon beauty, he held out to them the possibility that for some brief bit of time they might be in possession of it, too.

He was wearing only a pair of cut-offs and a sleeveless T-shirt, both of which he quickly discarded once he'd reached the end of the pier. Though he knew that all eyes were on him, he refused to acknowledge the scrupulous appraisal he was undergoing. It was really no problem for him; whenever he needed to, he could always block out the rest of the world. Spreading out his blanket, he lowered himself down on the pier and lay supine, allowing the sun to deepen still further his golden tan.

He was only feigning sleep. Meanwhile, through half-slitted eyes, he made a quick survey, seeking among all those collected there the one man who might offer him the succor, the beauty, and the love he had looked for everywhere in the world—in Rio, in Hamburg, in Port-au-Prince, in San Francisco. But it had begun to seem that, once real love and contentment had slipped from his grasp, he was never going to find it again. Its absence embittered him and kept him locked in a terrible solitude.

He was confident that he could have whomever he wanted. Apprehensions about disease, about death, came and went but had no power to defeat desire. The beauty that he offered could not be put off; it would live on, an aching memory of opportunity lost, if it were refused. There was no question of rebuff; there never had been. But that wasn't the point. That was never the point.

He began to scan the faces offered up to his view once again. Despairing of finding in them the love he was seeking, he was looking for something else. He was looking for someone who wanted to die.

It wasn't long before he spotted him. He was a slender blond with boyish midwestern good looks. Although he sat with a friend, he was really alone, only half listening to what his friend was saying. He couldn't have been more than twenty-three. He gave off an aura that indicated he was new to the city; he was reaching out, experimenting. But there could be no doubt, not in the mind of somebody discerning enough to pick up on these things, that he was despondent, that there had been more than one suicide attempt, and that, sooner or later, there would be another, successful one. From time to time he would shut his eyes and lift his face up to the sun. His friend was older by ten or fifteen years and could hardly believe his good fortune in making this catch. But there was no chance that the blond would stay with him. This afternoon together would be their last. Already the blond's eyes were straying, seeking out an alternative to the infatuated lover whose hands were smoothing lotion into his back. Inevitably his eyes met those of the man who meant to take his life. But he didn't know that—not consciously. He would see only excitement being held out to him, a prospect for great sex. He smiled and his lover— his killer—smiled back.

It wasn't much of a pretext to begin a conversation, but that hardly mattered. He asked to borrow some of their lotion. "I didn't think the sun would be this hot today."

He could see the pleasure in the blond's eyes that his presence evoked. The friend didn't miss the look they exchanged, and he glowered.

"Would you mind putting some of this gunk on my back?" he asked the blond.

The friend's expression darkened.

"My name, by the way, is Darryl," he said, introducing himself. It was a fitting name, he thought, at least for this afternoon, at least for this blond.

"I'm Patrick, and this is Mitchell."

Mitchell nodded glumly, watching helplessly as Patrick fell into a slow, modulated rhythm in applying the lotion, taking his time about it.

When he'd finished, Darryl remained motionless, his eyes closed. But he was acutely alert, knowing every step of the way he was about to traverse.

It wasn't long before Mitchell took some action. "Come on, Patrick, let's get out of here. Look at me, I'm all burned. I can't stay here another minute."

"You go on ahead, Mitch. I'll meet you later at Uncle Charlie's."

"Hey, what's this? Come on, Patrick."

"No, I want to stay here a little longer. It's okay. Believe me, Mitch, I'll see you in an hour."

Mitchell was in an impossible position. Now that he'd committed himself to leaving, it would be too humiliating to say that he'd changed his mind. Throwing Darryl a malign look, Mitchell put his clothes on and stalked off without a word.

"Well, that just leaves the two of us," Darryl said, winning an appreciative look from his new friend.

Patrick's was like a thousand other stories Darryl had heard. He began it on the pier and he resumed it, once they'd dressed, at the Ramrod, a suitably grungy bar close by habituated by gays, rough trade, and hustlers with predatory good looks. Darryl bought him several drinks, a little surprised at how plowed Patrick was getting. No doubt he was drinking to cover his nervousness around his new friend.

Patrick said that he was a waiter at the Twentieth-Century Cafe in the theater district; naturally he was struggling to be an actor. As Darryl had surmised, he'd come from the Midwest—from Indiana. Indiana bored him. He was sharing an eight-hundred-fifty-dollar-a-month studio with another unemployed actor who had been his lover but with whom he'd had "a falling out." He hated the idea of going home because the atmosphere was filling with tension. "I'm looking for another place, so if you hear of anything . . ."

Darryl told him he'd keep an eye out.

When he'd become a little more drunk, Patrick confessed that he was desperately unhappy and was having second thoughts about New York and a career in acting. He felt alone and adrift. He wanted Darryl to know that it wasn't often that he could talk to somebody so openly and say just what was on his mind. There were so few people that he could find in New York who really understood him.

Saying that he'd come into money, Darryl offered to treat Patrick to dinner at a small intimate French café he knew. Darryl felt it was necessary to go through the motions of an intimate romantic evening with him, God knows why.

At the café Patrick began to show signs of slowing down. He was clearly no longer capable of absorbing great quantities of Greyhounds. But Darryl didn't stop—he couldn't stop.

"And what do you do, Darryl?" Patrick asked. "I've done all the talking."

Darryl reached across the table and entwined his fingers with Patrick's and said, "I'm a collector."

"Of what?"

"Art, antiques, coins, stamps—anything that catches my fancy." He gazed at Patrick, giving him a look filled with longing.

"Where do you keep all your collections?"

"I can show you if you'd like."

"Yes," said Patrick happily, "I'd like that very much."

It was something that Darryl had found with just about all of his victims; they were in a hurry to get to their deaths.

CHAPTER FIFTEEN

"Well, my friend, it's all very strange." Ambrosetti didn't look as though he was alarmed. On the contrary, he seemed rather pleased. "Strange" must hold an attraction for him.

They were meeting at Michael's—Alan's—apartment. Ambrosetti had expressed a wish to inspect the premises where the "incident," as he called it, had taken place. He dropped down on the bed, keeping his doleful gaze on the spot where Alan had been found by Stopka weeks before.

"To tell you the truth," Michael said, pulling up a rattan chair opposite him, "I wasn't sure you'd come up with any-thing. Nothing against you personally, but so little has hap-

pened that I began to think maybe it never would. I used to
think that in a city like New York everything moves in high
gear. Now I wonder."

"Only when it suits somebody's purpose. Believe me. But
Nick Ambrosetti delivers, you can be sure of that." He tore
his eyes away from the floor and looked back at the well-
thumbed notebook in his hand. "Remember I told you
about those tests yesterday?"

"The paraffin and neutron tests, yes, I remember. Don't
tell me you found out they never got around to doing
them?"

"Well, they did some of the tests, anyhow. But they're far
from satisfactory. It's ambiguous whether the residue tests
were positive for just the left hand or for both. The neutron-
activation analysis came up positive only for the left hand.
No mention of the back of the right hand. And it's negative
on both palms, which is really weird. Alan was right-
handed, right?"

"Yes, he was."

"All we know for sure is that only the back of the left hand
proved positive. The report says that it's 'consistent with
amounts detected on the hand of a person who has discharged a firearm.'"

"Could you explain all that to me? What does it mean,
exactly?"

"It means shit. What Magnus is saying is that there's nothing to rule out Alan putting a gun to his head with his left
hand and shooting himself—twice. It can happen, but knowing the facts, it sure ain't likely—not if he was right-handed."

Michael could feel the excitement building in him. This
was getting close to something. They were approaching new
territory.

"But why would the test prove positive for the left hand?"

"Let's say that somehow Alan does use his left hand to
hold the gun. A positive swab still doesn't prove conclusively that the person discharged the weapon himself. It
could be something else."

"Like what?"

"Like he was in close physical proximity to the firearm when it was discharged."

"So what can we do with this?"

"I'm not sure. Let me go on. There was a Walker test done—that's for nitrate—and minimal traces of gunshot residue were found. Which doesn't help us much one way or another. But there are some real interesting aspects to this report. For instance, are you aware that most people who shoot themselves twice usually do it in the same location?"

"Supposing Alan had shot himself in the chest and was still alive and in terrible pain . . . ?"

"Then he puts the gun to his head because he wants to make sure it'll be over fast? I see what you're saying. Could be, okay. I don't buy it, but you could make a case for it." He flipped to another page. "About what time did you say Magnus phoned your parents to tell them he'd concluded the autopsy?"

"I told you—it was around two-thirty."

"I just wanted to make sure I got it right. According to the official report signed by Magnus himself, the autopsy wasn't completed until three-forty. Here's something you can think about. A *Times* reporter, Tom O'Neill, contacted the communications room in the M.E.'s office a little before one A.M. to make an inquiry about Alan's death—the call was logged in; there's a record of it—and he was told that the autopsy had shown that the death was a suicide."

"But hadn't the cops gone on record that it was a suicide by that time?"

"We're dealing with the M.E.'s office here, not the cops. What the cops did or did not say isn't relevant. We have documented evidence that the M.E.'s office was anticipating Magnus's ruling in the case by almost three hours. It means that the suicide verdict was a foregone conclusion, and it suggests a cover-up on the part of both the police and the M.E.'s office."

"Jesus! But what the hell do we do now?"

"Before we can do anything, there are a hell of a lot of other things I have to check up on. I want to trace the chain of evidence—see what happened to the clothes Alan had on, for instance. There's a request I saw for a chemical analysis on the shirt he was wearing, but I couldn't find out whether the analysis was ever done. So we're just at the beginning here, but from what I've seen we've got something to work on."

"What about Ginny Karamis? You find anything out about her?"

"I haven't had a chance to start looking yet. I'm still working on the paper trail at this point."

Again Ambrosetti's eyes sought the spot on the floor where Alan had been discovered. "That detective you mentioned, Mackie, is supposed to be on vacation, celebrating his retirement from the force. The only other official at the scene was the medical investigator. Her name's Ives—Gail Ives. She's a resident at Bellevue, works in the emergency room. I couldn't locate a copy of her report, but someone might have it. I'm not sure whether it would help us or not, but I'd like to take a look at it if it still exists."

"Are you going to talk to her?"

"I tried. She doesn't want to talk to me."

"Doesn't she work for Magnus? If there's a cover-up, she might be in on it."

"I don't know about that. See, she only works for Magnus on and off. They don't have enough full-time employees at the M.E.'s office, so they use interns and residents on a part-time basis. It's strange, though, that they'd use her in a case where foul play might be involved. Usually a medical examiner would be assigned. That's what I wanted to ask her about, but she says she doesn't want to get involved, that it's not her position to comment on coroner's cases. That's what she says, anyway."

"Is she important to us?"

"She could be helpful, but she's not our only source. We can live without her." He rose from the bed, finished with what he'd had to say. "I'll be in touch, let you know what progress I'm making."

Early in the evening Michael decided to take a walk, hoping to calm his turbulent feelings. Though what Ambrosetti had told him had momentarily lifted his spirits, the sensation hadn't lasted. Something else had moved in on him that he began to identify as the beginnings of a heavy depression. If he gave in to it, there'd be no telling when he'd be able to shake it off. Heavy depressions took up a lot of time, he knew. His mind wandered; he kept seeing Colin Gray swimming off to Ireland.

He felt that he must be to blame, that by divulging his name to Max Farrell he'd put a curse on him, pronounced sentence over him. He wondered what had gone through Colin's mind in those final moments before he went under for good. But he knew he couldn't allow himself to think that way. He'd only drive himself crazy and hasten the pall of depression that was ready to descend at any moment. He had to get out, had to commit himself to some action, do something besides sit there in the darkness of his brother's apartment.

Michael walked. He walked with a resolute stride, quickly, decisively, and with the purposefulness of someone who knew where he was going. Michael did not. Not until he was south of Thirty-fourth Street. Then it came to him. He would stop by the emergency room at Bellevue Hospital and see if he could find Gail Ives. Maybe he could succeed where Ambrosetti had failed.

The emergency room was in an uproar when Michael walked in—which he supposed was to be expected at nine on a hot Saturday night. Wherever he looked he spotted cops. Some held themselves alert as if they were still primed for an emergency call. Others were joking with the nurses while they waited to find out the resolution of the cases they'd brought in. Nurses and residents in iodine-and-blood-stained whites moved at a frantic pace back and forth, their eyes anywhere but on the great tide of patients and patients' families that occupied every free bit of space in the E.R. Paramedics materialized, wheeling in a black youth on a gurney, all covered with blood. Somebody had stuck him or shot him or something. His shrieks were demanding attention that nobody seemed likely to give him. Everybody had other pain to contend with and had no time to spare for his.

Michael had been in emergency rooms before, but not in this one, and not on a summer weekend night. With the tension and passions generated in the crucible of a dank, humid night like this, was it any wonder that violence would erupt? Was it any wonder that people went berserk with heat and rage? No, it made perfect sense, it was nothing unusual.

There must be some kind of order there, Michael decided as he observed the commotion, but it would take somebody with a more practiced eye than his to figure it out. A man with a grotesque birthmark covering half his face, carrying himself with odd dignity, approached Michael. A woman's pocketbook was clutched in his hand. Maybe he needed somebody to talk to, and Michael happened to be it.

"I've looked everywhere for her," he said gravely.

"Excuse me?"

"My wife. I brought her here two hours ago. She was complaining of stomach pains. Now I can't find her." He spoke calmly, resignedly. "I've looked everywhere, but nobody seems to know what happened to her. She can't go anywhere. See, I have her pocketbook. She doesn't even have any money for the subway and we live in Brooklyn."

He didn't seem to expect Michael to reply—what could he say, after all?—and now that he'd gotten his explanation off his chest, he walked away, his eyes filled with hopelessness. It was as though he'd had the feeling that something like this was bound to happen sooner or later.

Michael approached the nurses' station. When he managed to get someone's attention, he asked for Dr. Ives.

The nurse was prepared to make out an admission form for him until he told her that he wasn't a patient.

"Oh, then you're a friend of hers?"

It was clear that she needed a category into which she could slot him. "Friend of a friend," he said, a relationship that appeared to satisfy her.

"You can wait right here, sir. She's in one of the examining rooms, but she should be out shortly."

"Would you mind pointing her out to me?"

It was all the same to her.

Michael figured on a long wait, but not more than ten minutes passed before the nurse said, "That's Dr. Ives, right there."

If Michael had pictured her in his mind at all, it was as a pale, thin, and harried woman, neither pretty nor plain. The Dr. Ives who appeared before him now, however, bore no resemblance to that image at all.

The first thing about her that caught his eye was the way she moved; she was all motion, long legs propelling her forward, arms swinging, hair in great disarray, dirty-blond strands of it dropping into her eyes, temporarily obscuring her sight. And then he gave her face a more careful inspection. These were serious good looks, he realized. The light blue of her eyes was all the more striking in contrast to the dark circles surrounding them, no doubt the consequence of going for days with little sleep.

Although Michael was staring intensely at her, she didn't notice him any more than she noticed the rest of the teeming crowd piled into the E.R. Her attention was focused exclusively on the chart she held in her hand. She stepped over to the nurses' station and spoke to the nurse to whom Michael had spoken. He couldn't catch all she said, but it seemed to have something to do with a Mrs. Hersh who was now in holding. "With these grimmies," she was saying, "I never know whether to admit them or release them. I suppose we can watch her for a while and see if there's any change."

When she finished, the nurse said, "There's a gentleman who wants to see you. He says he's a friend of a friend." Ives turned, for the first time laying eyes on him. She frowned in puzzlement.

"Yes? Can I help you?" She hadn't made one step in his direction. So he bridged the distance.

"I'm Michael Friedlander."

The name made no impression on her.

"Do I know you?"

He shook his head. "No, but you did have . . ." Now he was stumped for words. Surely he couldn't call it an acquaintance. "You examined my brother . . . Alan."

This didn't help her. There was no sign of recognition in her eyes. "Was he a patient of mine? I see a lot of people, so I'm afraid I have a hard time remembering—"

"He wasn't a patient—not when you saw him, he wasn't. He was killed. You were the medical investigator on the case, I'm told."

Now she knew to whom he was referring. "Oh, yes, I'm sorry. I remember. I told that man who came around yesterday—"

"Nick Ambrosetti."

"Yes, that's right. I told him I didn't want to discuss that case."

Michael supposed that she seldom, if ever, had to deal directly with the families of the deceased. That was somebody else's responsibility—the police or the medical examiner's office.

"I'm really sorry about what happened to your brother, but I'm afraid I can't help you."

Obviously in a rush to get to her next patient, she was anxious for him to leave. Michael represented another world, the world of the dead, and the world here was one in which people wanted to go on living.

"Would you mind if I took a few minutes of your time?" he asked, growing painfully aware of how uneasy he was making her feel. "A few questions, that's all. You'd be doing me an enormous favor."

"Look, I'm sure you can see I'm terribly busy. I've got a million patients I have to examine. I'm sure if you talked to the medical examiner's office they could—"

"No, they won't. They're the problem, as they say. Not the solution. It really won't take long—a few minutes. I'll buy you dinner."

"No, thanks."

"Do you take bribes?"

She laughed. She had a terrific laugh. "Look, I'd love to help you, but I can't. I said everything I had to say in my report."

"Nobody can find your report."

She shrugged. "It happens all the time," she said wearily. "Charts, reports, prescriptions are constantly being mislaid. Or somebody throws them away by mistake."

"Do me a favor, just tell me what you put in your report. How long could it take? Otherwise, I'll keep coming around and pestering you. I can really be a persistent son-of-a-bitch. Take my word for it."

"I can believe that, all right."

He was making headway, he could tell. She was close to giving in. She'd talk to him if only to get rid of him.

"All right," she said, "but you're going to have to accompany me on my rounds or wait until I'm finished."

"When will that be?"

"Tomorrow morning at seven."

"Is it okay to go with you on your rounds?"

"Why not? I'll get a white coat for you. Anybody asks, I'll say you're my assistant."

"Won't the people in charge here object?"

She gave him a strange look. "What do you mean, the people in charge here? Do you see anybody in charge?"

Her next patient appeared to be sleeping soundly. He was packed in ice as if he were being made ready for a journey of several million light-years to a distant galaxy. Ives felt his forehead and then shook him until she succeeded in waking him up. "Mr. Alfano, how are you feeling? Are you feeling better?"

Groggily, the man murmured a reply that Michael gathered was favorable. Gail made a notation in his chart.

Michael picked up on the disdain in her voice. "What's his problem?"

"Oh, he took some heroin and Elevil earlier today, and then he fell asleep on a car radiator. When he came in here, he had a temp of a hundred and seven. So we packed him in ice." She seemed about to say a further word to the cooling Mr. Alfano, but he'd already dropped back to sleep.

She glanced at the list of patients still to be seen—more all the time. "Let's see what Luisa Marchado's problem is." On their way to the next examining room, Gail said, "Speak to me."

Michael had to be careful how he framed his questions. It would be self-defeating to let any trace of anger or accusation slip into his voice. If there had been a cover-up or just a bad mistake on somebody's part along the way, she might have been part of it. He had to remember that.

"The official autopsy report said that my brother committed suicide. Was that what it looked like to you?"

"That's kind of a broad question, isn't it? Appearances can be a hell of a lot different from reality. I'm sure you know that."

"You're not answering the question."

She gave him a hint of a smile. They were facing the door to another examining room, shielded by an opaque plastic curtain. "It's a little more complicated than you probably realize."

"Yes or no? No one's going to hold you to it."

She scrutinized his face. "Oh, is that so? You know, I really shouldn't be having this talk with you."

"Am I making you nervous?"

Without replying, she proceeded into the examining room, where a pale, almost emaciated girl in her late teens was sitting on the end of the bed.

"Luisa?"

The girl scarcely raised her head. She was one of the world's defeated, accustomed to mistreatment and disaster and stupidity. Her frailty was not just physical, it went deeper than that. A sudden gust would take her away for good. Gail took a look at her chart. "You're nineteen?"

The girl nodded. Her hair was so blond that it was nearly white. Her fingernails were painted a lurid red. Half of her face, now that she turned it toward the light, was bruised and still raw and bleeding slightly. The wound descended down her neck, turning from pink to purple.

Her hair was matted with blood as well. Gail explored for the source and found it quickly enough. It was a small wound that didn't want to stop bleeding. "He stabbed me there with a nail file," she said dully. There was shame in her eyes and pain that had nothing to do with the hideous abrasions.

"Who stabbed you, Luisa?" Gail's voice was calming but insistent. Michael realized he was interested in how she was going to handle this patient.

"My husband."

Gail nodded; she wasn't surprised.

"He's never done this before," the girl protested, suddenly finding her voice. "Really, I swear. He was drunk, that's all." She was fighting back tears and needed to make this doctor understand that it was all a mistake, an aberration.

"How did you get this?" Gail indicated the bruise alongside her head. "What exactly did he do to you?"

There was a long interval of silence. Then the girl answered, "He knocked my head against the sidewalk."

"Where is your husband now?"

A shrug; she didn't know.

"It says on your chart that you're ten weeks pregnant."

The girl nodded and lifted up her johnny so that if Gail wanted to, she could inspect her stomach. The swelling, to Michael's eyes, was slight. But that wasn't why she was exposing her stomach. Two ugly pink abrasions were visible. Blood was welling out of them. As Gail cleaned the wounds she observed tooth marks.

"How did this happen, Luisa?"

She received only silence from the girl.

"You were bitten, weren't you, Luisa? These are tooth marks."

"Dogs?" Michael asked, leaning closer to examine them. He couldn't imagine what other horrors might await them if they continued to undrape her. Her body was a collection of stigmata.

"No, humans. They're human bites. Luisa, who bit you?"

"Some girls," she said in a voice that was almost inaudible. "I was coming downstairs to mail some letters, and these bitches attacked me. They bit me and pulled my hair." Her face contorted in anger. "I know what you're thinking. It wasn't Don, it wasn't my husband." She was becoming vehement.

"No one said that it was."

Luisa glared at Gail and then at Michael, as if somehow they were to blame for her predicament.

Turning to Michael, Gail said, "All things being equal, I'd prefer to treat dog bites."

"Why is that?"

"Because dogs are better at keeping their teeth clean than most humans."

"You can't give her antibiotics for these wounds, can you? Not when she's pregnant."

Gail looked up at him in surprise. It was the intended effect. "You're right. I'll have to give her antitetanus. How did you know?"

"I studied medicine once upon a time—at Columbia Med. Then some things happened. It was the sixties." In some circles, that was enough of an explanation.

"I was in elementary school in the sixties," Gail said evenly. This didn't seem to call for any comment.

Meanwhile, Luisa was staring listlessly off into space; they might have been carrying on their conversation in another room—in another world, for that matter.

Once she'd dressed the girl's wounds and administered the antitetanus, Gail asked her where she planned to spend the night.

The question seemed to anger the girl. "In a hotel," she spat out. "I'll find a hotel."

"I tell you what I can do, Luisa. You're free to go if you like. There's no medical reason to keep you. But I can arrange for you to spend the night here. Is that all right?"

Luisa didn't respond immediately. Then sadly she nodded in agreement.

They left the room. Michael said, "I liked the way you dealt with her."

She looked sharply at him. "Are you flattering me because you think I'll give you more information?"

She was prickly, on the lookout for trouble. He suspected that she had some temper.

"Does that mean you're not going to?"

She shook her head, a motion that released more mutinous strands of hair into her face. She was having the damnedest time keeping it out of her eyes. "Okay, listen to me. This has to be off the record, all right?"

"All right." He could picture a time when she'd have to be hauled into court on a subpoena to testify, but for now he had no choice but to play along.

They were standing in the corridor outside the examining rooms, with hardly any space to move, while nurses and orderlies rushed by them.

"When I saw your brother, it was my impression that he'd been shot elsewhere and moved."

"Moved? Why do you say that?"

This was the first time that anybody had ever suggested this possibility.

"Because there was dirt on the rug and dirt under his nails. And the blood pattern indicated that the body had been moved."

"There aren't any witnesses, though."

"You asked me what I saw. I can't say conclusively that he was moved. That's for the police to decide."

"They're finished with their investigation. He shot himself. The end." He leveled his gaze at her. "Do you think he shot himself?"

She wasn't exactly looking at him.

"Well?"

"No, I don't."

"Did you write that down in your report?"

"Yes, I did."

"Dr. Magnus saw it?"

"I assume he did. Look, you've got to understand, Michael. This is my job, here in the E.R. Occasionally I do per diem work for the M.E.'s office, but I'm not in the position to follow up on the cases I investigate."

"I understand that. But you do know that Dr. Magnus ruled it a suicide?"

"If he did, then that's probably what it was. He's had a great deal more experience than I have. Usually in a case like your brother's, either Magnus or another medical examiner would have shown up. I don't investigate cases on my own where foul play may be suspected—not as a rule."

"Why did you in this instance?"

"I don't know. It was a summer weekend, people were away. I suppose I was the only one around to do the dirty work."

"You don't happen to have a duplicate of your report, do you?"

"No, I don't. I told you before, reports are always getting mislaid. It might turn up yet, you never know."

"When are you next scheduled to work for the M.E.'s office?"

"Whenever they call me. But maybe as soon as tomorrow night. The way they keep changing my schedule, I never really know. Why?"

"I was wondering if you'd mind doing me a favor and try to find a copy of that report for me."

She was shaking her head determinedly.

"Won't you let me buy you dinner? How about lunch? Cocktails?" It wasn't just for a copy of her report that he was making these offers, he realized.

She was still shaking her head. "I don't have time for the drinks or dinner. I'll look for the report. If I find it, you can have a copy, but I'm not promising anything." She dropped her eyes to the assignment list. "Look, Michael, you're going to have to excuse me. I've got a thousand people to see and I'm running way behind."

"When can I see you again?"

"Let me have your number. I'll give you a ring if I come up with anything."

"Promise you'll call no matter what you find?"

"Promise."

"Because if you don't, I'll be back. Count on it."

"I'm sure you will." Then she turned and headed back toward the nurses' station. He watched her until she was no longer in sight, admiring her legs, the movement of her hips, the hopeless attempt she was making with her hands to organize her hair.

After he left Bellevue, Michael felt compelled to walk by the chief medical examiner's office. It was so close he couldn't resist. As he passed by, he happened to see out of the corner of his eye a BMW double-parked in front of the building. He continued on, thinking nothing of it. Then something caused him to stop and go back to have another look. No, he hadn't been mistaken; he did know the man in the car. It was Ray Fontana.

CHAPTER SIXTEEN

Awakened by the phone, Michael groped for it, his eyes barely open. The readout on the clock said that it was after ten. A bright lavender light was in the room, cut up into sections by the slats of the blinds. He'd slept later than he'd planned. The phone was insistent. He was sure that it had to be either Ambrosetti or the real estate agent. He was wrong. It was Max Farrell.

"We should have a talk, Michael. How soon do you think you can get down to my office?"

"You've found something?"

"I think you'll be interested in what we've got, but I don't want to go into it on the phone."

"Give me an hour," Michael said.

* * *

Because it was Sunday morning Michael wasn't surprised to find the Fontana offices mostly empty. No phones were ringing, and there was no overweight receptionist to greet him. As soon as Michael entered, he heard Farrell call to him from in back. "That you, Michael? Come inside."

Michael hadn't slept well. He was feeling shaky, unaccountably on edge. Though he was anxious to learn what Farrell had pieced together, he was beginning to think that he'd have done better to postpone their meeting until the next day. It might have been wiser to consult with Ambrosetti first. Too late now.

Farrell had his legs up on the desk, reading the Sunday *Daily News* sports section. He looked unusually relaxed. Motioning Michael to sit, he asked if he would like some coffee.

"None for me, thanks." He was jumpy enough already.

Farrell put down his legs, assuming a more businesslike posture. "I didn't want you to think we'd forgotten about you." From his top desk drawer he pulled out a file labeled FRIEDLANDER, A.

"I'll try to make this brief and to the point."

It occurred to Michael that maybe he wasn't going to like what came next.

"First things first. A few days ago a body was fished out of Broad Channel—a woman. She was shot once in the head and gutted."

Farrell was watching Michael guardedly, the way someone might gaze at a dangerous caged animal.

"Ballistics tests were run on the fragments found in the victim's brain," he continued. "It was from a thirty-two."

"The same caliber gun Alan was shot with?"

"Better than that. It was from the *exact* same gun."

"What? You're joking!"

Farrell's expression was appropriately somber; it was no joke. "We have all the documents here. You can take a look at them if you'd like. Am I right in assuming you've seen your brother's autopsy report, Mr. Friedlander?"

"I read it over a few times, if that's what you mean."

"You might recall from Dr. Magnus's report that your brother had type-A blood?"

Actually Michael didn't remember, but he assumed that Farrell had gotten his facts straight.

"Were you also aware that Dr. Magnus noted type-O blood on your brother's body?"

No, Michael admitted, that was something he'd missed— or forgotten.

"Well, maybe it would interest you to know that this woman—the corpse they fished out of Broad Channel— also happens to be type-O."

Two and two makes four, Michael thought. "I'm not sure I follow you." He had the feeling that if he didn't find an anchor to grab on to very soon, he would fall off the edge of the world. He was perilously close to it now.

"What I'm getting at here is that it looks like your brother might have killed this woman before he took his own life."

"This woman is Ginny Karamis, isn't it?" Now he was falling off.

"No positive I.D. has been made. So maybe she is, maybe she isn't," Farrell said. But his manner left no doubt that he was convinced that it had to be Ginny.

"I can't believe my brother killed someone."

"Of course you'd say that." Farrell spoke with just a trace of condescension in his voice. "In this business, a hell of a lot of things don't make sense. But the circumstantial evidence points to a murder-suicide."

Michael needed air. He needed to get out and think this through. When he'd started out with his investigation, it was with the intention of proving that his brother hadn't committed suicide. Now it seemed that he was going to have to prove that he hadn't committed murder as well.

"But I don't want you to get the wrong idea. There are any number of ways we can play this—it depends on you."

"What do you mean, any number of ways we can play this?" It seemed to Michael that he must be missing something here. This was all going over his head.

"As of now, no positive I.D. has been made of the woman.

As far as I'm concerned, she can stay Jane Doe. She was a fucked-up broad. Nobody'll miss her."

"How can you do this?" He couldn't even begin to imagine how many laws Farrell was suggesting they violate. Not that he was ever any stickler for the law. Still, this was some serious shit they were getting into.

"What did Ray tell you? What did your friend Lou Waterman tell you? You're dealing with the best investigators in town. We have the pull; we can do these things. We can do this thing now. We can even make it so that your buddy Colin Gray is charged—posthumously—with making off with the company funds."

As soon as Farrell said this, Michael knew—he *knew*—that if Farrell didn't have a hand directly in Gray's death, he must have scared the poor bastard something terrible, done something to cause him to start swimming to Ireland. But what could he say? He had no proof. Besides, now he had his own ass to look after.

"Think of what happens if we let things take their course. Okay. It comes out that your brother was dicking this bitch, he was playing games with the company money, maybe she knew about it, maybe she was involved. Then he wastes her. Maybe it's remorse or maybe he can't see any way out, but whatever it is, he puts a gun to his head. Bam! And that's not the end of it; it won't just stop there."

He leaned back in his swivel chair and looked across the desk at Michael. At that moment he seemed to have reverted to his former role as cop, laying out the grim options open to the suspect he was grilling.

"Your father's an attorney, isn't he?"

His father? Where the hell was this leading?

"His firm does business with several major clients, doesn't it? AT and T, Intel, Hewlett-Packard, Sony." He'd done his homework. "But if I'm not mistaken, his biggest client—his firm's biggest client—is the City of New York. Now, how do you think it would affect his business if something like this came out? You've been away for a while living out there in Vermont—"

"New Hampshire."

"New Hampshire." To Farrell it was all the same difference; it was either New York, Chicago, L.A., or no place in particular. "But even so, I'm sure you realize how delicate some of these legal relations can be. Any taint of wrongdoing—"

"This has nothing to do with my father."

"Mr. Friedlander, this has everything to do with your father because it would get into the papers. How long do you think it'd be before the mayor and his legal counsel decided to take their business elsewhere? And you know what happens. One client leaves, next thing you know they're all jumping ship. Do you honestly think your father's partners would stand by and watch their major clients bail out? Do you think they want to open their morning papers every day for months while this thing drags on and see that their partner's in the news again?"

Michael stared blankly at him, hesitating to say anything at all. His stomach was heaving, and he wondered whether he could keep his breakfast down.

"Well?"

Some sort of response was necessary. "If that could be avoided . . ."

Farrell smiled, suddenly agreeable. "Yes, if that scenario could be avoided, everybody would benefit."

"What would you like me to do, then?"

"Nothing."

"Excuse me?"

"I don't want you doing anything at all, Mr. Friedlander. When you came to us, you told me you were anxious to get at the truth. I understood your concern. Well, it seems to me we succeeded to a large extent. The truth, as it so often does, turns out to be . . . unpalatable. The truth turns out to be shit. So now you know. Take it further and it can only get worse—for everybody. For your brother's reputation. For your whole family. For you."

"Let me get this clear. What you're proposing is that I forget about it and go back home."

"To New Hampshire, yes. That's it. It's a simple enough

thing to do." He shot Michael a reproving look. "And make sure you don't go hiring another investigator. That wouldn't do at all."

Was this meant to refer to Ambrosetti, or was this just a general warning? Whatever it was, it had the desired effect on Michael. It scared him shitless.

"And in return, what do you do, exactly? Clear the decks? Rub the slate clean? What?"

"In return we make sure you can sleep at night," Max replied calmly.

What Farrell had done was to offer Michael a radically different version of events than he'd been prepared to accept. Yet it was a version that had a certain chilling credibility to it, one that, for all Michael knew, might even be able to stand up to the withering scrutiny of a judicial proceeding. Michael didn't buy it. Certainly he didn't want to buy it. But what did it matter whether he bought it or not? These people had the power, they played their games in a whole different ball park than any he was used to. No matter how he looked at it, he was fucked.

The only thing he could think to do was call Waterman. It was Waterman who'd turned him on to the Fontana Security Agency. Maybe he had an idea what was going on, maybe not. But those long years on the bench must have given him a finely tuned capacity to discriminate between what was real and what was not. Michael would, in any case, like to hear what he had to say.

Isabel, Lou Waterman's housekeeper, took the call. "I am afraid that the judge is unavailable," she said in her melodic Caribbean voice.

"Well, could you tell me when he will be available?" Michael had forgotten it was a Sunday. Why should he expect anyone of means to be in town? Waterman was doubtless in the Hamptons or upstate somewhere.

"I can't tell you that. The judge, he is ailing, he is in the hospital."

"I'm sorry to hear that." He was more than sorry.

"When he is getting out, I do not know."

"Is it possible to visit him at the hospital?"

"Maybe yes. It is New York Hospital. You can try calling them and they will tell you."

Michael did not call; it was late in the afternoon, and he assumed that visiting hours were still going on. He decided to go directly to the hospital. Upon learning the judge's room number at reception, he proceeded directly to the elevators. He didn't want anybody to tell him that the judge couldn't receive visitors.

As he approached Waterman's room—a private one on the fifth floor—a man was just coming out of it. He was generously proportioned, with piercing eyes that found Michael from behind wire-rimmed glasses. There was something familiar about him that Michael couldn't place. But the man seemed to know him.

"Friedlander? Michael Friedlander?"

"Yes." Even closer, Michael couldn't say for sure who this was. He was in his early fifties, wearing a charcoal-gray jacket, a lemon-colored tie, carrying a bag. Unquestionably a doctor. "I'm sorry, I don't . . ." he started to say. Then it came to him.

"Dr. Shannon?"

Michael had taken a class in internal medicine with Ed Shannon either in his first or second year at Columbia; he couldn't remember which. Shannon hadn't been a particularly demanding teacher, but he was capable enough. Michael had not done well in the course and even now felt somewhat ashamed of his dereliction.

They shook hands. "It's been a hell of a long time," Shannon said. "Where have you been hiding yourself? You dropped out, didn't you?"

Michael was used to editing down the history of his life to such an extent that he needed less than a minute to account for the last fifteen years. He didn't sense much interest on Shannon's part anyhow.

Shannon's life, by contrast, was one filled with honors,

appointments, and fellowships. He enjoyed an association with Rockefeller University in addition to Columbia. He was directing a program at Mount Sinai, the nature of which Michael failed to comprehend. Dr. Shannon had returned from Paris, where he'd attended a conference about modern drug therapy, and sometime in September was scheduled to deliver a paper at a seminar in San Diego.

He was married—happily, if he was to believed—"to someone who I think was in your class, Sandra Raab."

The name didn't ring any bells, but then, when it came to Michael's recollections of his time at Columbia, his memory was pretty much a blur of upheaval, drugs, sex, and failed exams.

"Kids?" Michael asked politely, anxiously eyeing the doorway from which Shannon had just emerged.

"Three—two boys and a girl. The oldest is eleven."

"Congratulations!"

"You?"

Michael shook his head. Not only didn't he have any career or honors to pull out of a hat for him, but he even lacked the consolation of a family of his own. Shannon gave him a look that was at once bewildered and patronizing. Avoiding the obvious question as to what he was doing with his life, Shannon asked when he'd gotten back to New York. "You've been gone for several years now, haven't you?"

"I wouldn't be here now except for my brother."

"Your brother?"

Michael told him.

"Jesus! I didn't know. I'm awfully sorry. What a tragedy. You read about these things in the papers, but you never expect it to happen to anybody you know." He hurried on to the next topic. "So what are you doing here at New York Hospital, anyway? Visiting somebody?"

"Judge Waterman."

Shannon frowned.

"He's a family friend."

"Ah," he said. "What a coincidence. I'm treating Lou." He

sounded proprietary, as if the judge were solely his territory.

Michael had somehow assumed that Shannon had been brought in on a consult; it had never occurred to him that Shannon was Waterman's doctor. "How is he?"

"Not good," Shannon said in a low voice. "Actually, Michael, although I'm sure Lou would appreciate a visit from you, I don't think it's advisable right now. Later, maybe, when he's feeling up to it."

Thinking that his words might not be persuasive enough, Shannon draped an arm over Michael's shoulders and began to steer him back in the direction of the elevators.

"He's under sedation now," he went on, "and so the best thing to do is let him get some rest."

"What about tomorrow? Do you think he might be up to seeing visitors tomorrow?" But Michael could tell by the grim expression into which Shannon's features had arranged themselves that tomorrow—like today—was out of the question.

There was no choice but to accompany Shannon down in the elevator and go through the awkward formalities of saying good-bye. No sooner was his former professor out of sight than Michael retraced his steps and returned to the fifth floor.

There was no one to waylay him now. But once he'd gotten to Waterman's room, he saw that nothing was going to come of his evasive tactics. Just as Shannon had said, the judge was in no condition to see visitors. He looked terrible; his skin was pasty white, and his eyes seemed to be fighting their way back into his skull. Asleep, he resembled a dead man. The only signs of life were the short, rasping breaths that escaped from him now and again.

"May I help you, sir?"

Michael turned to find a nurse standing behind him, a reproachful expression on her face.

"No, thanks," he said, slipping away. "I've seen everything I wanted here."

CHAPTER SEVENTEEN

Once or twice while recounting his meeting with Farrell, Michael would notice Ambrosetti's attention wandering. Ambrosetti had developed a cold since they'd last met; his nose was bright red and raw, and his eyes were watery, so maybe it was the miserable state of his health that was causing his distraction. Still, it was unsettling. This was the man on whom Michael had placed all his bets. As far as Michael could see, the detective was probably the one person left he could count on. He wanted his undivided attention.

When he was through with his story, Ambrosetti lifted his bleary eyes to him and said, "That's it?"

"Isn't that enough?"

Ambrosetti hadn't seemed to have heard him. He was busy signaling to a waiter for another soda.

They seemed to know Ambrosetti in this place, a darkened saloon in Midtown Manhattan where in years gone by he'd no doubt put away enough boilermakers to stop an army in its tracks. He had that kind of look to him that only decades of persistent drinking could produce. But he seemed really content there, settled in, as if this bar was like a second home to him.

"Well?" Michael asked when he didn't immediately elicit any response.

"Well, what?"

"What do you think—about what I just told you? What do you think I should do?"

"What did you tell this guy Farrell you'd do?"

"I told him I'd think over what he'd said and get back to him."

"Hold off getting in touch with him for a while. We're making progress here. No sense letting some joker bollix up the works. So long as he thinks you're going along with him, what the fuck, huh?"

Michael wasn't so sure it was that easy. "What about Ginny Karamis?"

"What you've got to ask yourself is whether Farrell was bullshitting you or not. But let me check it out, okay? See if that stiff they took out of Broad Channel was Karamis. Your problem, Michael, is you worry too damned much. You want to worry, I'll tell you when to worry. I'll give you the signal, okay?"

Michael nodded his agreement. But all the time he was thinking that the problem wasn't that he was worrying; the problem was that Ambrosetti wasn't. One thing, though— Michael was beginning to see how Ambrosetti worked. Once he'd sunk his teeth into an investigation, he wasn't about to allow anybody to interfere, not even the person who'd hired him. Maybe he didn't have a strategy, maybe he had no plan, but he gave every appearance that he did, and for the time being that would just have to do.

Now that the detective figured he'd assuaged his client's rattled nerves, he forged ahead. "I did some more checking," he began, squinting against the gloom to see what he'd written down in his notebook, "and what I found suggests to me that we have a few problems more serious than your Mr. Farrell. Oh, Lord, do we have a few problems! Yes, sir. I believe I mentioned before that there was a property receipt filled out for the pullover your brother was wearing?"

Michael vaguely remembered. What report or fragment of evidence loomed as important—even as crucial—at one moment seemed to recede into insignificance the next. His brother's bullet-ridden pullover could be the key to the whole thing, he guessed, or it could turn out to mean nothing.

"There was supposed to be a chemical analysis done," Ambrosetti continued. "It was requested, anyway. But it never happened."

Another page: "Also, it seems that your brother's sweatsuit jacket is missing. We're seeing critical evidence vanish into the black hole of the Manhattan criminal justice system. It's nuts."

"What else is missing?"

"Let's see what else we've got. Ah, yes, no scrapings. Total absence of scrapings. Since I can't get hold of that medical investigator's report, I have no way of knowing whether the scrapings were taken. They should have been, though—it's routine in cases like this."

A little hesitantly, Michael said, "I went to see her—the medical investigator, I mean." He wondered whether Ambrosetti would react the same way Farrell had.

Ambrosetti's thick eyebrows shot up. "Oh, yeah? What did she tell you?"

"Nothing much. She said she'll try and get hold of a copy of her report for me."

Ambrosetti seemed relieved. Clearly he was dismayed by the idea that Michael might beat him at his own game. "Well, we'll see . . ." he said, doing nothing to cover the doubt in his voice. He returned his attention to his notes.

"Oh, yes, here," he said, drumming a stubby finger against the pad. "This is good; I like this one. We have another property request for latent processing—fingerprints—for the thirty-two-caliber revolver and shells. There's a notation here—'Process negative dispo to Detective Mackie, Homicide.' But nothing seems to have been done about it. I couldn't locate any official request for latent processing in the police files." He glanced up at Michael. "What that means is that we don't know—we may never know—if there were any other prints on that gun besides your brother's. It might not matter. It's a bitch trying to get latents off a gun, anyway. But the fact that nothing was done about it does raise some interesting questions. In fact, just about everything in this case raises some interesting questions."

As added emphasis, he unfurled his handkerchief and sneezed into it with a convulsive shudder of his body.

"Where exactly does all this leave us?"

"That's not a question we can answer yet, Michael. The stage we're at now is collecting the pieces. Later we can try and put them together and see what it adds up to."

"I'd like a copy of everything you've found so far, if that's all right."

"No problem. You're paying me, aren't you?" Then he said, "What we're seeing here is a definite pattern."

"A pattern? What kind of pattern?"

"This isn't the first time the M.E.'s office has queered an investigation—not by a long shot. I did some research. I found three other cases that stank. My guess is if you dug far enough, you'd find more. We've got one case last December involving the shooting death of a punk named Lucas Cato in the Bronx. Magnus submitted a report saying he'd gone to the scene, but the police who were there testified they never saw him. Oh, it was a real mess—blood samples and broken teeth found in the apartment were never tested to see whether they came from the victim. But more important, Magnus never tried to determine the time of death."

"And why did that matter?"

"It meant that the suspect's alibi held up—that's why it matters." Ambrosetti went on to enumerate the other two cases. One involved Tino Ojieda, a notorious drug dealer who had no compunction about wiping out whole families, kids included, to settle a score. He was strangled to death in the Bellevue psychiatric ward by two attendants—that was what the evidence showed, anyhow—but the attendants got off.

"Magnus put down as cause of death aspiration pneumonia and hyperpyrexia in 'undetermined circumstances, pending further investigation.' You can bet your sweet cookie there was no further investigation."

"How the hell can he get away with something so blatant?"

"Isn't it obvious? Nobody wanted those attendants put on trial for the scumbag's death. Magnus saw to it that they weren't."

The third controversial case had occurred the previous April and involved the slaying of a young woman named Cassie Epstein. Her killer claimed that it was an accident. The gun had gone off accidentally when he took it out to clean it. "Without going into all the grim details, the case came down to what position the killer—her boyfriend—was in when the gun went off. Everything hinged on the trajectory of the bullet and the location of the entrance wound. In his report, Magnus placed the wound about half an inch below where the bullet actually went in. Even though he was called on it in cross, he somehow managed to convince the jury that the wound had to be accidental."

"The killer got off?"

"Yes, indeedy."

"So you're saying that Magnus has been deliberately falsifying autopsy reports all along?"

"It sure looks that way, doesn't it? Of course, we got to ask ourselves what good does it do Magnus. Why the questionable autopsy reports? Why the missing evidence? The guy's not incompetent. Far from it—he's got a reputation as one of the best pathologists in the business. He's called on to testify as an expert witness all over the country. Which leads me to conclude that it can't be anything other than deliberate. But that still leaves the question of why."

"How do we find the answer?"

"We go through these cases, maybe we come up with a couple of others I missed, see how they relate to one another—*if* they relate to one another. What we've got to do is decipher the pattern. Find out who Magnus answers to."

"And then what?"

Ambrosetti laughed. "Then we're probably going to have to run for cover."

CHAPTER EIGHTEEN

It had been a rough night. For one thing, nobody knew what to do with Tony Morgantini. No sooner did Gail believe that she was rid of him than he was back from the psych ward, O.D.'d on Placidil. She returned him to the psych ward, but psych couldn't figure out what to do with him and put him back on the street. Then she'd spent an hour trying to staunch the bleeding from a knife wound that had very nearly skewered the chest of a youth named Vinny Senzel. It didn't seem to matter to him that he was bleeding to death; what bothered him was the tube they had to put in his nose and down his throat. "Let me die, I don't care!" he kept screaming. "Just take that fucking tube out! I want to go home!"

If Vinny wasn't bad enough, there was Wu Chang with whom to deal. Somebody had given poor old Wu Chang a barium enema hours earlier, but he had no idea who or why. A big problem was that he couldn't speak a word of English. His mind was lost. He looked ready to fade away right in front of Gail's eyes. He was jaundiced—yellow on yellow—ravaged with pancreatic cancer.

Then there was Josephine Perez: another O.D. case. When enough saline and charcoal had been forced down into her stomach, she came to. The first words out of her mouth were addressed to Gail. "You fucking bitch!" she said. "What the fuck did you wake me up for?" That was gratitude.

At seven-thirty Monday morning Gail emerged into the brilliant sunshine, blinking furiously with the shock of the light. She heard her name being called. Wheeling around, she saw a man with thick, curly black hair wearing a T-shirt and jeans—whom she supposed she should recognize. Squinting, she could better make out his features. God, she thought, it was that guy who came around the other night to ask about the Friedlander case. Michael, she remembered—that was his name. Michael Friedlander.

He ran up to her. "I was waiting for you," he said.

"It certainly looks that way. I'm sorry, but I don't have that report for you."

Actually, the truth was it had slipped her mind.

"I know. You said you didn't know when you were next scheduled to work for the medical examiner's office."

"So what do you want, then?" She was being rude, but she was too exhausted to be polite. While it would take some time for her to wind down enough so that she could sleep, she was in no mood for conversation, especially not with a stranger.

"Could we go somewhere and talk?"

She shook her head, continuing to walk at an accelerated pace. What did she think she was going to do, outdistance him? Maybe so. "Can't it wait? I'm about ready to drop."

"If it wasn't important, I wouldn't bother you, believe me."

"Important to you, you mean." She shot him a dirty look. But it didn't matter; she could see he wasn't going to be so easily put off.

"Important not just to me. Important to a lot of people. It's about Magnus."

Somehow this didn't surprise her. Friedlander might be a paranoid. A nut case. Paranoids and nut cases abounded in the city. They made for a continuous traffic in and out of the E.R.; some formed a strange attraction to her and came back repeatedly, hoping that she would see them. If he'd ambushed her at night, she might have reacted with panic, unsure of what motives lurked behind those intense brown eyes of his. But with the sun pouring down on him, he seemed unthreatening. Just a bit erratic, the kind of person one didn't want driving if one was in the car with him.

"I can't help you," she said more emphatically, hoping that in spite of her weariness she sounded firm enough. "I'll see what I can do about finding that report, but that's the end of it."

"Let me buy you breakfast."

"I'm not hungry."

She turned the corner at Twenty-second Street. Somewhere in the next three blocks she was going to have to get rid of him. She didn't want him trailing her all the way to her apartment.

"What about coffee? Listen, Dr. Ives—"

"I'm off duty now, so you can call me Gail."

"Gail, listen, give me five minutes, ten minutes—"

"And then you'll disappear?" She was becoming exasperated. Now that she thought about it, she didn't see how she could lose him. He was so goddamned persistent.

"Then I'll disappear, I promise." He smiled, then thought to add, "For now."

"All right. There's a coffee shop back in the other direction. We can go and talk there."

He was crazy, she was convinced. Not crazy like Raoul DeLeo, who suffered from inexplicable fits, or the man who swallowed a whole bottle of iodine and then refused to take a starch solution to counteract it because he said it was against his Jewish faith. No, this, she decided, was another brand of craziness. His was a craziness that was more peculiar to true believers and religious fanatics. He had a cause, the cause possessed him, and he had no room inside him for anything else. She wasn't prepared to admit it, not to him, anyway, but she sort of admired that. She almost wished she could be so fervent about a cause herself.

Numb from treating patients in the pit for thirty-seven hours, it was almost impossible for her to concentrate on what Michael was saying. Her attention was caught not by his words but by the expressiveness of his face, by the way he moved, keeping his hands in constant motion, dancing in the air. So much passionate conviction. She marveled at it. But what the hell was he saying? She ordered another cup of coffee, hoping that it might succeed in accomplishing what the last two cups had not, and make her more alert.

"Three cases, four if you count my brother's. Who knows how many others there might be? If you could get into the records and see what's there, it would be an enormous help."

"It'd be illegal. I couldn't do that." She didn't know that for certain, but it sounded illegal. A convenient excuse. She had to watch what she was getting into with this guy.

"These autopsy reports are public," Michael protested. "If you can't take them out of the office, you can look at them, can't you? You can make copies."

"But what good would it do?" Maybe he'd already explained, and she'd just failed to hear or understand.

"Until I take a look at them, I won't be able to tell you."

"Didn't you say that you've got a detective working on this for you? Why do you need me?"

"You work for Magnus; you're on the inside. It'll be easier for you to get hold of those records than it would be for my detective." Then suddenly he seemed to lose all of his energy. His shoulders sagged, and he looked terribly deflated. "You're not going to do it, are you?"

Up until this point she'd been ready to tell him to take a hike. It was none of her business. Not that she doubted that there wasn't a good deal of incompetence in the M.E.'s office or that evidence couldn't go astray. But it was inconceivable to her that some kind of criminal activity could be taking place. It was beyond her; it had nothing to do with her.

But on the other hand, she didn't like people anticipating her response. Michael seemed to have sized her up and found her wanting. His fierce conviction lent him a superiority to which she couldn't measure up. That infuriated her. But she replied in an even voice, "I didn't say I wouldn't do it. I didn't say yes *or* no. Give me the names of these cases you're talking about, and if it's possible, maybe I'll find out something about them. But no guarantees, okay?" Even as she said this, she was only digging a hole for herself. This couldn't lead to any good.

"I don't expect guarantees," he said. "Not from anybody. If you can't do it, you can't. It's just nice to know that you'll try."

He handed her a piece of paper with the names—Lucas Cato, Tino Ojieda, Cassie Epstein—and Alan Friedlander. Pieces in a puzzle, he told her. All pieces in a puzzle.

In the end she capitulated and let him walk her home. It seemed like the thing to do. No sooner had she gotten inside her apartment than her phone started ringing. It was as if somebody knew exactly the moment she'd walk in. When she answered she didn't know whether she was surprised or not to hear Kurt Magnus on the other end.

CHAPTER NINETEEN

Three hours after a mortuary hearse had removed the unidentified remains from the extreme southern end of Riverside Park were they had been discovered, Magnus began the autopsy. Gail strode into the autopsy room to join him and his assistant, Francis Holmes. She was wearing a short-sleeved shirt, drawstring pants, and a plastic apron, with her unruly hair pushed up into the confines of a cap.

Collected on the corkboard beside the hexagonal table were the tools of the trade—saws, chisels, knives, trocars, an Osterizer knife sharpener, and a pair of special long-bladed scissors for cutting away the brain.

Ordinarily Magnus would not have rushed to perform the post. One hundred twenty-eight refrigerated compartments were available to house the bodies until Magnus or one of his deputies had the time to examine them. But these remains had a high priority. Magnus suspected that they were the work of the Chopper.

Was it because Gail had been in on the examination of an earlier victim that Magnus wanted her in attendance now? Whatever the reason, she was there reluctantly—responding to his personal request. Again and again she directed her attention to him. Criminals and conspirators, she understood, bore no mark to identify them. Still, she realized that she was looking for a sign, some intimation of guilt, some furtiveness in his behavior.

But on the contrary, he acted with the same efficiency and sense of authority that he always did. His interest was concentrated wholly on the cadaver beneath him, his gloved hands gripping the knives, anxious to begin their work. In his melancholy eyes Gail discerned only a terrible knowledge of the world, but no guilt or criminality. She almost resented Michael for causing her to think ill of the man.

Magnus greeted her perfunctorily, with a wan smile. In this case, Gail sensed, there would be no lightness whatso-

ever, no gallows humor so commonplace among pathologists. Gail believed the air of solemnity that hung so heavily
in the cold, ventilated air of the autopsy room was at least in
part occasioned by the urgency of the case. Word of the
macabre discovery in the park had naturally gotten out, and
the story was already being aired in special news bulletins
on TV. Gail had seen the gathering of newsmen and photographers in the lobby on her way in. Animated and boisterous in their impatience for results, they looked as if they
were there for a party, not for an autopsy finding.

The shroud was drawn away to reveal a head and a
trunk—and nothing else. The head was grotesquely damaged, but the trunk had been spared all but a few abrasions
and some bruising where the frayed strands of rope binding
the deceased had been drawn taut. Where the amputations
had severed the arms and legs the skin was singed, suggesting that the wounds had been cauterized. Only where the
penis had been removed was the wound left open.

"Nice," said Holmes. His expression changed not at all,
except when his eyes lighted on Gail. And then he stared,
unashamedly, with undisguised lust, almost as if she were
another body to be examined and dissected. That she was
alive was only incidental.

But what Gail found most unnerving about the deputy examiner was how immune he seemed, how indifferent, finally how estranged he was from things that suffered, from
things that lived.

"Death, we estimate, occurred about twelve to fourteen
hours previously," Magnus told Gail. "What do you notice
here about the skin?"

For the moment his eyes were fixed on her, not the cadaver. "There are goose pimples all over."

"Why goose pimples?"

"Water . . . mud, maybe."

"So we can conclude that the body has been immersed
for how long?"

"I'd say a few hours. Otherwise, the body would be much
more wrinkled."

Magnus nodded. She'd gotten it right. "What inference can you draw about the bruises surrounding the ties?"

"That the deceased was still alive when he was bound. An absence of bruises would have meant that the blood had stopped pumping by then."

"Good," Magnus said. "Now let's begin."

But the questions didn't stop. Magnus proceeded in much the same way that he had in the railroad flat on Twenty-fifth Street, alternately coaxing and demanding answers from her, occasionally offering a hint when she was stumped. He seemed to be drawing her into this thing in a way that she could not quite fathom. It seemed to her that he was trying to initiate her, as if into a cult or a religion of some kind, though it might very well have been a religion all his own. But gradually she began to feel that in some way her presence there made her Magnus's accomplice—as well as the murderer's.

During the next hour they managed to reconstruct the murder in detail. Working backward from the tiny petechiae—hemorrhages—in the eyelids, the finger "blob" bruises, and nail impressions on each side of the neck, they deduced that the assault had begun with an attempt to strangle the victim, but that the murderer had decided to resort to other means. For there were no voice box fractures or any material asphyxial changes. Cause of death was most likely trauma to the head, accomplished with a heavy instrument. The whole left side of the face had been crushed, sunken into the skull, forming a crater of bruised and abraded skin from which one eye stared up at them.

"It appears to be direct impact," Magnus said. "You'll observe the crushing of the edges along the wound, the way in which the hairs have been driven into the skull, and the damage to the surrounding skin. The wound is jagged, completely shattered, and depressed. Fragments of bone have become separated here and driven into the skull so that we can presume bruising of the brain as a logical consequence."

Soon his face was soaked in sweat as he labored to open the skull. Bone chips scattered all over the place as he cut, using first the drill, then the saw, then the chisel at three-centimeter intervals along the line of the saw cut, then the dura elevator. Finally, losing patience, Magnus used his own fingers to pry the cap of the skull off. As he scooped the brain out of the skull, Gail said she would have to excuse herself.

It wasn't that she didn't have the stomach for this any longer; it was just that if she was ever going to look for the files Michael wanted, it ought to be done now. She didn't know whether she would ever again have either the opportunity or the resolve. Magnus cast her a reproachful glance, no doubt surmising that her nerves, or her constitution, or *something* had suddenly failed her.

Finding the records she was after wasn't going to be easy. Not because of security; that wasn't what she was so worried about. It was the sheer disorder that prevailed throughout the M.E.'s office, much of it she knew blamed on Magnus. People who worked here full-time claimed that he was a terrible administrator. She'd heard all sorts of grotesque stories, about how blood was seen dripping from storage cabinets and how refrigeration units were so cramped for space that body parts often had to be stored out in the hallways, creating one hell of a stench. Somebody even asserted that he'd seen body parts stuffed into ordinary black trash bags before being sent to the incinerator. Maybe some of these stories were exaggerations, but nonetheless Gail believed there was some truth to them. She herself had seen cockroaches in areas of the building and—once—a rat brazenly exploring a room full of specimens as if it owned the place. She'd also seen the dumpsters around in back with bags torn open, exposing needles and vials of blood and body fluids. She was appalled; disposing medical waste like that was entirely against regulations, but she decided that, as a part-time worker, it was none of her business. Now she wondered.

The records were another problem. Months went by before full autopsy reports were completed. A terrific backlog of over three thousand cases had developed in the last year. The police needed only short reports with the most salient facts. Families and insurance companies were another story. They were often compelled to wait months for complete reports—compared to a national average of two weeks. So Gail really had no idea whether she would find the records she was looking for or in what state those records would be if she did manage to locate them.

The vast bulk of the autopsy records was maintained on the second floor. But some of the more recent records were temporarily stored on the ground floor, beyond the communications room and the office cubicles where autopsy findings were transcribed. There, in the records room, statisticians labored to analyze and classify the data, determining trends in mortality—drug addiction, alcoholism, vehicular accidents, disease, and murder—to understand better how New Yorkers were being carried off year by year.

The room was open. One other person sat at a desk, a man in shirt-sleeves and a loosened tie. Gail was still wearing the garments she'd put on for the autopsy, and bone dust had collected in her hair like dandruff. But there was nothing she could do about making herself more presentable now. A shower would only delay her. What counted was that she looked as if she had a right to be there. The man nodded to her and then went back to punching data into his computer. The radio was on, low in the background, tuned to Lite FM.

She was nervous, and her heart was pounding. It didn't matter that nobody was watching her, that as far as she could tell she was perfectly free to look in the records. At the same time she realized that the danger, however ambiguous or imagined, exhilarated her. Like riding the Cyclone at Coney Island or scaling a dangerous peak. The adrenaline pumping, the blood roaring in her ears, she sifted through the files—Franks, Frascall, Frayer, Frazee, Frederick, Fredman, Freeman, B., Freeman, R., Freid, Friedenberg, Friedlander . . ."

It was there, after all. Thank God. Sure that by now somebody must be staring at her, she scanned the room. But there was just the lone statistician typing in data, and he couldn't care less.

Opening the file, she looked for her own report. It was there, all right. Only it wasn't what she'd written. Her signature was on it, but the words had been altered. How the changes had been made she had no idea, because there were no obvious erasures or corrections. But all the same, it had been done. There was nothing about the scrapings she'd taken. Her notations about the blood spatter had been changed so that all the evidence indicated that Friedlander had shot himself in the bedroom.

"Motherfucker!" she muttered, but not as softly as she thought, because the statistician suddenly looked toward her, a puzzled expression on his face. She smiled back at him and then walked to the copy machine to make a duplicate of the material.

It came to her then why she'd been sent to Alan Friedlander's apartment to investigate his death. It hadn't been a mistake, a result of bureaucratic error. Magnus needed someone who was inexperienced, who lacked credibility, who, in all probability, would never question his findings. Why else the strange interest he was taking in her? He must have believed that she'd back off and do the sensible thing and avoid any trouble. There was no question in her mind what had taken place—she had been set up.

CHAPTER TWENTY

Gail was furious, and her rage seemed to electrify the air. There was no possibility of her stopping to catch her breath. She was pacing back and forth, pausing occasionally at the window to look out. Michael, sitting by the coffee table in her living room, was astounded, even a little awed; it was like finding oneself in the middle of a violent hurricane. The only thing he could think to do was batten down the hatches and wait until the storm abated. And she'd struck

him as so controlled, so accustomed to dealing with crises
that nothing could faze her.

He'd come at once when she called, never thinking that
she'd actually gotten hold of the files he requested. Not only
had she obtained the report on his brother, but she'd also
come up with copies of the documents relating to Ojieda
and Epstein. Lucas Cato's file she said she couldn't locate.

She continued to fortify herself from a bottle of Absolut.
Serious stuff. But the vodka wasn't doing much of a job of
settling her nerves; then again, she didn't seem interested in
settling her nerves.

"Goddamn him!" she kept saying, half to Michael, half to
herself. "Goddamn that son-of-a-bitch! What does he think I
am? Some pretty, empty-headed girl he can fuck around?"

Michael had the feeling that this wasn't the first betrayal
she'd suffered. Others—parents, lovers, friends, associates at
work—must have let her down badly. He knew how it
worked from both sides. But he couldn't say he was displeased by what had happened. She seemed now as violently opposed to Magnus as he was.

She looked around the apartment distractedly, as if she
was searching for something that, once found, might put
things right again. "The hell with them," she said. "I don't
need the money that badly. There are other ways to make
money, right?"

"Of course," he said. But the truth was he didn't want her
to bail out—not now when there was so much at stake.
Events had conspired to make them allies. They were on the
same side. By continuing to work for the M.E.'s office she
could still be of help to him.

"I have to go wash up. I stink of formaldehyde. I can't
stand myself," she said.

The heat of her anger was beginning to slacken. Idly un-
doing the first two buttons of her blouse, she said to
Michael, "Make yourself at home." Then she turned and went
into the bedroom. She put on some music, Janis Joplin.
Michael couldn't remember how long it it had been since

he'd last heard Janis. It took him back in a way that it never could for her.

When he went to pour himself a couple of shots of the Absolut, he caught a momentary glimpse of Gail standing in the shadows of the bedroom, letting down her hair over her naked back. Then she disappeared into the bathroom.

While she took her shower, Michael looked over the copies of the files Gail had made, beginning with his brother's. But if he was expecting to find anything revelatory, a forthright admission that Alan couldn't have committed suicide or even some expression of doubt, then he was in for a big disappointment. Everything in the file, including Gail's altered report, supported Magnus's—and the police department's—conclusions. There was a lot that wasn't in the file: no results from the neutron or paraffin tests, no chemical tests on Alan's clothing, no scanning electron microscopy and energy-dispersive X-ray spectroscopy tests on bullet fragments requested by FBI headquarters in Washington, D.C.

Nor could Michael find anything in the file on the drug dealer Tino Ojieda that gave him heart. The report was heavy going like the others and required a clinical vocabulary to interpret it. Without his medical school training, however distantly recalled, phrases like "upper cervical transverse necrotizing myelopathy" and "ischemic cerebral necrosis" might just as well have been in a foreign language. What was in plain English wasn't much clearer, though. At the end of the report he found what would appear to be a conclusion—but a conclusion of the most tentative kind:

Circumstances undetermined, pending further studies and pending investigation.

This was crazy. It was as if after going to such trouble to collect all the evidence necessary to determine that the man had been strangled, Magnus had suddenly balked and said that he hadn't the faintest idea why the man had died.

More puzzling still was the handwritten notation scrawled at the bottom of the autopsy report:

Advised by Dr. Magnus to leave cause of death as is and make notation when police report is received.

It was unsigned, and no police report had been included.

Michael turned finally to the Epstein file. His eyes were growing bleary, and a headache seemed to be building in the back of his head. His concentration was off; he kept having the feeling that he was overlooking something essential in these documents that would make it worth all the trouble Gail had gone to to get them.

What the Epstein report said was barely different from what Ambrosetti had told him. Half a page was devoted to the locations of the entry and exit wounds and the track of the fatal bullet. There was nothing obvious in the file that indicated that Magnus's conclusions in the case were ever questioned. It was dry, technical data that for the most part Michael could make neither heads nor tails out of. But then he came upon some information that he'd never thought to ask about before—the name of Cassie Epstein's killer. To his astonishment it was someone he'd met. It was the head of Ray Fontana's trucking company, Frank Brice.

As far as Michael was concerned, there was no question: The autopsies had been falsified on Ray Fontana's orders. The evidence seemed to him incontrovertible. The very presence of Fontana in front of the M.E.'s office seemed to Michael to implicate him. This surely must be the pattern Ambrosetti was hoping to find. Michael decided to call him at once.

As soon as he had the detective on the line, Michael proceeded to tell him what he'd uncovered—or thought he had, at any rate. He realized that in his enthusiasm to get everything out all at once, he wasn't exactly making sense. Several times Ambrosetti had to interrupt him in order to clarify what he was saying.

To Michael's surprise, Ambrosetti knew of Frank Brice. Apparently the man wasn't nearly as obscure as he'd imagined.

"A big earner," was how Ambrosetti referred to him.

"Excuse me?"

"Brice is known as a big earner—it's mob jargon for someone who brings in a lot of money. From what I understand, he controls Kennedy Airport."

"I don't know about that. He told me he runs a trucking firm."

"You met him?"

"Once, with Fontana."

"Well, his trucking business is mob-owned. All the hijackings of trucks you read about at JFK? They're all set up. Drivers leave their keys in the ignition, then tell the cops they don't know what happened to their loads. They work for Brice. That's why he's such a good earner. Guy was in jail at sixteen. I understand he did hits for the mob while he was still in the big house. When he got out, his career was set."

"Jesus!" If Brice wielded so much authority on his own, what did that say about Fontana? "It all comes back to Fontana, Nick. He keeps putting people in his debt. It's as clear as day."

"Sometimes things aren't so black and white. I'll have to look into it. But you may be right, the guy does seem to have a lot of markers out. Let me see what I can come up with, and I'll get back to you."

The problem wasn't that Ambrosetti was indifferent to what Michael had said; it was that he just didn't seem to have gotten very excited. Having expected the detective to embrace his hypothesis, Michael had to admit he was disappointed at his tepid response.

He turned to see Gail emerge from the bedroom, wearing a pair of white shorts and a sleeveless T-shirt promoting a beach club in La Jolla. A dolphin was riding the crest of the waves above her breasts, loose under the thin fabric. Her legs were lean and muscular. It was all that exercise, he imagined, standing up for hours on end, running from patient to patient. Free of her uniform, she seemed transformed. She smelled of soap and hair rinse, the residual odor of formaldehyde scrubbed away. Her hair was hidden in the turban she'd made of her towel.

"Who were you talking to just now?"

"Nick. I think we've got something here."

He handed her a glass with more Absolut and tonic in it. She looked as if she was still in need of some. He poured more for himself while he was at it.

"Oh, just what is it you think you have?" She sounded dubious.

He told her about the link he'd established between Epstein and Brice—and between Brice and Fontana, in turn.

"And what about your brother? Was there anything in those reports I brought you?" She sat down on the couch, looking as if she was steeling herself for bad news.

"Nothing I didn't know already," he conceded.

"But you think Fontana must have had something to do with his death?"

"It's possible. I'm sure there's a link and that it probably has to do with the money. And with Ginny Karamis."

"Who?"

He told her. It wasn't a long story. Ginny was as much an enigma in death—if she was dead—as she'd been alive.

"Can you prove that Fontana was involved? I mean legally prove it?"

"I don't know about that. I'll have to have a long talk with Nick."

"What about Dr. Magnus? Why would he be falsifying these autopsies for Fontana? What possible motive would he have?"

"I assume Fontana has some kind of a hold over him."

She looked as skeptical as she sounded. "I don't know, Michael. It seems to me you're making a lot of assumptions here."

"I'm just filling in what blank spaces I can. There are a lot of blank spaces left to go. What's wrong? You're looking at me like I'm out of my mind."

"What's wrong is I don't see how you can do it. If it is

Fontana, if he has the power you say he does, how the hell are you going to be able to do anything about it even if you do prove he killed your brother? And don't tell me that your detective will take care of it. He's not a miracle worker."

"Somewhere there's got to be a chink in their armor. It's just a matter of finding out where Fontana is most vulnerable." And he firmly believed that. "Structures collapse of their own weight, they become bloated and lazy. Look at Watergate. How many asses can you cover indefinitely?"

"Well," she said, beginning to become amused, "it looks like you've given this a lot of thought. Maybe you could teach a class in political theory. Fire up the students with some of your revolutionary fervor."

He sat down next to her. "You think that's what it is—revolutionary fervor?"

"I'm not knocking it. I think it's admirable. It's just that sometimes I have this feeling you get carried away. You're not someone who thinks things through."

"But you do?"

"Me?" She threw her head back, laughing hard. "Whoa! Have you got the wrong idea! You are talking to one crazy broad here. Want to take bets on who's loonier? Only with me, the way I operate, see, people don't realize it. They look at me, they find out I'm a doctor, they think: professional, serious, sober-minded."

Seeing how little remained in her glass, Michael said, "Sober. Right."

"More, please, sir."

"You're getting drunk."

"And why not? Any objection?"

"Hardly. In fact, it makes more sense than anything else I can think of at the moment."

It occurred to him that he was actually enjoying himself. It had been a long time since he'd enjoyed himself.

"To your health," she toasted, clinking glasses loudly, "to your enterprise."

"How about to our enterprise?"

He won a smile from her. "To our enterprise."

It was hard to say who moved first, he or she. But he knew absolutely that he would have to kiss her. It was among the imperatives in his life. She appeared to be waiting for something to happen; there was such expectancy in her eyes. They were drunk and getting drunker and laughing and talking, though he, for one, couldn't put his finger on what their conversation was about. Did it matter? Not particularly. He was more intoxicated by her than he was by all the vodka he was putting away.

He kissed her and found a kiss waiting for him in return. A good sign. He heard her say something that, if he'd made it out properly, was, "This isn't such a good idea, Michael."

And he said, "No? Why not? I think it's a great idea."

They kissed again, deeper this time. Longer this time, too. Kisses hot with vodka.

"Yes, but you don't know what you're getting into here, Michael. Maybe . . ."

No, of course he didn't know what he was getting into. Neither did she. Wasn't that the point?

"Maybe what?"

If she had an answer, it was lost in another kiss. His hands were restless, wandering all over her back. Her skin was wet and warm. Her hair, freed from the constraint of the towel, came tumbling out, and when it did, it got all over the damned place. Soon he had strands of her hair *and* her tongue in his mouth. But it was generally all right with him, what was happening.

"Hey!" she said, laughing. "What's this?"

They were rolling. Too late he tried to stop them from falling off the couch, and they landed clumsily on the floor. He brought his hands around to cover her breasts. Her legs hooked him. This close, her face looked positively different, unknown, the face of a stranger. Which, he supposed, she was.

One button, as far as he could make out, was all that prevented her shorts from slipping down her hips. She hadn't troubled to wear anything underneath. He reached down, his touch causing her to gasp. She was very wet. Her eyes had a completely different cast to them, cloudy, unfocused. She was saying something, but he couldn't quite hear.

"What?"

"Don't you think the bed would be a better idea, all things being equal?"

They picked themselves up and went into the bedroom, leaving their clothes behind them.

Michael was asleep when the revolution broke out. Gunfire, grenades, bombs detonating all over the city. It was no dream. He could hear them clearly. They were making his head hurt more than it already did. Which was plenty. Gail, next to him, was returning little by little to consciousness. She looked at him in bewilderment, but he didn't know whether her mystification was due to the uproar outside or to her disorientation at discovering this strange man in bed with her.

Then she leaped out of bed. She moved to the window and drew the curtains apart enough to peer out. Light from the streetlamps played on her skin, dappling it with amber spots. Her face was in shadows. *What a fine piece of work she is*, Michael thought, almost transfixed at the sight of her. It wasn't her nudity that made the sight of her so erotic but the lack of self-consciousness she displayed, as if he wasn't there at all. For that moment he couldn't care less about the revolution.

It was a revolution, all right, but one that had already taken place two centuries ago. Michael got out of bed and went over to stand beside her.

"God, I'd forgotten," Gail said. "Tomorrow's the Fourth."

The sky was bathed in a reddish-pink light that was caused partly by the explosions, partly by the relentless summertime pollution. Michael guessed that someone with a bit of money had gotten hold of a small arsenal of fireworks and was setting them off above the East River in a private celebration of his own. It might not have been the most spectacular display he'd ever witnessed, but it was one of the most persistent. It went on and on and on.

After a while Michael grew tired of watching and went back to bed, expecting Gail to follow, but she remained at the window. Maybe she was afraid of missing something. Michael's eyes went to the clock on her side of the bed. One-twenty. Then his gaze fell on a laminated photograph; it was a portrait of a young man with a nicely trimmed blond beard and eyes bluer than Gail's.

"Who's that?" he asked. He was afraid of what the answer might be.

Slowly turning toward him, half her body becoming sub-merged in the shadows, she said, "That's my husband."

"Your husband?" He wasn't sure what to say.

"His name is William."

"What happened to him? Where is he now?"

"He's dead," she replied softly.

CHAPTER TWENTY-ONE

It wasn't until much later that night that Magnus had the op-portunity to compare specimens from the still-unidentified female found in the railroad flat on West Twenty-fifth Street and the grossly mutilated remains of the male Caucasian re-covered earlier that day in Riverside Park. The identity of the deceased had positively been established by the Missing Persons Bureau two hours before as Patrick Nelson, twenty-two, whose last known address was a tenement apartment in the theater district. For purposes of examination, the specimens, embedded in wax and mounted on a glass slide, had been finely sliced so that they could be viewed in cross section through a comparison microscope. When it came to studying specimens of hair, there were three basic features to look for: length, color, and texture. Each hair fol-licle was composed of three portions: the core or medulla; the cortex, which surrounded it; and an outer layer or cuti-cle covered by tiny, overlapping scales. These scales were used to match and identify different strands of hair and at the same time distinguish between the hair of a human and the hair of an animal.

Magnus undertook his examination in a laboratory on the fifth floor of the medical examiner's office. Arrayed before him on the slides were six specimens of hair follicles—three from the female murder victim, three from the male. Magnus was easily able to separate out four of the follicles. They had come from the head and pubic region of the two victims.

He concluded that the two remaining hair follicles must have come from the murderer. One had been removed in a swab of the vagina of the female, the second in a swab of the anus of the male. The match was perfect. One man had killed them both. The murderer was the same. The Chopper did exist.

"Dr. Magnus, is there any other evidence besides the hair follicles that will help in tracking down the killer?"

Magnus scanned the faces of the newsmen crowded into the lobby. They'd waited until the early-morning hours for him to appear, which was as much a measure of his importance as it was of the story he had to convey to them. Standing next to him was the man the police had assigned to the case—Inspector Lawrence Kohler, a solidly built man with prematurely white hair and the high coloring of someone who had spent most of his life out of doors.

"I can't speak for Inspector Kohler, of course. I'm certain that he'll be glad to inform you of whatever progress the police are making with this investigation. But I can assure you that the medical examiner's office is in possession of additional forensic evidence that we hope will aid us in identifying the killer."

"Could you say what that evidence is?"

"I'd rather not disclose that at this point. There's no sense alerting the perpetrator to what we may have on him."

He was making it sound as if they'd uncovered some bit of damning evidence, when all they had were impressions of teeth marks and a single rust-colored wool fiber found in the scrapings under the nails of the female victim. All in all, it wasn't much with which to work. But the idea was to convince the murderer—and the public—that they were further along in the investigation.

"Dr. Magnus, you said in your statement that the matching hairs came from the vagina in one case and the anus in the other."

"That's correct."

"So we can conclude that the assailant raped both victims before he murdered them?"

"Rape might not be the proper word. In the case of the female victim, decomposition in the vaginal area was too far advanced to make that determination. In the case of Patrick Nelson, we found no evidence of recent injury to the rectal wall. That would suggest that any sexual activity which took place was consensual."

This caused a flurry of excitement among the reporters; the story was becoming more sensational, more lurid, with each succeeding revelation.

"Now, I'm afraid, ladies and gentlemen, that I have to go. Inspector Kohler will take any additional questions."

"One further question, Dr. Magnus!"

"Yes? What is it?" He turned to face Sal Martin of CityVision Cable TV.

"Most serial killers have a tendency to select one type of victim—prostitutes, say, or elderly women. Is it your opinion that the Chopper targets any one type of victim?"

"There's no way to be sure. At this time we have definitely linked this killer only to two victims."

"But, Dr. Magnus, on the basis of the evidence, would you say that he goes both ways?"

"If you mean sexually, then the answer is yes."

When he returned to his office, Magnus found a message waiting for him from his wife.

He returned her call. "What is it, Barbara?"

"It's Valerie," his wife said flatly, the agitation clearly evident in her voice.

"Christ! Can't it wait? I've got some work here I want to finish up."

"No, Kurt, it can't wait. I wouldn't have called you if it could wait. It's serious."

"She didn't—?"

He had no need to finish the sentence. She knew what he was referring to. "No, thank God, but it's bad, Kurt. The police are involved."

"I'm on my way."

Of all times for his daughter to fuck up, he thought. But when had there been a good time? It was always bad, it was always going to be bad. There seemed no end to it.

Kurt and Barbara Magnus had been married for twenty-seven years when he was appointed chief medical examiner. The achievement followed a succession of increasingly prestigious postings: pathology resident at Mount Sinai; deputy chief medical examiner in Brooklyn; deputy chief medical examiner in Nassau County; director of operations, chief medical examiner's office, Dade County, Florida. It was no secret that his current appointment had saved his marriage. During the year they were in exile—exile *was* what it really amounted to—in Florida, Barbara had repeatedly threatened to leave him. It wasn't only the appointment that had changed her mind. Certainly the $125,000 salary was a factor, and so was the handsome brick house he'd bought on a maple-lined block in Forest Hills and the summer house he'd bought in The Pines on Fire Island. He'd never cared a great deal about money before nor even given it much thought until now. If he had, he would have certainly known that with the kind of lifestyle he'd adopted, $125,000 could never be made to stretch far enough, certainly not with the murderous taxes he had to shell out.

In her forty-sixth year, Barbara Magnus had kept true to the promise of her youthful beauty and grown older with grace and style. Though some gray strands had appeared in her hair, age had scarcely tampered with her face. Vigor and light still showed in her eyes. Magnus could see why men would be attracted to her. As for himself, he was no longer interested.

Magnus walked in to find his wife on the phone. She hung up as soon as she heard him. "That was Al."

Al was Al Silverstein, their lawyer.

"What did she do now?"

"Valerie was at a party earlier tonight at a friend's house in Manhattan. It seems that the party got out of hand. Apparently there was no supervision—the parents were away. The neighbors complained, and the police were called. About half a dozen kids were arrested."

"For a goddamned party?" He wanted to know what she was doing at a party anyhow after they'd expressly forbidden her to attend a party of any kind, unchaperoned.

"There were drugs—what do you think?" Barbara spoke without emotion. She'd gone through this too many times before to become overwrought. It seemed to Magnus that she'd decided she just didn't want to handle Valerie anymore and was leaving her to him to deal with.

"What kind of drugs?"

"Cocaine, I suppose . . . grass, pills, maybe. What difference does it make?" she snapped.

"But what exactly did Val do? What did they arrest her for?" He felt that if he knew the facts, then he could assess the situation and make some sense of it. Maybe it wasn't so bad as all that. His heart was racing; a pain he hoped that was more imagined than real seized his chest. He had to sit down.

"Possession of a controlled substance. Resisting arrest." She seemed deliberately to be avoiding his gaze. "Indecent exposure."

"What? What's that supposed to mean?" This somehow sounded like a more serious charge than the others.

"That's what the police told Al when he phoned. They didn't give any details. No doubt we'll find out." She made a racket putting away the dishes. Her face was taut with anger. When he didn't immediately respond, she went on to say, "You were wrong, you know, Kurt. You should never have been so liberal with her. You indulged her too much. I told you that time and again, but you didn't listen. You never listen."

"What do you mean, I'm too liberal with her? Where the hell were you today when she took the car? Why weren't you paying closer attention to where she went?" Magnus made himself a drink—a rye-and-soda, quickly thrown back and replenished. It seemed to do nothing to soothe his nerves or extinguish the pain burning in his chest.

"Of course, it's all my fault. She and her friend, that slut Carla, tell me they're going to the movies. What am I supposed to do— say no, you can't go? I can't hold her prisoner. She's seventeen years old, for Chrissakes. If something was going to be done to put some sense into that child, it should have been done long ago. After what happened, you should've let her take the punishment. Then we wouldn't have to be going through this now."

After what happened. That was as close as Barbara would ever get to referring to the incident that had occurred three years ago. He could understand her reticence, though. He could barely even bring himself to mention it. It was why they'd left the city and laid low in Florida for a year. But even then they went to great pains not to bring it out into the open. There was only one reason they had to speak about it, and that was to wound each other.

"You seem to forget, Barbara, that if we let her take her punishment, it would have finished me . . . and you wouldn't have this house or the cars or any of it."

She shot him a dark, aggrieved look. She was tired of being the pillar of the family without whose loving and resolute support the whole edifice of their lives together would come tumbling down. "You forget, Kurt, that I could have all the houses and cars I wanted—it just wouldn't be with you, that's all."

Expecting another outburst from her, he was surprised and unsettled by the silence that followed. Turning the dishwasher on, she now began to sponge off the counter with brusque, agitated strokes. Seeing her husband pour himself another rye-and-soda, she couldn't restrain herself any longer. "I wish you wouldn't drink so much. It doesn't help the situation at all."

God, he wished he was back at his office; there he had authority, there his word carried some weight. "Let's not start that business again. We've got Valerie to worry about now. Where are they holding her?"

"She's being held by police in the Nineteenth Precinct— on East Ninety-fourth Street."

"You instructed Al to bail her out?"

"No, I didn't know whether that was such a good idea, Kurt. We need to teach her a lesson. *Somebody* has to teach her a lesson."

"Christ, Barbara, I'll be damned if I'm going to let Val languish in a holding cell overnight. What's got into you? What kind of lesson do you think the child is going to learn from this? That her parents don't give a shit about her?"

"I would think quite the opposite," Barbara said. "And I wonder how much you're thinking of Val anyway. You don't want anything about this getting into the papers, do you? That's your main concern."

"Look, Barbara, of course it's a concern, you know damned well it's a concern. How could it not be? But that doesn't mean I don't love my daughter, does it? Goddammit, Barb, I don't want Val to have a record! For what? For doing something a million other kids around the country are doing on a Saturday night?"

"A million other kids don't kill somebody, Kurt." There, it was out. Barbara's face reddened. She hadn't meant to go so far. The words seemed to hang in the air like a malediction. She turned away. "Besides . . ." she said, her voice husky with tension.

"Besides what?"

"Besides, Al said they won't make it so easy for her. They'll check, if they haven't already, and find out that she's been in trouble with the law before."

"What are you saying?"

"I'm saying that Al isn't so sure what he can do for her— for us."

Magnus said nothing. He was thinking.

"Kurt, talk to me. What do you want me to do?" Her voice was quavering. She sounded as if something had broken inside.

"I don't want you to do anything, Barbara. Just don't do a goddamned thing, all right?"

"Where are you going?"

"I'm going to make a phone call."

He got up from the table and went upstairs into the bedroom and shut the door. He supposed he should have expected something like this to happen. Val was beyond his disciplining now; she was in a state of perpetual rebellion, an easy prey to temptation—just like her father. And it was possible that his wife was right, that he was terrified that everything would be lost because of something like this—something that crept up on one from behind and took one unaware. What was so horrible was that it would take so little to destroy his life now. Everything hung in such a delicate balance.

He knew what he had to do. He'd known since Barbara first broke the news to him. There simply wasn't any alternative; he couldn't depend on Al Silverstein to do what was needed. And he knew that every minute he allowed to slip away because of his hesitation might be fatal.

There was really no reason for him to look up the phone number—he knew it by heart—but he was so nervous that he could no longer count on his memory. He dialed the direct line, and when somebody picked up, he said, "Yes, this is Kurt Magnus—Dr. Kurt Magnus. Would you please tell Mr. Fontana that I need to speak with him?"

CHAPTER TWENTY-TWO

The electronic whir of the garage sliding open brought Ambrosetti awake instantly. He glanced at the clock on his dashboard. It was a little past five in the morning. He reasoned that something must be up; ordinarily Magnus didn't leave his house until after eight. And why he should be going anywhere on the Fourth was even more puzzling.

Ambrosetti's attention was so riveted on Magnus that it took him a few moments to realize he wasn't the only person interested in the movements of the medical examiner. He looked again, but he still didn't believe what he was seeing.

Just up the block, relying on the shadows of an ailanthus tree to keep him inconspicuous, was Michael. What the hell was he doing there? It made Ambrosetti furious that his client was homing in on him like this. Magnus had been backing out of the driveway. There was no time to waste. Ambrosetti was about to follow Magnus and leave Michael behind, but then he realized that Michael had spotted him. Too late.

As soon as Magnus's Seville had reached the corner of the street, Ambrosetti leaned out the window and motioned frantically to Michael, who came running up to him.

"Get the hell in, would you, for God's sake?" the detective said, beginning to maneuver out of the parking space even before Michael could get the door shut. The white Seville, meanwhile, had disappeared from sight.

"If I've lost him it's your goddamned fault, you know."

Michael chose not to respond.

It was amazing what Ambrosetti could make his battered blue Toyota do when he had a mind to. It vibrated like crazy with the acceleration but it didn't conk out, which was the main thing. And there was hardly any traffic at all. A couple of blocks farther on and they had Magnus in view again. Ambrosetti breathed easier.

"Now, do you mind telling me what the hell you were doing back there? You could have queered this whole investigation."

"I just had to see where he lived. I wanted to talk to him." Michael looked away. He must have known how lame that sounded.

"You wanted to *what?* You're fucking unbelievable. How long were you standing out there?"

"Since sometime last night, I don't know."

Ambrosetti identified the smell on Michael's breath. "Let me guess. You got smashed somewhere and this idea—this inspiration—flashed into your head. You just have to confront this son-of-a-bitch."

When Michael didn't answer immediately, Ambrosetti knew he was right.

"Jesus, why don't you go home and get some sleep? You look terrible. I'll let you off at a subway stop."

"I want to see where he goes," Michael said flatly. The look of determination on his face discouraged Ambrosetti from trying to persuade him further.

"All right, but please do me a favor and try to keep down if we get close to him. He might recognize you."

Michael nodded. But Ambrosetti still wasn't convinced he wouldn't do something to ruin his morning.

As they started across the Queensboro Bridge, they were greeted by the spectacle of a score of boats assembling in the East River: tall ships, sloops, yachts, yawls, tugs, powerboats, fireboats, sailboats. Above this makeshift armada there was still more activity as the sky filled with helicopters, observation planes, and two blimps, one from Firestone, one from Toshiba. And this was only the start. By the time the July Fourth festivities began in earnest, there'd be many more craft putting in an appearance, crowding into the harbor and the skies above it.

Once he was on the Manhattan side, Magnus turned uptown on the F.D.R. Drive—away from his office. Ambrosetti noticed that Magnus was making mistakes, driving through lights or hesitating too long after they'd changed. At one point Ambrosetti clocked him at nearly fifty miles per hour. Having spent the last two days tailing him, Ambrosetti had figured him to be a careful driver, scrupulous about adhering to the rules of the road. Certainly the erratic behavior he was exhibiting this morning suggested that something must be amiss.

Magnus exited the F.D.R. Drive at Seventy-second Street. He continued along Seventy-second until Third Avenue, where he turned north again, stopping when he reached Eighty-fourth. There he found a parking space.

Ambrosetti found a space closer to the corner. While he and Michael watched, Magnus got out of his car and walked quickly to the entrance of a restaurant called Natchez. Its windows were shielded by intricate beige netting, and its door was locked. Magnus knocked and waited. A few moments passed before he was admitted.

"Who do you suppose he's going to meet?" Michael asked.

"Beats the hell out of me. But I don't think he's here for breakfast. You stay here. I'll be right back." He regarded Michael dubiously. He was still waiting for Michael to do something seriously deranged.

Crossing the street, Ambrosetti approached the restaurant, pausing in front of it, as if he were an early-morning stroller who had nothing better to do than study the menus of a place he couldn't afford to go into.

He allowed his eye to wander, trying to see in through the glass-paneled door, but the glass was dark, the interior darker; it was hopeless.

Ambrosetti stopped into a deli, the only place open at this hour, and bought some coffee for Michael and himself. He felt lousy, and no wonder; besides the indignity of his summer cold, his back was killing him, probably due to his habit of sleeping upright in his car during these interminable vigils. Half of his life was spent waiting for something to happen. Now it seemed that something finally was.

Just when he'd settled back down in his car, the door to the restaurant came open.

"Could you hand me that camera?"

Michael reached over to the dashboard and found it. A small and ingenious device, it was capable of taking shots at virtually any distance: long shots, medium shots, closeups. The damned thing could even shoot around corners. He trained it on Natchez's open door.

Four men stepped out into the daylight. None of them

looked remotely like restaurateurs. A couple of them clearly were muscle. Ambrosetti could always tell when people were packing heat; they tended to wear their jackets one size too large for them so that their pieces wouldn't bulge. From all appearances, they were also Zips—native Sicilians imported to bring new lifeblood to the mob. The Americans were getting too soft, too high on drugs, so they had to call on talent from the old country to help them out nowadays. The man they were looking after followed them out.

"Jesus! It's Fontana," Michael said incredulously.

Ambrosetti couldn't say that he was surprised to see Fontana there. Natchez, he suspected, was probably one of his bases of operations; it was possible he owned the place.

Fontana was deep in conversation with Magnus. He didn't exactly look worried, but concerned, like a priest hearing a confession. And maybe it *was* a confession he was hearing. In any case, it was clear that Magnus was a man in trouble. His discomfort was obvious from the quick, nervous way he moved his hands, from the imploring look in his eyes. Ambrosetti shot his picture. Then Fontana reached for Magnus's hand in what seemed intended as a reassuring gesture. Magnus nodded curtly and made a move away from him. Ambrosetti got off another shot, a third, a fourth.

Michael had been onto something when he'd linked Fontana to Magnus, though Ambrosetti wasn't about to give him the satisfaction of saying so. The fact was that he'd been trying to locate Fontana for days without success. Fontana was an elusive bastard, never where he was supposed to be. Ambrosetti was becoming convinced that he was the key, not Magnus; he was the real source of power, the power behind the power.

Until he'd taken on the Friedlander case, Ambrosetti's knowledge of Fontana had been limited to half-baked stories, insinuations, and tantalizing rumors. That the man was wired into City Hall was well known to observers of the local political scene. To what extent he wielded influence over City Hall, though, was a mystery, but no more so than the nature of the ties he was reputed to have with the mob. Ambrosetti had heard that his agency had actually been contracted to carry out hits for the Gambino and Lucchese families, and this was the very same agency that recruited retired cops as detectives. In fact, cops seemed to love him; every couple of years the Policemen's Benevolent Association gave him awards. He broke up street-corner fights and pursued felons halfway around the world. It was said that he'd even thwarted a hijacking. He ran for office and he owned a cable television station; he pretended to be a legitimate businessman, investor, and real estate developer. Probably, Ambrosetti thought, he just wanted his share of the American Dream, like everyone else.

He was so heartened at seeing Fontana that the detective momentarily forgot about his bad back, his exhaustion, his cold. He could even bring himself to forgive Michael's presence in his car and barely protested when Michael insisted on accompanying him wherever the chase would lead them. Forget Magnus; Fontana was the one they followed— he was the one, after all, who held the key.

Fontana could move. This was a man with a million places to go, no matter that it happened to be a holiday. With a chauffeur available to drive his bright red BMW, Fontana had the luxury of being able to sit in the backseat, making any number of calls on his mobile phone, so as not to waste time between appointments.

Fontana's odyssey took him all over the city, beginning with a twenty-four-hour coffee shop in a shopping mall within sight of the Whitestone Bridge. Then it continued on to Joe Nina's Ristorante under the Westchester Avenue el; to the Palma Boys Social Club on East One Hundred Fifteenth Street in East Harlem; the Queens Palace Restaurant on Hillside Avenue in Jamaica; the Café del Viale on Knickerbocker Avenue in Brooklyn—Bonnano territory; Ponte's Restaurant at Desbosses Street in downtown Manhattan; the Fourth Street Saloon; the Raverite Social Club on Mulberry—Giotti territory. It was like a Cook's tour of organized crime. If Ambrosetti ever managed to find out what was discussed at all these meetings, he was sure it would make for one hell of an interesting story—the kind of story that grand juries were impaneled to hear.

Some of these appointments lasted no more than five or ten minutes while others went on for more than an hour. Fontana was always in the company of his bodyguard. Invariably Fontana's driver would remain behind the wheel of his BMW, feigning boredom while his eyes continued to search the street for any sign of trouble. He was another Zip, with his black cap pulled over his brow—Ambrosetti could always tell. No doubt he hung out at one of the Italian cafés on Knickerbocker or Eighteenth avenues, knocking back cups of espresso, waiting for an order to go out and whack someone.

Michael probably never believed that detection work could be quite so tedious, hour after hour of doing nothing but waiting. Yet whenever Ambrosetti suggested he leave everything up to him and go home, Michael would insist that he was fine just where he was, that he wanted to stay for the entire show. Ambrosetti reminded him that in this business, sometimes there was no show.

At approximately five in the afternoon, Fontana headed downtown along Broadway. Closer to the South Street Seaport the traffic became snarled, nearly impassable. Some sort of harbor festival was going on. Vendors were out in force hawking souvlaki, falafel, kebab, and Mexican shit. It was a mess. Frustrated by the lack of progress, Fontana and his bodyguard decided to get out and walk, leaving the driver to find a place to park. Ambrosetti didn't have the same luxury; he pulled over at the first convenient spot. He'd had his car towed at least a dozen times before; it was getting to be so expensive retrieving it from the police that he began to think it would be cheaper simply to leave it next time and buy another.

Michael and Ambrosetti began to trail them. With the throngs of people packed into the South Street Seaport, there was little likelihood that Fontana would notice. Ambrosetti carried his camera and an equally compact cassette recorder, uncertain as to what use he'd be able to put either. Lamentably the world no longer seemed made for a man of Ambrosetti's size and age. Everywhere he looked he saw only very young people. It was as if a law had been imposed banning anyone over fifty from coming to the Seaport.

Fontana and his guard had begun making their way along the perimeter of the piers where people were busy gorging themselves on junk food and beer in the shadows of the tall ships tied up there. From the pace the two were keeping, it was obvious they were in a hurry to get to a specific place. At Pier 17 they halted. A man wearing a light navy jacket greeted them and helped them into a motor launch; they were the only passengers.

The launch's destination lay in the waters off Governor's Island. It was a yacht, measuring at least ninety feet from stem to stern. Surrounded by hundreds of vessels, ferries, tugs, Coast Guard cutters, and sailboats more modest by far, the yacht made for a majestic sight. Signal flags were strung up and down the length of it; lights blazing from the bridge showered the decks in gold and silver. From a distance the yacht appeared to be hovering over the water, as though it was this brilliant light and not gravity that was keeping it suspended, like something magical and unreal.

After dropping off Fontana and his bodyguard, the launch turned around and headed back to the pier to pick up new arrivals. Already a dozen couples had gathered, and there were more people joining them all the time. Most of the men were wearing black tie, while the women had assembled themselves in seductive summer dresses, strapless or backless, either white or black, made more dramatic by the luster of their expensive tans and the glint of their jewelry. They represented the elite—the aristocracy. But Ambrosetti didn't need to judge on the basis of their clothes alone. He recognized many of their faces.

And what a strange crew it was: the fraternity of the elect, the kingmakers, legal advisers, urban buccaneers. Among the guests he spotted Jason Parnase, first deputy mayor;

Harry Irwin, Queens borough president; Vincent Reppetto, the head of the municipal unions; Hiram Goldstock, representative from the Nineteenth Congressional District; and Susan Brenner, head of the mayor's office for cultural affairs. He even spied Manny Arnoff, the real estate developer who was under indictment for racketeering, and Tom Abner, who only a month before had been released from Lewisburg after serving eighteen months for tax evasion. Apparently it didn't matter a damn which side of the law they came down on, so long as they were in possession of power and enjoyed the friendship of Ray Fontana.

Ambrosetti had spent years nursing his hatred of these people. It was the hatred of all outsiders who'd once been inside. Years ago, as a cop in Sunnyside and Corona Park, he'd developed a knack for knowing where—and how—his bread was buttered. He'd had a family to support then; he'd never considered it being on the take; he never thought of it as graft; it was just a way of getting along. It was chomp change next to what was really going down. The real money, the serious money, went to the construction unions, to the fire-code inspectors, to the state liquor authority, to the guys who decided which companies could wire which boroughs for cable TV and ruled on zoning variances. It was a time when one could buy a seat on the circuit or appeals court bench if one was in with the right people. Which was how Michael's friend, Lou Waterman, had probably gotten his appointment—through a friend, now gone to his reward—for $85,000. In 1967 it was a bargain . . . or a steal.

It was only after he'd lost his job and his family and emerged from the alcoholic cocoon that he'd wrapped himself in for so long that Ambrosetti had gone straight. Now he wanted to get back at the people he blamed for all those losses. People like Fontana and his guests. But he wouldn't say any of this to Michael; it wasn't the kind of thing he wanted to broadcast.

But he did identify them for Michael's benefit, reeling off their names, credentials, and indictments. He almost made them sound as if they were all his long-lost friends.

"What happens now?" Michael asked.

"They go have a party is what happens."

"What about us?"

"We wait. When the party's over and they come back to shore, then maybe we'll pick up where we left off."

Michael didn't seem very happy about that. "Why don't we try and get on board?"

"Sure, easy as that. You got a black tie in your pocket? Come on, Michael, you're not being reasonable." Sometimes, Ambrosetti thought, this guy didn't operate with a full deck.

"I want to try it."

"You want to try it?" Ambrosetti rolled his eyes heavenward. "You want to get yourself killed?"

"I don't think that will happen."

It was the innocents—especially the innocents who believed themselves invulnerable—who proved to be the real fuck-ups in the world. He shook his head. "Take my word for it, you don't want to do this. You may think you do, but you really don't. I've been in this business for a long time; just listen to me."

But Michael was adamant. "I don't need your permission," he pointed out.

"No, I guess you don't," Ambrosetti conceded.

"Can I borrow your camera and the tape recorder? Maybe they'll come in handy." When he saw that Ambrosetti was going to refuse, he tried to sweeten the deal, offering to pay for them.

Ambrosetti was too tired to argue. He just wanted Michael to leave him alone. "You don't know when to stop, do you? Tell you what, I'll lend you the tape recorder. The camera's too expensive; I can't let you have that."

Michael agreed. "Show me how it works."

Ambrosetti did so, but without any confidence that Michael would ever have the chance to put his lesson to use. In fact, when Ambrosetti handed over the recorder to Michael, it was with the expectation that he'd never see it— or him—again.

CHAPTER TWENTY-THREE

For more money than Michael could really afford, he found someone with a small powerboat willing to take him out into the harbor. The owner of the boat, a bony man with sunken eyes and cracked lips, no doubt figured that he had only this one day a year in which to make a killing.

Michael's arrival, he hoped, should just about coincide with the start of the annual Macy's fireworks display scheduled for nine o'clock over the East River. That should provide some distraction, anyway. One thing was already working in his favor, though—with so many party boats at anchor, no one was likely to notice his approach. He was certain that if he could get on the yacht, he'd be all right. He'd crashed parties before, to be sure never one like this, but he assumed that the same strategy should apply—act as if he belonged.

They were still some distance from the yacht, but the sound of percussive music and laughter from the decks was already reaching Michael's ears.

At five past nine, the first rockets went up, bursting into patriotic colors over Brooklyn. The detonating fireworks were synchronized, or should have been synchronized anyhow, to a medley of martial airs, Sousa marches, and fanfares. A reddish haze was rapidly settling over the water.

They were now close enough to the yacht so that Michael could make out the name on the hull: *The Wild Card*. Appropriate, he thought. His nerves were so shot, after his drinking spree of the night before, that it was a wonder he could register any sensation in them at all. One thing was certain: He was nowhere as confident as he'd been onshore that he could pull this off. On the contrary, he was growing very worried. No, he wasn't worried, he was scared shitless. He considered asking the boatman to turn back, but the idea of having to acknowledge failure to Ambrosetti was too humiliating for him to bear.

The boatman was steering around to the starboard side of *The Wild Card*, where the upper and lower decks were virtually deserted, except for one couple groping in the shadows, too undone by lust to bother with the fireworks. The rope ladder used hours earlier by the guests to clamber aboard was still dangling from the side. As Michael reached for it the boatman said, "You want me to come pick you up?"

"I don't know when I'll be finished. I'll try to get back on my own."

"Suit yourself," the boatman said, then pushed off.

Michael watched him for a moment or two as he guided his boat out into the smoky harbor. He wondered if he wasn't cutting off all avenues of escape. Well, he'd made his decision.

At least he'd gotten this far—further than Ambrosetti had dared to go. That gave his self-confidence some small boost. Assuming that a security guard would be by before long, he sought a stairway to take him below. He'd be safer, he thought, when he could lose himself in the party.

With the thud of explosives ringing in his ears, Michael descended the stairs, wondering where belowdecks he'd end up. He found himself in the middle of a saloon, big as a basketball court, gaping at a buffet table laden with lobster tails, roast beef, big bowls of salads, and heaping desserts, with a pair of white-capped chefs waiting to serve it all. A bartender, looking as if he'd give anything to be elsewhere, was standing by a prodigious selection of spirits and wine. In the meantime a rock band, whose members included a blonde in black leather, was in the process of setting up for the post-fireworks entertainment.

After several minutes had gone by, the sound of explosives began to die away and soon the room was filled with guests who, now that the show was over, remembered their stomachs. Although Michael was hardly dressed appropriately for the occasion, nobody seemed to notice. They probably assumed he was a guest, maybe one with questionable taste in clothes, but still with as much right to be there as anybody else.

Fontana was nowhere in sight, though; nor could Michael

see Arnoff or Irwin or Goldstock or any of the others Ambrosetti had pointed out on the pier. The idea that he'd gone to all this trouble to get there and come up with nothing distressed him. What was he going to do, gorge himself on this food and go back? He had to prove to Ambrosetti that this wasn't some empty gesture he'd made to defy him.

He went over to the bartender, reasoning that in this world bartenders were more likely than not to be in possession of information, and asked him if he knew where he could find Fontana.

"I think he's in his cabin. It's somewhere aft," the bartender told him. "But I doubt you can see him now; he's holding some kind of meeting there."

Michael thanked him. Thinking he had little to lose by exploring further, he began making his way toward the stern. At least he thought that was where he was going. There was really no telling where he was. Staterooms opened up on either side of him. By accident he stumbled into a room with a Jacuzzi that could comfortably accommodate a dozen people, though there was only one elderly man in it now, naked and contemplatively smoking a cigarette. Everywhere Michael looked he saw himself, a hapless and disheveled figure with bloodshot eyes, reflected in the many mirrors that lined the walls and even the ceilings. The color scheme was predominantly red and pink and chartreuse. All this plushness was too much for him; *The Wild Card* looked as if it had been designed to be a seagoing brothel. Maybe it was.

Somewhere just ahead of him he was able to detect the sound of voices. Michael turned down a passageway and stopped. A man who looked as if he was dying to get out of his tux was standing in front of a door, arms akimbo, watching movements in and out. Michael was all but certain that this must be where Fontana was holding his meeting.

If getting inside the cabin was clearly out of the question, Michael thought there might still be a way to tap into it and record the proceedings. He continued aft until he came to a spiral staircase that ascended to a glass-enclosed atrium.

There was a door located next to it. Michael tried it and found himself staring into a stateroom done up in a wholly different style, this time emphatically masculine with lots of suede and leather furnishings and ash-gray walls. He reasoned that this stateroom should be directly adjacent to Fontana's cabin. He went in and shut the door behind him, hoping he wouldn't be disturbed by the person whose clothes he saw scattered all over the place.

Planting his ear against the wall, he could barely make out anything more than a babble of voices. But that could be fixed if the recorder worked as well as Ambrosetti claimed it did.

The recorder came with a spike mike, a microphone element that looked like a phonograph pickup mounted on a hollow spike. A miniature integrated-circuit amplifier was contained inside it. Once the spike was nailed into the wall, Ambrosetti had told him, it should be able to pick up the sound vibrations and resolve them into distinguishable voices. The detective had cautioned him that the reproduction wasn't perfect but that it should be adequate for his purposes. Michael drove the spike into the wall, started the tape, placed his earphones on, and then began to listen.

Fontana was speaking. His was one voice Michael recognized right away.

"No problem . . . All right, everybody got what they want? Nobody need anything else? Okay, no, fine, thanks . . . Harry. What I was saying just now is that we all know we have a problem in this city—a problem with crime. That's no reflection on you people in the law-enforcement business. We all appreciate your efforts. We all know how hard it is. I know I do."

This was incredible. Michael didn't think Fontana had become so emboldened he would talk openly like this to elected officials, people whose reputations were on the line.

"What are you suggesting, Ray?" someone asked.

"Listen, Harry, I've been able to get things done for you in the past. Who was it who took that fuck Luis Zanna out for you? The cops couldn't do it, even the Gambinos couldn't find him, and you know how tight he used to be with them. No, it was my people."

Well, Michael thought, this was something. While he had no idea what mischief Luis Zanna had perpetrated in his lifetime, he had no doubt that it was considerable. But that Fontana would admit to being responsible for his execution—with these people as his witnesses—staggered him.

"I don't need to remind you about Tom Genovese or Tino Ojieda," Fontana continued.

Genovese Michael had never heard of. But Ojieda's name struck home. The inference was clear; Fontana had had him killed, then somehow influenced Magnus to falsify the autopsy report to thwart any investigation that would lead back to him. He prayed that the tape was getting all this.

"Look, Ray, we're here because we like you. We know what you've done for the city," another voice broke in. "But we have to make it clear that we can't condone vigilante action."

From the way this man was talking, it sounded as if he was covering his ass. A more telling statement followed: "However, the mayor wants you to know, Ray, that he appreciates the work you've been doing on behalf of the city. We don't want to discourage private enterprise, after all."

Scattered laughter greeted this remark.

"Hey, Jason, I don't want you to misunderstand me. We're in this fight together, we want the same thing. Isn't that right, Jason? We're on the same side or what?"

If Michael remembered correctly, this must be Jason Parnase, the deputy mayor.

"Of course, Ray, I'm not saying we aren't on the same side."

"Sometimes what happens, through no one's fault, you get an entrenched bureaucracy. You deal with it every day. The police have a lot on their hands; they don't have the manpower to cope with the shit that goes down in this city. We're a private agency, and that gives us a certain advantage. What we do, just so you don't go away with the wrong impression, is fill in the cracks. We supplement the work of the police. That's all. Look at it this way—is there anything wrong about bringing terrorists and gangsters like Cato and Ojieda and Zanna to justice?"

It didn't seem that Fontana wanted anyone to answer his question. He was just getting going.

"Of course not. We can't let these men destroy our city. They're scum, they're predators, they're animals! If we don't destroy them, they will destroy us and all that we have worked so hard to build. Does anybody here doubt me? Has anybody here at this table lost sight of what we want for our city, for our families, for our country?"

He was really getting wound up; it was an amazing performance. He was the evangelist calling down God's eternal damnation on the sinners, and they were his followers, his penitents, hoping through him to be saved.

Abruptly, dramatically, his voice fell, became more insinuating, friendly, cheerful. "Now I know you all want to get back to the party, but we've got a few more things I'd like to discuss with you before we do. Let's not beat around the bush, shall we? We all know the names of the people who are ravaging our good city. Why not say them?" His voice grew stronger as the passion came back into it. "Let me name one to start—Gerolamo Albinese. It's no secret that Albinese has begun moving drugs into suburban neighborhoods. It's not just the blacks or Hispanics anymore. He's dealing his fucking crack to our kids, white kids, middleclass kids. . . ."

He let that sink in for a moment before continuing.

"But what's being done about it?" Another rhetorical question. He wasn't about to allow anyone to interrupt him now. "I'll tell you what's being done about it. Not a goddamned thing! The son-of-a-bitch remains at large. And why? Not because the police are derelict in their duty. They're doing their best. You won't find a man more supportive of the cops than Ray Fontana. The problem is evidence. The problem is making the evidence stick in court. Well, I'm here to tell you that

I'll personally see to it that Albinese is brought to justice. At no cost to the taxpayers, I'll get all the evidence necessary to put him away in the can for life. It's my gift to the city of New York."

"We're always grateful for whatever you can do," said Parnase breathlessly, probably afraid that if he didn't get in a word now he never would, "but we don't want you to go berserk on us. The last thing we need is a situation where the state can't make a case because of some technical violation."

"Hey, Jason, I understand. I wouldn't want to see anything like that develop. Put you in an embarrassing situation like that? Are you crazy? Did you hear what I said before? We're on the same team, Jason, we're in this together. I'm not going to do anything to jeopardize our relationship."

There followed for a few seconds a rattle of glasses and then an eruption of coughing.

"Let me go on to another piece of business," Fontana said, modulating his tone. "I'm sure you've all heard about this fucking nut case, this creep the papers call the Chopper. Now I know we all want to see him off the streets. I know you're working on it hard as you can. And I know that you've got the best man on the force in charge of the investigation—Larry Kohler. What I'm asking you to do, gentlemen, is to take into account what Inspector Kohler manages to accomplish in the weeks to come. I've met Inspector Kohler; I've talked to him at length. And frankly, gentlemen, I can't remember when I was so impressed by an officer in his position."

"Nobody doubts Inspector Kohler's competence. No one is questioning his reputation," said a voice Michael couldn't identify.

"You're not listening to what I'm saying." For the first time there was a trace of irritation in Fontana's voice. "I'm not suggesting that anyone is questioning Inspector Kohler's reputation. I'm only offering my personal opinion, that's all. Now, you are entitled to disagree with me, but, as a friend of the police, I happen to think that the man who currently serves as commissioner isn't the best man for the job. He's a good man, an able man, but he hasn't proven to be commissioner material. I know how politics operates, but sometimes politics has to take a backseat in an emergency. And an emergency is what we have right now in our streets. Watch Larry Kohler, let him prove himself, and then consider who would be the best man to be commissioner. That's all I'm asking, ladies and gentlemen, give him the consideration he deserves."

"Ray, listen to me," Parnase said. "If Kohler can apprehend people like Albinese and the Chopper, I'm certain everyone at this table—everyone in this city—will be grateful. And while I couldn't make any guarantees—"

"Nobody is asking for guarantees, Jason, I know that."

"Well, fine, just so long as that's understood. But while I can't vouch for the mayor, I know that if Inspector Kohler succeeds in bringing the Chopper to justice, it would be inconceivable to me that the mayor wouldn't look favorably on such an appointment."

Michael had always known about furtive deals struck in smoky back rooms and dark conspiracies hatched among politicos in coatrooms and hotel suites, but he'd always believed that the transactions were somehow more subtle, a matter of insinuations, inferences, things hinted at but left unspoken. That deals could be struck this brazenly astounded him. But then, what did he know, living in New Hampshire?

He was ready to go on listening, perversely fascinated by the process by which webs were woven and marks were debited and credited, but just then he was alerted to the sound of voices in the passageway. His heart lurched and something seemed to drop in his stomach. He pulled off the earphones and quickly buried the recorder in his pocket.

Opening the door to peer out, he was prepared to say that he'd mistaken the location of the head, but luckily he saw nobody in the passageway. *Act casual*, he told himself, *act like you belong*. He started down the passageway, quickening his pace until he saw several disheveled guests standing around, their talk and laughter indicating that they'd already drunk way too much. Before Michael could advance any farther, he heard his name called out.

No, he thought in horror, *it couldn't be. I must have imagined it.*

But he hadn't. Somebody had said his name. Convinced that the game was up, he turned to see a man coming toward him. At first he wasn't sure he knew whom the guy was at all, not until the man took his hand and pumped it furiously, a fearsome smile on his reddening face.

"Frank Brice," he said. "Don't you remember?"

Michael managed a smile, thinking, *Jesus! This guy did hits for the mob when he was in his teens and arranges truck hijackings for a living.* "Sure I do. How are you?"

"So Ray invited you, too," Brice said. Obviously he was under the impression that Michael was a guest, which was just fine with him. The only thing he hoped was that Brice wouldn't think to mention it to Fontana later.

"You remember Sofia?"

Sofia? Michael was thinking. *Who the hell was Sofia?*

Brice beckoned to a woman wearing a low-cut dress made out of material so sheer that she might just as well have gone naked. Michael remembered her immediately. She'd been the woman who was with Mario the night they all ended up at the Zulu Lounge. Evidently, from the way in which she slung her arms around Brice and rested her pretty head on his shoulder, Mario was a thing of the past.

"Do you remember Michael Friedlander?" Brice asked her.

"Oh . . . oh, yes," she said dubiously. The process of recognizing him appeared to be very painful for her. Suddenly she lit up and decided to greet him in a more appropriate manner, throwing her arms around him as if he were a long-lost lover and giving him a moist, liquored kiss that he returned awkwardly. "How are you, love?"

He said he was okay. His uneasiness was only heightened by Brice's insistence that he get him a drink. He couldn't count on Fontana's meeting going on forever; his high-placed friends would surely be eager to return to the festivities. And once Fontana spotted him, he knew he'd be lost. He would not want to deal with an angry Fontana. But on the other hand, he wasn't anxious to offend Brice, either, and so he accepted his offer of a drink.

Brice was trying to engage him in conversation, but Michael's mind was on escaping. He saw that people were making their way up the stairs where a line was gathering on the decks for the launch back. It was imperative he join them.

"If you would excuse me," he said, "I have to . . ."

"Answer the call of nature?" Brice said. "It's down there."

Sophia looked after him with strange interest. He moved toward the head. A whole group of people were coming down the passageway in his direction. He saw Fontana and he froze. All he could do was go back the way he'd come.

Brice and Sophia were locked arm in arm now, half dancing, half holding each other up. Sophia noticed Michael, not Brice, whose eyes were glued to her mostly bare breasts. She and Michael exchanged a glance, the significance of which even he was at a loss to interpret. But she did nothing to alert Brice to his presence, and that was what counted most of all. He seized the opportunity and darted up the stairs. Mingling among the other departing partygoers, he silently thanked her for letting him escape. It was likely that tomorrow Sophia would forget that he even existed, but for tonight he was deeply grateful to her. *You can never tell where your savior is going to come from next*, he thought.

Everyone around him was all flushed and keyed up. Where before they might have smelled of perfume and cologne, now they reeked of sweat and stale champagne. In the confusion, Michael went happily unnoticed. If anything, he fit in better than he had at the beginning of the party.

It was Michael's intention to go straight home and contact Ambrosetti later, let him know just what incredible luck he'd had. He couldn't remember when he'd felt so pleased by what he'd achieved.

But no sooner had he gotten off the launch than he discovered that Ambrosetti was standing waiting for him in almost the exact same spot where he'd left him.

Exhilarated by his success, Michael didn't even think to hold anything back. Ambrosetti listened without interrupting, his sad eyes never leaving Michael's face.

Then, when Michael was finished, Nick said, "Let me have the tape." Just like that. No congratulations, just, "Let me have the tape."

Michael bristled. This was not the reaction he'd been expecting. After having gone to such trouble to get the tape, he was hesitant to turn it over to him just like that. "I don't know whether I should. . . ."

"You don't trust me, is that it?" Ambrosetti snapped.

"No, it's not that." And it wasn't. He just had a bad feeling about parting with the tape so easily.

"Look, until I listen to what you've actually got there, I can't say whether it amounts to anything or not." Before Michael could challenge him, he rushed on. "But let's say it does, let's say it does have all this explosive information on it. Do you know what to do with it? Do you have any contacts in this city? Do you know the reporters, the D.A.'s, the people who could help you nail Fontana and bust your brother's killer?" He waited for Michael's reply, which he knew wouldn't come. "But, you see, I do. Let me decide what to do with the information, how we can use it to maximum advantage. There's no way you would know what to do with it."

Reluctantly, Michael had to acknowledge the truth of what Nick was saying. He gave him the tape.

Ambrosetti clapped him on the shoulder. "It'll be all right, you'll see. You did real good. You've got more balls than I suspected." It was as much of a concession as Michael was ever likely to receive from him. "Can I offer you a ride somewhere?"

Michael said no, he'd rather walk; there were some things he needed to think about.

"We'll talk tomorrow," Ambrosetti said. Maybe he thought Michael needed further reassurance, because he added, "Things are finally looking up, count on it."

CHAPTER TWENTY-FOUR

As it turned out, though, Ambrosetti wouldn't have been able to give Michael a lift even if he'd wanted one. When he went to return to his car, he found that it wasn't there. That was what he got for leaving it in a tow-away zone. Crowds were still circulating through the Seaport area; they were raucous celebrants who were loaded to the gills. Smoke that carried the smell of sulfur and cordite hung thickly in the air from thousands of cherry bombs, ashcans, M-60s, and M-80s that had been set off that night. And there still was no letup; the hiss and crackle of firecrackers followed him wherever he went. Skyrockets, shot into the poisonous atmosphere, exploded into red, white, and blue pinwheels and sputtered out. Other skyrockets, more elaborate still, shone with a spectral light that persisted for too long a time, as though they were meant to illuminate a battlefield. It was a hell of a job just trying to dodge all these incendiaries, let alone push through the crowd.

Piercing sirens only added to the racket. All over the city tonight there was an emergency demanding immediate attention. Ambrosetti walked faster. Every so often he'd pat his pockets to reassure himself that he still had the tape and the film he'd shot earlier in the day outside Natchez. Repeatedly jostled and buffeted by people on all sides of him, he was worried about pickpockets.

He would have loved to find a taxi, but it was out of the question. The subway stations he passed as he walked up Fulton were jammed, and he didn't think he had the patience to stand and wait for a train in any case. It was after midnight; the subways would be running on off-peak schedules. Better to continue walking uptown in hopes of finding a taxi where there would be fewer people to compete with for it.

Despite his disgruntlement with the lack of transportation, nothing could dampen the elation he felt, elation that he'd carefully kept hidden from Michael. If even half of what Michael had described was captured on tape, then he was looking at a beautiful future; it was as good as winning the lottery. This tape could forever alter the equation of his life. He would have the power to throw City Hall into turmoil, maybe unseat the mayor. The evidence on tape could lead to indictments; it could turn the insiders out. He was so unaccustomed to having such power in his grasp that he could hardly contain himself. *Oh, Jesus,* he thought, *you can come back, this is your shot at the big time.* He wasn't even certain how he planned to use the tape; he would have to sit down and carefully work out his strategy, calculate the odds, make the right moves. This was a situation that didn't allow for any fuck-ups.

It occurred to him that he would finally be able to set things right in his life. Maybe his wife would let him see his children again, once he could persuade her that he'd shaped himself up. He could buy a house somewhere outside the city and put some money in the bank. Anything could happen; opportunities beckoned from all corners.

He was so carried away by thoughts of his immediate prospects—of coming into money and obtaining the respect of old adversaries and seeing his children once more—that he almost forgot all about Alan Friedlander. His death had led Ambrosetti so far that it no longer seemed to matter a great deal who killed him, or why, not when there was so much else at stake.

His excitement had fired him up enough to keep going for several blocks more before he realized just how winded and tired he was. He wasn't used to hikes of this length, and his cold was sapping him of any reserves of energy he might have had to call on. The smoke was a particular irritant, since he could scarcely breathe in the first place with his nostrils so clogged. He cursed himself for not having taken more decongestant, but then he'd needed to be alert—as alert as it was possible for him to get with a fucking cold.

At last he'd gotten beyond the tide of drunken humanity. About the only people he ran into now in these darkened streets skirting the edge of the East River were straggling kids clutching bottles of beer, barely able to put one foot in front of the other. Otherwise, he encountered no one. He began to grow uneasy. There were obviously no cabs to be had in this neighborhood. Somehow he'd let himself become distracted and had drifted away from where he'd wanted to be.

Though he wanted to stop and catch his breath for a minute, he didn't dare. Looking back at the dimly lit street he'd just come down, he strained to see if somebody might be following him, but he didn't notice anyone.

He knew he was behaving like an amateur, that if he'd had all his wits about him, he would have worked this through better in his mind. It was stupid of him to lose his sense of direction as he did. His cold was no excuse.

But his cold was dragging him down, nonetheless, and it was becoming more and more difficult to make any headway.

Suddenly he became aware of the sound of a car behind him. He turned to see it shoot out of a side street, bearing down on him. He was caught in the glare of its headlights. For a moment he couldn't move. Then he realized—too slowly—that it was about to run him down. Scrambling back onto the sidewalk, he flattened himself against the side of a brick building. The car was a blur of red as it jumped on the sidewalk, whipping past him by inches.

It was backing up. Ambrosetti recognized it—Fontana's BMW. He should have known this case wouldn't be so easy to wrap up. Then he began to run. *Get somewhere where there are a lot of people around*, he told himself. He reached the corner just as the car did. A man was leaning out of the open window, calling to him, "Nick, say, Nick, what's your hurry?"

Ambrosetti had a glimpse of a man in the backseat but didn't recognize him. Yet he knew it had to be one of Fontana's crew. Desperately he scanned both sides of the street, still running, his chest aching with the exertion. He looked up to see a couple arm in arm on the other side of the street, about half a block up ahead. He rushed toward them, thinking that surely in the presence of witnesses he would be safe.

Then he heard the shots. They sounded muffled, far away, two, maybe three of them. *They're shooting at me, the sons-of-bitches,* was what went through his mind first. Then he heard a scream, and for a moment he really wasn't sure whether it was coming from him or from the couple. They'd stopped about fifty paces from him and were looking at him, helpless, their eyes wide open, their mouths gaping. He staggered forward, no longer certain of his footing. A great weight was pulling him down. He was wobbling, he was wobbling, he was going down.

Goddammit! I've been shot, he thought. He was so furious with himself that he hadn't yet come to grips with the pain that was just beginning to take hold. Dropping his eyes, he saw blood soaking through his shirt. He knew the wound was bad, very bad.

But when he thought about the tape, he decided he'd be damned if he'd make it easy for them to get it. He tried to put himself in motion again. He could scarcely see, but all he knew was that he had to get away. He heard a car door slamming. Someone was getting out. He was so fucking dizzy, and it seemed as if the whole world was spinning. But the real trouble was that he couldn't focus; his vision was going and there was no way he was about to get it back. So really it was no surprise to him when his legs gave way and he smacked down against the ground, the old sailor's saying reverberating in his head: *Finished with engines, finished with engines.*

CHAPTER TWENTY-FIVE

Gail wouldn't have known it was Ambrosetti until one of the cops said the name loud enough so that it reached her. The name was unusual enough for her to recognize it immediately. He was being rushed through the maelstrom of the E.R. by paramedics, a big bleeding figure moaning on a gurney.

Three officers were moving with him, asking him questions. Did he get a look at his assailant? What kind of car was he driving? Did he have any accomplices? Gail used to think the cops had no business interrogating someone in such terrible pain. But supposing the victim crumped? This might be their last chance to get anything out of him.

But it didn't seem as though they were getting much out of Ambrosetti. He was incoherent, raving, possibly delirious. They wheeled him into the O.R., unstrapped him, and practically threw him on the table. The nurses then stripped him, tearing off the bloody clothes—the shirt, the jacket, the trousers, the blue boxer shorts that had filled with shit—and discarding them in a heap under the supply cabinet.

The room soon became crowded with people, not all of whom looked as if they belonged. Gail hovered nearby. There wasn't anything for her to do, since this wasn't her case, but she wanted to be able to tell Michael what happened. Phil Kinzer, the surgical resident on duty, took charge. He was a husky, bearded man convinced that he possessed immense skill and boundless luck. So far life had not disappointed him. Besides, in a situation like this, his arrogance was welcomed; it gave confidence to the others, who were jabbing needles into the wounded man, filling his blood up with painkillers and saline solution.

"Get me a blood gas!" Kinzer shouted. "Let's get an I.V. line in here. . . . Somebody take his blood down to the lab, and let's get it cross-matched. We're going to need at least three, four units. . . . Somebody get me a reading on his pressure. What's his pressure at?"

As Kinzer fired off his directives, the interns and nurses—Foley, Shapiro, and Nofziger—were running lines and tubes into Ambrosetti intended to keep him going until they could staunch the bleeding and go in and find the bullet or bullets. They forced a tube in through his nose and down his throat and threaded a catheter into his penis. In response he began to buck and thrash, for all the good it did him.

"Relax, just relax, you're doing okay," Kinzer was saying. "Take it easy."

There was no telling whether his words were getting through to him, though.

"Okay, what about X ray? Anybody get in touch with radiology?" Kinzer looked about, ready to chew out anyone who was handy, most likely a nurse like Foley or an intern like Nofziger, who was hanging back from the table. Kinzer had a temper and he was anxious to use it. It didn't matter on whom.

But Nofziger wasn't going to allow him the satisfaction. "X ray's on the way. Should be here any minute," he said.

The imminent appearance of the mobile X-ray unit succeeded in emptying the room, except for the lead-aproned radiologist and the gunshot victim.

Once outside the O.R., Gail spied one of the cops who'd brought Ambrosetti in. He was sipping coffee from a cup while he made out his report.

"How did this happen, Officer?" she asked.

He was a thick-jowled cop with a neatly trimmed moustache. At her question he looked up, his eyes traveling from her jacket, splattered with Ambrosetti's blood, to her breasts, then to her face. He liked what he saw.

"We got a call from somebody, said there was a guy lying out on the street, shot."

"No witnesses to the shooting itself?"

"Not so far. We're still looking." He directed his eyes toward the closed doors of the O.R. "Doesn't surprise me, though."

"What doesn't surprise you?" Gail asked. The anxiety was building in her.

"I heard about this guy, Ambrosetti. He used to make a real pest of himself. He set himself up as a private dick, but he never could get a license, not in this city. Fuck, he was thrown off the force."

"Oh? How did this happen?" Why hadn't Michael mentioned any of this to her—or didn't he know? He should have known. Somebody should have cued him in about the man before he went off half cocked and hired him. Of course, it was just like Michael to go on his impulses. What else could she expect?

"Sure, the guy was on the pad. The only reason they didn't put him in the slammer was because he ratted on the cops he was working with." He looked back at Gail. "You know what the prognosis on him is yet?"

It was too soon to tell, of course, but Gail hadn't the slightest doubt what this cop hoped it would be.

CHAPTER TWENTY-SIX

Michael had come as soon as Gail had called him with the news about Ambrosetti. But when he arrived at the hospital, expecting the worst, she had nothing more to add. Ambrosetti was still in surgery, the outcome was guarded, and the only sensible thing to do was go home, wait, and hope for the best. A colleague of Gail's promised to call with any word.

Gail dropped off to sleep while Michael was still talking to her, her head cradled against his shoulder. Michael held her until his arm became so cramped that he had to free it. She merely shifted position but didn't awaken, her rumpled blouse sliding up her back with the motion. Michael stared at the narrow ribbon of skin left exposed. He loved the look of her skin, its feel, its smell. He could go on staring at her like that for hours.

An unsettling stillness had settled over this part of the city, in contrast with all the uproar earlier that night. Now, apart from the occasional pop of a cherry bomb or the beseeching wail of a fire truck, there was nothing to be heard. Although the clock told him it was morning, it was still dark outside, a peculiar kind of New York darkness, filled with a garish pink light.

Michael couldn't sleep, not while he was waiting for the call from the hospital. He tried to imagine why the operation was taking longer than had been predicted. Or maybe it was so up in the air whether Ambrosetti would make it that no one could chance calling the outcome yet.

He couldn't understand why Ambrosetti hadn't been

more careful. He'd almost been convinced that Ambrosetti had known what he was doing. Now he'd never forgive himself for giving him that tape. Whatever happened to that detective, the tape was irretrievably lost, he knew that. And he knew also that there was nobody he could go to with the information he'd collected. Who would listen to him? What credibility did he have? What proof? Even Gail hadn't been quite as responsive as he'd hoped. She had no interest in Fontana's conspiracies; all she wanted to know from Michael was why he'd done something so foolish, taken such a risk. It seemed as if she believed that he had a death wish or something.

His one remaining hope was that Ambrosetti might pull through. Maybe together they could somehow salvage something from the situation. He refused to believe that all was lost.

His eyes continued to return to the phone as if his concentrated attention might set it ringing. But to look at the phone meant that he had to look at William Ives, and he didn't really want to have to do that.

Death had found William Ives in a sudden storm, Gail told Michael one day. It was a story she'd held back until she was certain that he would understand.

The storm had come up out of nowhere, attacking them halfway up a mountainside. It was a mountain out west somewhere, maybe in the Grand Tetons. Gail was the mountaineering enthusiast, and William had wanted nothing to do with climbing. She'd been scaling peaks in Wyoming and Colorado since she was sixteen. It was like therapy for her. She delighted in taking friends and lovers up to the mountains and sharing her fascination with them. In some way she was testing them, she admitted. After marrying William she naturally insisted that he come climbing with her, too.

At first he'd refused; there was something about great heights that spooked him. Eventually, though, he gave in to her entreaties. She broke him in gradually with easier climbs that required no rappelling, no dangerous negotiation. He'd acquitted himself well enough the first few times she took him up. Their fourth climb together had promised to be as uneventful as the first three—until the storm came up. It was a late-spring storm, but evil enough. Half blinded by the snow swirling about them, she couldn't see a foot in front of her. She lost track of William completely. She cried out for him, but with the wind shrieking there would have been no way to hear his reply even if he was there. But he was not.

He'd slipped off a ledge and gone careening down the slope, and with nothing to break his fall, he did not come to a stop until he was a long way down.

That was the worst thing of all, she'd said, not to be able to see him, for him not to be there anymore. With the wind and the snow lashing her face and the ice forming so fast underfoot, it became impossible for her to go in search of him.

Even after the storm had passed she couldn't find him. She was compelled to go back down and seek help. A rescue team took to the air in a helicopter. They discovered him half buried underneath a drift, mangled and dead. She and William had been married for less than two years at that point. Gail had never gone back to the mountains since.

Michael doubted that it was love that caused her to keep his picture by her bed. More likely it was guilt, though she would never admit it. He just wished that one day he'd look and the photo would be gone.

The phone began to ring. Gail stirred, made a kind of whimpering noise, and rolled over. Michael took the call.

"Hello, is Dr. Ives there? This is Jill Foley."

Michael shook Gail. She groaned and took the phone. Michael watched her apprehensively, fearing the worst, trying to read in her expression what the news was. When she put the phone down, she offered him a drowsy smile. "They had a hell of a time finding the bullets and getting them out of him, and he needed five pints of blood," she said, "but it looks like he's going to be all right."

Chapter Twenty-seven

It wasn't with the expectation that Ambrosetti could tell him what happened that Michael went the next morning to his room at Bellevue. But he believed it was important that he drop by and let him know that he was concerned, that he was prepared to offer what help he could.

Though it was her day off, Gail insisted on accompanying Michael, pointing out that so soon after surgery his doctors might not approve of Ambrosetti's having any visitors.

"We'll put one of those white coats on you again, and you can come and go as you want." She proposed that they meet afterward at the coffee shop across the street.

As Gail had predicted, no one stopped Michael or asked him what he was doing. His white coat seemed to lend him all the authority he needed.

At first he thought he had the wrong room. The patient occupying the bed nearest the door definitely was not Ambrosetti. He was a thin man with an alarming pallor, wracked with a painful cough. Beyond the opaque curtain that served to partition the room in two, there was another patient. It took Michael a few seconds to realize that the voices he was hearing from behind the curtain were coming from the television. He walked in and looked. It was the right room after all.

Nearly half a dozen tubes and catheters sprang out of Ambrosetti's body. His chest was swathed in bandages; one of the wounds was still draining. His eyes were open, but they didn't seem to be responsive. He looked like someone who'd gone into a trance. Michael's entrance failed to gain the detective's attention. On the television, contestants were anxiously observing the letters Vanna White was turning over on the board. She was dressed in a form-fitting pink dress with a low back. "I'll spin," one contestant said. So "Wheel of Fortune" was on in the mornings, too, Michael thought. But why would Ambrosetti be watching it, no matter how incapacitated and bored he was?

"Nick," he said softly, reluctant to disturb him.

Nothing.

"Nick," he said again, louder. "It's me, Michael Friedlander." For all he knew, a trauma such as the one the detective had sustained might have shaken his memory.

Still nothing.

Michael approached the bed. "Nick," he repeated. "Nick. Look at me, Nick."

Ambrosetti did not respond. His eyes remained motionless in his head.

Michael reached down, taking his hand, feeling for a pulse. There was none. Or maybe there was, and he just wasn't picking up on it. "There is one p," the host of "Wheel of Fortune" was saying. Applause. The words that followed next were drowned out by a spasm of coughing from the man in the other bed.

Michael tried feeling for a pulse a second time. He was sure now. He rushed from the room.

Spotting a nurse at the far end of the corridor, he yelled out, "Nurse! Nurse! You've got an emergency here! Room six-oh-seven—Nick Ambrosetti!"

The nurse hurried toward him, screwing up her face in consternation, saying not a word as she scrambled past Michael into the room. A moment later she came out, obviously alarmed.

While Michael lingered by the door of the room, a Code 99 was broadcast over the public address system. In less than a minute, doctors were racing into the room with a crash cart, mobilized to go into action.

A cluster of formless silhouettes against the opaque curtain, the emergency team moved around the bed. It was like watching some weird Japanese noh play. Hardly a word was spoken. Everyone understood what he or she had to do. Having witnessed attempts at resuscitation before, Michael knew what was happening. They'd massage his heart, pound it, shoot it with adrenaline. If these measures didn't work, they'd try to jolt him back to life with electricity.

As intently as he was listening, Michael could scarcely make out what was being said. He could hear "Wheel of Fortune" much more clearly: "I'll take the Toshiba digital monitor-receiver for one thousand . . . and the Bonaire air purifier for three hundred." He wished to God that somebody would have the good sense to shut the damn TV off.

Then Michael heard, "Okay, everybody, stand back!"

That meant they couldn't get his heart going again manually or with adrenaline. All they could do now was to try to shock it into life with four hundred watts from a defibrillator. Michael cringed at the sound of the protesting springs as Ambrosetti bounced back down on the bed. The man in the next bed seemed determinedly uninterested in what was going on, his hooded eyes resting fixedly on his open palms as if he were trying to read his fortune in them.

"All right, let's try it again. Stand back, people."

"And I'd like to spend my last three hundred on the Panasonic deluxe powerhead canister vacuum."

Ambrosetti bounced a second time. There was a sudden quiet. And then one of the doctors said, "That's it, let's call it. There's nothing more we can do for him."

They were sitting in the same dismal coffee shop across the street from the hospital—and the medical examiner's office—where Michael had met his mother right after Alan's death and where later he'd persuaded Gail to help him. As depressing a place as it was, it seemed to be playing an unusually significant role in his life.

"What the fuck was your friend talking about; he was going to be okay?" Michael knew he was raising his voice and drawing strange looks from the other customers, but he couldn't help himself.

Gail frowned. "Don't yell at me, Michael. All I know is what I told you. Jill was in the recovery room with him. She spoke to Phil Kinzer, who did the operation. They took two bullets out of him and left a fragment in his gut. They said that he could live with it. They'd gotten the bleeding under control. There were no vital organs affected. Something must have happened for him to crap out like that."

Michael couldn't believe it. The realization hadn't sunk in yet. He was so overwhelmed by what he'd seen that it didn't occur to him until too late that he'd just succeeded in scalding his tongue with coffee.

"What? What could have happened?"

"It could be one of a hundred things, Michael. You were in med school, you know that. Maybe they didn't stop all the bleeding like they thought, or maybe he began hemorrhaging during the night. What difference does it make? He's dead. I'm sorry it happened, but it did and there's nothing we can do to change it."

"They killed him." It seemed plain as day to him.

Gail's brow furrowed, and she studied him gravely. He knew what she was thinking: He'd taken leave of his senses, seeing conspiracies everywhere, a captive of paranoid fantasies.

"Don't you see, Gail? They knew they fucked up. When they found out he had a chance of pulling through, they decided to take him out in his bed. Don't you think it's possible?"

"It's possible, I suppose." She was willing to give him that much. "But it's like everything else—you're never going to prove it."

Michael realized that she was probably right, but it seemed important to try; it was the only thing that he had to hold on to. "Who did you say his doctor was? Maybe he'll give me more details on Ambrosetti's condition."

"Phil Kinzer was the one who performed the surgery."

"You don't think it's going to do any good to pursue this, do you?"

She was tired and listless, and at least Michael had enough sense to know how wearing he could be.

"No, frankly, I don't. If he was killed, then I can't imagine that his killers wouldn't cover their tracks pretty thoroughly. It stands to reason."

"You know where it has to end, don't you?"

She remained silent, but she knew.

"You want to take any bets that Magnus will be given the autopsy to do? They can't cover their tracks without him."

"You want me to try to get in on his autopsy, don't you?" She sounded angry, put upon.

"Well, yes, I do. You're the only one I know who has access to Magnus."

"It wouldn't work," she said. "Magnus wouldn't let me anywhere close to that autopsy if there was some sort of cover-up in the works; you know that."

"But wouldn't it be worth a shot? Don't you see, Gail? What we're after is some hard evidence proving that Magnus has been deliberately falsifying autopsies. That's all we need. It could be Ambrosetti's case or my brother's or Cassie Epstein's. That's not what's important. We've just got to show that it was done once."

"Oh, Michael," she said in that exasperated way she had. "You're grasping at straws now, you know that, don't you? I could stand right next to Magnus at the post and still not be able to spot anything he was doing wrong. He's smarter than that. How could I possibly prove that Ambrosetti didn't die of complications from his gunshot wounds?"

He knew she was right, though he was loath to admit it. "I'm going over to see Kinzer now," he said, getting up from the table. "I'll talk to you later."

"Don't get crazy over this, Michael. It's not worth it."

He turned, holding her steadily with his gaze. "You don't have any fucking idea what it's like," he shot back. "What if it was your brother, Gail?"

He knew he'd hurt her—he saw how her face flushed and how the anger flashed in her eyes—but he didn't stop to hear what she had to say in reply. He wanted to hurt her; at that instant he wanted to hurt everyone, and that included himself.

Only when he got out onto the street did he realize that of course she knew very well what he was talking about. Hadn't she lost a husband? He had half a mind to go back and apologize. Then, thinking she'd run out after him, he stayed where he was for a while. When she did not appear, he decided the hell with it, he could straighten things out with her later.

Michael found Phil Kinzer at the end of the afternoon. He was coming out of the O.R., looking curiously invigorated as if several hours spent in resectioning and suturing had had a tonic effect on him, like forty laps in a pool.

"Oh, so you're Gail's friend," he said in a manner that suggested he had some idea as to exactly what kind of friend he was.

"I was also a friend of the man you operated on last night."

"I operated on five people last night. Three citizens and two SHPOSes."

"SHPOSes?"

"Subhuman pieces of shit," Kinzer replied without any trace of humor in his voice. "We get a lot of them in here."

Michael wondered under what classification Ambrosetti fell but decided not to ask.

"Who's your guy?"

"Nick Ambrosetti."

"Oh, right. The gunshot wounding. We sent him upstairs. What about him?"

Michael was stunned to realize that the surgeon hadn't been told what happened to his patient. "He's dead. He died early this morning."

Kinzer pursed his lips, a look of annoyance crossing his face. "Dead? How the hell did that happen?"

"Don't know. I was told the surgery had been successful."

"It was, goddammit!" He was indignant. "This shouldn't have happened! Fuck! Who's his doctor?"

"I thought you were."

"No, not me. I just dug the bullets out of him. That was the beginning and end of my responsibility. Once he was formally admitted, somebody else took charge."

"Do you have any idea who that might be?"

Kinzer shrugged. "No, but I can find out. Let me make a call. Stay here, and I'll be back in a minute."

When Kinzer reappeared, he said to Michael, "You're right,

your friend did crap out." Apparently he'd needed the confirmation before he was willing to take Michael at his word.

"You find out how he died?"

"The resident I talked to up on six couldn't tell me. Anyone who was treating him has gone off duty by now."

"What about the records? Wouldn't the person who pronounced have to note the cause of death?"

"The records on this friend of yours aren't available, though that's not so unusual. The best thing to do is check with Ambrosetti's doctor. He should know what happened."

"Did you find out the doctor's name?"

"Yes, I did. He's from another hospital. Maybe he was your friend's personal physician. I wrote it down for you." He glanced at a scrap of prescription paper in his hand. "His doctor's name is Ed Shannon. Mean anything to you?"

CHAPTER TWENTY-EIGHT

"You'd think that the property would be divided up equally—isn't that what's supposed to happen? But, no! She gets it all. What kind of bullshit is that?" Tommy Christopher regarded the bartender, seriously expecting him to answer.

The bartender, whose name Tommy had forgotten, shrugged and said, "No divorce is easy, Tommy. The lawyers are the only ones who come out ahead."

Tommy ordered another bourbon-and-Coke. He'd lost count of how many he'd had. Didn't matter, really. What mattered was that in this particular saloon, whose name he'd forgotten as well, they let him drink. He'd been banned from just about every other bar in the Village. He was a lush, he grew loud and obnoxious, and he antagonized people. That was just how it was. The bartenders in this joint, though, put up with him, mainly because of the generous tips he lavished on them, he figured.

But everyone in the Village knew who he was—that was the important thing. They'd all heard his song: *Soon as you're gone, I'll get it all worked out, so long, baby, good-*

bye ... It was a light, upbeat, almost ethereal song, with lyrics he still believed were poetic and insightful. Why, there was a time one couldn't turn on a Top 40 station anywhere in the country without a chance of hearing "Comedown (So Long, Good-bye)." Tommy had gone on Merv Griffin and Johnny Carson. He'd become famous.

True, none of the songs he'd composed afterward had gone over nearly as well. He didn't know why he couldn't recapture the spirit of that first one. But even now, more than twenty years later, people remembered "Comedown (So Long, Good-bye)"; that fleeting interlude of fame had brought him lots of money, a condominium in Manhattan, a house in Malibu, two wives, and three daughters. When he got around to it, he'd try his hand at something new, but it never seemed to work.

Mostly what he did these days was drink. Which was nothing new—he'd been drinking since the late sixties. It showed, too; he'd grown thick in the middle, and his face had lost much of its definition, puffing up enough so that he felt he might look better with a beard.

He wasn't aware of the woman until she'd sidled up to the stool next to his. When he turned to inspect her, she smiled back at him. This was going to be interesting.

She was an exceptional-looking girl, with the flaring eyes of a Gypsy bandit, long glossy black hair, and a body to kill for, barely contained by a black dress that in front was demure enough but in back dipped to a vee, almost to her crack. Fucking amazing.

"The name's Tommy Christopher," he said, confident that she'd know it immediately. But to his disappointment, there was no sign of recognition.

"Hello, Tommy Christopher," she said. "I'm Dana Forest." It sounded as if she had an accent, vaguely European but definitely very classy.

She held her hand out. He leaned over to kiss it.

"You have a delightful smile. Allow me to buy you a drink."

"White wine, please."

He began to tell her about his divorce settlement; it was what was uppermost in his mind, and somehow he could think of nothing else to talk about. "How do you like that? I support the broad nine years, and she gets the rights to my house, half the income from my publishing company, custody of our kids. I tell you, it's criminal what she did."

Saying nothing, Dana listened, offering him a sympathetic smile.

"You sound like you've got a lot of money," she said.

"Oh, but I do. I do have a pile of money. You ever hear the song 'Comedown—So Long, Good-bye'?" He began to sing in his dry, croaking voice, " 'When I woke up next morning, I knew I'd never have a night like the one I had with you again.' " He threw her a questioning look. She had to know it, she just had to.

She gave him a quizzical smile. "I'm sorry," she said, "it was probably before my time."

"Oh, shit. Do I look that old to you? Do I look like ancient history? I mean, really."

Her hand reached to his wrist and rested there briefly. "Oh, no, I don't think you're ancient history. Not at all, Tommy. This is fascinating. Tell me more."

He did. He didn't know when to stop. He kept on ordering drinks—for him, for her. God, the broad could drink. Her allure only increased the more wine she put down. It put a flush to her face, caused her bandit eyes to sparkle. God, she was beautiful. One way or another, he vowed he'd get into her pants that night.

Finally he remembered to ask her what she did. "You a model? You look like a model."

"Is that what you'd like me to be, Tommy?"

This got him angry; this pissed him off. "What is this shit? I'm asking you a question. What are you?"

"It's all right, Tommy. I'm kind of a model. I used to model. Now I'm an actress. Don't jump down my throat."

"Okay," he said, "okay, okay. Well, I can see where you'd do real well as a model. You know, I have friends—

photographers, producers, good friends. If you're interested—"

"I might be," she said coyly. "Say, Tommy, why don't we get out of here?"

"Sure, sure we can get out of here. I know a place—" In truth, besides his apartment he didn't know many places right around there where they'd let him in. And he wasn't certain he could prevail on her to go back to his apartment, not yet.

"Would you mind if I suggested a place?" she asked.

"Well, yeah, why not? Sure, okay. What place do you have in mind?"

"Come with me and I'll show you."

A smile like that; how could he resist?

More time had passed than he'd imagined. Hours and hours. It was almost two in the morning. Not that it mattered. When had time actually mattered?

They took a cab somewhere west in the Village. He'd have known exactly where he was if it were day and he wasn't so fucked up. It wasn't that he was so drunk, though that was a part of it. It was all that fine toot she kept coming up with. No telling how much of it he did in the cab. He guessed half a gram.

Now they were out of the cab and walking. He wondered why she'd left the cab so far away from where she lived. But hell, people were entitled to their strangeness.

He stopped to kiss her, on the lips, at the base of the neck. But when he lifted his eyes toward her face, instead of the pleasure that he expected to see, he saw a certain confusion, as if she could not quite make out why he had done this.

"Come on," she said, breaking the mood, "let's go. It's not far."

They were walking toward the river; the smell of it reached them long before the sight of it. The streets there were quiet, almost entirely given over to brownstones and new brick-face condominium complexes.

They came to a building that looked noticeably aged, its red bricks discolored and chipping, blackened in spots from fire or tar. Six stories tall, it was located diagonally across the street from an elevated trestle that once might have connected one factory to another but now served no useful purpose at all from what he could see.

The few successful models he'd met had lived in expensive high rises on the Upper East Side. This was neither the kind of building nor the neighborhood he imagined a woman like Dana to be living in. But then, it was always possible that she'd lucked into a rent-controlled apartment, and then all bets were off. No one gave up a rent-controlled apartment.

"Hope you don't mind the climb," she said once they were in the lower hallway. Paint was peeling there. Names on the mailboxes had been scratched out, and the boxes themselves hung open. A sign was posted on the door: PLEASE DO NOT LEAVE CHINESE MENUS HERE. But Chinese takeout menus were visible just the same, half a dozen of them lying strewn on the tiled floor. Maybe, Tommy thought, the kids who distributed the menus couldn't understand enough English to interpret the sign.

She lived on the fifth floor, up steep flights of stairs that must be torture for anyone moving in—or out. Had the building been any higher, by law the owner would have had to put in an elevator.

There were only two doors on each floor—front and rear. Dana lived in the rear.

"What's that strange smell?" Tommy asked. He tried to identify it; he knew it from somewhere, but it wouldn't come to him.

"Maybe somebody's cooking," Dana suggested without displaying the slightest bit of interest. Of course, if one was used to something, it stood to reason one wouldn't notice it.

Once she got the door open, the smell was even more pronounced. There was no question it was coming from her apartment. The room that presented itself to view looked immaculate, however—white walls, white ceilings. Even the windows were papered over with thick white cloth so that there was no possibility of seeing out or of receiving any light during the day. The room was as sparsely furnished as any that Tommy had ever been in. There were just a couple of folding chairs, an empty bridge table, and a couch. The couch was the only piece of furniture with any character. It was obviously an antique, with red upholstery that was all the more startling because of the white backdrop against which it was placed. Otherwise, there was nothing Tommy could see that gave so much as a hint as to the personality or taste of the woman who lived there.

Tommy just stood where he was and looked at her uncertainly. Her smile hadn't changed since they were at the restaurant. "Make yourself at home," she said.

He looked about in wonder. This place did not seem like one where it was possible to make oneself at home. He took a seat on the couch and proceeded to tap out a line of her coke while she watched him expressionlessly. It was hard to tell what she was thinking. He raised his eyes toward her, appreciative of how her dress had swept up on her thighs.

Now that he had possession of the vial of coke, he offered her a hit, but she begged off. "Oh, no, thanks, Tommy, but you go ahead."

She was looking at him in a way he found disconcerting, as if she could see places inside of himself he'd rather not be seen.

"You know, Tommy, forgive me for saying this, but I think you're really a very unhappy person."

He couldn't believe what this broad was saying. "Oh, shit, I'm the happiest guy alive. What are you talking about?"

She gave him another one of her weird smiles. "I'm going into the bedroom to change. Is that all right, Tommy?"

The abrupt change of subject threw him. "Sure, sure it is. But before you go, tell me why you think I'm so unhappy."

"Oh, forget I said anything. It doesn't matter."

"What the fuck do you mean?" He was a prisoner of the coke now and he wasn't so sure he wanted to be there with a broad so crazy. Which wasn't to say he still didn't want to get into her pants.

"Tommy, forget it. We'll talk about it later." And with that she rose from the chair, the silk rustling around her body like a whisper, and swept from the room.

After ten minutes had gone by he began to wonder what was taking her so long. He looked down the length of the narrow corridor that led to her bedroom. Two doors were in view, one to his right and one at the very end of the corridor. Both were shut.

Suddenly the apartment filled with music. It didn't seem to be coming from anywhere in particular; it was just everywhere all at once, engulfing him. It was music unlike any he'd ever heard in his life; he couldn't even say for sure what instruments might be producing it: possibly out-of-tune guitars. He imagined it might be Japanese or else some avant-garde piece. Whatever it was, it sounded to Tommy like the whine of a car alarm that nobody was in any hurry to shut off. He clapped his hands over his ears, but that didn't do much good. "Could you make that a little lower?" he called out, unsure whether he'd made himself heard.

Receiving no response, he started down the corridor. There was something sticky on the floor that made it feel as though he were walking on a layer of gum. His hand groped along the wall for a light switch. There was some unidentifiable substance on the floor, dull yellowish in color, fat or grease maybe, that accounted for the stickiness. Only then did he notice the chart Dana had hung on the wall. Since there was nothing else hung on the wall, it was hard to miss.

It showed a human form in elaborate anatomical detail. Several arrows were pointing to different parts of the figure: the back of the neck, behind the ears, under the shoulders, the flat of the wrists, the groin, and other areas. For an instant Tommy thought it was a chart for medical students or artists. But they would have to be Chinese medical students and artists, because all the writing on the chart was in Chinese.

He was still staring at it, doing his best to ignore the demented music, when he felt Dana's hands slip over his eyes, blotting out his view. "Just keep your eyes closed, okay, Tommy?"

He did as she asked.

"Do you want to feel something?" Giving him no chance to reply, she kissed him on the lobe of his ear, then kissed him again, on the back of his neck. And as he delighted in the sensation these kisses were producing, she grasped hold of his wrists and squeezed. Pain, like an electrical jolt, shot up both his arms. He gagged and almost doubled over.

"Don't open your eyes yet, Tommy. Do as you're told."

"Don't, please, that hurts." Oh, this broad was twisted, she was really nuts. But she was strong, too. He wished he weren't this fucked up. No broad could get the better of him like this.

She was so close to him now that he could feel her leg rubbing against his in a motion insistent enough to cause an erection. "Let me . . ." he started to say.

"What's wrong, Tommy? Don't be like that. Do you know what else I can do? If I just put a little pressure on this spot right here"—he registered the touch of her fingers on his temple—"I can kill you."

"This isn't funny anymore, Dana. Stop playing these fucking games!"

"What's wrong with games, Tommy?" she asked.

As soon as he freed himself, he decided he'd throw her to the floor and ream her good. She was asking for it.

And then she did something—it was like lightning, that quick. He had no idea what it was, but all of a sudden he felt light-headed, he could scarcely breathe, scarcely see. It was a peculiar sensation, unlike any he'd ever felt before in his life. He couldn't understand what had just happened. "What the fuck are you doing to me?"

She let go. He tottered a step back, a step forward. Pain shot through him; it was amazing how much pain there was. Then he tried to look at her. It was difficult, almost impossible, with so many lights flickering in front of his eyes. And when at last he did catch a glimpse of her, he was certain that something was terribly wrong with his eyesight. Because how else would he see a man standing there and not a woman?

And then gradually he began to sink to the floor, into the thick, gummy substance that seemed to welcome him into its midst.

PART TWO

PART TWO

CHAPTER ONE

How Gerolamo Albinese acquired the sobriquet "Fast Boy" was something that even Ray Fontana wasn't even sure of. He suspected, though, that it came not from the cars he liked to race when he was younger, but from his ability to get away in the flash of an eye whenever things were about to go truly bad on him. Nowadays there was certainly nothing about Gerry Albinese's appearance that would suggest that this was a man with speed. The good life had gotten to him; things had come easier, and he'd put on weight. Dissipation showed up in his eyes, in the broken blood vessels in the thick of his nose, and in the flesh that drooped from his skull. Fontana could always sense when somebody had lost the edge. And it was certain that Albinese, now that he was getting on in years, had lost the edge.

There he was late of a weekday night polishing off a plate of ribs at Victor's, expressing his happiness over the Cuban cuisine, continually urging Fontana to eat what was on his plate and keep up with him. Maybe he resented Fontana's thinness, his youth, his ambition. But he'd come to rely on Fontana; he couldn't say no when Fontana called. Otherwise, he might have had second thoughts about appearing in public like this. Actually, Fontana was surprised that he'd had so little difficulty luring the man out from whatever rock under which he'd taken cover.

Seated next to Albinese was his bodyguard and shadow, Paolo, a hustler Albinese had picked up from the dregs of Copacabana Beach. Paolo had been with Albinese for well over a decade. Two additional goons from Albinese's legion of the damned were seated at their own table strategically situated so that they had an unrestricted view of the entrance.

There was a lot of booze being drunk at Albinese's table. Paolo could drink like a fish, which he had to do if he had any hope of catching up to Albinese. They were now working their way through their second bottle of Rémy.

For maybe an hour Albinese was able to maintain the appearance of sobriety; one would hardly know he was smashed unless one analyzed a sample of his blood. Then, without warning, it hit him. Suddenly he became expansive, full of good feeling for all mankind. He began toasting Fontana, clinking glasses hard enough to shatter them. "You're like my brother, Ray. I want to drink a toast to my brother." Turning to his bodyguard, he insisted he do the same. "Come on, Paolo, drink to my brother. Let's all drink to my brother!"

Paolo reacted with barely concealed disdain. He didn't like having to join in with these toasts. Anyhow, he really wasn't interested in them; he only had eyes for the waiter who, as the night went on, began to respond with some soulful stares of his own.

"You've done a lot for me, Ray. Don't think I don't appreciate it."

"I know how you appreciate it, Gerry. We do favors for each other—it works both ways."

Fontana was growing anxious, wondering whether something had happened to gum up the works. They couldn't expect him to keep this crazy guinea there forever. The food was gone, Albinese was picking at the scraps now, and once they were finished with the Rémy he'd want to move on. There was no guaranteeing when Fontana would be able to pin him down again.

"You know, Paolo, this man, my brother Ray, I'd do anything in the world for him. Know that, Ray? Any fucking thing in the world. There were some jobs you did for me I'll never forget. You know, Paolo, this guy is maybe the only guy in the world who could have taken out the Duesenberg and lived."

The Duesenberg's real name was Rubin D'Amico. He loved to collect antique cars—big, beautiful Hispano-Suizas, Mercedeses, Bugattis, Silver Arrows, and, of course, Duesenbergs, all in mint condition. What he also loved was to fuck with the Fast Boy, who at the time was farming out his services to the Colombo family. A fat contract was put out on him, and it was Fontana who took it, not so much because of the money, though the money was always a consideration, but because inevitably the credit for the hit went to Fontana, not to Albinese. It wasn't such a big thing as the Fast Boy seemed to think it was.

"So what is it you wanted to talk about, Ray? What is it?" Albinese seemed to be coming back to earth. So far as Fontana was concerned, this was not a good thing to have happen. Albinese must have noticed the darting movement of Fontana's eyes toward the door, because he said, "What is it, Ray? Something the matter? You expecting somebody?"

"I'm expecting the ghost of Christmas past, what do you think?"

Fontana had to work this very carefully; it was like performing a complicated dance step in time to music that was constantly changing tempo. Slip up, do anything to arouse Albinese's suspicions, and he was fucked. Paolo might take him out on the spot. He was entirely dependent on his wits; expecting to be frisked, as he was, he had brought no weapon to this meeting.

But Albinese was laughing, exhibiting no special concern. "We're all waiting for the ghost of Christmas past. Fuck, if he ever comes we're in deep shit. Ain't that right, Ray?" He was drinking his brandy as though it was second-rate Chianti. Belching quietly, he adjusted his posture and said, "Ray, there's something I been meaning to ask you."

"What is it, Gerry?"

"It's just something I heard. You know the way people talk; maybe there's nothing to it."

Fontana wondered whether now was the time to get worried. Possibly word had gotten out on the street that Albinese was marked. Parnase or Harry Irwin, even that DiNapoli cunt—the leak could have come from any one of them.

"What did you hear, Gerry? Tell me."

"They say that that Karamis broad was whacked. They say your boys were the ones who whacked her."

Much better by far that they discuss Ginny Karamis in the time left. "Maybe there's something to it," Fontana said guardedly.

"Too bad," Albinese said without the slightest trace of sorrow in his voice. "Nice piece of ass. You were fucking her, too, weren't you? We were all fucking her. It was like some graduate course we all had to go through." He broke up laughing over that. "What happened you had to whack her?"

Albinese had something of a vested interest in Ginny; she'd been one of his best mules, carrying toot, which, depending on the circumstances, she smuggled inside her bra, her panties, her stomach, in her crack—anywhere she could get it to fit, actually—thousands of miles across Bolivian, Colombian, and U.S. borders. Albinese had loaned her out to Ray to use. So it was natural he'd want to know why Ray had disposed of her.

"She fucked up, Gerry. She decided to cut herself in in a major way on a deal I was putting together."

"She wasn't smart enough to do that."

"No kidding. That was why she went in with some asshole I was using to wash my money. He got in way over his head. And he thought he was the brains of the operation. He and Ginny could make off with my bread. Imagine doing that, Gerry? With my money? It's fucking nuts."

They had a good laugh over that.

A couple of minutes later, the waiter Paolo had been watching all night came over to their table. "Call for you, Mr. Fontana," he said. "You can take it at the bar."

Fontana excused himself and casually walked over to the

bar. Picking up the phone, he looked across the floor to the booth where Albinese and Paolo were sitting. They were lost in conversation, though, paying not the slightest attention to him. Then he looked the other way to where Albinese's two goons were sitting.

Only they weren't there any longer. Their chairs were empty. Christ! Where the fuck were they?

"Yes?" he spoke into the phone, his voice sharp. He knew who it would have to be.

"We're going in."

"You're late, you bastard," he said to Kohler. "Another couple of minutes and you'd have missed the asshole." He hung up. A moment later he became aware of a disturbance in front of the restaurant.

Albinese was on his feet, scrambling for the exit. Paolo was right behind him, his face tense with anticipation. It seemed that Albinese could still move like hell when he had to. A tray full of cocktails went flying from a waiter's hand as the Fast Boy barreled past him. Fontana registered the anxiety coursing through the other diners. They sensed that something was going down, but of course they couldn't possibly have had any idea what it was.

Fontana tore out of the restaurant, cursing Kohler for fucking up. Anything could happen now.

Had Kohler organized the bust the way he should have, they'd have taken Albinese inside the restaurant, quietly, discreetly—no problem. Now there was a problem. Albinese was running, keeping to the shadows, ignoring warnings boomed through a megaphone to give himself up. Nobody was firing yet, not with a possibility of somebody innocent getting caught in a crossfire. Albinese was nuts, thinking he could somehow escape. One look at this dramatic show of firepower—a platoon of plainclothesmen and uniformed police wielding shotguns—should have told him as much. Squad cars, police vans, and ambulances blocked the street, their lights flashing in the drizzle that had begun to fall. Fifty-second Street was taking on the look of an armed camp.

Glancing up the block, Fontana saw one of his blue-and-white CityVision News trucks. A man carrying a Minicam was just emerging from it. CityVision was entitled to the television exclusive on this story as a favor to Fontana. Arrangements had been made to pool whatever footage they obtained to all the other local channels. The idea was to persuade the folks at home, in dramatic fashion, that Larry Kohler was a man who could get things done, a man who should have their vote of confidence as the next police commissioner. The way this was developing, though, there was every chance that he'd end up walking a beat in Spanish Harlem.

Albinese and his men had taken refuge behind two parked cars. No one had expected him to resist; no one had anticipated a stalemate. Kohler must have reasoned that Albinese was washed up, *finito*, and that surely he must recognize that and give himself up. Kohler had reasoned wrong.

Seeing Kohler across the street, Fontana started toward him. It was then that he observed a photographer, maybe a freelancer. He wasn't authorized to be there, and there was no controlling what he might shoot. Right now he was trying to take a picture of the inspector. Fontana strode up to him and knocked him over, ripping the camera from his hands at the same time. When the photographer began to protest, Fontana gave him a withering look that silenced him immediately. "Get the fuck out of here," he said, tearing the film from his Olympus before handing it back to him. The photographer was a sensible fellow; he took his camera and promptly disappeared.

All at once there was a burst of fire—a fusillade that couldn't have lasted more than a few seconds. There was a scream. Fontana spun around, incredulous. A cop was down. What was happening? Several more shots came in quick succession. There was no telling who was firing, or from where the shots were coming. People were dropping to the ground, crawling behind cars, crawling under them. Real panic was setting in. Fontana, however, remained where he was standing, trying to make out in all the confusion what had happened to Albinese.

But it was Paolo he spotted, not Albinese. Paolo was taking aim at another cop but had no chance to get off so much as a single round. Spattered with gunfire, he was thrown back against the fender of a Chevy and sank soundlessly to the ground.

There was more shooting. A round shattered the window of a tan Olds behind Fontana; another put a crater in its rear fender. Somebody was crying out in pain. Fontana looked to see a detective, his jacket covered in blood, sprawled in a puddle about ten paces from where he stood. Paramedics rushed to his side. Cops were in motion all over the place. Sirens signaled the imminent arrival of reinforcements. Everyone was screaming and shouting, trying to make themselves heard at the same time. It was sheer pandemonium.

Things seemed to have turned around. Kohler looked as if he were the man under assault, not Albinese. Rage and frustration had twisted his features into an ugly mask, and he was dripping with sweat. Fontana walked over to him.

"We got two men down. We got to end this," Kohler muttered. He was ready to take Albinese out if he had to.

"Give me five minutes with the son-of-a-bitch, I'll end it," Fontana said. Acknowledging the doubt in Kohler's eyes, he added, "Listen, Larry, I started it, didn't I? Well, I can end it. Don't worry, you'll still get the credit. I want you to have all the fucking credit."

"Hold your fire! Everyone hold your fire!" Kohler shouted into the megaphone as Fontana calmly crossed the street toward Albinese.

It was possible Albinese would fire on him. He had every reason to, but aside from the satisfaction it would give him, it wouldn't do him a hell of a lot of good; certainly it wouldn't save him.

"Hey, Gerry, I want to talk to you," he called over in Albinese's direction.

The uproar of a couple of minutes ago had subsided so

that now his words could be clearly heard up and down the block. It didn't take long for the answer to come.

"You set me up, you fuck! I'll wipe the street with your ass!"

Fontana detected a certain weariness in his voice; the threat carried no conviction. "You do, and you get nothing for it. I can help you out, Gerry, I can make everything go easier for you."

"You? What the fuck you talking about? You really are something, Ray."

Meanwhile, Fontana continued slowly advancing toward the Hertz rental van that Albinese and his goons were using as protection. Fontana kept his hands in view so that Albinese wouldn't get the idea he was armed. "You want to talk or not? It's your only chance."

Silence.

Fontana continued moving forward until he was at the van. Its whole side was punctured by bullet holes; there wasn't much left of the windshield, either.

"It's up to you, Ray. I might decide to blow you the fuck away, after all."

"I know, Gerry, I can understand how you feel."

Fontana walked around to the other side of the van. One of the goons was on the ground, his forehead bloody from a scalp wound. The other one, however, was in good shape, just winded. The Fast Boy seemed tired. He was breathing hard. All this strenuous exercise after a big meal wasn't healthy. He cast Fontana a despairing, hurt look. "After all these years, Ray."

"These things happen. There was nothing I could do about it. They had me by the balls. It got to be too big for me to control anymore."

"You take me for such a sap to believe that some fucking cop forced you into setting me up?"

"I'll be straight with you, Gerry. See that news truck over there?"

"That TV news truck? What about it?"

"What do you think this was all about, Gerry? You think this was cooked up by the Feds? What you see here, Gerry, is bullshit. It's media hype—that's all it is." He neglected to mention that it was *his* media hype.

"Throw the Fast Boy to the wolves for the eleven o'clock news is what you're saying."

"That's one way of looking at it. But once the cameras are turned off, you can walk. That's the beauty of it."

"What do you mean, I can walk?" Albinese was obviously having a hard time putting all this together.

"That was the whole idea, Gerry—until your boys went nuts and fucked it up." This remark drew a look of reproach from the one bodyguard who remained unbloodied.

"Shit!" said Albinese. He spat out a scrap of food that had gotten caught in his teeth. "Why me? There are a thousand wiseguys you could've set up. Maybe you're in show business, but I'm not. I got other things to do with my life." Then, his voice lower, sadder, he said, "I can't walk now. Not with a couple of cops down. They're not going to let me walk."

"Yeah, and who shot them? Fuck, we'll pin it on your boy Paolo. Won't be any trouble for him."

"Paolo," said Albinese, almost in awe. He liked the idea. "But suppose they run a ballistics test, prove that I was the shooter?" It went without saying that the goons were dispensable.

"That's not going to happen, Gerry."

Albinese frowned. "Yeah? You going to guarantee it, Ray? After what you did to me? You going to guarantee I get out of this shit?"

"You have to trust me, Gerry, you got no choice. What are you going to do, shoot your fucking way out of this? Take a look."

But the Fast Boy didn't need to have a look to know that he was ringed by cops and that he was a dead man unless he played along. "All right, Ray, you win, you fucking win."

Although Kohler was informed of the agreement that Fontana had reached with Albinese to obtain his surrender, it was clear he wasn't happy. Two of his men were shot, one was dead, and one seriously wounded. How could he be happy? He could have blamed himself for fucking up. Instead, he berated Fontana. "You could've told me this fucking guy was going to come out shooting like it was the fucking O.K. Corral. 'Nothing will happen,' you told me. Nothing will happen, bullshit!"

Fontana answered calmly, recognizing the need Kohler had to vent his anger. "If you'd gotten your act together, maybe this wouldn't have happened. But I keep telling you, there's nothing to worry about. I'll supervise the editing of this footage. Believe me, you'll come out of this looking like a hero."

Kohler was dubious. It didn't matter; Fontana was sure he'd come around.

In the meantime the cops were moving in—cautiously—on Albinese and his men. They slammed them up against the side of the van, then frisked and handcuffed them. Fontana had to stay out of it now; this was Kohler's show to run as he saw fit. He'd done all he could.

The cops treated Albinese especially roughly. He was the one they blamed for gunning down two of their brethren. Four cops were on him, twisting his arms behind him so that he cried out before he was cuffed. There was one cop—a sergeant—who appeared to be taking charge of the arrest. He was cursing out the Fast Boy, insulting him—him and his mother. Maybe the cop forgot that this was all being recorded on videotape. Maybe he didn't give a shit.

With each curse Albinese spat out, the more incensed the sergeant became; he seemed to be fueling his own anger. Three times he swung at Albinese with his stick, catching him in the ribs, causing Albinese to double up and retch.

It was all so incredibly unnecessary, but Fontana resisted the urge to intervene. That would only antagonize the cops further. He had to stay out of it; everything would be all right as long as this show of brutality could be edited out of the final footage.

With his club pressed against the base of Albinese's neck,

the sergeant began to steer him toward a waiting squad car. Then he shoved Albinese inside, the door slammed shut, and the Fast Boy was gone.

Keeping to his promise, Fontana returned to the studios of CityVision Cable Company on West Sixty-eighth Street to oversee the editing of the footage personally. Fontana was after footage that would be dramatic and entertaining enough for stations outside of the city to pick up for broadcast. At the same time Fontana had to make certain that Kohler emerged as a heroic figure, a man the public would welcome as police commissioner.

CityVision Cable—Channel 19—occupied half a floor in a building owned by Capital Cities Broadcasting. Its studios were modest, its signal was weak, and the quality of its programming indifferent. But just as Natchez did in its own way, the station was useful as a vehicle for certain projects Fontana was interested in pursuing. Like this one. He'd appointed himself president of the news division, which didn't mean much except that it entitled him to a press pass, another useful convenience when he needed to cross police barricades or gain admittance to openings and celebrity parties.

Walking into the editing room, he observed that the arrest was being run backward on one of the monitors. One moment Albinese was a prisoner, his eyes bulging, his jaw slack, the tendons of his neck swelling in response to the pressure of the club; the next he was a free man contemplating the odds.

The editor glanced up at Fontana and nodded. "Looks pretty good. We've got calls from Channels Two and Seven so far. They heard about what happened and they're chomping at the bit to get hold of this. Just so long as we can get them the tape in time for the eleven o'clock."

"What time are we running it?"

"In twenty minutes—at ten. We'll beat the big boys by an hour. What use is an exclusive if we can't show it first, right?"

"Okay, let's run this through once in its entirety," Fontana said just as the phone lit up.

The editor took it. "For you," he said, handing the receiver to Fontana.

It was Kohler on the other end. "Bad news, Ray."

"What is it?" He expected that the second cop had died on the operating table.

"Albinese is dead."

Not much could shock Fontana. This did. "What are you talking about, dead?"

"He's dead, Ray. And it looks like we were the ones who killed him."

CHAPTER TWO

She was a spirited girl, and Magnus liked that about her; in some way, she reminded him of his daughter. Which wasn't really so surprising since she was only a few years older than Valerie. And she was pretty—that counted for a great deal, too. Set off by a thick tangle of hair that was blond in one light and red in another, her face offered a promise that he realized could never be delivered. There was something hard about her, an edge that Magnus occasionally found enticing but more often found just irritating.

A week had passed since he'd last come to see her at her apartment in Brooklyn Heights. She was used to his erratic appearances and didn't seem to mind them. She said she understood how with his schedule he could never predict when he'd be free to see her. She'd welcome him whether he turned up at three in the morning or three in the afternoon; it apparently made no difference to her. She always seemed to be awake, with nothing better to do than entertain him. All she asked of him was that he call her an hour before he came so she'd know when to expect him. He suspected that she needed the warning to make certain that there weren't any awkward encounters with her other friends. He never asked about that, probably because he didn't really want to know.

By the same token, Kate never expressed any curiosity about his family. Usually he tried to keep them out of the conversations he had with her; Barbara and Valerie belonged to another part of his life. Nothing meant so much to him as keeping his family together. He needed a place to go back to—a home, the solace of the familiar. It seemed less and less important that Barbara and he no longer shared any love so long as they stayed together, giving comfort and support. Barbara was his anchor. If she stood by him, then he was not wholly lost.

But he needed Kate, too. Or, rather, he needed women like Kate. Or like Ginny Karamis. There'd been six since he'd begun his association with Fontana. This didn't include the women he might have partied with; he couldn't count how many of those there were, much less recall with any precision what they'd looked like. It was compulsive behavior on his part, he realized that; but like any other addiction, it had assumed a momentum, even a life, of its own, and he could no more think of abandoning it than he could his family or his job.

Kate Farrell was Fontana's. She was only on loan to Magnus; that was understood. He'd met her father on the occasions when he'd come around with money for him at the examiner's office. But Max had given no indication that he had any idea of the association Magnus enjoyed with his daughter. By the same token, Kate almost never mentioned her father. Tonight was different, however. Something had moved her to talk about her past; God only knew why.

"We were running a motel down south of Orlando," she began. "Oh, it was about '83 I guess when we were down there, Max and me."

She was sitting in front of the mirror, grimacing as she tried to comb out the tangles her hair had gotten into during their lovemaking. All she had on was a beige silk robe that she'd made no effort to close. Magnus had only to look into the mirror to have a view of her heavy pink breasts; gliding in and out of the robe, they still glistened with perspiration. It wouldn't be long before he wanted her all over again.

"I wouldn't take shit from anybody. I mean, when your dad's an ex-detective, why should you put up with it? These guys, black guys mostly, they'd rent out the rooms, they'd have to leave a four-dollar deposit. Couple of hours later they'd come out and ask for the four bucks back, and I'd go, 'No way.' I'd go, 'You see that sign in your room, says "Authorized Occupants Only"?' I'd go, 'You can't bullshit me, I watched. You had seven people in there with you.' Oh, they'd party, you know, they'd fuck, do some coke. You should've seen them, they'd insist on getting their four bucks back. I go, 'No way, man, you want to fuck with me, meet me when I get off work. I know how to use a shotgun, I'm not afraid.' "

Her vehemence was what got to Magnus, the absolute conviction in her voice. He wondered sometimes whether he should tell her about what happened to Ginny Karamis. But then he decided not to; it might get back to Fontana, and that would not be good.

"Your father teach you how to use it—the shotgun?"

"Yeah," she said. "But there are a lot of things I picked up on my own."

"I can imagine."

"Then one day I was riding around with some friends, and somebody shot at us."

"You're joking?" He knew she wasn't. At that moment he had the urge to gather her in his arms and shelter her from all the terror and violence in the world, protect her just as he wanted to shield his daughter but could not.

"No joke. Three times."

"Were you hurt?"

She swiveled around on the stool, shaking her head, an expression of annoyance on her face. "Of course not. Nobody was hurt. A window was broken, that was all."

"You see who did it?"

"No, no, it all happened too quick. We were pulling out of a parking lot. It was someone in another car, and he was just gone like that."

"And you think it was over that four-buck deposit?"

"Sure, that's what it was."

"That's not a lot of money to shoot at somebody for."

"That part of Florida, you didn't need a lot of money to shoot somebody over. Trouble was that in other parts of Florida people had too much goddamned money, nothing to do all day and too much money. There was no way to compete. You can buy one or two drinks, but the jerk sitting next to you can buy sixty. It was all coke money. Guys taking me out on their boats never did an honest day's work in their life. I was happy when we quit the motel business, moved back up here."

"Your father didn't like it anymore?"

"He went nuts. Fifty-two years old, hell, he wasn't ready for retirement and he sure wasn't cut out for managing some fucking motel outside of Haines City, Florida. It was Ray who convinced him to come back, set him up here."

"Set you up here, too," Magnus observed.

"Really."

"Your father know anything about what you do?"

"It's not any of his business. He'd probably kill me if he found out. At heart he's really a conservative. Born in County Galway, what do you expect? You know? But just in case, I have a boyfriend. I call him my boyfriend, anyway. I bring him out for special occasions—Christmas, Thanksgiving, you know. He makes a good impression."

"What's he do?"

"He's a lawyer. What a joke, huh?" She finished with her hair, then rejoined Magnus on the bed to get it all tangled up again.

When the telephone rang, Magnus asked her not to answer it.

"No," she said, "I have to." And she pulled away from him quickly, almost as if the call was a welcome interruption.

"Hello," was the only word out of her mouth until right at the end of the call when she said, "Okay, I'll tell him."

Without looking at Magnus, she reached down for her robe. "That was Ray," she said. "He wants to see you."

"Where is he?"

"He's across the street. He was calling from his car." The

way she spoke, it sounded as if this was something that happened all the time.

It was no use trying to discover how Fontana located him. Fontana always knew where to find him, just as he knew how to find Kate or anyone else he needed.

As much as he depended on Fontana—more so all the time—Magnus also went to enormous lengths to avoid him. Having to endure Fontana's presence made him sick—literally physically ill. The reaction was nearly instantaneous; the roiling in his stomach had already begun. It was so bad that he thought he might have to throw up.

But he couldn't allow Fontana to see his weakness so openly displayed. He had to keep in mind that Fontana needed him, perhaps as much as the other way around. Still, it was all he could do to pull himself together and get dressed.

Kate had retreated into the bathroom and was running the shower. Magnus felt as if he were being dismissed; when he called in to her, she didn't answer, or maybe because of the shower she just didn't hear. Parting the lace curtains enough so he could see out into the street, he took in the red BMW idling in the shade of an elm. It was time.

"Know something, Kurt?" Fontana said. "Half of Brooklyn Heights is being taken over by Jehovah's Witnesses."

Magnus looked at him as if he were crazy. He couldn't imagine why Fontana would want to talk about the Jehovah's Witnesses. "You don't believe me? You know where the Watchtower is, down by the river?"

"It's hard to miss."

"Well, what I'm told, they have tunnels running underneath the streets connecting the Watchtower to all the property they've bought up around here. People are moving back and forth all the time underground. Don't you find it interesting to think that there's this other life, this second life, this Jehovah's Witnesses life, going on all around you? You know it's there, but you can't see it."

"I guess," Magnus replied in a neutral voice. Far from putting Magnus at ease, Fontana's comments about the Jehovah's Witnesses—their tunnels and their real estate—only made him more anxious.

"So you haven't told me how your wife is. She okay?"

With the smell of Kate still on him, Magnus did not much feel like talking about his wife in these circumstances. "Yes, she's all right."

"And your daughter? What's her name?"

"Valerie."

"Right, Valerie. She okay, too? All that trouble taken care of?"

"Yes, everything was taken care of. There won't be any record. They let her off with a warning. I appreciate everything you did." He knew that he didn't sound especially grateful.

"Well, I'm happy to hear that everything's been taken care of. Girls that age, they run around, you shouldn't be afraid to discipline them. But really, Kurt, any time you run into a little problem like that, be sure and call me. Don't hesitate, okay?"

"What can I do for you?"

"A little favor, Kurt. You can do me a little favor. I don't know whether you heard, but earlier tonight this wiseguy, Gerry Albinese, was picked up by the cops. Things got a little out of hand. A cop was killed. Albinese was taken into custody, but—"

"But what?"

"But it seems he died while he was being taken to the station house."

"How—how did he die?"

"He was choked. The arresting officer was holding a club up against his neck. You know, to restrain him? And maybe he pressed it harder than he meant to. It happens. One of your friends is wasted, another is put in intensive care. You can see why somebody might overreact."

"And you want me to find what?"

"I want you to find whatever the official statement says he died of."

"And what's that?"

"Coronary, brain hemorrhage, fatal stroke. Take your pick. Look, the guy was getting on, he was overweight, drank too damned much, health was bad to begin with. A trauma like this, you can imagine the effect the shock would have on somebody in poor shape."

"It has to stop, Ray. Somewhere it has to stop. I did what you wanted on that detective. Can't you leave it alone?" Magnus said this quietly, almost to himself. "You don't have any idea of the risks I'm taking each time I do this."

Fontana rolled his eyes as though he could not believe Magnus was raising such preposterous objections, especially at this late date. "Jesus! You'd think I'm asking you to do this out of the goodness of your heart. Tomorrow, after this gets taken care of, you can expect to see Sam with five thousand. Hell, let's make it six. That sound okay to you?" He waited to see if Magnus was going to say anything before adding, "Of course it does."

Sam, sometime bagman, sometime driver, did not react to the mention of his name, keeping his eyes fixed on the brownstone Magnus had come out of. It was undoubtedly smart of him not to take too great an interest in Fontana's affairs.

Magnus didn't move. He didn't know whether Fontana was finished with him or not. Fontana gave him a puzzled look. "Anything the matter?"

There was, but Magnus could not go into it now. His head was throbbing. All he wanted to do at the moment was get away from this man. "No," he said, "nothing's the matter."

"Good. Then I'll see you. Remember what I said, Kurt. Any time you have a problem, just give me a call. I'm always there for you."

Whatever the reason, Albinese's body had not turned up yet. Holmes was anxious for Magnus to take a look at another case. It was past one in the morning. Magnus hadn't eaten earlier, and now his appetite was gone. His stomach was in worse shape than ever; he'd go to the john and sit on the toilet, but nothing would happen. He took some Valium, thinking that it might help. It didn't seem to.

"Can't you handle it, Francis?" he said. "I'm waiting for a case to come in any minute. I'm sure you can do the post without me."

Holmes looked mildly aggrieved, which was about as much emotion as he ever allowed himself to display. "Just take a look at this one, Kurt. It's all I'm asking. You might know what to make of it. I'm at a loss."

Magnus agreed. They descended to the basement and proceeded into the first autopsy room.

"This is a derelict the police found in the street tonight. No I.D., probably in his early fifties."

"Any injuries?"

"Some lacerations on the stomach and groin, abrasions on the legs. Nothing serious, though."

"Acute alcohol poisoning?"

"The alcohol level's high, but I don't think that that's what did it. You see, Kurt, his penis is carbonized."

"His what?"

"His penis is carbonized. It's fried almost completely black."

"He was burned, then?"

"Burned, yes, but curiously this was the only area of the body affected."

An assistant stood over the cadaver in question. He broke into a grin at seeing Magnus but said nothing.

The cadaver was small, nearly emaciated, the ribs protruding against sallow skin; the eyes were sunk into hollows that looked as if they'd been scooped out with a penknife. The hair was sparse, the bald spot in the middle of it reddened from prolonged exposure to the sun. Pus had congealed in an open sore on his groin. Much of his body was covered with scratches and bruises, brown and pink and purplish. His had been a dreary and anonymous life. And now he'd had an equally anonymous—if peculiar—death.

One glance at the man's penis, and Magnus was certain he knew what had happened. It no longer resembled any human organ; rather, it was a shriveled blackened crisp of a thing, like a strip of bacon kept too long on a burning grill. "Electrocution," Magnus said. "This man was electrocuted."

"How could he possibly have gotten electrocuted . . . there?" the assistant asked.

"From time to time you'll see cases like this—derelicts, mostly. They have too much to drink. Then when they have to urinate they stand over a subway grating. Sometimes if their urine strikes the third rail they can electrocute themselves. It's like lightning, but from below ground, not above."

What a way to go, Magnus thought, zapped without a second's warning. And so what if there was no dignity to it? Had there been any dignity for this man in life? It was quick, the pain could not have lingered more than a moment or two, perhaps not even that with so much alcohol in his system to anesthetize him. Only the surprise would have registered in his mind. That and maybe relief that his ordeal was at last at an end.

CHAPTER THREE

Waiting in the austere surroundings of the reception room of the law offices of Kroll, Friedlander, Geddes, and Lichter, Michael tried to puzzle out all the ramifications of Ambrosetti's death in the hospital. He wasn't doing too well.

For one thing, Ed Shannon was out of town and his secretary had said there was no way to get in touch with him until the following week. It was only Tuesday; it was much too long a wait for Michael. Still, he couldn't imagine that it would make much of a difference. Michael wasn't so naïve as to believe that even if he found his former professor he'd succeed in wresting a confession from him. No doubt existed in his mind that Shannon was involved in Ambrosetti's murder. Maybe if he weren't so exhausted he might have been able to fathom the intricate connection that must exist among Lou Waterman, Ed Shannon, and Ray Fontana, but he could not do it.

The receptionist called over to him to tell him that his father was ready to see him.

He dreaded this meeting. The summons from his father was terse, and terse was bad. It meant there was something that his father felt was too important to communicate over the phone. Feeling as if he were being led to his execution, he walked slowly down the corridor leading from the reception area to his father's office, a carpeted path that he was familiar with from childhood, passing the same framed portraits and landscapes that had been there since he could remember.

Paul Friedlander was on the phone when Michael walked in. "It won't be possible to take those depositions Friday," he was saying. "It'll have to wait until next week." He listened for a moment with growing irritation. "Listen, I don't give a damn whether Friday happens to be convenient for your client. I can't get out to the Coast until Tuesday. You want to do it Tuesday afternoon, fine. . . . All right, see whether you can't rearrange it and let me know."

Michael observed that something had been changed in the office and decided that it was the color scheme; once a shade of beige, it was now more a creamy white with a touch of pastel gray. Through the window there was little else to be seen besides the tops of glass-sheathed buildings and a patch of sky.

His phone conversation concluded, Paul Friedlander directed his gaze toward his son. "How are you, Mike?" he asked.

His father looked worn and in some way defeated, Michael thought. It wasn't just the pain of his younger son's death that had wounded him so deeply; it was the restraint he was exercising to keep that pain from showing that put such desolation into his eyes.

"All right," Michael said.

"You don't talk to us much anymore. We always have to get in touch with you."

"I call when I have anything to say."

His father nodded, his hands riffling through papers on his desk. "Everything's settled. We're closing the deal on Alan's apartment at the end of the week."

Michael had had a feeling that would happen; it was inevitable that sooner or later the sale would go through.

"The new owner would like to start work in the apartment beginning next Monday. So you'll have to be out by then."

Michael hadn't expected it would be so soon. He had four days left before he had to scramble around for a roof over his head—or simply decide to bag it and go back to New Hampshire. "Was that what you wanted to see me about?"

"No, no, it wasn't."

Michael didn't think so; this was information that he'd have had no difficulty relaying over the phone.

"I received a call yesterday from a man who said that his name was Max Farrell."

A wave of nausea assailed Michael. He felt as if he were going to be sick. He sat there rigidly, struggling not to betray himself. In recent days, he hadn't given much thought to Farrell's threats. He supposed he'd always believed that Ambrosetti would take care of everything. Only, Ambrosetti wasn't around anymore to take care of everything.

"Mr. Farrell identified himself as an employee of the Fontana Security Agency." His father was speaking deliberately, seeming to weigh each word, as though Michael were a client whose defense depended on an understanding of every subtlety and nuance. "He told me that you had sought out his services and that in the course of his investigation he'd come on some very disturbing information about Alan." He looked across the desk at Michael. "Is that true so far?"

Michael nodded, unable to speak.

"He also raised the possibility that this information might have to be 'journalized,' as he put it, if you continued your efforts to reopen your brother's case. I presume that he said as much to you."

Michael allowed that he had.

"You didn't think that this was something you should have brought to my attention? You went ahead on your own without considering the damage you could do to me, to your mother, to everyone around you. But then, perhaps I was overestimating you."

"I'm sorry you feel that way." Michael didn't want to be drawn into an argument he couldn't possibly win.

His father shifted position in his chair, which Michael knew was a signal that his father was about to change his line of attack.

"Now, Mike," he began, using the same tone of voice he had when Michael was in high school and showing no improvement in his grades. "I've always tried to encourage you to tell the truth, to fight for what you believe. Is that true?"

"Yes," he said.

"But I've also tried to impress on you the reality that you can't fight every battle, that there are limits. You have to decide where to fight, what battles matter."

"Isn't this a battle that matters? We're talking about my brother here—your son."

Instantly he regretted his words; it was as though he were accusing his father of not caring, and he knew that wasn't true. It was something else. He waited for the storm to come; Paul Friedlander was a man capable of erupting into a terrible rage that could cause opponents—in court and out of it—to cower and run for cover. But not this time. Instead, his face went slack, and his gaze wavered. For a moment it seemed to Michael that an incredible transformation had come over his father; it was as if he'd turned into another man, a man who was on the verge of tears, a man paralyzed by such immense grief that he found it impossible to communicate it to anyone, even to his surviving son. "You don't know," he said in a voice that was scarcely audible. "You have no idea what you're doing."

And then this man unknown to Michael, this other father

of his, was gone, and the Paul Friedlander he'd held for years in his memory reemerged in full command of himself.

"It's gone far enough, Michael. I want you to quit it. Nothing good can come of this."

"And if I decide that this is one battle I have to fight? What happens then?"

Paul Friedlander stared at him, perhaps unable to comprehend his son's defiance. "You can't mean to go on with this, Michael, can you? Do you have any idea of the position you're putting yourself in, let alone your family?"

"It's all right for me to fight for what I believe in as long as I don't take any risks—is that what you're saying, Father?"

Now, finally, his father was becoming angry. Having resolved to say nothing to aggravate him, Michael was reverting to form, falling into the old pattern. They had been carrying on the same impossible argument for years. It didn't matter whether they were together or thousands of miles apart. Only the specifics of the dispute had changed, nothing else.

"You are, I suppose, perfectly free to take what risks you want on your behalf. Nobody can stop you—I can't, certainly. But what right do you have to take risks on the behalf of others? None that I can see. And that is exactly what you are doing, Michael, exactly." Then he said in a lower voice, "Besides, I don't want to lose another son."

Leaving his father's office, Michael felt like a cripple, barely able to walk, to function. He was empty; he was one of the hollow men, the stuffed men of Eliot's poem. The world was made not of the malleable material he'd believed it was, capable of being reformed, but of some rocklike substance one could chip away at for years without its making the slightest bit of difference. Though Michael couldn't bring himself to say so, it was possible his father was right, that he had no business dredging up the past, sifting through its artifacts in hopes of hitting on an absolute truth. At that moment he was filled with self-loathing. He made up his mind: He would leave, he would go back home—with no good-byes.

Returning to The Brandenberg, he began packing at

once, throwing himself into the task with frenzied haste. He was not neat, he was not organized; whatever he could cram into a couple of suitcases and a Pan Am travel bag would go. Everything else, as far as he was concerned, could stay, and it didn't particularly matter to him which was which.

Somehow his bags seemed heavier now than when he'd arrived, although he couldn't remember adding anything significant to their contents. While he waited for the elevator to arrive, he heard the door behind him open. Turning, he found himself looking into Mrs. Moskone's puzzled face.

He had only a nodding acquaintance with the woman. Michael had her pegged as a recluse from the first moment he moved in. Sometimes she left under his door copies of a magazine called *Plain Truth*, which maybe she thought he needed for his salvation. Whatever global problem the magazine took up, the solution seemed to lie in Jesus's return to earth. It never said what anyone should do in the meantime. It was apparent to Michael that Mrs. Moskone had long ago abandoned hope of finding anyone to befriend or understand her; she'd embraced her isolation with the ferocity of a lover. Michael had made it a point to steer clear of her, sensing trouble.

When she saw the suitcases, she frowned. "You moving out?"

He nodded.

Of her tired crinkled face Michael could see only an eye and part of a nose and mouth through the crack in the door. The chain remained in place.

She beckoned to him, whispering to him as if she were afraid somebody might overhear. There was, however, no one else in sight.

Michael approached her door. "What is it, Mrs. Moskone?"

"You'd better watch it," she said. "Don't leave anything behind. He's a thief."

Michael had no idea what she was talking about. "Who's a thief?"

"Stopka, the superintendent. He steals you blind. I watched

him take all those things out of your brother's apartment before the police came."

"What? What things?" He imagined her isolated in the prison of her apartment, spinning out paranoid fantasies in which neighbors and the super played a variety of villainous roles.

"Television, radio . . . big things, expensive things. He sells them, I know this for sure."

"Why didn't you tell me this before?"

"I'm just an old lady, I'm defenseless. If he finds out what I tell you, he'll do I don't know what to me. This Stopka is a crazy man, he is a monster."

It was only then that Michael recalled the missing VCR and computer. Was it possible that Mrs. Moskone was right, that Stopka had made off with them while Alan's body was still sprawled out on the floor?

"So you don't want to leave anything behind. He'll grab it all, I'm telling you."

"Thank you for letting me know this, Mrs. Moskone. I appreciate it."

"Sure, no problem. I don't want people getting robbed blind. I'd tell the managing agent, but then Stopka will find out. Then I don't know what he'll do to me. I'm an old lady. What can I do?" As she was about to shut the door completely, she said, "You sure you don't want to come in for a drink or something? Maybe a glass of Scotch. I think I have some rye."

Michael told her that he'd have to pass on the invitation. Instead, he put his bags back in the apartment and went down to the lobby and knocked on Stopka's door.

It was opened by the super's wife, Maria, a woman of plump dark beauty who reminded Michael of one of the Tahitian girls Gauguin used to paint. She shooed away a small child—male or female, Michael couldn't tell—who'd come to the door along with her.

"He isn't here now, my husband. Maybe he is in the basement. You can try looking there."

* * *

The basement was reached through a fire door. Michael had never been down in it before; certainly he had no idea that it would be so large, so cavernous. It was well lighted and kept fairly clean, even if it held the damp, musty odor peculiar to subterranean places. But the most astonishing thing about it was the number of paintings, potted plants, and pieces of furniture that were stored here. It was like a gallery operated by a man with profligate and eccentric tastes. There were so many couches, divans, settees, love, seats, high risers, beds, leather chairs, glass coffee tables, kitchen tables, cribs, crutches, cabinets, bureaus, baby carriages, and strollers that they crowded one another out, leaving practically no room to maneuver around them. Michael couldn't imagine where Stopka could possibly fit anything else.

The cellar unfolded itself, revealing yet another room the farther into it Michael went. Paintings—some of them cheap prints, others displaying remarkable workmanship that might actually turn out to be worth something—had been hung all along the plaster walls. A miniature jungle took form wherever Stopka had found space for the towering palms, cacti, philodendrons, Dieffenbachia, and ficus plants that tenants had abandoned when they'd moved out. Or died.

After a while Michael began to notice that there were fewer plants and furnishings and more televisions, radios, tape decks, and VCR's. Maybe he'd been wrong to compare this place to a gallery; it now reminded him more of a department store. Maybe what Mrs. Moskone had told him was true; Stopka might have stolen some of these items for eventual resale. In the confusion of a move, with doors left open and cartons crammed full of goods left unattended, it shouldn't prove too difficult to lift something without anyone's catching on.

For all he knew, one of these VCR's might have belonged to Alan. But that wasn't what he was hoping to find there. It was Alan's computer he was really looking for. Suddenly he picked up on the sound of footsteps behind him. Glancing around, he saw Stopka making his way through the bric-a-brac and furniture, coming in his direction.

"Yes, hello!" he said, his voice bouncing off the high ceilings. "What can I do for you?"

Stopka wasn't a big man, but he was powerfully built, and Michael would never have welcomed a fight with him. Nor was he interested in antagonizing him; that wasn't going to help him get his brother's computer back—if Stopka had, in fact, taken possession of it.

"I see you have quite a collection of things down here, Stopka." Nobody, so far as Michael knew, ever called him Mr. Stopka or even addressed him by his first name.

"Quite a collection, yes, it is," Stopka said, pleased that Michael had credited him with assembling it. "People leave this building, you'd be surprised what they don't want anymore. Maybe you would like to decorate your apartment. You see here anything you like? This painting, maybe?" He pointed to a framed rendering of a martyred saint, possibly Sebastian, bleeding from a dozen arrow wounds.

"Not my taste, really."

Stopka nodded, as if this confirmed in his mind something he'd always believed about Michael. "Anything you see here, you can borrow."

"What if I wanted to buy?"

"Want to buy?" Stopka repeated. He made it sound as if this were a new concept for him. "Maybe. I am selling nice televisions, color, stereo. With VCR. I make you good price."

"What about computers? Do you have any computers?"

Stopka lit up. If he had any suspicion that Michael might be onto him, he failed to show it. "Yes, computers. What kind of computer do you want? Come this way."

He led him into yet another part of the cellar, where a new smell took over. It was noxious and pungent. Michael realized that it must be from the poison laid out for the rats. Stopka unlocked a door and switched on a light.

What were black metal boxes in the gloom revealed

themselves in the light as MacIntoshes, IBM PC Jr.'s, Compaq's, NEC's, Apples, and Ataris: computers, monitors, keyboards, printers, modems. . . . Some of the equipment looked used; much of it, though, seemed barely touched. "My God, Stopka, you ever think of opening a store?"

The super laughed, stroking his chin, happy that he'd managed to impress one of his tenants.

"What type computer you would like? I have everything here." He began to list the brand names, putting special emphasis on IBM and Apple because he obviously expected that those brands would have the most appeal.

"I tell you, Stopka, I'd like to have the same kind of computer my brother Alan had. If possible, I'd like to have the exact same computer Alan had." He tried to make this sound as casual as he could.

Stopka's face darkened; his smile was still in place, but that was only because he'd forgotten to remove it. "Are you accusing Stopka of stealing?"

"Oh, no, Stopka, God forbid. I'm not accusing you of anything. For all I know, Alan might have sold his computer to you because he was interested in buying a more expensive model."

Of course, Michael didn't for one moment believe this scenario. And it was apparent that Stopka didn't think that Michael believed it either. It was such a convenient pretext, however, that Stopka seized on it at once. "Yes, that is possible, maybe he did this. You see, my wife, Maria, one day she tells me out of the blue she has four children. All this time they are waiting for her to send for them in Santo Domingo. Stopka loves his wife, but now this love is getting expensive. My tenants see what I can do for them, they are sorry for me, they wish to help out Stopka. They sell things to me, like these computers, for practically nothing!"

As he went on, his voice began to resonate with growing conviction that what he was saying was actually the truth. Michael didn't think of contradicting him. Producing three crumpled tens—about all he could spare for baksheesh— he said, "If Alan did sell you his computer, maybe you could rent it to me for a day or so. Then I'll give it right back to you."

Casting a covetous eye at the money held out to him, Stopka nodded gravely. "You wait for me in your apartment. I will look, and if I find, I come to you half an hour from now, okay?"

True to his word, Stopka was ringing Michael's bell half an hour later. With a Compaq computer cradled in his arms, he said, "It is a miracle how I find it."

"You're sure this was my brother's?"

"Oh, yes, Stopka is sure."

Stopka had also brought along with him the necessary peripherals to operate the system, which he then proceeded to unpack from Styrofoam-filled cartons.

The computer held a forty-megabite hard disc. What Michael was hoping was that there was something valuable on that disc. It was possible that its memory had been erased or that, lacking the right password, he couldn't access it. A third possibility suggested itself: Maybe there were no records, no trail of documentation that would reveal what had happened to all those millions of dollars his brother had funneled through his accounts.

Once Stopka had gone, Michael sat down at the keyboard, fortifying himself with strong Colombian coffee as the night wore on. To keep himself alert, he realized that another substance from Colombia might be more effective, but coffee was all he had available.

Using a software manual he'd discovered among Alan's books, he managed to bring up the directory—the disc drive's table of contents—on the screen. Over one hundred and fifty files were listed, each coded according to a sequence of letters and numbers Michael was unable to interpret. What was B68DAV, B90DAV, or C10AL supposed to signify? Methodically, he called up each file in turn, trying to make sense of the names and numbers that filled the monitor's screen. His eyes hurt from the strain, and his mind refused to function except in fits and starts. The coffee stopped having any impact except on his bladder. It was two in the morning. It grew later still.

He continued to search for a name, a pattern, something, anything at all that might act as a landmark, provide him with a point by which he could orient himself. But so far he'd come on nothing like that. He had half a mind to give up.

He rose from the table, massaging his stiffening neck, and walked around the room. Whenever he closed his eyes to ease the strain, all he could see was the same hazy greenish light he'd been staring at all night long. Forty-two files done, a hundred-plus to go. It was murder.

Light was beginning to seep into the sky by the time he reached the seventy-ninth file. The first thing that caught his eye was the Nassau, Bahamas, address of Bank Leu, followed by an account number. Several transactions were listed over the last several months. Deposits were for sums never less than fifty thousand dollars and withdrawals for never less than one hundred fifty thousand. As Michael continued to scroll down, he discovered the names of additional banks—all foreign: ANZ Bank, Sydney; Union Bank, Zürich; Midland Bank, London. There were listings of transactions on the Comex in gold, platinum, T-bills, North Sea Brent, and West Texas Intermediate; there was an additional list of nearly sixty transactions on the London, Tokyo, and Hong Kong stock exchanges that involved a bewildering variety of companies—Sun Hung Kai, China Light, Mitsu Chemical, De Beers, Gold Field, Plessey, Nippon Oil. . . .

But what particularly drew his attention was the list of companies and individuals that indicated where the profits generated from all this frantic financial activity had ended up:

3.10 Natchez	rec. $ 8,450.95
3.13 CityVision Cable	rec. $14,445.00
3.13 F. Brice	rec. $ 2,335.00
3.14 Quick Auto	rec. $ 1,010.75
3.17 K. Magnus	rec. $ 5,500.00

The list went on and on. Maybe it wasn't the solution to the riddle of his brother's death, but it was surely a step in the right direction. It was the kind of hard evidence that he'd been driving himself crazy trying to get hold of. It was, goddammit, a beginning. He decided that maybe, after all, New Hampshire could wait.

CHAPTER FOUR

Francis Holmes lived in a residential hotel uptown that was in the same state of genteel decline that its tenants appeared to be suffering from. The hotel's lobby was going to seed, but unhurriedly, almost at a dignified pace. Ancient ladies sat on overstuffed sofas talking in hushed tones, while men, equally ancient, read the morning newspapers, savoring each word for fear that by finishing too quickly, they'd have to confront the emptiness of the day that much sooner. Visitors had to announce themselves at the desk. When Gail arrived, there were no other visitors besides her. She guessed that most of the hotel's occupants no longer knew anybody who wanted to come see them.

It was easy enough for her to avoid the desk and proceed directly to the elevators; the man sitting there was inattentive and stricken with the same terrifying boredom as everyone else in sight.

Gail felt that she would get further with Francis if she took him by surprise. He lived on the fourteenth floor, at the end of a long dingy corridor.

His eyes widened and his mouth gaped open at the sight of her. He seemed to be on the verge of saying, "I'm afraid you must have made a mistake," but for several seconds he was speechless, staring at her. While he obviously recognized her, he seemed incapable of fully absorbing the reality of her presence.

"Dr. Ives?" he said at last, as if he needed to reassure himself that it was truly she.

"I'd like to talk with you if you have a few minutes. May I come in?"

He was wearing a robe, although it was mid-afternoon. The smell of brewing coffee reached her when she entered, confirming her suspicions that he'd just gotten up. It was his day off; there was no need to keep to any schedule.

"How did you find me?" he asked, immediately turning away from her and stepping into the kitchen. Well, it wasn't exactly a kitchen, it was more like a nook with a small gas stove and an even smaller refrigerator.

"Somebody at the M.E.'s office told me where you live."

He mumbled some response that Gail couldn't quite interpret, but it was her impression that he wasn't exactly pleased to learn how free people were with dispensing his address.

Gail had somehow expected Francis's apartment to look like this, meticulously clean and filled with ponderous dark wood furniture that glowed from all the polish that had been applied to it. Not a single plant was in sight. But he did own a small yellow parakeet that observed her silently through the bars of its cage.

Francis came back into the room with only one cup of coffee. He didn't ask whether Gail might like some. His eyes took her in more scrupulously now. Having had the chance to accustom himself to her being in his apartment, he now seemed to be considering what advantage he might be able to draw from it.

"So, Dr. Ives, to what do I owe this . . . this honor?"

She was scared, there was no getting away from it. Friends of hers from her climbing days used to tell her she was fearless, when the truth was that she was just reckless. For years she'd managed to rein herself in, but meeting Michael—becoming entangled with Michael—seemed to have triggered off those old impulses in her. She was a sucker for excitement—that was the problem.

After taking a deep breath, she said, "I wanted to talk to you in private because I think we both may be in trouble."

He gave her a coldly appraising glance. "How so?"

"It's about the Friedlander case. Do you remember the post you did on him? He was brought in as a suicide."

"I can't remember every case I do. I've done thousands of cases." He wasn't denying he remembered, he just wasn't admitting to it.

"Well, there seems to be some problem with the autopsy—in fact, with the whole investigation."

Her throat was dry, her breathing was shallow, and she was certain her anxiety was communicating itself to him. But she kept on, and what came next was the hardest part, the beginning of the roller coaster ride. "I was approached by a man from the Manhattan D.A.'s office. He said that they've gathered evidence that indicates Alan Friedlander didn't commit suicide at all but was murdered. Anyone involved in the case—including the two of us—is being investigated for participating in a cover-up."

Pausing, she looked across the room at Francis, wondering what effect her words had had on him. Though he didn't speak for a moment, she noticed that in setting down his cup on the saucer he spilled some of the coffee. Then he said, "A cover-up? This man from the district attorney's office told you specifically that our office was implicated in a cover-up in the Friedlander case?"

Gail nodded. When she'd rehearsed the story in her mind, it had seemed plausible; it was, after all, a very real possibility. For all she knew, the D.A. *was* conducting an investigation into irregularities at the M.E.'s office.

"Well." Francis rose from his chair. "Would you care for a drink? I would like one. I think I should like one very much. All I can offer you is whiskey. Is that all right?"

She said that whiskey would be fine. Her story, plainly, had gone over.

The first sips of the whiskey put color into his pallid face and relaxed his posture; it seemed to make him come alive. "What did you tell them?" His voice hinted at alarm.

"I said that I stood by my report, but then I went back and looked at my report and found that it had been changed."

"Changed?"

"Changed so that my findings would conform to a determination of suicide."

"I see." He poured out another whiskey for himself. "And do they think that I had anything to do with this . . . this cover-up?"

"I only know that they wanted to talk to you. I thought that I should warn you. I mean, we are in this together."

"Yes, yes," he said abstractedly. He was thinking hard, his eyes closing for a moment, as if the sight of Gail posed a needless distraction. "I've been in the employ of the M.E.'s office for seventeen—nearly eighteen—years now. I have always been scrupulous about my work. Nobody has ever accused me of incompetence. I am good at what I do; I am not incompetent."

"Nobody said you were."

"However, I must say that others in the M.E.'s office are not so scrupulous. They make mistakes because they're careless or lazy or tired. We have had problems, certainly we've had problems—the storage facilities are inadequate, and at least fifty refrigeration compartments aren't functioning. We have criminal elements in our employ who've stolen gold teeth from the deceased. Did you know that?"

Gail had heard rumors of such things, but before this never had them confirmed.

"You work as a resident, don't you? So you must know how easy it is for people to make mistakes, even criminal ones."

His repetition of the word *criminal* interested her. "Yes, I do. It happens much too often."

"Of course, there is a middle ground—a gray area. Honest men can differ. To one, the signs point to a suicide, to another, a murder. I may think one way, but if it is not my case, well, then, I defer to whoever is in charge."

"Particularly if it's Dr. Magnus?"

"Just so. Although . . ." He hesitated.

He was petrified; she could see the fear bright in his eyes. The whiskey was bringing it out in him.

"Although what? Please go on."

"Although last night I saw Dr. Magnus do something that . . . well, to be candid, it jolted me. It really upset me. I shouldn't be telling you this. But perhaps if, as you say, I am to be questioned anyway . . ." He let the words hang.

"What did you see?" She hoped that he was about to reveal information pertaining to the Ambrosetti post.

"Certainly, Dr. Ives, you have witnessed enough procedures yourself to appreciate to what lengths we go to ensure that the deceased is not mutilated or disfigured in any way. The cadaver is treated with dignity; it is one of the principles of our profession."

"I know."

"There was a case brought in late at night. A criminal, a mafioso. I recall seeing his name in the papers. His name is Albinese . . . Geralamo Albinese. There was no question about the cause of death. It was clearly a result of asphyxia. The signs were clear: dusky skin on the head and upper neck, many small hemorrhages on the face, especially in the whites of the eyes. We found evidence, too, of a deep cyanotic congestion of many of the organs. There were hemorrhages of the lungs, heart, brain, stomach, and small intestines. But the most telling sign of all was that the hyoid bone was crushed, and that almost never happens in the absence of strangulation."

"Is that what Dr. Magnus ruled? It was Dr. Magnus who performed the post, wasn't it?"

"Yes, just the two of us." Francis fell abruptly silent. It was difficult for him to question the actions of a man he'd served loyally for so long. It was almost impossible for him to do so openly, with someone he barely knew. More whiskey was necessary before he was ready to continue. "You must understand that sometimes these findings can be tentative, pending lab tests and additional police reports, but his initial determination was that the deceased, Albinese, suffered cardiac arrest and that there was no evidence of any physical injury that would have caused his death."

"There's nothing you saw that would lead you to any other conclusion?"

Francis sadly shook his head. "I couldn't believe that Dr.

Magnus could have overlooked so many obvious signs of asphyxia."

"But you didn't say anything?"

"It is not my case," Francis declared flatly. "It is not my report." That in his own mind must have justified his decision to do nothing. "But . . . but what I was starting to tell you is last night Dr. Magnus did something that was totally out of bounds, absolutely unforgivable!"

He was becoming excited. Rage, which was usually so foreign to him, had the effect of turning his face redder still. His hands fluttered in the air, his thin lips trembled.

"You can't imagine what he did." He paused, looking at her as if he were daring her to guess. Then he said, "He cut out the man's eyes!"

"Cut out the eyes?" She was surprised.

"Such disfigurement is never done. There is almost never any reason for it in an autopsy procedure."

"And why would it be done in this case?" Gail thought she knew but preferred to hear it directly from Francis.

"Because, I assume, that the petechiae, those hemorrhages, in the whites of the eyes provided the most clearly visible evidence that strangulation would have to be the cause of death. Any pathologist could see it plain as day."

"What did he do with the eyes?"

"Why, he placed them in formalin solution. Are you aware that formalin solution has a bleaching action?"

"Which means that the hemorrhages will vanish?"

"Just so."

"Would it be possible to recover those eyes before the formalin bleached the hemorrhages out completely?"

Francis looked baffled by the question. He emptied his glass and then immediately replenished it. Gail had lost count of how many whiskeys he'd had in the last half hour, but it had to be a dangerous amount. "What are you suggesting?" he asked warily.

"If we could get hold of the specimens from the Albinese post—or any specimens from the Friedlander case—it might help us."

"Help us how?"

"With the D.A.'s investigation."

"Ah, yes, the D.A.'s investigation." There was now an unsettling skepticism in his voice. Was it possible that, having bought her story sober, he was now reconsidering its veracity in the light that only a generous dose of whiskey could bring?

"Once Dr. Magnus gets wind that there's an investigation, he'll destroy the evidence—if he hasn't already," Gail said. "What you saw last night should have convinced you of that. But if we can provide the D.A.'s office with the evidence—"

"Make a deal with the state, turn state's evidence ourselves? Is that what you're saying?"

"Yes, that's exactly right."

"And you want me to help you gain . . ." His brow furrowed as he picked out the right word from his increasingly sodden mind. "Access . . . you want me to help you gain access to specimens from the Albinese case, and I suppose from this Friedlander case as well."

"I'd be very grateful if you could. I can't get to them myself, but you have the authority, you know how the system works."

There were specimens from other cases, too, that she would have liked to lay her hands on—Ambrosetti's especially—but she knew enough not to press her luck. Any cooperation from this man would be welcome.

"And you think that in return for my cooperation I might be able to avoid prosecution for complicity in a cover-up?"

Gail was convinced that she had him hooked. "I can't imagine why not. You'd be one of the principal witnesses against Magnus."

"No."

"Excuse me?"

"I won't do it. To begin with, I'm doubtful that the eyes would be useful at this point. The formalin would already have done its worst." He shook his head vigorously.

"What about the Friedlander specimens? I can give you the names of four or five other cases that are probably under investigation."

"Impossible."

"You don't believe me?"

"If there is an investigation, I shall have no choice but to let it run its course. Later, maybe, I will make up my mind. I can't act precipitously." He stood up. "I am not someone who believes in responding according to impulse." He made it sound as if it was a dogma. Maybe for him it was. "Pardon me for a moment." He tottered for a few steps, then recovered and proceeded to the bathroom.

When he came back, he made himself another drink and tossed it back almost immediately. He remained standing, looking expectantly at Gail.

"What is it, Francis?"

"I was thinking . . . possibly I could help you."

"Oh, yes?"

"Yes, perhaps, it might be . . . possible." He was silent for a moment. Then he resumed. "Could I tell you a story?"

Whatever it took, she decided. "Sure."

"I once had a friend who was a Vietnam veteran. He'd served as a medic during the war, and what he told me was that in the army hospitals sometimes when the men were brought in, often in terrible shape, as you can well imagine, barely able to function, often quite paralyzed, the nurses . . . well, they had compassion for these wounded men."

He stopped dead, as if he'd forgotten what he was going to say next. His eyes were fixed on the wall behind Gail, never on her. Then he began again with a quaver in his voice.

"You see, if they had any feeling left—the wounded, I mean—any feeling at all, down, well . . . below the waist, these nurses . . . not all of them, but some of them . . . would at night come and . . . well, help them, feeling that they were deserving of some small pleasure after what they'd been through . . . and what I was thinking was if I were to give you the help you want from me . . . well . . . then if you could show to me the same compassion that those nurses showed for those men, I should be very grateful indeed."

CHAPTER FIVE

Their bodies were so slicked down with sweat from their exertions that Michael could almost believe they were in the process of liquefying. Their breath came rapidly in shallow gasps. For several minutes they lay with their arms around each other, too exhausted to move. He was half in her, half out of her, submerged in fluids. Her hair seemed to be everywhere, pasted by moisture to his skin as well as to hers. Her face was blurred, indistinct, and it wasn't just because he was so close to her or because of the uncertain lighting in the room. Passion seemed to have softened her features, smoothing out any hard edges. Her eyes were luminous and moving over his face, studying him intently.

"What is it?" he asked, unnerved by the steadiness of her gaze.

"Nothing," she replied. "I was just looking at you."

Then she stopped looking, finding the ceiling more interesting. Her breathing was returning to normal. Abruptly disengaging herself, she turned away. Her face disappeared from view.

"Something the matter?" He reached over to her but elicited no response. What was this? How could she be so ardent one moment and then so indifferent the next? The speed and suddenness with which her mood had changed dismayed him, and there was no way he could account for it.

"Michael."

He didn't like the way she pronounced his name; it was like an accusation.

"What? What is it?" He switched positions so that he could see her better.

"I have something I want to show you."

"Sure."

"I wasn't going to . . . because it doesn't matter anymore."

"You're not making any sense." It seemed as if a terrible

weight had been clamped on his chest; each word he ut-
tered was a strain. Something was about to happen any second now—something bad. He knew that with an amazing
clarity. He wanted desperately to do something to stop it,
but it was beyond his control. He knew that, too.

She slipped on the T-shirt that an hour before had been
flung in a frenzied haste to the floor, and got out of bed. She
was gone from the room for less than a minute. When she returned, it was with a jar.

The overhead light she snapped on blotted out his vision
for an instant. When he could regain the use of his eyes, he
discovered that he was looking at a specimen of some kind.
He realized it was a brain floating in solution, gelatinous
and grayish-pink, but badly damaged, with much of the rear
portion missing altogether.

Michael lifted his eyes to inspect Gail's face. Her expression was impassive, unreadable. He could not believe how
desirable he found her.

"It's Alan's?" He glanced back down at the jar. It surprised
him that he didn't feel anything. This wasn't Alan anymore;
this wasn't even a part of Alan, it was just a specimen—a vital piece of evidence. This could not be the bad thing he
sensed was coming.

"How did you get hold of it?"

"That's not important," she said curtly. "It doesn't matter
how I got it. I got it, that's all." Lowering her head so that he
could no longer see her eyes, she said bitterly, "It doesn't
mean shit."

"What do you mean? Gail, what is it?" He was astonished
that she'd extended herself so much on his behalf; he
wanted to hold her, to somehow make it clear to her how
grateful he was.

"It's not Alan's brain. It was labeled 'Alan Friedlander,' but
it's not his. I examined it. There were two bullet wounds, not
one. They substituted it, don't you see? It's useless as a piece
of evidence."

It didn't surprise him. Since Magnus had shown no compunction about tampering with reports and evidence in the past, why should he act differently in this case? He wasn't nearly as disappointed as Gail seemed to be.

"We've still got the information I found on Alan's computer. That's something. It's not like we're back where we started."

In fact, he was so afraid of losing the material that he'd downloaded the entire list of transactions onto a floppy disc that he carried with him everywhere. He didn't want to lose it the way he'd lost the tape.

But either Gail hadn't understood the potential significance of the financial record Michael had discovered, or else she didn't care one way or another.

"Michael," she said again, resting the specimen on the bed table, "I have to tell you something."

This, he had a feeling, was where it became very bad. The tone of her voice told him what must be coming next. Bile rose into his throat, and fear silenced him. He could only wait helplessly to hear what she had to say.

"I can't go on," she said almost in a whisper. "I wish I could—God, do I wish I could." She sat down on the bed, but almost on the edge of it, widening her distance from him. His eyes were held by the revelation of her body by the light filtering through the fabric of the T-shirt. Painfully, his weary cock was becoming erect again.

He found his voice. "Go on? Go on with what? I don't understand."

"I'm getting in too deep with you, Michael. I'm doing things I don't want to, things that disgust me."

"Like what? Gail, come on, please tell me."

She was shaking her head and scattering strands of hair over her face. "I can't talk about it now. But listen to me, please, Michael, try to understand." When she turned her face toward him, he could see her eyes, and how much pain was in them. She seemed to be gathering her will. It was tough for her. For an instant he forgot his own pain and let his heart go out to her.

"What? Tell me, Gail, what?"

He grasped hold of her hands.

"I don't want to see you again, Michael. I sometimes think I love you, and maybe if this wasn't all happening we could make something work between us. But it *is* happening, you see, and I can't stand it. I just can't live like this anymore." Her eyes found the gruesome specimen.

"You don't have to, Gail, sweetheart, you don't have to be involved. It's my problem, let me deal with it. Just don't leave me. I need you."

"You don't need me," she said willfully. "You do surprisingly well on your own, really. This is your trip, Michael. I can't be a part of it, and no matter what you say, you will always try to make me a part of it. It has to end."

It wasn't love that they had made, then, he thought, it was more in the way of a good-bye fuck.

A long, painful silence had fallen between Michael and Gail. He didn't know what to say, and it seemed she didn't either. Then, when the silence became too unbearable, she said, "Please go, Michael, please go now."

She wasn't crying. He might have taken heart if there had been tears, but she was composed enough to see this through. And if she intended on doing any crying, she was damned if she was going to allow him to see it.

Just as he reached the door, racking his mind frantically for some words to say that could set things right or at least exact from her hope that she might change her mind, the phone rang. The real world was intruding, shutting out Michael even more. He tried to hear what she was saying, but her voice was muffled, confidential. He imagined that it was another man on the phone, a prospective lover, somebody who wouldn't complicate her life any further, somebody who was just fun to be around. He realized it was stupid to hang on there. The words he wanted to say to her wouldn't come; they might not even have existed. While he still could, he moved. He opened the door and walked out.

Chapter Six

They were headed downtown, weaving through ill-lit streets that would eventually lead to the river. No one would tell her where they were going, though, or just how soon they would arrive at their destination.

Gail knew that whatever she was letting herself in for, it couldn't possibly lead to anything good. She should have refused Magnus when he called, had nothing more to do with him. Why, then, was she sitting next to him in his car—or someone's car, a sleek gray Cadillac driven by a man she'd never seen before?

What compulsion held her in sway like this? It wasn't going to end with Michael, she knew that. Apparently she had adopted Michael's cause as her own. In a way that she couldn't quite fathom, it had to do with William and the malign fate that had sent him crashing down the mountain to his death. She wanted to scream, to hit somebody, to leave town. But instead she was there with Magnus.

His face was haggard and pale except for a ragged band of red on his brow where the sun had burned him. Nicks were conspicuous on his neck where the shaving had not gone well. Gail could tell that he was struggling to maintain appearances, to keep himself under control.

"I know what you've been up to, Gail," Magnus was saying to her. He was no longer doing her the courtesy of calling her Dr. Ives. Apparently they were beyond that now.

"Oh, I see."

Her eyes were on the street, not on Magnus. The driver was now taking them along Fourteenth Street, picking up speed the farther west he got.

"I know that you took those case records from the M.E.'s office."

There was no particular rancor in his voice, and it didn't seem as if he was accusing her. He was just making a statement of fact.

"I know you went to Francis Holmes," he continued.

She shot a questioning look at him, thinking to read in his eyes what he might have discovered about their meeting. But his eyes gave nothing away.

"And I also know that he helped you to remove certain specimens from the M.E.'s office without authorization."

Gail would have preferred that he express his indignation, that he threaten her with judicial proceedings. She understood that there had to be some sort of reckoning. She'd rather it be now so she could get it over with. That was one of the reasons she'd agreed to accompany Magnus—to get the damned thing over with. But it seemed more that he just wanted to make certain points clear to her, maybe with an eye to laying the groundwork for what came next.

And what, she wondered, did come next, exactly? At Washington Street they turned downtown. It was very late on a quiet, muggy night, and there was hardly any traffic.

"Have I said anything that isn't true?"

"No," she said, thinking that she must have been an ass to believe that she could have escaped with impunity. The thought occurred to her that maybe she didn't want to. Was it possible that she'd wanted to be found out?

"I know that you can't think much of me," Magnus went on.

She had to keep in mind that whatever she'd done could scarcely begin to compare with the criminal acts for which he'd been responsible. It was just that he had the power and influence to avoid the consequences, and she did not.

At the moment she thought she would have liked to hear music—something upbeat and danceable. It would have cut through the lugubrious atmosphere. But the driver continued in silence.

"I like you, Gail. I want you to know that. I don't hold anything against you for what you did to me. I think that if I were in your position, if I were your age and in love—"

"I didn't do anything for love, Dr. Magnus. I did it because I wanted to. For myself."

The defiance in her voice startled him. "Whatever your motivation was, it isn't relevant now, Gail. What I'm asking you to do is try and understand that nothing is quite so black and white as you may imagine. There are things at stake that you have no idea about. By insinuating yourself in this situation, you've only made things that much harder. You haven't helped anybody."

"What happens now?"

"Now?" The question seemed to surprise him. "Now you will assist me one last time in your capacity as medical investigator. When that is done, you will of course return the specimens and any copies of any records you took from the M.E.'s office and make no further mention of these cases."

"And that's it?"

"That is it. I don't think that it would profit either of us to involve the police, do you?"

"I guess not. But—"

"But what?"

"But why do you want me to help you on this case? There are other more experienced investigators you could bring in."

He gave her a thoughtful look. "Because your education isn't finished yet."

They were only a couple of blocks from the Hudson River now; it was just visible at the end of the street. It was a street as empty of people as it was of traffic. The buildings in view looked uninhabited, their windows almost uniformly dark. Either everyone was away for the summer or else they were asleep.

Gail was expecting to be greeted by the sight of squad cards and ambulances, with a full complement of police keeping the curious at bay. But there was no sign of a police presence at all. Magnus, his gaze fixed squarely ahead, ignored the look of puzzlement she cast him. But he must have known what she was thinking.

Once they got out of the car, Gail followed Magnus up the steps to the vestibule of a six-story apartment building. A sign was posted to discourage the distribution of takeout Chinese menus. Another sign alerted tenants to the times when they should leave their garbage out for pickup. The door leading into the building was open. "We're going up to the fifth floor," Magnus said.

The smell caught up with them by the time they reached the fourth floor. It was a smell that was familiar, yet mysterious at the same time, poisonous and sweet. It was not just that it was a smell of decomposing flesh, something to which Gail was accustomed. It was different this time—it was the smell that only human flesh could have when it has been put to a fire and burned.

CHAPTER SEVEN

The door was already ajar, perhaps because the medical examiner's arrival was expected. Pale light trickled out through the gap. Gail detected voices of two men inside. They must have heard their steps in the hallway, for now the door opened wider, and a good-looking man—smartly dressed in an expensive-looking white jacket and matching slacks—appeared in the light. A gold necklace shone at the base of his neck.

"What's she doing here?" he asked.

A broad-shouldered man, with a bullet-shaped head, nowhere as nicely dressed, stepped up behind him.

"From what you told me over the phone, I knew I couldn't handle this on my own, Ray. I needed an assistant." He turned toward Gail. "This is Dr. Ives."

Though he may have been put out at seeing her, the man quickly bridged the distance separating them, extended his hand, and offered her a practiced smile. "Ray Fontana," he said. "A pleasure."

So this was Ray Fontana. What would he be doing there? She avoided his gaze, afraid of showing any sign of recognition.

Fontana's insouciant attitude was amazing. He was acting as if they were at a cocktail party, not at an abandoned apartment pervaded by the smell of scorched flesh. He gestured behind him to his companion. "Kurt, I believe you and Max have met."

Magnus gave Max a strange look and nodded. Gail recalled that she'd heard about this man from Michael as well. What was going on here? It was obvious that she wasn't going to be let off as lightly as Magnus had led her to believe.

"It's a fucking mess in there," Farrell said. "Never saw anything like it."

As they followed the two men farther inside, Gail whispered to Magnus, "Where are the cops? These men aren't cops, are they?"

Magnus slowly shook his head. "Later maybe we can talk," he said quietly. "Right now we do what we would do in any investigation."

Only at that moment did Gail understand how really powerless Magnus was. All this time she'd been looking on him as the source of corruption, the manipulator, the seducer. But now she saw that he was a pawn as well, another player in someone else's game, not unlike herself, and she was strangely moved.

They found themselves in a room of immense whiteness. This whiteness was disturbed only by streaks of blood; still drying, they trailed over the walls and the wood floor like a road map of some unknown territory.

"How did you find out about this?" Magnus asked.

"Owner of the building contacted the police," Fontana said.

"And just where are the police?" Magnus pressed him.

"The case is under Kohler's jurisdiction," Fontana replied, as if that should explain everything.

"And Kohler wouldn't make a move without checking with you," Magnus said, filling in the blanks.

Fontana allowed a smile to settle in on his face; further affirmation wasn't required. His eyes were trained on Gail, who couldn't help but pick up on the exchange.

"Where's the owner now?"

"It's none of your concern, Kurt. We're taking good care of

him. Why don't you just get on with it, and then we can all get the hell out of here."

Gail looked from one man to another. A thousand questions flashed through her mind, but she knew enough to keep silent. Magnus motioned to her. It seemed that he had an idea as to what awaited them. "The smell," he said to Gail.

"What about it—except that it's godawful?"

"Most of the victims are young."

"How do you know that?"

"The young putrefy more quickly—less body fat."

Then they got on with it.

In contrast to the spanking whiteness that dominated the decor of the front room, the rest of the apartment was practically buried in darkness. What few lights there were, were naked bulbs—energy savers with odd wattage: twenty-three watts, forty-one watts, sixty-seven watts.

As soon as Gail stepped into the passageway leading off the front room, she felt her feet dig into a thick, gooey substance that she thought at first must be gum. But even in the dim lighting she could see that the substance couldn't possibly by gum—not any kind of gum with which she was acquainted. It was yellowish, the color of consommé soup. There were small chunks of something embedded in it, more of them the farther down the passageway they went. Then Gail realized what they were—bits and pieces of a human being.

Magnus identified the substance. "Melted body fat," he said, almost with a certain wonder in his voice.

They found the first body in a room off to the left. It was a room infested with fleas, roaches, maggots, and flies too sated on the remains to trouble to move at their approach. It was also knee-deep in litter: syringes, torn mattresses, shredded clothes, yellowed newspapers, hat boxes, nylons, panty hose, and the uneaten remains of a meal that might have been only a day or two old. It was, Gail noted, a takeout order from a Chinese restaurant.

The body was a female. Headless and armless. Her legs were intact, though, and splayed in a posture that suggested sexual intercourse. Magnus made a hurried inspection. He asked Gail to take notes while he dictated, his voice authoritative and emotionless.

"Fingertip bruises are present on both thighs. More bruises can be observed along the muscles around the entrance to the vagina. A ball of pubic hair is present at the top of the vagina, which could only have been carried to the site by the insertion of either a penis or a finger. There is no question that force was used during intercourse, but it's likely that the deceased consented at first."

"Why do you say that?"

"You'll observe that the outer sides of the calves are soiled. That indicates that she'd been lying with her legs flat on the floor and wide apart. The positioning of the legs and the soiling that resulted suggest that at first there was no resistance.

"Put down that the body is too maggot-ridden to obtain swabs of semen, but that I am removing six strands of hair from the vaginal region for analysis."

They continued with their grisly survey. A large black trunk in the corner under the window yielded easily to the pressure that Magnus applied. Once opened, it revealed additional remains: the organs of a human chest and abdomen, removed in a single mass, along with several large pieces of skin and muscle. Magnus had only to give a cursory glance before announcing, "We might never know who this was. Even the sex is impossible to identify."

In yet another room, somewhat smaller in size, they came upon a pelvic bone with which Magnus had more luck. A telltale groove in it meant that it was female. But unless he was able to find other bones that he could match it to with any certainty, the identity of the woman might forever be unknown. Gail, in leaving the room, accidentally knocked over a blue hat box; it turned out to contain a filmy pink nightgown that might have come from Frederick's of Hollywood. There were, in addition, at least twenty pieces of flesh turned the color of rust from decay.

It got worse, if that was possible, when they entered the kitchen. On the stove lay a saucepan half filled with a reddish fluid that wasn't quite the color of blood. A layer of grease floated on top of it. With a pair of prongs Magnus lifted out of it a piece of boiled human bone. Some of its flesh was still clinging to it.

The air was stifling, and Gail tried to throw open a window, only to find that it was nailed shut. By tearing at the cloth that had been used to block the sunlight, Gail succeeded in exposing a view to the outside. But the only thing to see was an airshaft, a brick wall coated with soot.

In some way, Gail sensed that for all the gore and terror that this apartment held, Magnus felt safe carrying out his work, exercising his skill at coaxing secrets from these mutilated remains. For this was his dominion, this was his place in the world. It was with the people who were alive that he was all at sea.

Opening the refrigerator, Magnus exposed seven green plastic trash bags and a carton of Half-and-Half. For some reason he examined the label on the Half-and-Half. "Expired," he said.

Then he cut a slit into one of the bags with a knife. "Bones," he observed. He opened a second. "More bones."

Turning back to Gail, he asked her to inspect the contents of a large bulky green duffel bag propped up against the wall near the sink. The thing weighed a ton, and it was all she could do to move it so she could take a look inside it.

It didn't surprise her to find still more body parts. They were all recognizably human—sawed but not boiled. Magnus lifted them out one by one. All together, there were five parts, all belonging to one woman, amputated at the shoulders and hip joints. The uterus was enlarged; she had been pregnant.

At the bottom of the bag Magnus found a cookie tin containing several human organs that, by some trick of the lighting or Gail's wearying eyesight, seemed to be moving. She hastily put the cover back on, a gesture that Magnus failed to notice because his attention was now diverted by Max Farrell's appearance.

"There's something we want you to take a look at," Farrell said.

It would seem that they'd seen enough already; it was hard to imagine that there could be more.

They walked back out into the hallway. Seeing them, Fontana slid open a black metal panel on the wall. "The incinerator," he said.

Using a flashlight, Magnus peered inside. Gail, directly behind him, could make out an abundant heap of ash from which hundreds, possibly thousands, of splinters of calcinated bone stuck out. "We might be able to reconstitute some of these bones for identification purposes," Magnus said.

"Forget it," Fontana told him.

Magnus glanced up at him in bewilderment. "What do you mean, forget it?"

"I don't give a shit who these people were. They're dead; they don't count anymore."

"But we've got to try to make an I.D. of these victims. It's the least we can do," Magnus protested.

Fontana wouldn't hear of it. "I remember a time, Kurt, when you weren't so hot on the idea of anyone making a positive I.D."

This cryptic reference was lost on Gail, but it had the immediate effect of silencing Magnus.

"What I'd like you to do, Kurt, is for you and . . ."—he turned his gaze back on Gail—". . . your assistant here to gather up any evidence in that apartment you can that will help us find the motherfucker who did this shit."

"What happens if you do find him?" Magnus said.

"That's my business, not yours, Kurt," Fontana said. "I'd have thought that you'd be able to figure out the distinction after all this time."

CHAPTER EIGHT

Gail couldn't sleep. What dreams—what nightmares—might be lurking in ambush for her she didn't want to find out. The horror that she'd witnessed sooner or later must slip into her unconscious. Sometimes she wondered what she was losing by desensitizing herself so much of the time. But what other choice did she have if she was to carry out her work?

But whatever defenses she had relied on to get through the ordeal began to crumble as soon as she returned to the solace of her own home. She was shaking all over, and the Absolut she drank didn't help to stop it. Twice now she'd gone to the bathroom, certain that she was going to be violently ill, but she'd been unable to throw up.

She decided on a long bath, but no matter how much she'd scrubbed and soaked she still felt soiled, contaminated. There was no way to wash away what needed to be washed away.

Little by little she began to understand what had happened. Himself tainted by guilt and facing criminal charges should the cover-up collapse, Magnus had co-opted her. He had in effect made her into his accomplice by insisting that she aid him in securing evidence that should belong to the police. She was not just a witness but a participant. A court of law would find her as guilty of tampering with evidence and withholding information from the police as Magnus was. It was his way of ensuring her silence.

So it was no wonder that Magnus had exhibited so little concern; all he'd done, in fact, was to remind her to say nothing about the incident. And certainly she was aware of Fontana's reputation; she'd seen for herself what had happened to Ambrosetti. Yet, all the same, how could she go on as if nothing had happened?

How the hell was she going to get herself out of this mess? As powerful as the temptation was, she resisted the idea of calling Michael and asking for his help. This was her problem, and she would handle it one way or another. More Absolut seemed essential to make her decision. Finally she knew what she had to do. The following morning she would go to the police and tell them what she knew. It might lead to jail, to turning state's evidence, to testifying against Magnus and Fontana and putting herself in danger. But she had to do it; she couldn't live like this. The roller coaster ride was far from over.

CHAPTER NINE

What Fontana wanted Magnus to do was practically impossible, especially in the short time allotted. First Magnus had to separate out from the hundreds of specimens they'd gathered at the apartment only those that might lead to identifying the killer. Given the absence of all the evidence he was obliged to leave behind, it was likely to be a hopeless task. Even by sifting through all the tissue, blood types, clothes, hair follicles, scrapings, rotten food, and assorted vials and bottles, he doubted he would come up with any usable clues to the Chopper's identity.

Worse, he had to work alone, sequestering himself in his laboratory on the fifth floor. He couldn't risk anyone else in the M.E.'s office getting wind of what he was up to. He'd have to mislabel whatever specimens and samples of blood he needed to have analyzed so as not to alert the lab technicians about what he was actually engaged in.

He worked himself ragged through the night, aware that he was probably making careless mistakes, his inattentiveness due as much to panic as it was to exhaustion. He knew that he mustn't let himself think about the implications of what he was doing. There was no question that Fontana had a plan in which this psychopath had a role to play. But Magnus didn't want to ask; he was terrified of finding out.

After several hours of painstaking investigation he raised his eyes and glanced out the window, astonished to see that it was already morning. The sky was gray, and a drizzle was falling. It was ten to eight.

Relying on the previous matches he'd already made using the comparison microscope, Magnus finally collected twenty-eight hair follicles, all of which came from the same head of hair, and another fifteen pubic hairs, taken from swabs of three victims, all of which also formed a perfect match. While even a single hair follicle had been known to solve a crime, Magnus wasn't convinced that these specimens, any more than the ones they'd previously taken, would lead to the killer in this instance. And how much good would it do to know that the killer had type-A blood? It was something, but with a man this elusive, this cunning, Magnus wondered.

Nor was it much use to make a comparison of dental plates until a suspect was actually taken into custody. Once there was someone to match them to, Magnus had collected enough bite marks to make a positive I.D. What struck him particularly were the shapes of these marks; they were invariably the same: all elliptical, all love bites.

But from among the gruesome souvenirs recovered from the apartment on West Twelfth Street, Magnus did uncover a few articles of interest. One was a scorched shred of paper with an anatomical diagram of an arm and a trunk with words in Chinese. Arrows pointing to different parts of the anatomy appeared to indicate pressure points. It was the sort of diagram that someone interested in medicine or versed in the martial arts might keep around the house. The perpetrator's ability to overcome his victims, even younger men in good shape, might be accountable to an intimate knowledge of a human being's vulnerabilities—physical and otherwise.

That things Chinese might figure prominently in the killer's life was borne out by the discovery of three small bottles of Chinese medicine—Wanling Ointment for insect bites and skin irritation; Tujin Liniment, recommended for scabies and itchy toes; and Chung Wan Hung from the Tientsin Drug Manufactory, suggested for the relief of burns. In addition, Magnus found a mysterious substance that in color and smell was vaguely reminiscent of soy sauce; he suspected that it might have some kind of medicinal property as well.

Of the three labeled bottles, the killer had made most liberal use of the Chung Wan Hung. Magnus could only conclude that the Chopper, in his haste to burn the remains, had burned himself. He would advise Fontana to look for a man who had received serious burns, probably on his hands and wrists, and who was also a student of martial arts on an advanced level. And he would recommend that Fontana begin his search in Chinatown.

Having managed to determine this much about the killer, Magnus was pleased with himself. The pride he took in his accomplishment, however briefly, overshadowed the furtiveness with which he was compelled to execute it. It saddened him, though, to realize that no one else, certainly not Fontana, would ever appreciate the nature of his achievement.

When Magnus descended to the ground floor, nobody expressed any surprise at seeing him. He often worked through the night; it was nothing to provoke comment. Even his harried appearance was unlikely to cause a stir. Magnus knew that there were rumors floating through the office about him. People said that his health was seriously deteriorating, that he was on medication and that the puffiness in the face was from the cortisone he was taking. Others ascribed his exhaustion and distracted behavior to family problems and insinuated that a divorce might be in the works. But nothing had reached him so far to cause him serious alarm, nothing to suggest that anybody suspected him of meeting every few weeks or so in his private john with Farrell or Sam bringing him several thousand dollars in unmarked bills.

In the privacy of his own office, he put in a call to the Fontana Security Agency. It was Farrell who took the call. Apparently Fontana wasn't available. Magnus found it gratifying that Farrell should still have no idea that he was fucking his daughter. If he didn't have much power, at least he had that. It was something to hold on to.

When Magnus finished briefing Farrell on the results of his findings, Farrell said, "Ray says to tell you thanks and that you're to expect a message from a friend. It should be there any time now."

With that he hung up, leaving Magnus to wonder what kind of message—and what kind of friend—Fontana was referring to. He could only imagine that it must be money.

Money, aside from what it could buy, once had the capacity to lift his spirits. Just the act of taking possession of it was enough to get him through the darkest of days. Now, he realized, the prospect of getting more money no longer excited him. It was a need, a hunger, that must continuously be sated, but he couldn't muster any enthusiasm for it anymore.

He was on his way out the door of his office when one of the forensic pathologists rushed over to him. Though he'd appointed the man himself, Magnus could never remember how to pronounce his name. It was Nagayama or Nakayama, something like that. When he spoke, his cadence and his pronunciation made him sound as though he were still speaking Japanese, although it was apparent his words were in English. At first all that Magnus could make out was that a case demanded his urgent attention in one of the autopsy rooms, and that he had better come take a look.

As Nagayama or Nakayama continued talking, Magnus determined that the case involved a gunshot wound to the head, a possible suicide victim.

The cadaver was lying on an examining table, draped from head to toe by a sheet. Magnus stepped over to it and lifted the sheet. His heart skipped a beat, then exploded into a dangerously accelerated rhythm. His throat dried up, and he didn't seem able to breathe. Now he understood what Fontana had meant by his enigmatic message. The message hadn't been about money. The message was the cadaver right in front of him—Francis Holmes. He was the message and he was the friend.

CHAPTER TEN

Detective Jim Graczyk might have been capable of expressing astonishment, but there was no indication of it now as Gail proceeded to relate her story. Mild skepticism was about the only reaction she seemed to be evoking.

A man in his mid-thirties, a few years younger than

Michael, who wore his hair probably as long as police regulations permitted, Graczyk struck Gail as a man who was more comfortable dealing with felonies—robberies, car thefts, stickups—than he was with conspiracies. Every so often he'd look up from the notes he was making, his pen racing across the paper, to stare at Gail as if he couldn't quite believe what he was hearing.

Graczyk was particularly insistent on getting down details that related not to Magnus or Fontana, but to her own life. How long had she been working at Bellevue? How long had she been employed on a per diem basis at the medical examiner's office? Was she married? What had happened to her husband? They were questions she believed to be entirely irrelevant to the matter at hand.

But gradually she discerned why Graczyk was probing her background to such an extent; the allegations she had brought to him were so incredible, so outrageous, that he wanted to pin down what type of individual he was dealing with; he needed some way of assessing her credibility. It was hard to say whether she'd convinced him of her credentials.

"This man Fontana . . ." Graczyk lowered his eyes to his notes to make sure that he'd gotten the name right. "What I don't understand is the role he plays in all this."

Again Gail attempted to explain. The more she told the story, the less he seemed to believe her. Maybe, she reasoned, he was looking for holes, looking for a way of exposing her as mentally unstable so that he could dismiss her and get on with more pressing business.

"I told you before," she said with mounting irritation, "Fontana's the man who's organizing the cover-up."

"And you're saying the chief medical examiner takes his orders from this individual Fontana?"

It was never Magnus; it was "the chief medical examiner."

"Yes."

"And while you were present at this fifth-floor apartment on West Twelfth Street, you never saw any police officers?"

"Not at any time while I was there."

"Which was for how long, Dr. Ives?"

"Approximately an hour."

"When you left, did Mr. Fontana and Mr. Farrell leave with you?"

"No, they remained behind. Only Dr. Magnus went with me."

Graczyk wrote this down, although it seemed to Gail that he'd already recorded this information. "So it's possible that police officers arrived at the scene later."

"I doubt it. You must have a way of checking with the Sixth Precinct. In any case, something like this would have been on TV and in all the papers by now, don't you think?"

One of the problems, she realized, was that the very enormity of the horror—the bones in the freezer, the body parts in the trunk and duffel bag—made it more difficult to convey.

"And you are convinced that this mayhem you witnessed was the work of the so-called Chopper. Have I got that straight?"

"There's no question it was the Chopper."

"Have you discussed this incident further with the chief medical examiner?"

"No. We separated as soon as we left the building."

"Didn't he say anything to you at all?"

"That I should act responsibly and look out for myself."

"Those were his words?"

"More or less."

"And what did you take these words to mean, Dr. Ives?"

"I took them to mean that I should keep quiet about what I saw, that I shouldn't be doing what I'm doing now."

"But he didn't threaten you in any way, did he?"

"Not directly. But I sensed a threat."

"From the chief medical examiner?"

"No, from Fontana and the men who work for him."

"Fontana," Graczyk said, a certain exasperation in his voice. He didn't seem to know what to make of this man he'd clearly never heard of.

"Stay here for a minute, please," he said. He left her sitting in his cubicle surrounded by his cigarette smoke.

A few minutes later he came back. "You're right," he said. "According to the dispatcher at the Sixth Precinct, there's no record logged in of any visit by police to the West Twelfth Street apartment you described. There's no record of a U-sixty-one."

"A what?"

"That's a form that's filed any time we receive a complaint. If the owner of this building notified the police, there should be a U-sixty-one on it."

"So you see what I'm saying, then?"

"This doesn't confirm your story, Dr. Ives," he said. "The only way we can do that is obtain a warrant to inspect the premises."

"How long would that take?"

"It depends. I'm not certain that we would be able to obtain a warrant on the strength of your statement. But if someone like the super or the owner will let us in, that would be a different story. Do you know whether anyone will be available to open up for us?"

Gail said she had no idea.

"Well, why don't we drive over there and see?"

Obviously Detective Graczyk wasn't expecting anything out of the ordinary; he didn't even think it necessary to bring along another officer. "If something happens, I just radio in and I'll have all the backup I need in a minute," he assured her.

Gail had a feeling that if he hadn't found her attractive, as he apparently did, he might not have consented to go even this far in checking out her story. He seemed to be humoring her.

Long before they reached the West Twelfth Street address, she began to suffer from heart palpitations. Her stomach, though she'd put nothing in it, was in turmoil. She was more afraid now than she had been the night before with Magnus. It was worse now because she knew what to expect.

They pulled to a stop in front of the building. Without a word Graczyk got out and advanced up the steps, entering the vestibule. It was remarkable how undistinguished the building looked in the dreary morning light—it was anything but sinister. That people were carrying on with the routine business of their daily lives—walking dogs, wheeling strollers, and riding their bikes—only served to emphasize the prosaic nature of the setting.

Hesitantly Gail followed Graczyk into the building. She was beginning to think that she was all wrong about this. Although Graczyk had at no point insinuated that she might be guilty of any criminal action, she wondered now what would happen to her when he actually laid eyes on the hideous spectacle.

Graczyk was scanning the names under the bells. Most of the bells had no names under them at all. "You say there's no super on the premises."

"I got the impression that there wasn't. As I told you, they mentioned an owner, but I don't know where he lives."

Graczyk nodded, as if he wasn't expecting much in the way of concrete information from her. He pushed against the door leading into the building. Finding it open, he walked in.

As soon as they were at the fourth-floor landing, Gail asked him if he noticed the smell. It didn't seem quite as bad as it had last night, but it was still present.

But Graczyk said only, "I don't know. It smells crummy, but that's nothing. A lot of these old buildings smell crummy."

On the fifth floor she pointed out the apartment to him. "It's the door straight ahead of you."

Graczyk knocked, waited, knocked again. When no answer was forthcoming, he glanced back at Gail, shrugged, and tried the door. It opened, no problem. "Hello!" he called out. "Hello! Anybody here?"

His words echoed hollowly in the empty room. Opening the door wider, he stepped in. Gail was right behind him.

"You sure this was the place?"

The room was just as white as she remembered it, but now it was immaculate. The walls gleamed. There was another smell she became aware of besides the residual smell of death—it was the smell of fresh paint.

She rushed into the darkened passageway, searching out any sign of the carnage she and Magnus had plumbed through twelve hours previously. But the rooms were all spotless, all freshly painted. Graczyk, following her, looked more and more puzzled, even faintly annoyed.

The duffel bag was gone, the trunk was gone, and the refrigerator was empty save for two trays of ice. It was as if neither the victims nor their murderer had ever existed.

Although she couldn't be certain—her memory was indistinct, confused—she thought that the walls looked different. It seemed that they'd been plastered over. Lowering her eyes, she saw that the floor was tiled and she was sure—almost sure, anyway—that this hadn't been the case on her last visit. But what was she going to do? Start taking the place apart?

Graczyk was leaning against the kitchen wall, waiting for an explanation. But how could Gail explain that once there had been a past, and now that past was no more?

CHAPTER ELEVEN

The day was lost in drizzle and fog that erased the tops of the World Trade Center; the damp atmosphere leached the color out of everything until the whole world seemed composed of varying shades of gray. By early afternoon Fontana and Farrell had found their way to 69A Bayard Street in Chinatown. The shop located at that address did not identify itself in English, only in Chinese. Evidently the proprietors felt that little business could be expected from English-speaking customers. The shelves were crammed with Chinese medicines, herbs, laxatives, ointments, liniments, lotions, and teas—a whole exotic pharmacopeia intended to cure ills and ailments, some of them so rare that neither Fontana nor Farrell had ever heard of them.

But this was the only shop they'd found that carried Wanling Ointment, Tujin Liniment, and Chung Wan Hung. Fontana stepped up to the counter, which was tended by a middle-aged woman who offered him a quizzical smile.

"Do you know a nice-looking man, American, very soft-spoken, about thirty or so, who comes in here pretty regularly? He calls himself Dan or Daniel."

The description Fontana gave her had been supplied to him by the owner of the building at 358 West Twelfth Street, a thin, tremulous man whose cooperation was ensured as much by fear as it was by the cash that Fontana had lavished on him. The man they were looking for, according to the landlord, had never caused any trouble; he was quiet, unassuming, always very polite on the few occasions they had met. He paid his rent on time, was helpful to old ladies, and was known to have watched children while their mothers went out on errands during the day. The most exceptional thing about him, the landlord said, was his exquisite looks. He claimed that it was almost impossible to take one's eyes off him, making certain to add that he "didn't go that way," and had contempt for those who did.

After a moment or two of contemplative silence, the woman nodded and said something that might have been English or might have been Chinese; Fontana wasn't sure which.

Fontana looked at Max. Max shrugged. "Beats me what she said."

"Probably thinks we want to buy some of this crap." It was clear to Fontana that there was no use in trying to question this woman further about Daniel. He decided on another approach. Fontana produced the sample of the unidentified liquid that gave off a smell like soy sauce that Magnus had provided him. "Do you sell this here?"

The woman made a face, shaking her head.

Speaking slowly, clearly enunciating each syllable, he asked, "Do you know of any karate or kung fu school near here?"

This much at least the woman comprehended. "Kung fu, karate, yes," she said, nodding her head vigorously, smiling triumphantly now that she had finally caught on to what these two gentlemen wanted.

She came from around the counter and led them to the door of the shop. "Up there, you turn, okay? You go Pell Street, okay? This number, okay?" She scribbled 131 down on a piece of pink paper and thrust it into Fontana's hand. "Okay?"

"Okay, thanks very much," Fontana said, wondering whether they were actually getting somewhere.

"Yes, I think I know who you are talking about," said the man who greeted Fontana and Farrell at the Pell Street address. The floor and the walls trembled with the vibration of students advancing back and forth behind the flimsy partition, practicing their kicks, blocks, and punches, crying out every so often as they reduced their imaginary opponents to shreds.

"Does he study here?"

"No, I think not. This is a Northern Praying Mantis School. We emphasize kicking here. I think he does not feel that we can meet his needs. Perhaps you will try the Southern Praying Mantis School. This school you can find at Fifteen Doyers Street."

It was raining harder. They were getting soaked, but Fontana scarcely noticed. Nothing worked to mobilize him quite as much as a pursuit. Nothing gave him the lift; at no other time did he feel so alive.

The building they were looking for was practically next door to the Hip Kee Beauty Salon, where men in white jackets were busily cutting and setting hair. An open doorway beckoned; they ascended a set of stairs to the second floor, where they were again greeted by the rhythmic stomping of feet and the sharp guttural cries that punctuated the completion of each sequence of moves.

"This is it, I have a feeling," Fontana said. Noting the dubious look Farrell shot him, he added, "My feelings are never wrong, believe me."

They found themselves in a cramped room with sawdust

on the floor. Swords and chains hung on the walls; punching bags lay on the floor. But what caught Fontana's attention were all the anatomical diagrams and charts with Chinese inscriptions on display. It only heightened his conviction that they'd come to the right place. But nowhere could he see any student who even remotely resembled the man they had come to find.

The master turned out to be a husky figure with a shaven head and a sardonic smile. Every so often he barked out commands in Chinese, to which the students, who ranged in age from ten to about fifty, responded with precision and enthusiasm.

In the front room, where Fontana and Farrell found themselves, however, the atmosphere was more like a disorderly café than a martial arts school. Chinese kids were running around, giggling and shrieking. A slender young American woman of about twenty, who looked like the type who'd run off to join the Moonies, was offering almonds to anybody who would take them. It was interesting to see how upset she became when someone refused. She was the only person to pay any attention to the new arrivals. Otherwise, their presence seemed to have attracted no attention whatsoever.

Something that perched on the edge of a leaf of a potted plant in the corner caused Fontana to take a closer look. It was, appropriately, a praying mantis, but one far bigger than any he had ever laid eyes on before. On the screen, blown up a hundred times, it would have scared the living bejesus out of him. For several seconds man and insect stared at each other, sizing each other up.

"You ever wonder what must be going on in their minds?" he asked Farrell. But it was clear that Farrell couldn't understand what there was about a bug that should get Fontana so fascinated.

"No."

Fontana looked back at Max. "Wanna know what your trouble is, Max? No imagination." Then he became aware of something he hadn't noticed before and said, "You smell that shit?"

"Sweat. I smell sweat. Should I smell something else?"

"Soy sauce. You should be smelling something like soy sauce, Max." He scanned the room, his eyes alighting on a shelf full of tinted vials.

"Master Chu has balms for every type of pain," a man said, stepping up behind them. He was a student who had just completed his lesson, a tall youth with a vaguely Caucasian cast to his Chinese features. "He prepares these medicines for us; he can cure anything himself."

"He sounds like a remarkable man, your master."

"He builds confidence in us, he inspires us," the youth said. "Are you interested in becoming students here?"

"Not really. Tell me, is this one of Master Chu's medicines?"

The student took Fontana's sample and sniffed at its contents. "Yes, this is from Master Chu." He frowned. "Where did you get this?"

"To tell you the truth, we're looking for somebody we think is one of your students."

"Oh, and who would that be?" There was a trace of suspicion in his voice.

"He goes by the name of Danny, but I wouldn't know what name he uses here." Fontana thrust a card under the student's eyes, identifying himself as head of CityVision Cable. "We're doing a story about martial arts in New York, and we were told that he would be an interesting subject to do a profile on."

The student studied the card for a few moments. "What does this Danny look like?"

As Fontana described him, he could see the recognition come into the youth's eyes.

"The man you describe is named David. I don't know his last name. If you'd like, you may ask the master about him." Before Fontana could respond, the student motioned to Master Chu.

Master Chu greeted them with a slight bow of his head. He said something in Chinese, which the student translated. "The master would like you to hit him in the stomach."

The master's stomach protruded as conspicuously as a

pregnant woman's. Fontana exchanged a look with Farrell, who obliged.

Master Chu laughed.

"Fuck! It's like a rock."

The student said something else to Master Chu. Fontana could understand the word *David*. Master Chu's face brightened. He let out a burst of Chinese, keeping his eyes locked on Fontana all the while.

The student said, "Master Chu says that if you are a wimp and come to this place to learn, you will always be a wimp. Except you will be a deadly wimp."

Fontana wasn't certain he liked Master Chu's brand of humor. And he certainly hadn't gone there to witness demonstrations of Master Chu's formidable skills. "Ask Master Chu what he can tell us about David," he told the student.

Master Chu picked up on the name and said several words to his student, at the same time gesturing toward the anatomical charts on the wall in back of him.

"Master Chu says that David can use these pressure points to kill in a way that the victim would not know."

"And how is that?"

"David has learned from Master Chu the Dim-Mak. This is the ancient art that gives its student a secret knowledge of the nervous system. Very few people know this art. In the wrong hands, it is dangerous. Master Chu selects only his best students to learn the Dim-Mak."

Though it was unclear whether Master Chu comprehended any of this translation, he beamed as if each word his student was saying was pleasing to him.

"Do you believe this shit?" Farrell asked.

Though he'd directed his question at Fontana, the student chose to answer, "If Master Chu says that it is so, then it is so."

"When does David come in here to practice?" Fontana asked.

"He usually comes in around four or five in the afternoon. You can wait if you like."

Master Chu said another few words to the student, who proceeded to pass along his message.

"The master invites you to a free lesson this afternoon that starts in ten minutes."

"Can he teach us how to do this Dim-Mak?" Farrell wanted to know.

Once the necessary translations were made, the student turned back to them and said, "Master Chu says that this is advanced knowledge only for the most extraordinary disciples. You would have to study for years before he would know whether you were ready for this knowledge."

"Tell him thank you, but we haven't got the time," Fontana said. Before he and Farrell left, Fontana asked the student to say nothing to David if he should turn up. "We'd like it to be a surprise."

They waited across the street in the arcade of the Wing Fat Shopping Mall. Max knew how to wait, but not Fontana. Fontana needed action, he needed to keep moving, and his hands itched for a telephone. Doing nothing was driving him nuts, but he wasn't about to risk leaving now, not when they were so close.

An hour passed, two hours. The rain subsided, the street becoming shrouded in smoky fog. One had to be on one's toes; in weather like this, a man might easily disappear so that it would be impossible to tell if he was there in the first place. Long waits tended to dull the senses.

It was Farrell who spotted him first. He was walking with a long loping stride, hands buried in the pockets of his light khaki jacket. His hair was thick and wet, his face half hidden from view. But for one moment, as he hesitated at the door of 15 Doyers, he happened to glance over in their direction. And in that moment they caught a glimpse of his face. Fontana almost expected to see a hint of the evil that inhabited his mind, but all he saw was beauty, the face of a god come to life.

As Daniel turned to go inside, he lifted one of his hands

out of his pocket. It was partially swathed in a bandage. This was their man. Fontana motioned to Farrell. "Remember, I don't want him harmed."

"Oh, shit!" Farrell cried. "The son-of-a-bitch is getting away."

Maybe they'd moved too soon and alerted him—anything was possible. A man like Daniel would constantly be on his guard, going nowhere without having an emergency exit scoped out.

They took off after him. He was running down to the end of the block, past the post office, dodging traffic as he crossed Chatham Square, skirting the derelict shell of the old Pagoda Theater, rushing headlong into the middle of Catherine Street. Fontana was quicker than Farrell, who had more weight and years to carry with him. Now Daniel was turning up Henry Street. Fontana was right on his heels, his .38 held openly in his hand. He hoped to intimidate him, to force his surrender, not to actually shoot him. Farrell in the meantime was trying to keep up with Fontana. Fontana could hear his heavy breathing a few paces in back of him.

Daniel kept going, gaining speed. The man was like mercury on his feet, gone before one could mark him. A block north, at the junction of Henry and Market streets, he swung left. Just beyond the First Chinese Presbyterian Church he tore across the street in the direction of the el that led across the river to Brooklyn.

Farrell moved to cut him off. But Daniel was quicker, clambering up the steps to the el, taking two at a time. But then he stumbled over a heap of beer bottles, breaking his momentum. The few seconds it took him to recover was enough for Fontana and Farrell to very nearly overtake him.

With a surprising burst of speed Farrell shot ahead of Fontana, halving the distance remaining between him and his prey. A walkway followed the subway tracks the distance to the Brooklyn side. For Daniel there could be no way back.

Farrell continued closing the distance so that now only three or four feet separated the two. It was possible that

Daniel had twisted his ankle in stumbling, but in any case he was losing his advantage. Suddenly he spun around and whipped his right leg out, striking Farrell in the chest. Farrell grunted and reeled back. Daniel made a quick, decisive gesture with his hand. A moment later Fontana looked to see Farrell's face covered with blood. A knife glinted in Daniel's outstretched hand.

Daniel might have attacked again, but after seeing Fontana he began to run. Wiping the blood from his eyes, Farrell scooped up the gun that had been knocked out of his hand, dropped to a crouch, and sighted it on the receding figure.

"Max, no!" Fontana shouted to him.

A Brooklyn-bound train was rapidly approaching. Max's shout was drowned out by the train's clamor as it hurtled in their direction. Daniel, struck, lurched and staggered, desperately trying to keep his balance. Impossible. He toppled onto the tracks.

Max, half blinded, cursing in a frenzy, was stumbling himself, holding his hands to his face. Fontana raced past him, his chest tightening with the effort. The train was maybe fifty feet away from Daniel, barreling down on him, its horn wailing. Stunned by his fall, Daniel was struggling to lift himself up from the tracks, but he was too slow—there was no way he could make it on his own.

Fontana caught hold of Daniel's bruised hands and hoisted him up just as the train shot past them. But when Daniel looked up into the eyes of his rescuer, it wasn't with gratitude—it was with contempt.

CHAPTER TWELVE

Ushered into the bedroom by the housekeeper, Michael took one look at the man stretched out in the four-poster bed and thought that maybe he'd come too late after all. His face had already taken on the waxen pallor of a corpse, and he lay so perfectly motionless that Michael was unable to detect any sign of life. Learning that Louis Waterman had been released from the hospital and was back at home, Michael had assumed that his condition had improved. But it wasn't to recuperate that Waterman had come home, it was to die. The room itself had a funereal air; with the curtains drawn the sun barely penetrated. Possibly the sun was unwanted.

Somehow Michael's presence in the darkened room must have registered, because all at once Waterman's eyes flickered open and fixed themselves on his visitor. He said something.

"Excuse me?"

"Hand me my glasses, please, so that I can see you," Waterman repeated, gesturing toward the bureau top close to where Michael was standing.

His glasses on, Waterman directed his gaze to the several bottles of pills placed on his bed table. There were at least half a dozen of them.

"I forget which I should take when," he said almost apologetically. "Not that it matters much." His chest rattled with a thin cough, he squeezed his eyes shut against the indignity, then opened them again. "I'm glad you could come, Michael. Pull up a chair."

Michael did so, coming close enough to the bed so that he could breathe in the odor of disintegration from Waterman's body.

"It won't be long now," Waterman said with indifference. "I thought I'd mind, but curiously I don't, I don't mind at all." He peered at Michael through his thick lenses. "I understand you wish to ask me some questions."

Whatever anger Michael felt toward this man could not be sustained now that he was face to face with him. Michael could not look on him as an adversary; he was a dying man who tomorrow or the next day would cease to exist, and this was the only reality that seemed to matter.

"What is it you want to ask me?" Waterman pressed him when the silence between them had grown too intolerable.

Not knowing exactly where to begin, Michael said, "I found a record that my brother was keeping."

"A record?"

"A financial record that detailed how he was laundering money for Ray Fontana and where the money went." He looked to see whether there was any change in the judge's expression. There was none. He went on. "One of the names in that record was yours. It says that you received over sixteen thousand dollars from Fontana in the last year."

He was waiting for a reaction. Certainly there ought to be a reaction, but all Waterman said was, "It's not wise to assume anything. Haven't you learned that yet? Am I being charged with committing some crime?" His voice remained unsettlingly calm. Of course he would be calm, Michael thought. Death would claim him long before the justice system ever could.

"You must have known what Alan was up to," he said.

"At this late date I have no intention of pulling the wool over your eyes, Michael. It's true that over the years I've entered into many associations that some people would question. But what you should bear in mind is that I never forced Alan to do anything. I presented him with options."

"Options," Michael repeated. The word, coming from this man's dry, caked lips, seemed ominous.

"Yes, options. It was his choice to do what he did on behalf of Ray Fontana."

"But you set him up in the position to have the choice," Michael pointed out.

"I won't deny that it was through me that the contact was made."

Michael thought he had an opening there. "Then what happened? He got greedy, was that it? Or did he fall in with the wrong people?"

"Let's say a combination of both. I never believed, though, that it would get so far out of hand. I didn't think he'd kill the poor girl."

Suddenly Michael realized that Waterman's version of events was the same one that Max Farrell had wanted him to believe. He clung to this scenario of avarice and tawdry passion because it left him with clean hands. Michael was so enraged by this travesty that he momentarily forgot about Waterman's desperate condition and lashed out at him. "Don't you understand that Fontana had Alan and Ginny killed?"

Waterman gazed at him sorrowfully, the way a priest might look at a wayward parishioner who refused to return to the bosom of the church. "Michael," he said, his voice a croaking whisper until he could revive it with a glass of water. "Why do you think I steered you to Fontana's agency? I didn't want any harm to come to you—that was what was uppermost in my mind. But I was also anxious for you not to open up a can of worms. I thought you'd have understood and let Alan rest in peace."

He was holding tenaciously to this scenario, uninterested in what Michael had to say. The laundering, the payoffs, were nothing. That was forgivable. But to acknowledge, even to himself, that he'd had a hand in Alan's death was unacceptable.

Michael tried again. "Judge Waterman, I hired a private investigator of my own. Would you like to hear what he found out?"

Waterman remained silent, which Michael took as a sign of acquiescence. In telling his story—Ambrosetti's story as much as his own—he noticed the judge's attention flagging. How much of this, he wondered, was getting through to him? He realized he was in danger of tiring him out. But then, when would he have another opportunity like this?

Nothing Michael said, however, seemed to have any impact on Waterman. It didn't matter to him that Alan had delivered payments of several thousand dollars to Magnus following the autopsies on Tino Ojieda or Cassie Epstein. "Coincidence," he snorted. Nor did he express any surprise at hearing that his own doctor—Ed Shannon—might have been responsible for Ambrosetti's death.

Michael was growing desperate. He had to break through to Waterman somehow. Surely this man knew, or at least suspected, that Alan had been murdered, that it couldn't possibly have been suicide. But he might not have wanted to acknowledge or come to terms with his responsibility for it. Even on his deathbed he seemed determined to blind himself against the truth. Well, Michael would be damned if he'd let the judge off the hook that easily. He didn't care if he was dying; this was no time for indulging in pity—or mercy. He decided to tell him what he'd learned from Gail. And if he choked on it, well then he would choke on it.

"It didn't look like suicide to the medical investigator," he said. "There are ways you can tell whether a wound is a contact wound. You can tell from how far away a gun was fired."

"Perhaps the investigator was mistaken."

"Her report was altered without her knowing about it."

"I see."

"There's one more thing, sir. The last time my brother served as Fontana's bagman was two days before he died. He paid out seven thousand dollars, which he noted was delivered to Dr. Magnus. You know what I think that money was for?"

"I suppose you're going to tell me that it was for the purpose of falsifying another autopsy report."

"Not just any autopsy report. It was my brother's. Don't you understand what Fontana was doing? He put Alan in the position of becoming an accomplice in the cover-up of his own murder." He stopped to let the words sink in.

This time Waterman reacted. He sat up in bed, but maybe too abruptly, because the motion triggered a spasm of pain. He clutched at his stomach and made a disturbing sound in his throat as if he were going to vomit.

Michael sprang from his chair. "Is there anything I can do?"

The judge managed to shake his head no. After several torturous seconds went by the pain left him, and he drew himself upright again, his face drained of blood, still gasping for breath.

When at last he could speak, he said, "It's possible that what you say may be true. I may have made a terrible mistake, a terrible mistake."

"It isn't too late to do something about it."

Waterman seemed almost to recede in front of his eyes, fading into the gloom so that Michael had the feeling that all he'd have to do was blink and the judge would be gone. Waterman said nothing, enfolding himself in an unnerving silence.

Then he spoke. "I tell you what I can do. I can put in a call to the D.A.'s office. You can be assured that he will pay attention to what I have to say. I will tell him of my part in these things. That's the best I can do."

"Will you call him today?"

"I will call him now if you'd like. You can sit here and listen in." His voice might have been failing before, but it was now resonant and clear, full of authority. He reached for the phone.

He dialed with a palsied hand. "Yes," he said as soon as the phone was answered, "this is Judge Louis Waterman. Would you please inform Mr. Barbanel that I would like to speak with him?"

Michael was familiar with the name: Joe Barbanel was the Manhattan D.A.

After a few moments the judge said, "I see. Well, would you have Mr. Barbanel call me at his earliest convenience? Tell him it's important. . . . Yes, he knows the number."

He hung up and looked at Michael.

"He's expected back in an hour or so. You have my word that I will be perfectly candid with him. You may, if you'd like, give me a call tomorrow morning and I'll let you know what happened."

Michael was disappointed. Even now, with death so close, he suspected that Waterman was still capable of deceit. It was impossible to know just how much his conscience might weigh on him, or if it did at all. He wanted to take something more tangible from this room than a dying man's promise.

It could be that Waterman sensed Michael's dissatisfaction. The judge groped for the phone and dialed again. His eyes shone brightly with fever and perhaps a strange sure knowledge that he could still spring one more surprise on the world before he died. Keeping his gaze focused on Michael, he waited a moment until somebody answered and then said, "Yes, hello, this is Lou Waterman. How are you today, Dr. Magnus?"

Astounded, Michael leaned forward in his chair, anxious not to miss a word the judge said.

"I have with me a young man I believe you're already acquainted with," Waterman continued. "His name is Michael Friedlander. I'm sure you remember him. We've just been talking about his brother, Alan. He's supplied me with certain facts pertinent to his brother's case. . . . No, please hear me out, you'll have plenty of time to give your side of the story. . . . It seems to me that I would be derelict in my duty if I didn't communicate these facts to Joe Barbanel." There was a pause while he listened to Magnus and then he said, smiling for the first time since Michael had entered the room, "But you don't seem to understand, Dr. Magnus, that I no longer have anything to lose."

CHAPTER THIRTEEN

On examination, the wound in Daniel's leg did not turn out to be very serious, the bullet having just grazed the calf muscle. Undoubtedly he would have suffered worse if Farrell's vision hadn't been clouded by the blood from his facial cuts. At any rate, Ed Shannon was able to deal with the injury in his office, cleaning out and dressing the wound. About the only noticeable effect on Daniel was that he now walked with a hobbled gait.

Farrell, too, obviously required attention from Shannon; there was no question that he was incensed that Fontana wanted Daniel treated first. He was forced to wait and sponge up the blood with a towel until Shannon was ready for him. It was an insult, an outrage, but Farrell knew enough not to protest. In Fontana's view, the Max Farrells of the world—and their daughters—were replaceable. But the madness, the purity of evil, that Daniel embodied was almost unique in Fontana's experience. In the presence of such a man, Fontana felt almost reverential.

At no time in his ordeal did Daniel say a word. He responded to no questions posed to him by Fontana; he used silence as a weapon, scrupulous about giving nothing away. Fontana liked that. He also admired the way he reacted to Shannon's treatment. Though it must have stung terribly when Shannon washed out the wound, Daniel's expression remained impassive, almost serene. It seemed that he was immune to feeling; dead to remorse, to guilt, maybe to any emotion at all, he was no less dead to pain.

One-way mirrors strategically positioned in his richly paneled office allowed Shannon to inspect his patients sitting half naked in the examining room while they waited anxiously for his appearance. Fontana took advantage of this amenity to observe his captive. Daniel seemed oblivious to the indignity of having had his clothes taken from him. Nor had he made any effort to try the doors; he must have surmised that they were firmly secured. In fact, there was no sign of restlessness in him; if anything, he gave every indication that he was perfectly content to lie supine on the examining table, staring dreamily up at the lamp that gave his skin an eerie amber glow. His face was angelic, his body superbly proportioned. Fontana was unable to tear his eyes away from the perfection of the young man's limbs, the flatness of his stomach, and the suggestion of immense strength in the muscles of his arms and chest that was present even in repose.

This man was the closest a human being could come to being a superman, Fontana thought, since he was inhibited by no morality, no ideology, no love, and perhaps no hatred, either. To kill without hatred, to kill with utter indifference not only to the fate of the victim but to one's own fate as well struck Fontana as an achievement surpassing all others. It was no wonder he didn't trouble to ask them whether they were police or carrying out some private vendetta; he may not have cared what plans they had in store for him. He was an enigma, a cipher, a blank screen on which they could project their own images.

But Fontana believed Daniel's was a mystery that ultimately could be unlocked—if only one knew the trick, the right combination. More than that, he sensed that this man was a natural force, powerful and deadly as a hurricane or a typhoon and just as unpredictable. And because Fontana was who he was, because in spite of all this he believed himself superior to Daniel, he wondered what it would be like to try and control this force, bend it to his will. Over the years he'd known exactly which tactic to exploit to get his way; some people needed to be bribed, some blackmailed, some seduced, some deceived. No one resisted forever; eventually everyone came around. He was certain he could bring Daniel around, too, but how? This was the challenge. What did Daniel want that Fontana had?

As he continued to study him, the way an anthropologist might scrutinize a primitive being from the wilds of Papua, New Guinea, an idea began to take shape in Fontana's mind. He knew what he could use to lure Daniel, what temptation would finally bring him under his control, reducing him to the level of all the others—Magnus, Parnase, Kohler, and Shannon.

Turning away from the mirror, Fontana saw that Shannon was staring at him with the same intensity with which he'd been viewing Daniel. But he didn't mind. Like Farrell, Shannon knew better than to ask questions—even when they'd walked into his office with Daniel, leaving a trail of blood behind on his carpet. He'd reacted as if that was something that happened every day. It wasn't his place to criticize Fontana; as long as his money came in on time, he was happy. As lucrative as his Park Avenue practice was, he was still overwhelmed by expenses. It seemed an endemic problem in New York: People one figured were stinking rich complained incessantly that they didn't have what they needed to get by. Money was tied up, frozen; somehow it was never liquid enough. Shannon had made things worse for himself by thinking he could psych out the market. His ego was a frightening thing; having mastered the art of diagnosing diseases and prescribing cures for them, he assumed he could make a killing in undervalued stocks. He'd been mistaken.

In spite of the discretion that Shannon customarily exercised, he still couldn't entirely suppress his anxiety. His uneasiness showed in his abrupt movements and the brusqueness of his replies.

Once Farrell was patched up, his face now a crosshatch of bandages from which his eyes, nostrils, and lips peered out, Shannon figured that he'd done all that was necessary. He was ready to see the three of them out and get back to his other patients. But it wasn't in the cards. Fontana said that Farrell and their captive would be staying a while longer and that Shannon would have to turn one of the examining rooms over for their use.

"How long is a while longer?" Shannon asked irritably.

"I'll be sure to let you know," Fontana said, "but I should tell you who your guest is before I go."

"I don't want to know who he is," Shannon said. "Please don't tell me, Ray."

"You have no choice, Ed. I want to tell you, so you'll just have to listen." And then Fontana told him.

Shannon gaped at him. "You're not serious, are you?"

Slowly it dawned on him that this was no joke. "Good God!" he muttered. He found it necessary to sit down.

"And you haven't heard the half of it," Fontana added. Maybe he was being a little boastful, like an agent who by chance had come to represent a client with an incredible track record.

"What are you going to do with him?" Shannon's voice was about to break.

"I've got an idea, but I don't know whether it will work. That's why I'm going to need your help, Ed."

"My help? What the hell can I do?" He was growing angry now—panicking, too—resentful that Fontana was recruiting him into his program like this.

"Let me explain, Ed. I want you to test him. I want you to run a whole fucking battery of tests."

"What have you got in mind, Ray?" Perhaps Ed thought he could get out of this by demonstrating to Fontana that what he wanted was hopelessly unrealistic.

"I don't know, try doing an EEG on him, do a CAT scan, a PET scan, whatever they call it. Do whatever you can think of—that's your field, not mine. What I want to know is what makes this mother tick. I want to come as close as any man can to knowing what is going on in this man's mind."

Shannon threw him a puzzled look. "First of all, Ray, that isn't my field. What you want is a goddamned neurologist."

"Is that all you have to say?"

"No, no, it isn't. Why the hell can't you just hand the bastard over to the cops?"

"In time, Ed, in time I'll give Larry Kohler a buzz and set it up. I'll take care of it. Don't I always? But right now I need you to arrange those tests for me. I don't care how you do it just as long as no one knows who he is. And I want it done as soon as possible—tomorrow, the next day at the latest."

"Why, Ray? Why are you doing this?"

"You should know better than to ask me a question like that, Ed."

"You're not going to leave me alone with him, are you?" Shannon was aghast at the prospect.

"No, of course not, Ed, what do you think I am? Your ass will be covered, no problem. We'll have him under guard twenty-four hours a day. Your job will be to figure out a way we can control him."

"Control him? How do you mean?"

"Manipulate him, is what I mean. That's why I want him tested so we can pinpoint his weakness, where he's most vulnerable. There must be some psychotropic drugs you know of we can use to make him more pliable. What about biofeedback or some of that behavioral modification shit I'm always reading about? You're a good man, Ed, you can work it out. I have complete confidence that you'll come up with something."

Shannon was looking at Fontana as if he'd taken leave of his senses. "It's not as easy as you think. Hell, the CIA, the FBI, probably every damned intelligence service in the world has been trying to figure out how to do what you're proposing. You want to turn this guy into a robot. The man's a fucking menace—he should be locked away somewhere for the rest of his life. Hell, he should be put in the electric chair if they had one in this state. And you're talking about giving him a CAT scan and controlling him. You're crazier than he is."

"Maybe, Ed, maybe," Fontana said, absolutely unflappable, "but you do it for me anyhow. I'm counting on it."

Shannon wasn't ready to give up yet. "Look, Ray, it's not like I can devote myself full-time to this. I've got patients. I've got a heavy schedule."

"Ed, you know what you've got to do. I don't want to talk about it anymore."

Shannon bristled, but he knew that he'd lost. By pulling the plug on Ambrosetti he'd slipped over the dividing line; he was a murderer, a criminal, and as such he belonged to Fontana. The money was the least of it; the connection now ran much deeper than that.

Chapter Fourteen

There was no telling how long Magnus had been waiting for The Call. Nor had he any idea from whom The Call was going to come. Over the years The Call had begun to dominate his thoughts, turning into an obsession. It was much worse because he lived in constant expectation and fear of it. True, there were times when he'd convinced himself that The Call would never come, that he was being paranoid for no good reason. Or else he would think that no matter how bad things turned out to be, Ray would always know what to do.

Of all the people that he imagined would make The Call, Lou Waterman was not among them. In Magnus's mind, Waterman was already a dead man. How had he managed to hang on for so long? Magnus wondered. What streak of perversity had moved him in his final days to destroy the lives of people with many years ahead of them to enjoy? Did he begrudge them their health?

Maybe he'd gotten religion. That was a possibility. Terrified of meeting his maker with so many sins to answer for, he was putting his last hours on earth to good use, attempting to redeem himself and assuage his conscience.

So where did that leave him? Joe Barbanel was not, as far as he knew, beholden to Fontana. Magnus understood how these things worked: Once a leak had sprung, then it was only a matter of time before the dam collapsed. It didn't take long for the damage to work its way through the structure. What would follow, though—the headlines, the subpoenas, the impaneling of the grand jury, the indictments, the suspension from his job, the depositions, the hearings, the pillorying in the press—would take forever to get through. And what was there to look forward to when it ended? The best he could hope for was a fine and five years in a minimum-security federal prison, the loss of his reputation, debts he could never in his lifetime hope to pay off, and—without a doubt—the destruction of his family, which he'd gone to such pains to preserve.

He could only hope that out of his bag of tricks Fontana could find something that would once again hold back the tide. It couldn't go on like this indefinitely, but maybe this one last time . . .

After all, he considered, if he went, Fontana would not be far behind.

It wasn't a simple matter to locate Fontana. It never was. Magnus tried his office at the agency and then at the television station, then at Natchez, then at the trucking company, leaving messages everywhere. If anybody knew his whereabouts, he wasn't letting on.

While he waited for Fontana to return his call, Magnus prepared a stiff drink for himself; a triple shot of Chivas on an empty stomach went right to his head. It had been a long while since he felt so drunk. It was all right, though; he could face the world better that way. He was grateful that he had the whole house to himself and that Barbara and Valerie were still in the city. It wasn't so unusual for him to go out to Fire Island even in the middle of the week. His colleagues understood, even if his family did not, that he sometimes needed to escape the tension of work for what solace he could draw from the nearness of the sea. It was enough for him to say that he was going to recharge his batteries. There was no reason to tell his wife that The Call had finally come.

Magnus took a module phone out on the deck and rested it next to his drink. The deck looked out on a clump of trees through which it was possible to see patches of the ocean. The sky was clearing, and a constellation Magnus identified as Orion began to show through the dissipating cloud cover.

From time to time he spotted figures on the beach—joggers, lovers, solitary walkers—some wading into the surf. He was becoming lost in a reverie induced partly by the lulling rhythm of the tide, and partly by the Scotch he was throwing back with greater determination. So he was brought up sharp by the phone's intrusive fluttering. For a moment he couldn't recall why anybody would be calling him. But as soon as he lifted the receiver to his lips, he knew who it would have to be.

"Fontana here. What's up?"

"Trouble," Magnus said. "This afternoon I received a call from Lou Waterman."

"Waterman?" That Fontana sounded surprised portended nothing good.

Magnus went on to explain, pausing at intervals in the hopes that Fontana would reassure him as he always did. But Fontana kept silent, and that, too, portended no good.

It took him longer than it should have to describe the conversation he'd had with Waterman. The alcohol was slowing his thought process as much as it was his speech pattern. Finally he said, "What do you think I should do now, Ray?"

"Why don't we get together, sit down, and talk this whole thing through—say, tomorrow at Natchez?"

"I'm not coming into the city. I'm staying right here." Magnus was adamant about that; at the moment he was convinced it would be a mistake to leave. On the island he felt safe. Or safer, anyhow, than he would have in the city.

"All right, whatever you want to do is fine with me. Stay right where you are, Kurt, don't move. I tell you what I'm going to do. Tomorrow, first thing, I'll send somebody out there to see you, check on how things are. How does that sound?" He might have been calming down a young child after a temper tantrum the way he was talking.

"But what are you planning to do, Ray?" He hated how he sounded, so plaintive and desperate. "I've got to know what you're planning to do."

"Damage control, Kurt, that's what I'm planning to do. Just stay put and get some rest, okay?"

"Ray, listen, it's not enough to say damage control—" But then he realized that Fontana had already hung up.

Magnus fell into a tormented sleep. Repeatedly throughout the night he'd awaken, drenched with sweat, listening to the nocturnal sounds of his big, rambling house: the creak of knotted wood, the rustle of wind through open windows, and the slap of insects against the mosquito lights. When at last it grew impossible to sleep, he rose from his bed and dressed. He was woozy from the drinking he'd done, and was now at the mercy of a terrible hangover.

He walked down to the ocean. It was still gray and chilly in the hour before dawn. Though his condition was debilitated, he seemed to be able to think things through with much greater clarity than he had the night before. Now he was able to identify what had him so troubled.

When Fontana had told him over the phone that he was sending somebody out to see him that morning, he hadn't really thought anything of it; it was just Fontana's way of doing things: dispatch a messenger to soothe his rattled nerves, offer him advice and reassurance. But now, in the more sober light of a new day, he began to think that there might be more to it than that.

The memory of Francis Holmes rose up in his mind—a memory of Holmes stretched out on the autopsy table. Try as he might, he could not conjure up any memory of him alive. He was almost certain that what they had done to Holmes they would one day get around to doing to him.

Maybe that day was today. The more he reflected on the possibility that Fontana's "messenger" was on his way to Fire Island in order to kill him, the more likely it seemed. Putting himself in Fontana's position, he could come up with no scenario that made as much sense. He was a liability now, dangerously close to a breakdown; his usefulness—to Fontana, to anybody, really—was at an end.

He stayed on the beach for a few minutes longer, walking hard against the lashing wind, until he'd decided what had to be done. Then he returned to his house.

Knowing that he'd be waking up his wife, he telephoned nonetheless, uncertain whether he'd be in shape to call at a later time.

"What is it? Is anything wrong?" she asked drowsily.

"No, I was up and just needed to hear your voice," he said.

"Oh. Are you sure you're all right?"

"I'm fine. I just couldn't sleep, that's all." He hoped that his voice carried conviction. "How's Val?"

"She's okay. She's asleep. The whole world's asleep. Can you call me this evening? I've got to go into the city, but I should be back by six at the latest."

"Yes, of course, Barbara," he said. Then he added, "I love you."

"Oh, yes," Barbara said. "Love you, too." And she hung up.

Now Magnus tried another number, suspecting that the response would be little different.

"Hello, Kate, it's me, Kurt."

"Oh, yes," she said. "How are you, sweetheart? What's up?"

"Nothing really, I just wanted to call and say hello."

"Hi." She fell silent, waiting for him to fill in the gap.

"Are you all right?" he asked. He really wanted her to be all right.

"I'm great, I'm terrific, Kurt. Do you think we could talk later?"

"Do you have company?" He tried to imagine what the

man lying next to her would look like, but all he could see in his mind's eye was an amorphous figure, tall, muscular, and with a full head of hair mussed where her hands had run through it.

"Uh . . . no, no, I don't," she said in a way that told him clearly that she did. "But I'm wiped out. I have to go back to sleep. All right, darling, okay?" And then she hung up without giving him the opportunity to get in another word.

What had he expected? Words of love? Of consolation? It was too much to ask. Certainly it was too much to ask at six-twenty-five in the morning.

There was one additional call he felt compelled to make. But as soon as he heard her come on the line, her voice thick with sleep, he was stumped. He realized he didn't know what to say. "Hello? Hello? Who is this?"

Gently he replaced the receiver. What could he have possibly said to Gail Ives? That he wished things could have worked out differently? That he had long been attracted to her but had not known what to do about it? Or did he want to tell her that, however briefly, they'd been bound together—more intimately in a way than if they'd been lovers—in the fellowship of the dead? He supposed, finally, that anything he did say would be discounted or misunderstood. Anyway, tomorrow it would make no difference.

His first idea was the gun, a .22-caliber Ivar Johnson pistol, which he was licensed to carry and had never used—never thought to use until that moment. He sat down in a comfortable wicker chair in the living room and, cocking it, put it to his head, then to his heart, then back to his head again. He wasn't thinking of pulling the trigger just yet, but he was interested in seeing what the sensation felt like. The truth was it didn't feel very good at all. His heart quickened in response so that he wondered whether he might not kick off from a heart attack before he could bring himself to shoot himself.

Nor could he escape the memories that flashed through his mind of autopsies he'd performed on countless gunshot victims. The whole brutal messy business of their death deterred him from going further. He put the gun down.

He walked into the bathroom, and when he returned to the kitchen he had with him four bottles. He set them on the kitchen table along with a new liter-bottle of Chivas. Four small bottles all in a row: Tuinal, Seconal, Nembutal, and Tofranil. What he decided to take would depend on how fast he wanted this to happen. The Tuinal and the Seconal were short action; in two to three hours—less with the addition of the Chivas—he would be gone. The Nembutal would give him a few more hours, up to five or six. Unlike the barbiturates, the Tofranil was a sedative that would put him in an agitated state before it killed him, inducing hallucinations and possibly hypermania.

Soon he had spread out in front of him—neatly separated—pretty little clusters of red, blue, yellow, and white capsules, each containing the proper dosages to do the trick: one and one-half grams each of Tuinal and Seconal, two grams of Nembutal, and two grams of Tofranil. He poured himself out a shot of Chivas, forgoing the ice, and waited until the warmth from it radiated into his chest and dulled the headache pounding in his temples. Then, like a chess player contemplating the deployment of his pieces on the board, he looked over the selection of pills he'd laid out for himself and made his choice.

CHAPTER FIFTEEN

When it seemed to him that it was a decent hour and he wouldn't be at risk of disturbing the judge, Michael made his call. Though he was hardening himself to setbacks, he realized how much he was counting on Waterman to come through for him. In retrospect, Waterman's call to Magnus seemed more of an empty gesture to appease Michael—or worse: a warning to the M.E. to cover his tracks. The one call that mattered was the one to Barbanel. If Waterman actually had come clean to the D.A., then Michael would be satisfied.

Isabel inevitably answered. It was a little after eight, but she sounded hoarse, as if she'd just awakened.

"Mr. Friedlander?"

"Yes?"

"It will not be possible for you to speak to Judge Waterman."

"He's asleep?"

"No, I'm afraid he passed away last night."

"Jesus! I'm sorry. . . ." He let his words hang for a moment. "Could you tell me whether he managed to speak to the D.A.'s office, to Mr. Barbanel, before he died?"

It was hopeless, and he knew it.

"The judge made many calls yesterday, but I can't tell you to who. I'm sorry."

Michael was furious. It didn't seem right that he'd gotten this close and then had had the door slammed in his face. He looked up the number in the phone book and called the Manhattan D.A.'s office. Of course, no one was about to put him through to Barbanel, but he left a message, saying that it was in regard to Judge Waterman. See what good that did.

Then he tried Gail. He desperately needed to see her. There was no one else he could confide in, nobody who could understand what was going on better than she. At another time in his life maybe he would have backed off, given her time, given her space, given whatever people gave their estranged lovers these days. But not now. He suspected he was in love with her. He realized that this was the sort of thing a man should know with certainty; love should be something about which there were no doubts, no hedging, no ambiguities. But he didn't know; and that was the truth, and there was no getting around it. What he did know was that he needed her. For now such certainty would have to do.

But she wasn't at home, and he was damned if he was about to leave a message on her machine, afraid that she would become just one more person who would never call him back.

He had to do something. He couldn't just sit there. For the

hell of it he tried another number—the M.E.'s office. Without giving his name he asked to speak to Magnus, hardly daring to think that the man would agree to talk to him. It turned out not to matter. Magnus wasn't in the office; he was taking a few days off and wasn't expected back until the following week.

Michael thought he could remember how to get to Magnus's home from the night he'd gone out there, fired by alcohol and determined to wring the truth out of the man. While he recalled that it was in Forest Hills, Queens, he wasn't sure he could locate it exactly. Well, he had the address. He'd ask someone. One way or another, he didn't see that he had anything to lose. In the back of his mind, the hope lingered that the medical examiner might have reconsidered his position in light of Waterman's call and had at last made up his mind to reveal the truth. Stranger things had been known to happen.

It was a dazzling morning, dry and warm, the most benign weather Michael could remember since he'd arrived in New York. Half an hour after getting on a train at the Seventy-seventh Street IRT station, he was walking the unfamiliar streets of Forest Hills in search of Magnus's home.

The tranquility of this neighborhood unnerved him; it wasn't like being in the suburbs where his parents lived, but it wasn't like being in the city either. His pace slowed as he continued to look. He knew from the directions he'd been given at a newsstand that he was getting close. Soon he would have gained his destination, and then what?

It was just as he remembered it: the two-story brick house, the two-car garage, the sprawling maple that put half the lawn in shade. It was the kind of home every American family was supposed to have, or at least to desire.

This time, he resolved, he wasn't going to stand around for hours, paralyzed with fear and uncertainty. But even so, he still couldn't help feeling somewhat ridiculous as he walked up the fieldstone path to the door. What did he think he was going to accomplish by this? He imagined Ambrosetti's reaction right now. He was sure that at any moment somebody would call out to him. He knew that certain city officials were guarded. It was even possible that a cop might demand to know what business he had there. But there was no one around to stop him at all.

Once he got to the door he knew that if he hesitated, he would surely change his mind and leave. He rang the bell. It still wouldn't come to him what he would say if Magnus should actually appear.

There seemed to be somebody home; he thought he could hear the radio or television on inside. He rang again. Despairing of obtaining any response, he turned and was about to walk away when the door opened and a girl of about seventeen or eighteen peered out. "What do you want?" she called to him.

"I'm looking for Dr. Magnus. Is he at home?"

The girl opened the door another inch. She wore her blond hair cropped almost as short as a marine recruit's. Her eyes were violet, her skin frighteningly pale. Maybe she never ventured out into the sun. She was very thin. Shaking her head, she said, "Dad's out on the island."

Oh, so this was the daughter. Michael had imagined a wife, not a daughter or a son.

"Which island?"

"Fire Island. We have a place out there." Her enormous violet eyes were taking him in with some interest. "Who are you?"

"Michael," he said, seeing no point in giving her his last name, though he doubted that she would recognize it anyway.

"I know a lot of Michaels." Her voice was smoky, and the words came out slowly.

"Is he going to be out there long?"

"On Fire Island?" Suddenly she looked stumped, as if nobody had ever put a question like this to her before. "I couldn't say. I don't keep track of what my dad does."

"I see. Well, then could you tell me where his house is on Fire Island?" He realized he was slowing down his speech to be more in synch with hers. It occurred to him that she was extremely stoned.

She stepped onto the porch. All she was wearing was a T-shirt and shorts, and the T-shirt and shorts were both shredded. He suspected that this must be a style of fashion for her. It certainly couldn't be a sign of destitution.

"You wouldn't find it," she said after a long silence. "It's way at the edge of The Pines."

"Can't you give me an address, the name of a street?" Actually, he felt himself lucky to have gotten this far; somebody else would have sent him away without a word.

She laughed. "You don't know Fire Island, do you? There aren't any streets, and there aren't any cars. Believe me, you'd never find it."

He supposed she was telling him the truth. It had been years since he'd been out to Fire Island, and from what he remembered, it wasn't easy to travel from one community to another, especially if one wasn't sure where one was going.

"You got some cash on you?"

"Some. Why?"

"Because if you want to pay my way on the ferry, I'll take you out there. I got nothing else to do."

While he had his doubts about putting up with her company for the two hours or so it would take to get there, he couldn't see any other choice. He told her he was grateful for the offer.

"They'll kill me if I take the Porsche to Bay Shore, but then, my mom's not going to be back till late. She'll never know. And if she finds out, fuck her," she said. "You don't want to take the train, do you? The train's a fucking drag, man. There's only one thing."

"What?"

"You got a license?"

"A New Hampshire license. Why?"

"Because if any cop stops us, you're going to have to take the rap, okay? You're going to have to say you were the one who was doing the driving, okay?"

Her conditions kept growing more complicated. He didn't like them, but he agreed.

She smiled a wide, stoned smile. He asked her her name.

"Valerie," she said. "Michael and Valerie. Sounds okay, doesn't it?"

He wasn't so sure about that, but he didn't want to say anything. "The car's in the garage?"

"Yeah, but first let's smoke a joint, okay? No sense going anywhere without doing some weed, don't you think?"

CHAPTER SIXTEEN

Fontana had delayed making his decision until the very last minute. He would have preferred sending Farrell out to see Magnus, while he stayed in the city and dealt with Daniel. Magnus no longer held much interest for him; he'd gone from the credit side of the ledger to the debit side. There was no trusting his judgment or his sanity anymore.

On the other hand, it wasn't as if Magnus could be easily dismissed; Fontana recognized the danger to his operations that he presented. He had to be pacified and reassured, and no one could do that better than he himself. Magnus would listen to him; Magnus respected him. Above all, Fontana had to convince him that he was under no threat. There was still a chance the medical examiner could be of use to him. The important thing now was to retire him and get him off to safety—beyond the reach of federal authorities. Hell, it might even make sense to transplant Magnus to some little Caribbean or Mediterranean hideaway—any country with a hot climate and no extradition treaty with the U.S. Keep the man happy with Scotch, bimbos, and wads of cash. Maybe make him chief medical examiner of Far Tortuga or the Lesser Antilles. Surely people died in questionable circumstances in places like that. All that mattered was that he stay put and feel under no obligation ever to respond to any subpoena issued by a New York court.

Before Fontana left town, though, he stopped by Shannon's office to check on the progress he'd made with Daniel. Farrell occupied a seat in the waiting room, observing movements in and out of the office. With his face criss-crossed by bandages and gauze, he looked like another one of Shannon's patients.

"How's our friend doing?" Fontana asked him.

Farrell shrugged. Protecting the man who'd nearly taken his face off wasn't a job he particularly appreciated. "I don't know, you'll have to ask Ed. What the fuck are you going to do with the scumbag, Ray?"

"Oh, you'll find out soon enough. It'll be worth the trouble, believe me."

Fontana proceeded into Shannon's office. Shannon, who wasn't used to being interrupted without any warning, scowled. "Don't you bother to knock?"

"What would be the point, Ed?" Fontana stepped over to the mirror to see how Daniel was getting along.

He was clothed now and seated in the swivel chair that Shannon used to examine patients. A book was open in his lap.

"What's he reading?"

"A book he found on one of my shelves—it's a textbook on communicable diseases."

"He looks engrossed in it."

"I think that if you gave him a cereal boxtop to read, he'd be just as engrossed. It doesn't seem to make any difference to him. Nothing seems to make any difference, frankly. What an odd duck."

"What about that wound in his leg?"

"It's healing nicely."

"You do any tests on him like I asked?" He was expecting to hear that Shannon hadn't gotten around to them, but evidently he'd misjudged the man.

"I did an EEG on him and I've arranged to use facilities at a clinic where we can do a CAT scan and maybe a couple of other brain tests."

"I assume you've been discreet about this."

Shannon furrowed his brow, looking vaguely offended. "What do you think?"

"Okay, okay. What did the EEG show?"

"You want to take a look at it?" Shannon was prepared to roll out an endless printout for Fontana's benefit.

"I wouldn't know what to make of it, Ed. Just give me an idea what it says."

"His brain function is normal, absolutely normal. If anything, he seems to have a heightened sensitivity to certain stimuli compared to the norm."

In a way Fontana was almost disappointed, having held out the hope that Daniel's madness might be translated into a comprehensible pattern of brain waves and statistics; that way maybe he'd know exactly what he was dealing with. But the man continued to remain as unknowable as God.

"Did he eat this morning?"

"Three eggs over easy, cinnamon toast with marmalade, coffee, tomato juice. He displayed a ravenous appetite. The man seems to be in excellent health."

"He talk?"

"He thanked me for bringing him breakfast, if that counts."

"But he didn't ask any questions, like what we were planning to do with him?"

Shannon shook his head. "He seems content to stay put. It's strange. The guy gives me the creeps. Even if I didn't know what he'd done, he'd still give me the creeps. How soon do you think you can get him out of here?"

"When you've done everything I want you to do, Ed—not before. Have you given him anything?"

"Anything like what?"

"Like some kind of drug. What I asked you to do for me yesterday. Something that will give us some control over him, some power."

"I've started him on fifty milligrams of Chlorpromazine."

"What the hell's that do?"

"You've got to realize, Ray, that these psychotropic drugs are not miracle cures or anything like that. The effect varies from individual to individual. With something like Chlorpromazine it may take up to four weeks for it even to begin to have any impact on the guy. And without knowing what his problem is in the first place, it's like whistling in the dark."

"You still haven't told me what this Chlorpom shit does."

"Chlorpromazine. It's a neuroleptic that acts on the hypothalamus and the brainstem reticular formation—"

"I don't want a medical lesson. Just tell me what the fuck it's supposed to accomplish."

"It's intended to control hyperactive and hypermanic states. It acts to quiet the emotions, sometimes at the cost of producing an attitude of indifference."

Fontana cast another look at the subject. He was still intently reading his book about communicable diseases. "Have you noticed any results?"

"Did you hear what I just said? There may be no discernible results for weeks. I'm planning on increasing the dose and maybe experimenting with a few other drugs— Anquil, maybe, some M.A.O. inhibitors like Marplan or Nardil, throw in some Lithium, see what works, what doesn't. Could be I'll try out antiandrogen on him."

"What the hell's that?"

"Reduces the sex drive. From what I've read in the papers, this fellow seems to have a problem in that direction."

To Fontana that sounded more promising. He liked the idea; certainly it was one way of asserting control over the man. "I wouldn't hesitate to start him on the antiandrogen shit right away."

"There's one side effect I should tell you about."

"Oh? And what's that?"

"Enough of the drug and it will begin to enlarge the breasts in a male."

Fontana laughed. "Hell, I wouldn't worry about that. Somehow I don't think he'd really mind if that happened."

Fontana's entrance into the examining room failed to distract Daniel from his absorption in the book. Fontana seated himself on a leather-covered stool about six feet from where Daniel was sitting. He felt the comforting presence of his gun under his jacket. Daniel was a lethal weapon in and of himself; one blow from him, if delivered with the precision he was undoubtedly capable of, might kill Fontana or at least cripple him for life. It would require much greater dosages of Shannon's chemical arsenal to make Daniel as tractable as Fontana wanted. At the same time there was a danger of reducing him to a zombie. That wouldn't do at all, not for what he had in mind.

Fontana spoke gently to him, thinking that it might be possible to establish some communication, maybe even a certain rapport, now that Daniel had had several hours to adjust to his captivity. "Is there anything I can do for you?"

Daniel raised his liquid blue eyes, studying him as intensively as he had the book. "No," he said at last.

Gratified to have elicited even this much of a response, Fontana pressed him, inevitably falling into the role of the seducer. "Sure, now? Cigarettes? Something to drink? TV? Maybe there's something you want to watch?"

Daniel shook his head. "I'm happy with what I have."

Perhaps this was another form of resistance: refusing all offers to him except for food. He needed his strength. This way, even imprisoned in this small room, he still held power over them.

Reasoning that he wasn't going to make any headway by being nice, Fontana decided to see if he could provoke his captive instead. Maybe that would command a response.

"You enjoy killing people? You get off on it—you get hard, is that it? I'm just interested, see, I want to know how it feels."

Daniel seemed not to mind his attack. But at least he felt moved to reply. "You misunderstand. I don't kill people so much as I help them to die. I can see in their eyes that they want to die; I recognize the look. Sometimes they don't know themselves; sometimes they are under the illusion that they must hang on to life, though there is no longer any purpose in it. They call it a survival instinct for good reason—it's a primitive response, but for some people it means very little. Once they let go, they are happy."

His words were delivered calmly, gently, with the conviction of someone who would never entertain any doubts about his sanity. But Fontana was heartened; at least he'd gotten him talking.

"Then you slice them up? I just want to get this straight."

"You are acquainted with the idea of *mana*."

"Like *mana* from heaven, you mean?"

"No, *mana* is a totem—a sacrament." A certain disdain came into his eyes; it was as if he wasn't expecting that anybody of Fontana's intelligence could possibly understand. "*Mana* is the sacrament. It is a union with the spirit of the victim. It is the union that the Indian achieved with the buffalo he killed."

"What you're saying is you eat—?"

"I eat the flesh of my victims, yes."

He waited for Fontana to react, to say how disgusted he was, but Fontana would be damned if he'd give him the satisfaction. He had the feeling that Daniel was playing him along, twisting the truth, throwing out the most fantastic tales just to get a rise out of him. They were playing a game, each baiting the other.

He decided to go on. "Tell me, Daniel, can you look at somebody's picture and see if that person is ready to die? Can you do that?"

This was the test; this was where he found out whether he could control this man or not.

Daniel seemed to reflect on his question for a moment. "Sometimes I can, yes. Why?"

"Because I have a picture with me, and I want you to tell me whether you can help the person in the picture to die."

There was real interest in Daniel's eyes now. "May I see this picture?" His studied politeness barely concealed his mounting excitement. Fontana liked that. He was sure it was going to work.

Fontana drew the glossy out of his jacket pocket and handed it to him. Daniel examined it for several long seconds. "It could be that this person is ready to die." He looked up at Fontana. "Who is she?"

"Her name is Gail Ives," he said.

CHAPTER SEVENTEEN

Having no shades of her own, Valerie borrowed Michael's. This left Michael blinking furiously in the glare. The beach they were walking along was filled with roasting flesh. Many of the men and a fair number of women were nude, but it was Michael who, dressed for the streets of New York City, was the real object of curiosity. It was nearly eleven o'clock, and the day was growing hotter by the minute, a fact that Valerie endlessly remarked upon.

"I hate the fucking beach. I hate the goddamned sun," she said again and again.

A row of rambling beach houses, half-hidden by the swell of the dunes, provided Michael with his first glimpse of The Pines. They proceeded past knots of more nude sunbathers—men here, women there, seldom the two sexes mixed—until they came to a stretch of beach that was practically deserted. A streamer trailing from the back of a prop plane proclaimed "There's No Tan Like a Coppertone Tan" in the cloudless sky.

Now Valerie was leading him in toward the dunes where a set of rickety wooden stairs led off the beach. She stopped to put on her sneakers. "One day this whole fucking island will be gone. I can remember when this beach was out to there." She pointed to a point where the surf was rolling in. "One day, you watch, some big fucking storm's going to come up and there won't be a goddamned thing left." It sounded as though she'd be happy to see the island gone.

Though Michael couldn't say he especially enjoyed Valerie's company, it didn't turn out to be nearly as bad as he'd expected. At any rate, he was relieved that she never expressed any curiosity as to why he was so anxious to see her father. It wasn't that she was being discreet—this girl didn't have it in her to be discreet. Rather, she just wasn't interested. This was a lark, a little adventure. It gave her something to do on an otherwise boring summer day.

Actually, the more Michael thought about it, the better he

liked the idea of having Valerie along. It made the prospect of confronting Magnus that much easier, defused some of the tension. Even so, he suspected that later on, when her father got Valerie off by herself, there'd be hell to pay for bringing him out there. But if Valerie was concerned, she didn't show it. Maybe she was too stoned to let it bother her. Besides, there was every chance that she was already in such deep shit with her father that one more offense couldn't possibly make a difference.

They were on a dirt path that had been carefully tamped down. Houses for the very rich nestled in the shelter of pine trees on either side of them. What sounds there were came from the birds and the churning of the tides.

Valerie stopped. "There it is," she said. "What do you think?"

It was a roomy brown clapboard house with a deck in front that held a table and four white metal lawn chairs and a grill. The house wasn't all over the place like others they'd passed, it wasn't modern and filled with windows in whimsical geometric shapes, but in its quiet way it was impressive. It was the kind of summer home that Michael would like one day to have for himself.

Windows were open, but the door was not. "We can go around in back," said Valerie. "He never locks up unless he's not here. And there's no way he can't be here."

"How can you be so sure?"

"We were down at the beach. He wasn't there. Where else would he be? It's not like there's a fucking lot to do around here, you know."

In the back there was a smaller deck from which one could look out onto a copse of trees. Beyond that there appeared to be an untended field.

As Valerie predicted, the door on the back side of the house was open. They walked in, with Valerie leading the way, shouting out in her smoky voice, "Hello! Daddy? You have visitors."

They got all the way into the kitchen without hearing a reply before they saw him. His eyes were red and feverish, his face distorted with confusion or rage, maybe both. He was looking straight at them, but Michael wasn't at all certain that he knew they were there.

"Jesus! Daddy!" Valerie gasped. "We got to get you to a hospital."

He was teetering on his feet, and it was a wonder he could stay upright at all. But when she reached for the phone, he still managed to move quicker, grabbing hold of it before she could. "Bad girl," he said, "bad girl."

And that was when Michael spotted the half-drained bottle of Chivas on the table and the pills scattered all over the floor. Red pills, blue pills, yellow pills. They looked just like candy. Then he noticed the gun.

CHAPTER EIGHTEEN

It was only on the seaplane over to Fire Island that Fontana had the chance to read the story he'd fed Bernie Cook. The *News* played it up nicely, giving it front-page coverage. That made sense, considering the feverish interest people had in the Chopper.

NEW YORK EYE by Bernie Cook
POLICE CLOSING IN ON CHOPPER

For weeks the cops have taken a beating by the public. And no wonder. They capture a crook and dope peddler like Gerry Albinese in a dramatic shootout and then lose him a couple of hours later to "natural causes." Some natural causes. Meanwhile, mafiosi continue to litter the streets of Brooklyn and Queens with bodies, and hoodlums are still—hawking dime bags of heroin and crack in our schoolyards. No question that crime in this city is so pervasive and so routine that we no longer think of the cops in terms of stopping crime; we feel lucky if they can just keep it from getting worse.

Yet sometimes there are crimes that force their attention on us. There are those crimes that are personal—muggings, break-ins—and there are those crimes that are so hideous that our credibility is strained. How, we ask ourselves, can a human being rape and kill—and then cut up the bodies of his victims as if they were just so much meat? But that is exactly what's happening in our city; somebody like that does exist, he is real. His victims are mutilated beyond recognition, perhaps never to be identified. The next question we are likely to ask is: What the hell are the cops doing to find him? Days pass and nothing happens.

For once there is good news to report. Confidential sources inside the NYPD tell me that the investigation, spearheaded by one of the boldest and most imaginative cops we've got—Inspector Larry Kohler— is close to nabbing the ruthless serial killer known as the Chopper. If my informants are right and the Chopper is finally brought to justice, then you can bet your Lotto money that Larry Kohler will be tapped as our next police commissioner. And if you want my opinion, it won't be a moment too soon.

It all depended on just how well Daniel responded to Shannon's drugs as to when Fontana would put his plan into effect. He trusted that they wouldn't have to wait longer than a week before they could send their new, revised incarnation of David-Daniel out into the world for one last performance. Gail Ives was the principal target. But it was possible that there'd be others, Michael Friedlander among them, unless he had the sense to go back to Maine or New Hampshire or wherever the hell it was he'd come from.

And then, when Daniel's usefulness had inevitably come to an end, Kohler would be called upon to destroy the Chopper once and for all. Fontana pictured something suitably dramatic: the psychopath shot down while resisting arrest. The coverage of the event—provided of course by CityVision TV—would be unrivaled: The viewing audience would eventually span the globe. The most publicized killing in history, witnessed by millions. Nor would Daniel's death cause any outcry ; the public would be grateful not to have its tax money used to try him and put him away for twenty-five to life. That kind of hard time wouldn't satisfy anybody; besides, Daniel would probably use it to find somebody to ghost his autobiography.

The ingenuity of this plan delighted Fontana. It was a way of tidying up, of tying together loose ends, with no questions asked. A psychopath didn't need reasons to kill his victims. It happened. No one would think to try to prove a setup or a conspiracy of some kind. Best of all, the enterprise did not depend on Magnus for its success—for its appearance of randomness.

Fontana wasn't alone for this excursion to Fire Island. Accompanying him was one of his new employees, Ralph Mackie. He'd only begun working for Fontana's security agency in the last week following his early retirement from the force. He'd come highly recommended by Farrell, who used to work out of the same precinct—the 19th.

Like Farrell, Mackie owed a significant debt to Fontana. Wearying of marriage to the same woman for almost twenty years, he'd begun several heated affairs in quick succession, hopelessly complicating his life. He wasn't particularly good-looking, but women must have seen something in him that Fontana couldn't.

When Mackie finally broached the subject of divorce with his wife, she'd threatened to haul him into court as an unfit parent and make sure he never saw his kids again. That was much worse to his way of thinking than going after his money.

Ralph knew of Fontana's reputation when it came to solving problems as sticky as his. He was interested in seeing what in the way of a miracle Fontana could accomplish for him.

Fontana had delivered the hoped-for miracle. Now over two years had passed since anybody had last seen his wife. An official probe had turned up nothing. Fontana had been best man at Ralph's second wedding.

Of course, it wasn't as if Mackie hadn't helped Fontana

out in turn. Without his cooperation things would have been far tougher for Fontana in the Friedlander case. Eventually, of course, it became clear to both of them that Mackie was going to be of little use remaining on in the department. Already Internal Affairs was nosing about his activities. Better to get out while he was still ahead. Besides, retirement wasn't so bad, not when he had a pension to look forward to as well as a lucrative job waiting for him to step into.

Of all the assignments that had come Mackie's way since he'd joined the Fontana Security Agency, this would probably be the simplest. "I'm just going to baby-sit him, hold his hand a little," Fontana told him when they were within sight of Fire Island. Ralph could look forward to an easy day's work.

When they arrived at The Pines, the dock was covered with people. The outdoor bars that flanked the pier were crowding up with new arrivals who'd just stepped off their yachts at anchor in the harbor. Even in jeans and Lycra bathing suits, they looked tan and classy. More than that, they looked as if they belonged, not just in The Pines, but in St. Moritz and Positano and Cancún and the hundreds of other enclaves scattered around the world for those with the necessary money and cachet. They gave off a special aura; it was an aura that Fontana kept trying on to see if it fit. Somehow it never did. He envied these people, he longed to be one of them, and sometimes, like a light-skinned black mistaken for white, he managed to pass. But deep down he knew that he didn't belong, that these people would never fully accept him, maybe fearing that some of what he had might rub off on them, and he hated them for it.

After the two of them had had a chance to quench their thirst, Fontana decided on his plan. "Tell you what, Ralph, why don't you hang around here? Kurt may get spooked if he sees I've brought somebody along. I'm pretty sure you can amuse yourself in the meantime. Have a few drinks, enjoy the scenery."

"Lots of nice ass around here," Ralph noted, picking up on the kind of scenery to which Fontana was referring.

"I should be back in an hour—I don't expect this to take long."

Then he began on his way along the path through pines and brush that would take him eventually to Magnus's house.

Sometimes it was like being sucked down into the deepest sleep, he thought. Sometimes, though, it was more like a perilous amusement park ride with hairpin turns and sudden unexpected descents. From one moment to the next he didn't know what would fill up his mind, what thoughts would leap and dance through his head. But that wasn't what bothered him. What bothered him was that he could never hold on to any thought in particular. In his near delirium he kept having the feeling that he was close to getting the point—that amazing understanding that would make everything all clear for once—but then it would slip away again, just vanish, and that pained and puzzled him.

What was interesting was how nothing seemed to happen for the better part of an hour. He felt a little drunk, a little hypersensitive, nothing else. The Tofranil didn't seem to be having any effect, although he couldn't discount the possibility that he was already under the drug's subjugation, that it was the drug that was supplying him with this illusion that nothing was happening. He decided to keep notes. He was always keeping notes, clinical observations pertaining to the conditions of the cadaver at death. Why stop now, when it was the progress to his own death that needed recording?

7:30. Begin: Three jiggers of Chivas, no ice. Two 25 mg caps of T.

7:50. A little fuzziness, numbness in the back of the neck. Last night's residual hangover? Add five 25 mg caps T.

8:30. Three jiggers more of Chivas. Add ten 25 mg caps T. More fuzziness. Slurred words, but no matter: no one to talk to, no one to hear.

9:20. Nothing staying still. Floor moving, keep slipping, won't stay afloat. Like an endless earthquake. Ten maybe more 25 mg caps T. Can't see straight to count.

Now he could no longer write. Or write so that the words showed up legibly on the page. His hand shook when he held the pen, and letters mutated all of a sudden into swirls and lines that trailed off the page and continued onto the tabletop. It didn't matter, Barbara would be able to clean it up; the ink wouldn't settle into the Formica surface.

After a while it began to dawn on him that he was hallucinating. Somehow, while he was aware that it could happen, he wasn't prepared for it. Ginny Karamis was sitting at the kitchen table asking him if she could have some of his Scotch, telling him how terribly thirsty she was. At one moment she would appear to him the way she had many months ago, her eyes bright and wild, her lips as moist and open as she was between her legs. And then, while he stared at her, protesting her presence in the kitchen, shouting at her to go away because she had no claims on the living any longer, her face dissolved and all the flesh fell away from her body. But dead, she still moved. He closed his eyes, opened them again, and she still moved.

He walked away from her; he decided that this was his only choice. In the living room, though, he thought he saw out of the corner of his eye Francis Holmes coming down the stairs, unsteady on his feet, as if he'd been doing a great deal more drinking than he should have.

Magnus was thinking that this was all wrong, that he should have chosen the Tuinal or the Seconal, gone with something that would have been quicker and spared him from these unnatural visitations.

Maybe throw up. He couldn't make up his mind whether he was sick enough to throw up. Instead, he returned to the kitchen to take what remained of the Tofranil, expecting to see Ginny Karamis. But she had gone and been replaced by his daughter and a man he thought he recognized but whose name now escaped him. He strained his tired eyes in an effort to pin them down, but his vision was starting to fail. Whatever facility that enabled him to distinguish between what was real and what was merely a projection of his over-wrought mind was no longer working. It occurred to him that his daughter and this man were dead, too.

The girl was reaching for the phone. He knew what that meant. Police . . . paramedics . . . analeptics to get his circulation going . . . gastric lavage . . . headlines tomorrow . . . He couldn't allow that to happen. The phone, yanked out of the wall, crashed to the floor. Interesting, because he couldn't recall having had it in his hand. The phone, he was sure, must be real. And maybe this girl, his daughter, was real as well.

"Daddy!" she was saying. "What are you doing?"

She was moving to the table, maybe thinking that she would hide the pills and the liquor bottle. Now she was down on her hands and knees trying to scoop up the hundreds of pills that had somehow fallen there. "Help me, god-dammit!" Her voice was choking with sobs.

The man was slow on his feet, stunned, not knowing how to react. Magnus was embarrassed. He hated being seen like this. Too late, though. Too late to do anything. She could call, she could put the phone back in or go upstairs and use the phone there, call whomever she liked, he was through. He could sense something happening inside him that alerted him to the finality of what he'd done.

Maybe it was fear—panic, really—he was feeling, even more than shame. All at once he wanted to disgorge the pills and the Scotch, he wanted to undo his whole life, go back to where things had begun to turn wrong.

It was because of her, because of Valerie. He had never received any gratitude for what he'd done for her. All he'd gotten over the years from her was shit. "Bitch!" he cried. He was filled suddenly with loathing for her. He was slapping her, watching her face grow violently red and heated, but what was so weird was that she wasn't doing anything to resist. "You did this, you did this!" he was shouting at her. Or maybe not. Sounds were becoming distorted with the drug. He actually might have been speaking very softly or not at all. Really, he had no idea.

The man with her was trying to separate them. Magnus suddenly knew who he was. Michael... Michael... Michael Friedlander—yes, that was it. But what was he doing there with Valerie? It made no sense to him. Maybe it didn't matter; he was tired, he wasn't in the mood to struggle with him, and so he let him drag her away. "Watch it, you don't know who you're dealing with. She's a killer. If you don't believe me, go outside. Back in the field beyond the house. You'll see it."

Magnus had to lean against the counter to steady himself; it was no longer possible to stand on his own power. The world was turning colors. Then it would go black, and he would think this was the end. But after a time he could see again. However, now the world was floating; nothing would stay still, the kitchen had turned into a weightless environment; they were lost in space. He could not make out what had happened to his daughter. He was saying something important that he knew he had to finish. But what was it?

"Outside. You'll want. To see outside. Where flowers are growing taller. Know why? Weeds, too. Taller. Tell you why." He saw her again, like a specter, barely there. "Dead bodies make good fertilizer."

He couldn't go on; it wasn't the pain that was becoming so unbearable, because truly he didn't know whether what he was feeling was pain or not; rather, it was the agony of waiting this out. The goddamned Tofranil wasn't doing its job nearly as quickly as he'd hoped, even with the additional kick of the Chivas. If his goddamned daughter hadn't hidden the rest of the pills, he'd have taken the remainder and have done with it. Probably she flushed them down the toilet. God, he despised her, hated what she'd done to him, hated what he'd allowed her to do, fucking bitch.

The gun. Now the gun made sense. He wouldn't feel a thing when it went off. He was anesthetized already. He might not know when he was dead, his mind was so far gone.

Then the thought flashed into his mind to take his daughter with him. What good had she ever been to anybody? He could kill her, then himself. It was simply done; more than that, it deserved to be done.

He welcomed her cry, the anguish in her eyes, when he trained the gun on her. Finally something was penetrating her mind, finally he was able to draw some reaction from her. She couldn't run to her room and shut the door on him now.

Then, before he could squeeze the trigger, Michael jumped between them and tried to take the gun away from him. Weakened by the drugs, he tottered, fighting to maintain hold. He couldn't let this son-of-a-bitch take his gun. Valerie was screaming, hysterical with fear. Oh, yes, finally, he was getting through to her.

All at once he heard the screen door opening and somebody walking in. It wasn't the hallucination he thought at first, because Michael heard it, too, and was so surprised to see who it was that he loosened his grip enough on Magnus's hand to give him the freedom of movement he needed to aim the gun where he pleased.

He didn't think—couldn't think—he just pressed the trigger, and when the report came, it was incredibly loud and left his ears ringing. Suddenly everything he'd put in himself during the last few hours came rushing into his head. His heart stopped, and a stabbing pain seized his chest. This was where it came to a close, he knew. But at least before he dropped to the floor, he'd had the satisfaction of watching Ray Fontana thrown back through the screen door out into the summer day.

CHAPTER NINETEEN

Most of the time they left him alone. He knew the purpose of the mirror. They must be observing him through it—Shannon, Farrell, and, most of all, Fontana. He understood that they were experimenting on him with drugs that had already begun to have their effect. His vision was not as it should be, and his mouth felt half the time like cotton and the other half like some corrosive metal. He experienced dizzy spells and drowsiness. To fight off these debilitating symptoms, he concentrated on his exercises, using the examining room, his prison, as his dojo. He had to restore the proper flow of energy—the chi—if he was to have a hope of surviving.

He'd begin with limbering-up exercises, stretching, stretching, exhilarating in the pain he was drawing out of his thighs and pectorals. The pain felt good; the pain was needed to keep his mind sharp, to defeat the drugs. Then he would perform a series of lethal kicks and punches but slowed down so dramatically that they were transformed into something very much like a ballet: a ritual of harmony and grace. It was called the Flower Dance of Sai Lat. He wondered what his captors were thinking while they watched him.

Occasionally he would stop and just sit still, his mind not focused on anything at all, a blank slate waiting to be filled in. Even his meditation was a form of exercise. He could practice his breathing, sucking down his breath into his diaphragm, holding it in, holding it in, then expelling it in one single concentrated burst. It was interesting to discover what thoughts and images floated into his head at such times.

From time to time he returned to the picture of the girl Fontana had given him.

They hadn't supplied him with much information about her—just her address and the fact that she was a doctor at Bellevue Hospital. Why would they want him to put her away? There was more to it than what they'd told him. Perhaps she'd jilted Fontana, or else she stood in the way of something that he was desperate to have. Fontana was, Daniel thought, a very desperate man. But if he were to find her—if he were to kill her—then it wouldn't be because of Fontana.

What would make him go find this woman was something that struck him about her picture. It wasn't merely that she was attractive; the photo was unreliable in that respect and there were, besides, many hundreds of equally attractive young women in this city, a new crop every season. Rather, it was the dissatisfaction that he sensed from the wariness and challenge in her eyes and the combustible sexuality that was so evident in her posture. "Come and get me" was the message her body was communicating. There was a second message, too: "You're not going to win me, so don't even bother trying."

He liked the fact that she was a doctor, too, that she was familiar with the body and all the corruption to which the body's flesh was susceptible.

But he knew what he really wanted, what mattered beyond all else. He wanted to find the hungering beauty, the sad allure, that he remembered from his youth. When Byron's face came back to him, his eyes were feverish with desire. Everybody said that they looked like twins, not just brothers separated in age by a couple of years. And they were twins—under the skin, in their souls, where it truly counted. No one ever found out about all those times they spent in the darkness of the bedroom upstairs, discovering each other, driving each other crazy. The look they would exchange when the need came over them was sometimes all that was necessary, just the look, no words: the touching, the groping, the penetration that followed—it was delicious, it was ecstasy, but it was the look that held him even now across the years.

So why did Byron have to go and get himself killed, stuck in the gut with a knife in some North Beach saloon? It remained a mystery to him, but only because he'd let it be one, too afraid to question it. But finally he'd had to acknowledge the truth: Byron had died to escape him, to escape the terror of his own inexhaustible desire. It was a simpler way out. In dying, of course, his brother had made Daniel a captive of his love forever.

So he would go and see the girl and look for Byron in her as he had in the others. But he had a feeling that he wouldn't be there. Her beauty was not his, her love could not equal his. In the end, he'd find only what he'd find in the others: the same secret yearning for a way out.

But he'd made up his mind about one thing: He wouldn't wait for when his captors decided to send him to her; they must be stupid to believe that he would go along with their program, slip unresisting into whatever trap they'd laid for him. He knew better than that.

It was necessary to get out quickly—that very day. No matter how rigorously he pursued his regimen of exercises, there would inevitably come a time when the drugs would begin to sap his strength. What was worse, he might not know how much damage—permanent damage—they were doing until it was too late. He knew something about how these drugs worked, how they could linger in his system for months even after he was off them, how they could induce constipation or diarrhea and cause him to walk with a hobbling, spastic gait. Bad enough that he had this flesh wound in his leg to contend with. He couldn't allow them to tamper further with his brain or his body chemistry; he might never be able to restore his chi. That risk was unacceptable.

He hadn't the slightest doubt that he could overcome the two men responsible for guarding him. Farrell was the more dangerous one, but not because he held the gun. No, Farrell was more dangerous because Daniel sensed that he was indifferent to his beauty, which, he knew, was a weapon far more formidable even than his skill in martial arts.

Shannon, however, was another matter. While at first he might have been repelled by Daniel, he was little by little beginning to respond to him without having any idea that this was happening. Shannon, he was certain, would be the kind of man who, under different circumstances, would invite him to a party where all his friends and colleagues would be on hand. What an exciting, titillating guest he'd make—a serial killer, a butcher, but a killer with the looks of a matinee idol, articulate, well mannered, soft-spoken, supremely self-confident! The reactions from the guests would be predictable: They'd think that the police or the press had gotten it all wrong, that this wonderful young man could not possibly be the Chopper. Or else they would manage to separate the horror of the crime from the man himself, judging him only by their first—and misguided—impressions, their minds unable to bridge the gap between the criminal and the man who radiated such magnetism. The women would give him their phone numbers—excited by the danger he represented, convinced somehow that they might succeed in reforming him—while the men would extend invitations for him to come visit or join their health clubs, their games, their social circles.

So he knew very well the effect he was having on Dr. Shannon, even if Dr. Shannon did not. Dr. Shannon wanted his prisoner to appreciate what he was going through, what with these tests and the drugs he was obliged to administer. It was plain as day to him: Dr. Shannon wanted to be his friend.

It was nearly one in the afternoon. The light penetrating through the beige curtains was harsh. A sunny day. From behind the door to the examining room he detected movement, voices. It was time for another injection. Dr. Shannon and Farrell would be coming in at any moment. He held his body in readiness, his muscles tensed. There was no seduction more satisfying than the seduction that had death as its goal.

At first Shannon thought that there was no question but that Fontana was bent. Why else this obsession with Daniel? He couldn't figure it. But then he'd begun to have a glimmer of understanding, sensing in this killer something unique and unfathomable. A truly baffling disease, never before recorded in medical annals, resistant to every therapy doctors could devise, might ignite in Shannon the same hopeless enthusiasm that held Fontana in its grip. Shannon realized that if he'd been kept in the dark about Daniel's identity, he might even have grown to like him.

But once the knowledge was given to him, he could not shut it out again. Shannon noticed how Daniel looked at him; he was constantly sizing him up, not liking what he saw—that much was obvious. There was only repulsion in those dazzling eyes of his.

If Fontana ever suspected Shannon of crossing him, there would be hell to pay. He would ruin Shannon, destroy his career and his family. All he needed to do was tie him in to the death of Ambrosetti; it would be no problem for him. But for Shannon to allow Fontana to continue this devious experiment, whatever its ultimate objective, was unconscionable. Like everyone else in the city, Shannon knew what Daniel was capable of, what atrocities he'd committed, and would—if he had the chance—commit again.

So he'd hit upon a solution that seemed to him absolutely inspired. He had prepared an injection that was certain to throw Daniel's mind permanently out of whack, while at the same time disabling him physically. How the combination of Chlorpromazine, Nardil, Marplan, and various tricyclics would actually work was of course altogether unpredictable. Nor did he have any way of knowing how long it would require to take effect. But the dosage was so high that it all but guaranteed an acute reaction, one that was certain to render Daniel powerless. It was possible that he wouldn't even be capable of controlling his own limbs. The effect would be equivalent to shooting a bolt of lightning directly into an electric grid; it was how Ed Shannon planned to make Daniel's lights go out.

There was a further advantage to this solution. The M.A.O. inhibitors that Shannon had included in his deadly cocktail could kill Daniel if they were combined with such a commonplace food like cheese. A glass of red wine would be lethal. And the beauty of it was that Fontana would never realize that his captive had received an overdose. Hadn't Shannon warned him that these drugs varied from individual to individual? It was no one's fault, it was just an experiment that had gone bad.

To Shannon such an outcome was preferable to killing Daniel outright. Ambrosetti was the last one. He couldn't do it again. This was the only way Shannon knew to take back the power that Fontana had stripped from him, the only way Shannon knew to obliterate the loathing in Daniel's eyes.

CHAPTER TWENTY

"Oh, shit!" Valerie said, but no more emphatically than if she'd just spilled a glass of milk. She was looking down at her father's body, dumbfounded, apparently incapable of movement. "Jesus motherfucking Christ!" Her eyes shifted to the screen door, which was still banging open from the impact Fontana had made crashing through it.

Michael knew that he would have to do something, though in the heat of the moment it would not come to him exactly what. From the instant he'd walked into this house, nothing had seemed real; there was a dreamlike quality to it, a feeling that no action was possible, that he could only watch helplessly while events unfolded in front of his eyes. How long had it been? Five minutes? Ten? An hour? He couldn't figure it.

"I need to smoke a joint," Valerie said, fumbling with her pocketbook as she tried to open it and get one out. "I don't fucking believe this." She was talking to herself, not to Michael. It didn't seem as if she knew Michael was there any longer; her eyes were red and glazed, and there was every possibility that she was completely numbed by shock.

Michael tried to motivate himself. But his senses were overwhelmed, and it was really hard for him to put one foot in front of another. His mind kept giving him instructions, but they tended to contradict and cancel one another out: Find a phone, call the cops, call a doctor, calm down Valerie, just get the hell out of there—off the island, off the planet, if possible. In fact, he felt as if all he wanted to do was sit down and not move for another hour or two just to get his bearings.

Now he was edging toward the door, afraid of what he'd find once he actually reached it. He wasn't certain about what he'd just witnessed. The gun had discharged in Magnus's hand, and Fontana had tumbled out the door. He thought he'd seen blood on his face. Or maybe he'd imagined the blood. Certainly the bullet must have struck him, but was he wounded or dead? God, what a mess.

Looking back, he saw that Valerie was still having trouble getting the joint lit. But that was her problem. He couldn't worry about her. He stepped to the door and held back for a moment before looking out. He wasn't anxious to see anybody hurt, even if it was Ray Fontana.

He looked. Fontana was alive, moaning, in obvious pain, thrashing about on the deck, soaking blood into the wooden planks. It was impossible for Michael to say where he'd been hit; there was just a lot of blood and it was all over him. What an incongruous sight Fontana made for, Michael thought. The rustic setting in which he seemed to be dying was no less tranquil than before; birds cooed and shrieked in the treetops, and the sound of the tide coming in was as lulling as ever. Michael realized that he'd been expecting something in the landscape to have registered the violence that had just occurred. But it was all the same.

Returning to the kitchen, he found the phone and placed it back into the jack on the wall. "Valerie, do you know what number you dial for police here?"

Valerie didn't seem to have heard him. She was sucking on her joint with fierce determination, as if her life depended on it. Half of her thin body was shrouded in pungent smoke.

"Valerie!"

She looked at him, scared, jolted for the moment back into real time and space. "What? Oh, I don't know . . . I don't know." Then, as if she'd just comprehended the ramifications of what Michael was asking, she shouted, "Hey, wait a minute! You can't call the fucking cops. We can't stay here!"

Michael began to go through the thin phone book. There was nothing he could do to make his hands stop shaking. Christ! What a fuck-up! "We'll call them and then get out of here. We won't leave our names, okay? But we have to call them. We can't just let him die out there."

Valerie regarded him with bewilderment. It seemed to him then that she wasn't entirely unused to being in situations that ended as badly as this. "Christ almighty!" she muttered. "You know he didn't really give a shit about me."

"What's that?" He couldn't pay much attention to her; he had to focus his mind completely on getting just one thing done, which in this case was punching out the number of the police in The Pines. He supposed that there must be a number for emergency medical assistance, too, but he assumed that once he made his report, the police could handle that part.

"The thing was that Dad liked to think he was doing it for me, but he wasn't protecting me, not really. He was doing it for himself, for his goddamned fucking reputation!" Her anger burned through the barrier she was trying to erect with the weed.

She was screaming, and tears were running down her cheeks. In fact, she was making so much noise that Michael could hardly hear himself as he spoke to the police.

"There's an emergency at Dr. Magnus's house," he was saying. "Somebody's hurt. You've got to get a doctor here."

Whoever had picked up on the other end kept demanding his name, but he'd be damned if he'd give it to him. "It's not important. Just get somebody over here right away."

He hung up, thinking, *Fine, now I've done my duty. Now I can get the hell out of here.* He turned, just in time to see Valerie, her face contorted by rage, trying to lift her father up as if she meant to do—what? Pommel him? Spit at him? Talk to him? He couldn't tell, and it was likely she didn't know herself.

Michael grabbed hold of her, but she resisted and began showering him with blows. So he slapped her, unable to think of what else he could do to restrain her, to stop the hysteria from overwhelming her completely. Up until now he could have cared less whether she came with him or stayed there. But suddenly he was gripped with the fear of what might happen if he left her behind. She might become so unhinged—she might already be so unhinged—that she'd say anything to the cops, anything that would exonerate her, even if it meant accusing Michael of the shooting. And it probably wouldn't be the first time she found someone to take the fall for her, either.

His slap surprised her. Her bright, bloodshot eyes found his own, and then she sagged in his arms, her sobs muffled against his chest. She was whimpering and trying to say something at the same time, but he couldn't understand a word of it.

"We've got to get out of here, Valerie. The cops will be here any minute."

He hoped that that would mobilize her. And it sort of did. She separated herself from Michael, her body still wracked with sobs, and began to make her way slowly, with a weird somnambulistic motion, toward the door. Never once did she glance back at her father's prostrate form.

"Valerie."

"What is it?" She sounded like a small child denied an extra helping of cake.

"What was that your father said about the dead being fertilizer? Something about a field?"

She looked blankly at him, seeming not to know what he was talking about. Then she asked, "Oh, that. He must have meant the place where he used to bury all that shit."

"What shit?"

She shrugged.

"It's important, Valerie."

"I don't know . . . notes and shit, files . . . you know? He didn't think I knew, but I used to see him some nights. I knew."

"Can you show me where?"

She really must have thought him to be crazy now. "Hey! What the fuck? I thought you just said we've got to get out of here. What is it with you?"

"There a shovel around here?"

"In the closet." She was standing right by it, but she made no move toward it.

Michael got it out. It was heavy and encrusted with dirt, but it would do the job. "Now show me this place."

Valerie gave Fontana a look full of disgust as she stepped around him. His condition failed to interest her. He was moving around less. He was still alive, though, his eyes darting from side to side in mute appeal. Now Michael noticed that blood was pumping out of his lower neck; it was there that the bullet had entered.

Gradually Michael was emerging from his dazed state. It was difficult, even painful, because it required so much concerted effort for just the simplest task. And he had to watch Valerie constantly; she could go berserk on him at any moment.

They cut through the wall of trees and into the field. Suddenly they were surrounded by weeds and grass up to their ankles. The brush underfoot, bristling with thorns, lay in ambush for them, stinging and scratching at every turn, causing Valerie to cry out and curse and, periodically, stop to inspect her latest wound. "I'm bleeding, goddammit," she complained.

"Forget about your scratches. Let's go," Michael said, ready to propel her forward by force if necessary.

At least, Michael thought, she had something to focus her mind on besides the events of the last fifteen minutes.

Magnus's house was almost obscured by the trees that ran along the back of his property, which meant that they probably wouldn't be spotted by the police when they finally showed up.

After trudging through the undergrowth for ten minutes, they reached a stretch of land covered with dandelions and Queen Anne's lace. Valerie stepped up her pace. "There," she said, "there it is!"

Michael could detect some excitement in her voice. Maybe she was curious to find out what her father had been concealing after all.

He could see what Magnus had been referring to. In the

spot where Valerie was standing, the flowers and the weeds were growing thicker, taller, too, than the surrounding vegetation. Their leaves were a darker color; it was as if these plants were bred from a strain genetically altered to cause them to devour nutrients and sunshine at an accelerated rate.

"You're sure this is it?"

Valerie nodded.

"Well, then, I guess we start digging." He drove the blade of the shovel into the earth.

Michael didn't have to dig far down. What Magnus had buried there was only half a foot beneath the surface. He knew he'd reached it when his shovel met resistance, metal striking metal. He cast a sidelong glance at Valerie, but she seemed not to appreciate his discovery even after he'd exposed a steel case to the light. Her eyes had a peculiar faraway look that only shock and several joints of Jamaican grass could have produced. Under the harsh noontime sun, her skin was turning a violent shade of red, but she didn't seem to mind. After all that had happened, a bad sunburn was the least of her problems.

Brushing away the dirt that had hardened on the surface of the case, Michael undid the latch, which had become partly rusted. He could barely contain himself; his nerves were gone and he only hoped he could handle this.

The lid wouldn't budge at first, but finally it yielded to his exertions. He reached it. There were files inside, bulging with documents. Many were damp to the touch and badly deteriorated. There were pages and pages of notes in Magnus's hand as well as official autopsy reports with further corrections made in pen. Half a dozen dictabelts lay in the bottom of the case, but their labels, written in ink, had been blurred by moisture and were practically illegible.

Frantically he pored through the records, looking for names—his brother's name most of all. He noted *Epstein, C.* He noted *Ojieda, T.* He noted *Ambrosetti, N.* He noted *Holmes, F.* And then he noted *Friedlander, A.*

*   *   *

His eyes scanned the first page, catching the words ". . . inconsistent with finding of suicide."

This was it, this was what he wanted. It was like stumbling on an alternative universe, a mirror image of this one, where falsehoods and deceits were reversed, transformed into truth. Had Magnus thought to use these records for insurance, a way of keeping leverage for himself against Fontana? Did it give him some kind of security to know that these records were there, within easy access? What must have been going through his mind each time he furtively added a new autopsy report to his grim collection? Perhaps he thought of it the way a dishonest comptroller might, who maintained two sets of books, one to show to the IRS, the other to be consulted only in the dead of night, in private, when it was necessary to know what the state of his finances actually was like.

Valerie was getting edgy, her eyes gradually focusing, taking in the world and her place within it. "Can we get out of here now?"

The damp, moldy documents Michael clutched in his hands held no significance for her. Her father's final, ignominious legacy had nothing to do with how she got on with her own life.

"You want to take the fucking box with you, take it with you. But let's split."

Michael replaced the records and dictabelts and secured the lid, fully prepared to leave, when his eye was caught by something lying in the bottom of the hole he'd just dug out.

"Wait a minute, Valerie." He began to shovel deeper, widening the hole as he went.

"What is it? Why are you digging like that? Haven't you got what you came here for?"

Apprehension came into her eyes. She crinkled her nose and stared down to see what had drawn Michael's interest. "Eeecch!" she said.

It was a hand, still with some tatters of flesh hanging off it. Shoveling away more dirt, Michael exposed an arm and then a neck and then part of a head. Half the skull was shattered, one eye socket telescoped by the force of the blow so that it was little larger than a pinhole.

"Oh, fuck!" Valerie said, and quickly looked away.

Then, before Michael could reveal anything more of the body, she grabbed his hand, suddenly excited and desperate—more so than she'd been back at the house.

"Promise you'll never tell," she said. "You owe me that much, goddammit, you do!" She began to hit him on the chest—feebly, uselessly—until he could stop her.

"What is it? What are you talking about, Valerie? Whose body is that?"

She refused to tell him until Michael had covered up the body—haphazardly, quickly, because she was panicking and still queasy. Only when they were well away from the site did she begin. Even then her story emerged in fits and starts.

The remains he had uncovered—the fertilizer that caused the plants to grow so profusely, so abundantly—were those of somebody she once knew. His name was Eddie Lupica.

They had met four years before at a party and gotten stoned out of their gourds. Coke, weed, angel dust—whatever was around at the time. She was driving him home. Her home or his? She didn't remember, might not have even known it at the time. It was her car, though—she was sure of that. Her father's car, actually. Maybe she was avoiding another car or had dozed off at the wheel; that was something else she didn't remember. The details hadn't stayed fixed in her mind. Next thing she knew she was lying on the side of the road, all bloodied, the car smashed against an embankment. Everything was very quiet, very still. She was crawling, couldn't walk. Did he want to see the scars? No, he said, he didn't. She showed him some anyway. If he looked at her right leg, he could make out the way the skin had whitened and swollen. Or maybe he'd prefer to see the scars on her stomach?

He said he didn't think so. Later, maybe.

She lifted up her torn T-shirt anyway. "I don't want you to get the idea I'm lying to you," she said.

An ugly pink scar crept toward her pubis like a directional sign. "This nearly fucking killed me," she said, her voice filled with pride. Eddie was momentarily forgotten.

"And Eddie was dead?" Michael had already surmised the answer but decided to ask anyway.

"Eddie?" She looked confused by his question. "Why, he'd gone through a window. He didn't look much better than what you saw just now."

He supposed they were heading toward the bay. Certainly he hoped that this was the way to the ferry. She seemed to know where they were going, but that might have been wishful thinking. She might just be walking in any direction that happened to suggest itself to her, anxious to put as much distance as possible between herself and Eddie. All the time she continued talking. Now that he'd gotten her started, she didn't seem capable of shutting up; she apparently had a deep, insatiable need to tell him what had happened.

"They put me in a hospital," she said, "and when I wake up Daddy's standing there and he goes, 'It's all over with, honey, everything will be okay.' And I go, 'What about Eddie?' And he goes, 'What did I just tell you? Everything will be fine if you do what I say and don't ever say anything about him again.' He goes, 'I'll handle it.' And he did."

"And you never asked?"

"Why should I? I didn't want to fucking know about it," she snapped. "Would you?"

He didn't reply. But one thought dominated all others now: If it weren't for Valerie, Magnus might never have gone to Fontana for help. It was just possible that the long and tangled chain of cause and effect that would ultimately lead to his brother's death had begun with this wasted, sunburned adolescent girl.

"Jesus! I didn't know he was buried there. You think I'd have let you dig if I knew he was there? You think I'm crazy or something?" She stopped and gave him a funny look. "So you've got to promise," she said.

"Promise what?"

"That you won't say a word to anybody about Eddie. Deal?"

"Deal," he said.

CHAPTER TWENTY-ONE

Growing restless, Ralph Mackie decided that he'd given Fontana enough time. Nearly an hour had passed since Fontana had gone off to Magnus's house. Sensing that there might be trouble, Mackie decided to see if he could find Fontana. He should have known better than to let him go without getting directions. But he figured that it was a small community; somebody must know where Magnus lived.

His reasoning was right; it just took him longer than he'd thought it would.

When he got to within sight of Magnus's house, though, he was brought to a standstill by the sight of a couple of paramedics lifting Fontana onto a gurney while a cop looked on. Another cop was coming out the back door, shaking his head gravely. Obviously something had gone very wrong. Mackie decided to go no closer to the house.

Then he took in what the local cops seemed so far to have overlooked: the undergrowth close to the line of trees had been recently disturbed. A branch had snapped off, and leaves lay crushed. Taking care not to call attention to his movements, Mackie started toward the trees. A few minutes later he observed something else of interest: drops of fresh blood on the ground. He was on the right track.

Two sets of footprints—one produced by a pair of walking shoes, the other by sandals—were clearly visible in the ground. Mackie had no way of knowing whether the people he was trailing were Fontana's assailants or witnesses to what had happened. In either case, he wanted to have a talk with them—but on his terms.

It was only when he was well out into the field that Mackie caught sight of a couple—a man and a slender girl. They were a good distance away, headed toward the bay, obviously in a hurry, it seemed, to get away from something. The direction of the footprints into the field left no doubt in Mackie's mind that these were the two who'd come from Magnus's house.

Soon he came to a spot that showed signs of having been dug up and indifferently covered up again. The end of a shovel protruded out from the undergrowth in which it had been clumsily concealed. But unless he wanted to lose the couple, he couldn't take the chance of digging out the spot himself. Besides, he had the feeling that whatever had been buried there was now in their possession.

Mackie followed them all the way through The Pines, until they reached the pier where the ferries tied up. He kept well in back of them, but there was never any danger of losing them. Only one path led to where they were going. When the two got into line for the next ferry back to the mainland, he joined the line as well. His interest was focused on the gray metal case held tightly in the man's arms. He would very much like to know what was in that case. The girl, meanwhile, looked distraught, on edge. Any minute now she would fall apart—he knew the signs. But he decided to wait to make his approach until the ferry had started back to Bay Shore. She would make for an easy target.

No sooner had the ferry gotten under way than the girl started moving around. It seemed impossible for her to stay put. While her companion remained on the deck, taking in the sun, she went below, escaping the heat.

Mackie found her close to the bow, tearfully staring out the window at The Pines, which was rapidly disappearing from view. He came up from behind her, catching her un-aware. Even before she detected his presence, he leaned over to whisper in her ear, "What's your name, honey?"

She jumped. Her eyes went wide with apprehension. She couldn't get a word out. Her eyes darted this way and that, searching for an escape. It was a useless idea; Mackie had her cornered.

"Valerie . . . Valerie M-Magnus," she stammered. "Please don't hurt me." She was hugging herself, rocking back and forth.

So this was the chief medical examiner's daughter. "Tell me, honey, what's your friend's name?"

She told him that, too. "I'll tell you anything you want. . . ."

"Tell me what's in that case."

When she described its contents, he knew at once what he had to do. But it couldn't be done on the ferry, not with so many people on board. A plan was forming in his mind.

"If you be a good girl and do exactly what I say, nothing's going to happen to you."

CHAPTER TWENTY-TWO

When the ferry put into port at Bay Shore, Michael looked all around for Valerie. Failing to see her among the debarking passengers, he assumed that she'd gone ahead to the car. He was relieved that she wasn't his responsibility—not any longer. All he wanted out of her now was a ride into the city.

Once he was back in New York the first thing he intended to do was find somebody who could help him secure the documents he had unearthed. For the better part of an hour he'd been racking his brains, trying to come up with the name of a person he could rely on absolutely. But of all the people Michael could think of, only one could be trusted, and that was his father.

Apart from the fact that Paul Friedlander had a vested in-

terest in seeing justice done for his murdered son, he also
had the necessary connections, the power to get these papers into the right hands. The D.A. would certainly listen to
him; he had the credibility that Michael did not. No one
would question Paul Friedlander's credentials as they would
his. Michael counted on him to know what to do.

Of course, he had another compelling motive in seeking
out his father. These documents were his vindication. His father would have to acknowledge that maybe, after all,
Michael had been right to pursue what others regarded as a
lost cause. His life was not a waste; it took its meaning from
what lay inside this case.

But he couldn't do a single thing unless he could get back
to Manhattan. Certainly he'd feel a great deal safer in the city
than he did where he was, especially if someone should
have seen him close to Magnus's house at the time of
Fontana's shooting. For all he knew, Fontana might have
been conscious enough to identify him.

But he couldn't dwell on these things. His main concern
now was finding Valerie, but where the hell was she? From
the ferry station he walked into the parking lot. The Porsche
was not there. He looked and looked, but there was no mistake, the Porsche was gone. She'd obviously cut out on him,
leaving him stranded. She wasn't that far gone that she would
have forgotten him. After venting his spleen for a few moments, drifting back and forth across the lot cursing her, he
decided that he'd better find a way to get back to New York
on his own.

It was no problem obtaining a taxi to take him to the rail-
way station. Taxis were everywhere, shuttling people from
one end of Bay Shore to the other. The problem was the wait
he'd have to endure until the next Manhattan-bound train.
He didn't like the idea of standing around on the platform
with the case. As much as he realized he was being irra-
tional, he kept having the sense that people were staring at
him. He decided that he'd be safer—at least he'd *feel* safer—
if he went into the bar located half a block behind the station. Besides, he was badly in need of a drink.

It could have been a bar anywhere in America: dark, smoky, atmospheric, filled with carpenters and day laborers and men who were obviously out of work, drinking bottles of Bud and shots of whiskey. A big-boned middle-aged woman was supplying them with their fortification. Nobody was bothering with the pinball machines, but a woman with incredible tan legs and long auburn hair—obviously somebody who'd come off the ferry, too—was dropping quarter after quarter into the jukebox. Frank Sinatra was belting out "I've Got You Under My Skin."

A couple of minutes later there appeared another passenger he recalled seeing on the ferry. For an instant he stood in the open doorway, thrown into silhouette by the afternoon sun. Then he entered. Taking a seat about halfway down the bar from where Michael was sitting, he ordered a beer. He didn't look like a man who would own a house on the island or even know someone who did. Though the man seemed to be minding his own business, Michael could sense his interest in him and the case at his feet.

Michael was convinced that this man had to be a cop. Or maybe an ex-cop like Farrell. Michael had had enough experience with cops by now—mostly unpleasant—to sense when they were close by, even when they were out of uniform. Under the man's persistent scrutiny, he found it more and more difficult to affect an air of normalcy. He wished that he had the money to hire a taxi to take him into the city; it would have made things so much easier. But when in his life wouldn't money have made things easier? It was just more of the same.

Finally he couldn't stand it anymore. Though there was still ten minutes to go before the train was due to arrive, he abruptly got up and walked out of the bar. He didn't look back. There were more people on the platform now, and he took comfort in that. Eventually the pretty girl with the legs appeared on the platform, but there was no sign of the man. Maybe he had been wrong about him.

Though he expected that the train would be late, if only because nothing yet had gone right in his day, this didn't turn out to be the case. The train was on time. As he boarded, he looked up and down the platform, but the man definitely was not there. Maybe, in spite of Valerie, he could make it home in one piece after all.

Notwithstanding his determination to stay awake, he kept nodding off. The events of the day had taken a lot out of him. All that nervous energy and adrenaline constantly pumping through his body hadn't left him with much to go on. His body cried out for relief; he couldn't keep it in such a state of high alertness forever.

Only when the train, with a great grinding and clatter of gears, would suddenly lurch to a halt—something it did at regular intervals but seldom at a scheduled stop—would Michael come fully awake.

Somewhere beyond Babylon the power died. It came back after a short while, but after another fifteen minutes, farther up the line, it died again. Off went the main lights and the air-conditioning. And when the air-conditioning went, the air in the cars turned rank and stifling.

It was in this irritating stop-and-start fashion that the train at last reached Jamaica, the first stop in the city. Some people were getting off, but none that he could see were getting on. But then Michael looked up to see a balding man wearing a blue sweat shirt, baggy pants, and running shoes approaching him.

"Is this seat taken?" he asked, indicating the seat across from his.

"No, it's free."

The man allowed a smile and took the seat. "You know something," he said, "it's a bitch when you have to get back to the city on the train. You really appreciate the plane."

Michael mumbled some meaningless response. The train had set in motion again.

The man lowered his eyes to the case resting between Michael's feet, then returned his gaze to Michael. "You know something," he said, "you don't look anything like Alan. I don't see much family resemblance at all, as a matter of fact."

It wasn't the first time in his life that Michael had made a mistake. But never before had he made one quite so serious. This was the man he should have been on the lookout for. And here he had always believed he could smell a cop. When the gun appeared in the man's hand, it struck Michael that he was finally looking into the face of the man who had murdered his brother.

CHAPTER TWENTY-THREE

Hours before it came on the news, word had gotten around the hospital about Magnus. Gail heard first that he'd been shot to death in his house in Fire Island and was surprised—shocked, really—to learn when the news was aired on WINS at six that he was a suicide. But an exchange of gunfire was believed to have taken place, and a man, whose identity police were withholding, had in fact been shot and seriously wounded.

Gail didn't know whether she was relieved to hear this news or not. Would Magnus's death change anything for her? Was she off the hook completely? Or did she have it wrong? For all the trouble that Magnus had caused her, hadn't he gone out of his way to protect her from Fontana?

Whatever the case, she still could do nothing to shake the feeling that she was caught in an undertow and that it couldn't be long before she was dragged out to sea.

When she left the emergency room a little after six to start on her way home, the sky had turned overcast. The city already had the smell and feel of rain without any actually having fallen. Lights were coming on early in the buildings she passed, and people were picking up their pace, headed for shelter before the downpour. At every other corner fast-talking Senegalese men, who seemed to have sprung out of nowhere, were hawking umbrellas for three dollars apiece as if their life depended on it.

From every newsstand she rushed by the same headline stared back at her:

CITY CORONER KILLS SELF

Power Broker Felled in Mystery Shootout

She bought a copy and began reading, suspecting that she already knew the identity of this mystery power broker. Yet when she saw for a fact that it was Ray Fontana, she was thrown into more confusion than ever. Again she couldn't decide whether she should relax, let down her guard, and get on with her life. Or was there something still to come that she should be watching out for?

The story read, in part:

Fontana was rushed to Long Island Jewish Medical Center, where he underwent emergency surgery for a bullet wound in the neck. A mercurial entrepreneur with a penchant for outrageous behavior, Fontana is known to exercise considerable influence in New York City political circles. The exact circumstances of his shooting are still under investigation, police say. His condition is listed as critical. . . .

When she finished the story, she said a small prayer to herself; it was the first time in a long while that she'd said a prayer. It was a prayer that Ray Fontana would die.

When she got home at last and found that the door leading into the downstairs hallway was no longer functioning, she was furious. What was she paying fourteen hundred fifty dollars a month for if she couldn't be guaranteed any security? More dismaying, she discovered that she'd evidently forgotten to make sure the top lock on her own door was bolted when she left in the morning. But then all sorts of things had been slipping her mind lately, even the names of friends and associates. It was getting so bad that some days she had to examine William's photograph just to remind herself what, exactly, he had looked like.

She didn't want to be alone, not tonight. She felt anxious, spooked. Certainly it must have something to do with

Magnus's death. But it went further than that: Ever since she had been at that apartment on West Twelfth Street she had been filled with foreboding. She couldn't get the smell of it or the horror of it out of her mind. Seeing the place empty and spotless made no difference; it still wouldn't leave her. It continued to swim in blood and gore, but now that it was locked in her memory, it could never be made clean.

All at once she had the urge to be in some warm, congenial café where there were certain to be other people around. But as she was about to head back downstairs, the sky split open and the rain began pouring down. So much for the idea of going back out again.

She opened her apartment door and went in. A light was on in the living room, which was strange because she couldn't remember leaving it on. Panic, which up until then had been worming its way into her vitals, took hold of her, stunning her into paralysis. Somebody was there, she was sure of it.

Standing in the hallway, she peered into the living room, but there was no one to be seen. It was all that she could do to summon the will to venture farther into the apartment, her ears sensitive to the least little sound. It was only at that moment that she observed the gift-wrapped box sitting on the coffee table. What the hell was this?

There was no telling either from lifting it up or shaking it what might be inside. A thousand things went through her mind as to what it was and how it had gotten there. But until she actually opened it, one guess was as good as another. She ripped the silver foil paper, exposing a cardboard box with the words MEAD-JOHNSON LABORATORIES stamped on it, which didn't help her a bit.

Inside she found lots of Styrofoam packing. Only after clearing it away did she finally have a glimpse of exactly what kind of a gift this was.

She let out a scream and leaped back, the box tumbling out of her hands. A head rolled onto the rug, leaving a fresh ooze of blood on the carpet. Its face was looking up at her, the flesh waxen, like a mask, the eyes curiously alive, like those trick eyes in pictures of Jesus that followed one every-where around the room.

"His name is Dr. Shannon," she heard a voice say, and she spun around, looking frantically to see where it had come from. But she'd misjudged its origin. For suddenly he was there in front of her, an extraordinarily beautiful man with a curiously sympathetic smile perched on his lips. "And mine is whatever you'd like it to be."

CHAPTER TWENTY-FOUR

Michael wasn't nearly as afraid as he thought he would be. He had imagined a scene like this so many times that it was almost as if he had lived through it before. Now that it was really happening, he felt oddly calm. He'd had a similar feeling when he was behind the wheel of a car going into a skid. With no way to pull out of it, he would watch it happen the way he'd watch a movie, with the same eerie detachment. *Here it goes*, one would think. *What comes next?*

Well, he knew that he couldn't remain in this trancelike state indefinitely. He had a stake in this, after all. Action was going to be necessary, but he could not for the life of him figure out what action was possible under the circumstances.

"You could at least tell me your name," Michael said. It was important that he get the name of his brother's murderer exactly right. He could turn out to be his own murderer, too, he supposed.

The man hesitated, then shrugged as if it didn't make much of a difference what he said at this point. "It's Ralph Mackie," he said.

"You work for Fontana?"

"I used to," he said cryptically. "Now, please, the case."

Michael hesitated, realizing that if he were ever to shake his stupor, it would have to be soon—now, really. At the same time he was thinking, *Would this man actually use his gun in a crowded Long Island Railroad car?* He wouldn't put it past him. It was probably nothing to gamble on.

Mackie was reaching out his hand to grab hold of the case when Michael said, "Tell me something."

Mackie's free hand hovered in the air, fingers extended to receive the case. "What is it?"

"Did you kill my brother?"

"And if I did, would it matter all that much?"

"Yes, I think it would."

Mackie allowed a thoughtful smile. "It was funny, he barely protested when I wasted the girl. He even helped me get her to the end of the pier. She was bleeding like a stuck pig all the way down, but she wasn't dead yet. I guess he thought that it was the tradeoff he'd have to make—her life for his." He paused and studied Michael's face as if there was something there he needed to remember. "But he was wrong."

Michael wondered whether Mackie was telling him the truth. It was hard for him to believe that Alan would actually participate in the slaughter of his own girlfriend. But then, in the last few weeks there were any number of things he had learned about Alan he neither cared for nor understood. None of which took away from the fact that his brother had still been murdered.

"The case, please. Soon as I have it I'll go, and we'll never have to see each other again."

He seemed convinced that Michael would offer no resistance, not when his life was at risk.

Michael reached down under his legs for the case and was about to hand it over when something inside him recoiled. He just couldn't do it. The threat was nothing compared to his outrage. Surprising even himself, he sprang from his seat and ran, expecting at any instant to be shot.

Now Michael was alive in the world—he'd thrown off his stupor. He moved as quickly as he could, registering only shapes, lights, shadows in front of him, never daring to look behind to see how far back Mackie was.

He got through one car, then another, and was about to enter a third, wondering just how far back he could go and what would happen as soon as he reached the end of it, when the train shuddered to a halt—another unscheduled stop—causing him to lose his balance and pitch to the floor. Simultaneously the overhead lights flickered, dimmed, went out. The air-conditioning system sighed and expired.

Michael gathered himself up off the floor and kept pressing back farther in the train. In the near total darkness he tried to distinguish Mackie, but that proved impossible. Too many people were crammed into the aisles in back of him. There were too many people ahead of him as well. Making his way through the cars was growing more and more difficult.

Yet in his frenzied state he managed to get all the way through two additional cars, though not without a good deal of buffeting and cursing, before the power was restored and the lights returned. Only then did he risk looking back.

To his astonishment, Mackie had succeeded in keeping up with him in spite of all the irate passengers standing in his way. Michael could see him advancing up the aisle one car back. His eyes had a feral brightness to them, his lips were pursed in grim determination.

The train was beginning to move. Michael stepped out onto the small platform separating one car from the next. There was no point in continuing to the end of the train; then he'd have no way out at all. Dropping his gaze, he watched the tracks beginning to sweep by. As far as he could see, only one choice remained.

He put one leg over the protective chain, then the other. That done, he threw the case down, then jumped after it. As he came crashing down he heard—or thought he did anyway—the sound of a gunshot, half muffled in the pouring rain. Then the train barreled passed him and was soon lost in the thickening gloom.

Michael hurt all over. Most of all he hurt in his right leg, which had sustained the brunt of the impact. His pants were torn at the knees and darkening with blood. He could barely stand, let alone walk. But he'd just have to do his best. He had to get moving.

The rain was punishing, and he was almost instantly drenched. Limping along the tracks, he went in search of the case, praying that it hadn't broken open when it landed. The documents were sure to be destroyed if the rain had a chance to get at them.

He came on the case lying about a dozen feet from the tracks. It was still secured, still intact.

Now he had to find his way back into Manhattan. He knew that he was somewhere in Queens, but where in Queens he had no idea. Sooner or later, he reasoned, he should locate a subway station. But finding one turned out to be more of a problem than he'd anticipated. The neighborhood he was walking through had an ominously rundown appearance to it. In the faces of those who passed him, he detected menace and barely suppressed violence. Of course, in daytime, this might prove to be a perfectly fine area, inhabited by upstanding citizens. He would probably never know.

Once he got to a subway stop he had a chance to inspect his injuries. Just scrapes and abrasions, nothing serious. What troubled him most was that he couldn't run worth a damn. By the time he reached Times Square, it was almost ten. He phoned his father's office only to learn that his father was gone. What did "gone" mean, exactly? Was he at home? Was he at a meeting? The answering service said they didn't know. He tried his parents' house and received no answer. Perhaps they were out having dinner.

His father would undoubtedly turn up in time. But he couldn't simply hang around Times Square until he could get hold of him. Nor did he like the idea of waiting in another bar. And there was no sense in returning to the apartment; that would only make it easier for Mackie to find him.

Then it came to him what to do. He would go to see Gail. Simply show up unannounced. Otherwise, if he phoned ahead she might balk, insisting that she'd meant what she said, that she never wanted to see him again. She might not even listen to what he had to tell her. But he doubted that if he appeared in person she would have the heart to send him away—at least not without hearing him out.

CHAPTER TWENTY-FIVE

Knowing that her life depended on it, Gail was struggling to pay close attention to every word this man was saying. But it was becoming harder; her brain seemed to want nothing to do with this and simply desired to shut down. At first, in the hope that she could calm him, she had tried to get him to talk about himself. But the only information she'd succeeded in eliciting from him was his name, which he said might as well be Daniel as anything else. A strange reply. But then again, she could see what kind of man this was.

Certain that it was only a matter of time before he killed her, she was prepared for her life to flash before her. But that failed to happen. Even when she closed her eyes, all she saw was the same dissolutely beautiful face that was right there in front of her.

"Did you hear what I just said?" he asked.

Actually she had absolutely no idea what he had just said. But she wanted to do whatever was necessary to appease him, and nodded reassuringly.

She was suddenly aware of the color of his eyes. They were a color of blue that she'd never seen before; they didn't seem quite real, though. Nothing about his face seemed real, in fact. His perfection was horrifying.

"Usually the people I have to kill," he was saying as if he were only making casual conversation, "don't know who I am. They don't enjoy the privilege that you do. Usually before they die I let them look at themselves—in the mirror. The mirror of my eyes. I don't think they need to see me; they need to have that final glimpse of themselves, so that they can carry with them into the next world that understanding." He slumped back in his chair, his breathing coming hard and fast, as if the excitement was too much for him.

"If only people would understand . . ."—he started again—". . . that some of us carry death in our blood, like a gene. That's why we can recognize one another so easily, that's why we're drawn to one another, don't you see? We're all in this together, we're only half of this world. A part of us is already stepping out. Like Byron. He stepped out in San Francisco. Why would he do something like that to me? Because he was afraid? Because it was too unbearable for him? Why do you think?" He was looking straight at Gail, evidently appealing to her for some kind of response.

Who the hell was Byron? she wondered. What could she say to him? She tried to think quickly. She had to say something. But nothing seemed to come. She was blank, mute.

But then he began speaking again, as if he'd forgotten what he'd just asked her. "What we're in this for is . . ." he started, only to let his voice falter and die. It seemed he had lost his train of thought; his eyes narrowed in concentration as he struggled for his next word. But when it came it was garbled, unintelligible.

Then his eyes began to roll until only the whites were showing. His head sank down on his chest. Gail took heart. He seemed to be suffering from some kind of psychosis, possibly a drug overdose. She was sure that she wouldn't have an opportunity like this again.

Leaping off the sofa, she started toward the door. Amazed that she'd managed to reach it, she put her hand to the knob. But then he was on her, wrenching her arm back as he flung her to the floor. Before she knew what was happening he was on her, straddling her, pinning her arms down, allowing her no time to catch her breath.

Her attempt to escape seemed only to have unleashed his madness. His smell was stale and poisonous, but his smell was all she had to breathe. He was ripping apart her blouse, tearing at her skirt. If it was sex he wanted, if he was going to rape her, maybe, she thought, that would satisfy him; maybe that way he'd spare her life.

But then he stopped and began to examine her body, coldly, dispassionately, as though she were already dead. His words now were much clearer. "Sometimes I wait until afterward; sometimes, though, I do it before . . . little by little . . . just to see . . ."

She wasn't sure what to make of this until she saw the blade glinting in his hand.

Even before she could react, he'd put the knife to the base of her neck and began to draw it lightly down between her exposed breasts, so lightly that until she looked down and saw the blood she was certain he hadn't broken the skin.

She buckled, she heaved, she tried to fight him off. But it was no contest. All he did was bear down harder with the blade so that now the pain reached her, and she cried out. And then she heard pounding at the door and screamed for all she was worth.

The door flew open. Daniel, seeing Michael come in, was slow to react, but not as slow as Michael was; otherwise, he would have seen the kick coming that struck him in the gut and drove him halfway across the room.

CHAPTER TWENTY-SIX

No help could be expected from Fontana any longer. When Mackie phoned his security agency to find out how he was doing, he was told little more than he'd already heard on the news. His doctors believed that he would live, but it was likely that he'd be paralyzed from the neck down, a quadriplegic, forced to carry oxygen with him wherever he went because his lungs were no longer capable of doing the job alone. He might not even be able to regain the use of his voice, that was how bad it was.

Over the phone Mackie could sense the panic, the disarray, the incomprehension prevailing in Fontana's office. Up to this point it had been a one-man show; now that the show was over, nobody had the goddamnedest idea of what to do.

But Mackie had his own problems. If Friedlander managed to get those documents to the D.A. or to the press, then he was finished, no question. Visions of an indictment on murder one rose up in his mind.

Without the resources to track down Friedlander, he wasn't sure what he could do. There was no answer at his apartment. He could be anywhere. Possibly it was already too late. But it struck him that Max Farrell would know how to locate Friedlander; he'd handled his case and would have an idea where to find him.

As soon as he learned where Max was, he set out for Shannon's office. When Mackie got off the elevator on the ninth floor of the posh Park Avenue address where Shannon had his office suite, Mackie became aware of an eerie silence broken only by a ringing phone that nobody was answering. His suspicions already intensified by the events of the day, he took out his automatic, prepared to break down the door if he had to.

It wasn't necessary. The door was unlocked. As soon as he stepped in he was assaulted by an odor that he identified at once. Blood was everywhere. It was obvious what had happened. Farrell lay sprawled out on the waiting room carpet. The fucker had completely eviscerated him, as deftly as a butcher might gut a pig. In the examining room, Mackie found Shannon—or all of Shannon except for his head.

A further search yielded a syringe, a tiny drop of blood drying at the tip of its needle. Most of its contents was gone.

But it was the photograph, smeared with blood and stained with what might have been wax but that was more likely sperm long since dried, that arrested his attention. He recognized the woman, though for a few seconds it wouldn't come to him from where.

Michael couldn't have had any idea what hit him. Still reeling from the kick to his stomach, he wasn't ready when Daniel came at him again, delivering a roundhouse kick that struck him in his solar plexus.

"Daniel, no!" Gail shrieked, as if her protest could possibly have any effect on him. Daniel didn't appear to have heard her in any case.

Michael collapsed in pain. These blows might have

packed more of a wallop if Daniel had been in better shape. But they were strong enough, and it was clear to Gail that there was no way Michael could long sustain this kind of battering without sustaining serious injury.

His attention riveted on Michael, Daniel appeared to have forgotten completely about Gail. It was as if she didn't count in his demented scheme of things any longer. Or possibly the madness or the drugs—whatever was wrong with him— had erased her from his mind.

Gathering what little strength she had, she got to her feet, frantically scanning the room for something—anything, really—that she could use to attack Daniel. At that instant it didn't even occur to her to run for the door and escape.

The only thing she could easily lay her hands on was the mysterious metal case that Michael was carrying with him when he'd walked in and that now lay where it had fallen under the coffee table. All the time keeping an eye on Daniel, she crawled along the floor until she could reach out and grab hold of it. She was gratified to find that it was heavy enough to do some injury. Daniel still wasn't aware of what she was doing. Nothing appeared to interest him except for the task he'd now set for himself: securing Michael to one of her newly upholstered chairs with picture wire he must have brought with him. Just as he began to fasten the wire around Michael's neck, Gail risked standing up, the case gripped in both her hands. They were shaking badly, but she couldn't let that stop her.

Soundlessly she crept up behind him. Catching sight of her, Michael's eyes suddenly shifted. Daniel must have noticed. He started to look around just as Gail slammed the case as hard as she could against his head. Then she stepped back, astounded at what she'd just done.

The blow caused Daniel to lurch backward. Then he stopped, wobbling crazily on the balls of his feet. Blood began flowing into his hair. It seemed that at any moment he would fall, but infuriatingly he remained upright, shaking his head violently. Michael tried to get himself up from the chair, but everything he did was in slow motion; he hadn't had time to recover from the blows he'd received to act with any more speed.

As Gail lifted the case to strike him again, Daniel whipped around, casting her a hurt look, as if he could not possibly comprehend why she should want to do this to him.

Held by his gaze, she hesitated a second too long, only to realize that the opportunity had passed and that both she and Michael were lost.

He used picture wire to tie her up as well. It was this wire, knotted around their necks, that gave him the control over them he wanted. It wasn't enough to kill them. He had to control them first, tightening and relaxing the pressure of the wire at whim.

He'd occupy himself first with Gail, then Michael, then return to Gail again. Every time Michael felt the wire tightening, spots flickered before his eyes. It wasn't the pain so much that got to him, it was the inability to breathe. His head had begun to feel light. At any moment he might black out.

Suddenly the wire went slack and Michael slumped forward, gasping. Daniel seemed to enjoy taking them both to the brink, then pulling back just before he'd lose them for good.

"One of these times," he said with a certain amazement in his voice, "I'll go too far, won't I? I'll slip up, I'll hold on too long and then . . ." Did he stop because he'd made his meaning clear, or because it wouldn't come to him what to say next?

Michael no longer dared look at Gail. She was gagging and sputtering the same as he was, but even when the wire loosened she couldn't stop; there was no end to it. Her eyes were bulging grotesquely; a cyanotic blue cast had come into her face. It occurred to Michael that no one was in control there. Both he and Gail were powerless, but so in a way was Daniel, who seemed to be obeying forces that he could neither understand nor master. Chance ruled here; their lives—all of their lives—might just as well have depended on a throw of the dice.

CHAPTER TWENTY-SEVEN

He thought he was hearing things. He was not. The door was coming open. Hope of rescue caused Michael to open his eyes. Even with his vision blurring he could see that there was someone there, but could not make out who it was—not at first. But at least the tension on the wire had relaxed, and he could get air down into his lungs. He clutched at his stomach and slumped forward.

Then when he lifted his eyes, he saw who it was and despaired. What rescue he'd prayed for would not come from this man. It was Mackie, gun in hand. Gail's eyes were running, and she was clawing desperately at the wire, trying to loosen it. Maybe she hadn't become aware that anybody else was in the room with them, too absorbed by the need to suck in an unimpeded breath of air to understand.

Daniel wasn't much better off, Michael saw. He seemed stupefied, at an utter loss as to how to respond with Mackie standing less than six feet away from him; there was a threat he couldn't possibly have taken into account. Uncertainty was visible in Mackie's eyes, too. He was undoubtedly trying to judge how much of a danger Daniel represented. But he continued to keep his gun in motion, training it first on Daniel, then on Michael, then on Gail, as if he had no idea which one of them to shoot first. The four of them were frozen for an instant in this strange tableau, no one moving, no one knowing where to move.

Still, it was clear that Mackie believed he had the leverage; he was the one with the gun, after all. "You," he called to Daniel, "hands up or I'll blow your fucking head off. I'll waste you like you wasted Max."

So Max was dead, Michael thought. But he felt nothing—no satisfaction, no triumph, nothing.

Michael risked a glance at Daniel, who, even as he raised his hands, never removed his eyes from Mackie. Michael could see that he was assessing his options, making up his mind when to strike. No matter how groggy or crazed he might be, he was still canny enough to realize that Mackie had no intention of letting him live.

Gail gaped at the scene taking place before her, though she seemed unable to comprehend what was happening. At the base of her neck there was an ugly red welt where the wire had dug into it, and she was rubbing it absentmindedly. Her eyes were glassy, and she seemed removed from everything that was happening around her.

Mackie's gaze shifted for an instant to the case on the floor. Blood, Daniel's blood, was still drying on it. As he stooped to pick it up, he continued to direct his gaze at Daniel, who so far remained motionless.

Then he unlocked the case to inspect the documents, and it was at that moment that Daniel made his move.

He sprang forward, hurtling himself at Mackie before the detective was aware of what he was doing. Caught completely off guard, he stumbled back, almost losing his balance in the process.

Spinning on his heel, Daniel attempted to kick the gun from Mackie's hand, but the kick was a little off and Mackie managed to keep hold of his weapon. Before Daniel could attack a second time, Mackie reeled back and got off a shot. Daniel groaned and staggered away toward the bedroom, clutching his side. Then he collapsed and lay still.

With Mackie's attention diverted, Michael pulled the wire constraint off his neck, then sprang from the chair and threw himself at Mackie. He gave no thought to what he was doing; he didn't realize he was on top of Mackie until the man's hot breath hit his face. One look at Mackie was enough to see how much Michael's attack had taken him by surprise. In the few seconds that it took Mackie to recover, Michael began to pound him repeatedly.

Mackie fought to get Michael off him, but Michael was tenacious, out of his mind. He'd be damned if he was going to allow the man to overpower him. Michael was driven by fury, by rage, he didn't care, he wanted to pound this man into a pulp, stomp him, blind him, castrate him. And because he didn't care, he held the advantage. He gave no thought to what he was doing; the pain that wracked his body was gone, the fear that would have kept him paralyzed was gone, his identity was gone, and his sense of self was gone. Everything was gone except for this insatiable need to subdue this man who killed his brother. Nothing else mattered—not Gail, not Daniel, certainly not his own life. Only revenge mattered. He felt as if he had the strength of a hundred men. Mackie struggled crazily, ferociously. He tore at Michael's clothes, thrashed and punched and cursed, all to no avail. Michael was the madman now. It was as though Daniel's insanity had gotten into him. He swung repeatedly at Mackie's face, heartened to see his nose flatten and blood begin to flow into his open mouth. Gail was crying out, screaming to him, but he couldn't hear a word she said. Then the gun went off.

Michael stopped, releasing his grip on Mackie. There was a sharp pain in Michael's stomach, and he thought that surely he must have been hit; but then he saw that Mackie's eyes had suddenly gone hazy, and his body seemed to be convulsing. Michael realized that the pain had come from the recoil of the weapon, but he wasn't the one who was hit. The gun had gone off, that was all. Michael was lucky, Mackie was not. Michael drew himself up and watched stupidly while Mackie attempted to get himself off the floor, too. But it wasn't working, he couldn't make it. His mouth sagged, and he cast a look at Michael that was filled not with hatred so much as disgust. He seemed to be appealing to Michael to tell him why his luck had turned so sour. But his last glance was reserved for the documents exposed in the open case. He began to crawl toward them, his arm outstretched, as if he still couldn't get used to the idea that they would never be his. But he couldn't quite grasp hold of them. It was too far away for him, farther than the farthest star in the universe could ever be.

Michael waited for him to do something more, but there was no further movement from him. Michael turned his gaze toward Gail. She approached him like a sleepwalker, then fell against him, slumping into his arms. For a long time they held each other. She was wet all over, so that his hands slipped over her flesh, finding no purchase; she was no longer flesh but liquid.

He freed her to inspect the extent of the damage the blade had done. She opened her blouse and dropped her eyes to the wound. Blood had gotten smeared over her breasts and stomach in such a way that it looked worse than it actually was. The cut wasn't very deep at any rate. The way she was looking told him that she was putting herself beyond reach. "I should go shower," was all she said.

He was thinking that he should call the police. A shower was the last thing on his mind. But maybe nothing else struck her as important just then.

As she turned from him, she looked to the spot where Daniel had fallen. Only, Daniel wasn't there anymore.

CHAPTER TWENTY-EIGHT

In the pounding rain he wandered aimlessly, aware sometimes of the burning pain in his side, other times completely oblivious to it. He remembered receiving an injection hours or maybe many days or years ago. And he knew somehow that the condition of his mind must have been affected by it. Something was happening to him. The pain in his side didn't matter so much. He thought he could handle that. It was the taste in his mouth that he couldn't stand; there seemed to be no way that he could get rid of it. Soda didn't do it, and neither did beer and coffee. He supposed he might try wine next. Maybe that would help.

He was walking funny, too, with a weird shambling gait; there seemed to be no way he could make his legs do what he wanted them to. But it was his mind the drugs had affected the most. He couldn't keep it focused on any thought for more than a few seconds. His memory was almost gone.

Actually, he didn't know whether he remembered anything or not, whether what he believed to be his memories weren't memories at all but just bits and pieces of his imagination washing up on the surface of his consciousness. It was as though the foundation had all eroded, and it was only a matter of time before the rest of the house caved in as well. He did not remember who he was, what his name was, where he'd come from, or what he'd done in his life.

Every so often he would stop and look at the photograph he'd taken from a bedroom. It was very dim in his mind what bedroom it was, or who slept there. But he reasoned that it must belong to a woman named Gail because that was the name scrawled on the back. "To Gail with much love, William." He liked William. He wanted to meet him. He had such a sweet, melancholy face. He knew that William reminded him of somebody, somebody he'd loved dearly many years ago, but it seemed that it was buried forever in a part of his brain he would never be able to reach. Maybe, he thought, it was William he loved. Maybe it was William he was on his way to see.

Little by little he was becoming empty, blanking out, turning into a tabula rasa. He was a clean slate. It really wasn't so bad, he decided. In a way it was like being born into the world all over again.

EPILOGUE

Night and day didn't hold much meaning for Michael; the law offices, courtrooms, and holding cells that he kept being shuttled in and out of were all lit with artificial light regardless of whether the sun was shining or not. Often there weren't any windows to look out of, or when there were, the shades were drawn, as if the sunlight presented some sort of threat. He didn't know.

He couldn't say what the disposition of his case was. His father had hired a criminal lawyer for him, an influential figure—the best that money could buy, people said, a man who saw loopholes wide as the Sahara where others saw solid walls. But Michael had rebuffed him, refusing to cooperate, figuring that this was his own problem; if his family had balked at helping him before, why should he accept their aid now? He'd gotten himself out of worse jams; he told himself he could do without their charity. He reasoned that his father was motivated by a desire to spare the family name more embarrassment than it had already suffered as a consequence of Alan's murder, that was all.

When at last the great attorney realized he was going to get nowhere with Michael, he resigned from the case. For a short time afterward Michael felt that he'd achieved a kind of victory. It was perverse of him, he knew, even self-destructive, and he sensed he would come to regret his decision. But it gave him satisfaction just the same.

The court-appointed lawyer he was given instead proved to be an intense young man with thinning hair and an impatient manner. He inspired no confidence whatsoever in Michael, who had the feeling that any case more complicated than a traffic violation would leave the lawyer confounded. Michael's refusal to volunteer more than the bald facts—and even those he stinted on—dismayed and aggravated him. He repeatedly told Michael, "I'm not going to be able to help you if you don't help me. I can walk out of here, you can't. Don't forget that." But Michael wasn't moved to be more forthcoming.

He had to admit he was being fatalistic. At first he thought he was ready to accept his fate, even to embrace it. But, with so much time on his hands, he began to think otherwise. He remembered all the warnings he'd gotten from Ambrosetti about the kind of people he'd taken on—warnings Ambrosetti himself should have heeded. Michael wondered whether he'd wake up in his cell one morning to find a knife stuck in his belly. Fontana might be a vegetable, but he had friends who still owed him. And Michael had killed a cop, after all. A retired cop, but a cop nonetheless.

He wasn't certain who inspired more fear in him: the other prisoners who regarded him with undisguised suspicion—a rich white boy among people who were neither—or the men holding him who regarded him as a cop killer.

The day came for his bail hearing. His court-appointed lawyer told the judge that Michael was clearly no threat to society and was unlikely to flee. He asked for bail of five thousand dollars. The district attorney, however, recalling Michael's arrest nineteen years ago on drug charges, made him out to be a dangerous felon who had a history of being on the run—from life if not always the law. He asked the judge to set bail at a quarter of a million dollars. The only thing that came to Michael's mind at that moment was, while a quarter of a million dollars was a lot of money, it still wasn't enough to buy Alan's apartment.

The judge compromised: fifty thousand. It didn't matter. Whatever it would have been, Michael didn't have it. He was broke. He certainly couldn't turn to his father, not after dismissing his friend, the famous criminal lawyer. He was remanded into custody.

Michael must have dozed off sometime after being returned to his cell, because somebody was shaking him, waking him up. When he opened his eyes, he saw a guard standing over him. "You can go now."

"Go where?" He was having trouble clearing his head.

"You're free to leave. Somebody posted bail for you."

"Who?"

The officer shrugged. "How the hell should I know?" he said irritably. "Let's get going."

Michael complied, slowly though, thinking that this must be some trick, or a very sick joke his jailers had contrived to play on him. He followed the guard along the row of holding cells, distantly aware of the faces peering out at him from behind the bars, calling out to him. They knew his name, they knew who he was, and no doubt what he'd done. It unnerved him, all that knowledge about him floating around.

Still disbelieving, he went through the formality of signing for his possessions and then walked out into the main room of the station house. He hesitated for a moment. Across the room he saw his father. Paul Friedlander looked amazingly out of place, this dignified man in his three-piece suit making his way toward his son through a crowd of assault victims, busted hookers, pickpockets, and three-card monte dealers. Some were sobbing, some hurling obscene epithets, some just trying to get their stories across to anyone who would listen. His father ignored them all, his eyes fixed only on Michael.

When he was close enough, he held out his hand to Michael. Dazedly, Michael took it, unable to say a word.

Now that they were face to face, Michael could see how weary his father looked, how pale. "Are you all right?" he asked.

"Okay, I'm doing okay."

"The car's right outside." He turned and began walking toward the exit.

His father's car, he noticed, was parked directly in front of the 13th Precinct House in a place reserved for police. It wasn't like his father to commit so flagrant a parking violation, but then, it wasn't every day that he had to come and bail out his son, either.

"Did they treat you all right in there?" his father asked once they got inside the car. He put the key in the ignition but made no move to turn it on.

"It could have been worse." Michael realized that he feared his father more than he had the police or the other prisoners. He was waiting for the explosion.

"You know, you've made all the papers."

"Oh?" Somehow Michael hadn't expected this.

"And the TV stations. They've managed to get an old picture of you, God knows from where. It doesn't really look like you."

"What are they saying?"

"The reactions are . . . well, kind of mixed."

"That figures."

"Some are saying you're a hero. Others, including the mayor, are portraying you as a vigilante, taking the law into your own hands."

Which was the way his father must see him, Michael supposed.

"Of course, the mayor has his reasons for saying that," his father went on. "After all, many of the men you've exposed are his appointees, his protégés. You've caused him and his administration a great deal of embarrassment."

It sounded to Michael as though his father might not be so unhappy about this development. That was strange.

"I never really did like the mayor," the elder Friedlander added. "But I have to tell you, Michael, that the more I read and the more I listened to the news reports, the more confused I got. It wasn't until your friend, Dr. Ives, got in touch with me that I finally managed to get a clearer picture as to what happened."

"Gail called you?"

His father looked at him. "Does that surprise you?"

"Yes, a little."

"I don't see why. She seems to think a great deal of you."

Either she never made it clear to him, Michael thought, or else he'd failed to pick up on it. Probably the latter. He was very good at missing the point.

"She's quite an attractive young lady, too. Seems to be bearing up well after all she's been through."

"You saw her on television?"

"No, we met. She gave me the autopsy reports and the dictabelts you found on Magnus's property."

Michael had asked Gail to hold them for him, assuming that she'd find some way to get them into the hands of Joe Barbanel, but he never would have guessed that she would go to his father first.

"Did you look at those reports, Dad? Did you see Alan's?"

"Of course. I studied all the documents very carefully before I called Joe."

"And?"

His father's eyes shifted so that now he was looking out to the street, which was filling with long shadows and late-afternoon light. "And you were right."

He was right? He marveled at his father's words.

"I have to admit I'm very proud of what you've done. It took a lot of guts."

And stubbornness, Michael thought. And ignorance and foolishness, too. But what counted was that his father was proud of him. He couldn't get over it.

"But there are a lot of things to clear up. I don't know whether you realize how complicated your situation is."

It always was complicated, Michael decided, it was just complicated in different ways.

"But if we're going to resolve your case and get you out from under, we have to work together. Does that sound all right with you?"

Michael nodded. *Yes, it was all right.*

"I know you weren't too happy with my initial choice of counsel for you."

"Not really."

"But maybe if the two of us could sit down in the next few days and go over a list of prospects, we could come up with somebody more acceptable. I have a few ideas in mind."

"Sure, Dad, I'd be happy to."

"Good." His father allowed a brief smile, then leaned forward to turn on the ignition. "Let's get home, then. Your mother's anxious to see you."

T H E GRIEF SHOP
VICKI STIEFEL

Tally Whyte has seen a lot of dead bodies in her years with the Massachusetts Grief Assistance Program, but this is the first time a murder victim has been brought there by the murderer himself. During the night, someone broke into the Office of the Chief Medical Examiner, aka the Grief Shop, and left behind a tragic calling card—the body of a young girl, bearing a message that reads: Sins of the Father.

The girl's playmate is also missing. Could she be another victim? Or can Tally still save her before the killer strikes again? As the mysteries multiply and Tally's life is threatened, she scrambles to prevent yet another child from falling prey to a madman's warped sense of justice.

- -

DAVID HOUSEWRIGHT
TIN CITY

It started innocently enough. An elderly beekeeper asked Mac McKenzie to find out why his bees were suddenly dying. Asking a few questions isn't a big deal for Mac, but it looks like the beekeeper's neighbor, Frank Crosetti, doesn't like nosy people. Now he's disappeared, leaving behind a dead body... and a very angry Mac McKenzie.

With only a faint trail to follow—and some very suspicious federal agents gunning for him—Mac is forced to dive underground. But he'll find Crosetti even if it means sniffing around the Twin Cities' darkest corners. No one's going to stop Mac—unless of course they kill him.

Dorchester Publishing Co., Inc.
P.O. Box 6640
Wayne, PA 19087-8640

_____5762-X
$6.99 US/$8.99 CAN

THE BRIBE
WILLIAM P. WOOD

He was a war hero and a member of Congress. Now he's dead—shot down the day after he made a scathing speech blasting corruption in Washington. For Sacramento police detectives Terry Nye and Rose Tafoya, the investigation is a time bomb. They have just twenty-four hours to find out if the congressman was killed because of his speech…or something far worse.

Dennis Cooper is acting District Attorney during these critical twenty-four hours. He's in for the fight of his career and time is running out for everyone—and they know it.

FEAR & GREED

LAWRENCE LIGHT

It's the impossible dream of every trader and dealer on Wall Street—an accurate means to predict the ups and downs of the stock market. The Reiner sisters have made that dream a reality in the form of a computer program they call Goldring. The sisters have kept Goldring their little secret, even when a magazine story by financial reporter Karen Glick showcases their sudden wealth. Everything was working so well, but now one of the sisters has been found murdered, Goldring is missing— and Karen Glick has a hit man on her trail.